Juliet Bates was b   th-east of England. A er studying art and art histor   orked as cturer in   schools in the UK and now   e Colou   Juliet's sec   l novel; her debut, The   lin   he   by L   n Press in   09, and her short stories ha appeared in British and Canadian journals and magazines.

Praise for *The Colours*

'There is a delightful observational delicacy to Bates' prose, a careful cataloguing of the everchanging shades of the waves and the vivid red of the "clarty" sand of Teesby, where the novel is set. It's a quality that perfectly befits the two main characters ... Theirs is a story of illness, estrangement and misunderstanding'
Eithne Farry, *Daily Mail*

'*The Colours* is a sweeping family drama covering a span of several decades of the twentieth century from just before the First World War right up to the Royal Wedding of Charles and Diana in 1981. The imagery and descriptions in the novel are striking, closely observed and beautifully wrought'
Yvette Huddleston, *Yorkshire Post*

'Entirely absorbing ... *The Colours* is a fine novel'
Steve Whitaker, *Yorkshire Times*

The COLOURS

JULIET BATES

FLEET
2021

FLEET

First published in Great Britain in 2020 by Fleet
This paperback edition published in 2021 by Fleet

1 3 5 7 9 10 8 6 4 2

A CIP catalogue record for this book
is available from the British Library.

ISBN 978-0-7088-9939-7

Typeset in Caslon by M Rules
Printed and bound in Great Britain by Clays Ltd, Elcograf S.p.A.

Papers used by Fleet are from well-managed forests
and other responsible sources.

Fleet
An imprint of
Little, Brown Book Group
Carmelite House
50 Victoria Embankment
London EC4Y 0DZ

An Hachette UK Company
www.hachette.co.uk

www.littlebrown.co.uk

To I.J., for all the conversations

Contents

Ellen and Jack, 1981

Prologue

April 1982

Through the windscreen, smeared with drizzle and dead flies, is the sea, only the sea. The emptiness is uncanny, breath-taking; the metallic gleam of the water against the flat white sky.

'It's gone,' he says, turning to the girl in the passenger seat. 'You see, there used to be a ...'

He points at the windscreen, but she is twisting her hair around her finger, gazing down at her lap.

'There used to be ...'

He peers into the distance. The tower was on the far shore: a squat stone structure, two floors high – a watchtower, a look-out. Now that it has gone he can only visualise it as a pale blue silhouette.

'I'm going for a walk.' He reaches for his sketchpad on the backseat. 'Do you want to come?'

She usually stays in the car while he draws, biting her nails or reading a book, but this time she nods her head. 'Where are you going?'

'Over there.' He gestures at the space where the tower once stood. 'To look at the view.'

There is a new gate at the head of the track. Beyond it, emerging from the waves, is a windswept plane of shingle and sand. It is a narrow line that from this distance appears no more solid than the sea itself.

'We'll have to climb over the gate and walk across the marsh to get there.'

'But it says ...' She is pointing to a metal sign planted in the ground. She runs her fingers across the rusted letters.

'I know what it says.'

She takes a step away from him, stumbles over a stone. 'It says it's against the law.'

'But there's no one here. Look,' and he waves his hand at the grey horizon.

Ahead, on the track, a cluster of gulls are pecking at the soft-shelled crabs that have been washed up with the tide. As he moves towards the gate, the birds scatter and skim away across the marsh, then they settle on a far pool, eyeing him uneasily, waiting for his decision.

'There's no one here now.' He is attempting to convince himself as much as her. 'Look, nothing.'

She is standing by the sign with her arms folded. She looks cold – he should have told her to bring a coat – and she must have stepped in a puddle because her boots are damp and edged with sand.

'Let me give you a hand.' He reaches out but she doesn't move.

'If there's nothing to see I may as well go back to the car.'

He is not surprised. He remembers how it was.

'I won't be long then.' He watches her trudge towards the road, head down, hands in her pockets. When she turns the corner, a gust of wind makes her long hair coil into the air for a second or two, forming a brown halo round her head.

On the other side of the gate he walks cautiously, avoiding the deep ruts that have filled with salt water. With every step, lumps of silty gravel and pebbles tumble into the marsh: the track is slipping

4

away from him. It is only when he reaches the relative stability of the sea-spit that he turns to look at the town. He has never seen it from this angle before. He can make out the beach, the thin line of the promenade and the thicker band of Marine Parade. Looking back at the town is like peering at a distant star. If he had a telescope he would see himself, a small boy leaning against the railings of the promenade staring out to sea.

The wind blows. His eyes smart, his ears ache. He weaves through the clutches of marram grass and seakale to the shoreline. But there is nothing left of the tower, just a scatter of stones and a small patch of fissured concrete. A few steps away, half buried in the shingle, is a helmet from the last war, or the war before that. He touches it with the toe of his shoe and the brim shatters into red flakes that are swept away. Still hopeful, he stands for a while – listening, watching – but all he can hear is the shrill wail of the wind, all he can see are the waves.

ELLEN

1912–16

Home

Da said the Pearson family came out of the sand. He said they were born out of the red clarty sand that stuck to the soles of boots and the hems of frocks. On the beach, the women had deep frills of it around their skirts, so heavy it weighed them down. You couldn't just brush the sand away, you had to beat your clothes with the palm of your hand like you were smacking them for being naughty. You had to bang your boots against the doorstep and find a knife to gouge away the sand that clung to the heels and round the stitching. But however much you cleaned your clothes, it was always in the seams and the pleats and the pockets. It was in the bed too, trapped in the pillowcases and the folds of the sheets. On wash days, if you filled the basin with clean water and pushed your nightgown under the surface the water turned pink straight away. And afterwards, when the basin was emptied, there was a sulky red sludge in the bottom and a hard skim of red around the rim.

Teesby was covered in sand. It piled up in the streets and filled the cracks in the pavements and the gutters. It covered the front gardens and got caught in the long grass and the privet and the flower petals. When the wind was bad, the sand would swirl around your ankles, nip your legs and arms like a snappy dog. And when the waves were fierce, the sea would hurl fistfuls of it at the town, then the faces of all the houses were spotted with soggy gobbets of dark red sand.

Da told Ellen that the sand blowing over Teesby came from the Snook. He said the Snook was a sea-spit. The sea carried the sand in its waves then spat it out in the same place year after year. When the tide was high the Snook was an island, and you would have to swim across the bay to reach it. But when the tide was low, you could get there by crossing the river and walking along the causeway over the marsh.

Right at the end of the Snook was a tower. From a distance it was a short stubby thumb of a building against the pale grey sky.

'They built it to keep the Frenchies out,' Da said. 'That was a long time ago.'

If you climbed to the first floor, you could stick your head out of the window and look back at Teesby. From the tower, the town was just a dark-roofed cluster of small-windowed houses that looked like they were trying to ignore the view. But the Snook was different. It was unpredictable: glowing in the sunshine, glowering in the rain.

When Ellen was small, Da had said that the Pearson family came from the Snook. They had pushed their heads out of the sand and levered themselves into the world with their brawny arms. Every Pearson had Snook sand running through their veins, Da said, and Pearson blood was red like the colour of the shore when the tide was low.

But Da's blood was almost black. He kept coughing it up. She heard him in the night and when she went to his room in the morning, shiny clots were splatted onto his pillowcase and his nightshirt and there was a great streak across his mouth. Henry was leaning over him, dabbing at the drops, gleaming and bright, hanging from the bristles of his beard.

'Do you want the doctor, Da?' he asked.

Da tried to lift his hand that had been gripping the bedclothes and managed to wave his fingers a little. 'Don't fuss yourselves. I'll be all right.'

They watched him all morning – Ellen at the end of the bed

and Henry beside him – breathing in then breathing out again, labouring, as if he was climbing a steep hill. Sometimes he groaned gently and sometimes the air that came out of his open mouth whistled like the wind spinning round the trees on the moor behind the town. Then he stopped. Swallowed. Took a deep gasping rattling gulp.

'I suppose you could ask Aunt Minnie to come,' he finally said, his voice struggling through the thickness in his throat.

It was Henry who ran to the post office to send the telegram. Ellen was only twelve and didn't know what to do, so she stood in the bedroom waiting for something to happen. Da always got better in the end. He always cleared his throat and sat up in the bed and said something like: 'So how about a cup of tea, Nell, or a nice boiled egg.'

But he didn't move. He lay on his back, his breathing quietened now. It sounded like faraway waves, 'Shush, shush, shush, shush,' each one fainter than the last.

When Henry returned, he peered at the face on the pillow. Then he pulled away the sheet and grasped Da's wrist.

'I think he's gone, Nell.'

'Gone?'

'Gone to heaven. Didn't you notice, didn't you look?'

So this was it. This was what she had been waiting for. She held her breath and clutched her hands together until her knuckles turned white. If she didn't breathe or move or think she could almost believe that it hadn't happened.

'Nell, come here. Look.'

She edged slowly round the bed and stood beside Henry. He was right. When she leaned over her father she could tell that something had gone. The thing that was Da had slunk away, seeped out of him, leaving just flesh and skin and hair. She could feel the thing floating above them. She could see it: deep blue and glassy like sea water when the sun shines.

11

'Maybe we should let it out,' she murmured.

'Let what out?'

Ellen reached over to the window and pulled up the sash. The wind blasted through the room and ruffled the covers on the bed as if Da had kicked the sheets. And that was it. That was the end of it. He was gone.

Whenever something bad happened, Da always used to say 'life goes on'. Which was true, except for Da's life. Life went on but it was always a different sort of life. Endings became beginnings again.

This beginning began with Aunt Minnie standing on the doorstep in the dark: a great big shiny woman with a fat shiny face, patent boots and an enormous Gladstone bag.

'I'm not too late, am I? He hasn't passed on already? I had to change at York and at Darlington, then it was stop-start all the way here.' Aunt Minnie had a surprisingly shiny sharp little voice like tin. You could hear it ringing long after she had walked through the hallway and into the parlour.

Although she didn't stay shiny for long. You couldn't stay shiny in Teesby. As soon as she sat on the settee, the sand that lay on the backrest and the cushions rose up in a cloud and descended again, showering Aunt Minnie and her Gladstone bag and her neat little boots.

She flailed her hands above her head as if the sand was a swarm of flies. 'Enough to drive you mad all this sand,' she cried. 'It gets in your hair and your eyes.'

'And it's in our blood too,' said Ellen, solemnly.

They should have taken Da to the Snook. Instead they buried him in the churchyard next to Ma where the soil was boggy. As the undertakers lowered Da's coffin into the grave, the rain began to fall, light, warm, slanting rain that hit the sides of the mourners' faces. Damp coats flapped against damp legs, and handkerchiefs that were clutched between fingers quivered respectfully. Even the long grass and the cow parsley growing beside the old tombstones swayed from side to side. Only Father Scullion at the head of Da's grave was a solid black shape: unmoving and unmoved.

'May his soul and the souls of all the faithful departed, through the mercy of God, rest in peace,' he declared flatly.

'Amen,' mumbled the mourners. 'Amen.'

After the funeral there were sandwiches in the parlour: ham and cheese and egg and cress. The bread was dry and each time Ellen took a bite it crumbled away, taking little bits of yolk with it. She sat on the edge of the settee trying to hold the sandwich together and watched Aunt Minnie shining brilliantly in the centre of the room.

'Another cup of tea? Another iced bun?'

'And what about the children?' somebody asked.

'The boy's old enough to look after himself.' Aunt Minnie's voice soared.

'And the girl?'

'We'll see, we'll see,' she trilled.

Ellen placed her sandwich on the arm of the settee. The bread fell away from the egg. The two parts lay in dry isolated clumps on the green horsehair. She looked down at the mess and with a quick flick of her fingers she brushed the remains onto the floor then kicked it under the settee with the heel of her boot.

She found Henry in the hallway, leaning against the banister rail that was draped with the mourners' coats. He was biting his nails.

'What's going to happen to me?' she asked.

'You're to live with Aunt Minnie,' he said, pulling his finger from his mouth.

'And where are you going?'

'Mrs Veasey's boarding house on Marine Parade.'

'So I could come and live with you, then.'

'No, you can't,' said Henry dully, pushing his hands into his pockets.

'Da would have said—'

'Da's not here.'

Ellen glared at Henry in his best suit and his new black tie. He was blank-faced and calm. His calmness smelt musty and mothy like the woollen coats behind him. She could see their creased greasy collars and the sagging pockets filled with dirty handkerchiefs. Beyond them, she could see the brown flowered paper on the hallway walls and the linoleum floor that she had swept the day before Da died. She could hear someone clattering the dishes in the kitchen and Aunt Minnie's shrill sing-song voice, echoing through the parlour door: 'A cup of tea, Mrs Pym? Milk? Sugar?'

She despised the ordinariness of it all: Henry, the coats, the linoleum. It should have been a day that was far from ordinary, it should have been a day that was special. Something inside her began to lift its head, began to unwind. It spiralled upwards, knotting itself round her throat and her tongue before it spewed out of her mouth and into Henry's face.

'I hate you!' she spat at him. 'I hate you all!' she screamed at the coats and the clattering dishes and Aunt Minnie's piercing voice.

She darted out of the house and along the street. The rain had stopped now, the sun was strong. As she ran the sweat streamed down her neck, and the heavy velvet funeral dress beat against her stockinged legs. She made her way towards the promenade, then sprinted over the sand to the river, weaving round the ice-cream salesmen and the donkeys then dodging the noisy children with their buckets and spades. At the quayside the little ferryboat was waiting to cross the estuary. As she stepped aboard, the boat lurched queasily down then up again.

*

It only took five minutes to cross the river, but by the time the boat had reached the opposite bank, Teesby was far away, just a heat-hazed huddle of buildings in the distance. The tiny half-dressed figures on the beach were silent now, their excited voices muffled by the breeze. Ellen began to trot down the road towards the causeway, sensing Da beside her: a ripple in the air, a shadow on the ground. If he could have spoken he would have turned to her and said, 'You should calm down, Nell. Take a deep breath. Look at the view.'

He had said that to her after Ma died. They had stood together in the tower looking out of the window at the sea. 'Take a deep breath. Look at the view.'

'Look at the view,' she whispered into the breeze.

The Snook was just ahead of her, a wide red line: silty and pebbly and sandy, speckled with seakale and storksbill. She stopped running, moved slowly, picking her way over the causeway, careful not to step on the washed-up crabs. Her anger was beginning to retreat. She could feel it settling down, curling up like a cat, resting but still alert: one eye open, one eye shut.

On the Snook she skirted the clumps of yellow gorse that grew amongst the pebbles then slid down a bank of shingle to the shore. There were heaps of driftwood on the sand – sea-shaped tree branches, bark-stripped and bleached – that had floated down the coast from Hartlepool and Sunderland. There were other treasures too: bits of rusted metal, fragments of china, buttons from the clothes of sailors who had drowned. She crouched down and found slivers of jet like black fingernails and shards of rose-pink quartz. She collected the stones, along with a few steel-coloured razor shells and periwinkles. And when her pockets were bulging and her hands were full, she made her way across the shingle to the tower before the sun disappeared behind the hill.

Ellen returned to Teesby in the dark. The ferryman had already gone home by the time she reached the estuary: she had to walk a mile upstream to the swing bridge in order to cross the river. When she finally turned onto her street again, she could see them standing on the pavement: Henry stooping into the warm night, and Aunt Minnie spinning this way and that.

'Where have you been?' Aunt Minnie snapped as Ellen reached the front gate. 'Everyone saw you tearing along the street. Everyone!' Aunt Minnie was shaking Ellen by the shoulders, but Ellen didn't care, she was calm now. She watched the sand fly off her clothes.

The day after the funeral, Henry traipsed round the house, gathering things up: Da's old penknife, a clutch of Ma's embroidered handkerchiefs, and a dish from the parlour mantelpiece with 'Souvenir' painted on the side. He packed them into an old suitcase that he had found in the attic and when it was full, he carried it down the stairs and placed it carefully by the front door.

'You know where to find me, Nell. It won't be for long. In a year or two you can come back to Teesby. You'll be fourteen, old enough then.'

He heaved Da's best coat over his shoulders. Then he moved towards her and brushed his dry lips against Ellen's cheeks. 'Behave yourself, Nell. It'll always be easier if you just behave yourself.'

There were visitors to the house now that Da was gone. Ellen sat at the top of the staircase and watched them: the landlord, who skulked along the hallway, lifting up the corner of a rug and picking at the peeling wallpaper; and Mr Parry, the auction room manager, who turned up with a yellow pencil tucked behind his ear and a notebook in his hand. Mr Parry sped through the bedrooms and the parlour, muttering the names of things and writing them down: *Grandmother clock, silvered dial; set of brass fire irons; black lacquered bamboo what-not.*

16

Then, late on Saturday evening, Father Scullion arrived. He stood in the shadows by the front door while Aunt Minnie squeaked at him like a tiny shrew.

'What should I do? You know what she's like ... and my husband said ...'

Ellen heard Father Scullion rattle his rosary and say in a low dark voice 'Ellen Pearson' and 'Sacred Heart', but the rest of the words soaked into the gloom of the hallway, or got lost in the folds of Da's scarf which was still hanging on the hook by the front door.

Things were taken away or packed away and the sand that had been trapped behind the pictures and underneath the china figurines and in between the sheets and blankets, escaped and drifted round the house. Ellen could feel the sand, gritty between her teeth and salty on her tongue. When a grain got caught in her eye it was enough to make her weep.

The rooms were almost empty now. The beds had been stripped and the mattresses rolled. The settee had been carried away by Mr Parry's men, and the kitchen chairs had vanished late one afternoon. The only place to sit was in the hallway, leaning up against the door to the parlour.

On the other side of the door, Ellen could hear Aunt Minnie and Mrs Pym, their next-door neighbour. She could hear the clink of the last few tea plates and the clatter of the silver spoons. The spoons were being laid out like Da, ready to be swathed in shrouds of the *Northern Echo* and buried deep inside Aunt Minnie's Gladstone bag.

Through the lock, Ellen could even see the spoons on the newspaper, lying together, round bowl against round bowl. She had always liked the spoons. They were kind and easy-going, they used to hum when she polished them.

'Jam spoons, teaspoons, sugar tongs,' said Mrs Pym. 'And look, a whole set of Apostle spoons!'

'But it's out of the question ...' said Aunt Minnie. 'We live a quiet life and my husband says ...'

The spoons were swaddled in newsprint and bundled into the Gladstone bag. Now it was the turn of the forks: fish forks, dessert forks, meat forks. But the forks weren't like the spoons, they were sullen and quiet and watchful. The pickle fork was the meanest because it only had two prongs and spent its life in vinegar.

'Who'd have thought they'd have so much cutlery?' said Mrs Pym between the sound of the crumpling newspaper and the moaning forks.

Only the knives were left: butter knives, meat knives, fish knives. The knives were complicated and misunderstood. They could be sharp and clever, but if you took a knife apart, unscrewed the metal blade from the bone handle, you could make it useless, make it sad.

'Of course, I'd have taken her if she'd been a quiet girl,' muttered Aunt Minnie.

'... always a handful,' said Mrs Pym, from the other side of the parlour door. 'And the priest ... didn't he say?'

It was Ellen's turn. She was packed away, bundled into clean combinations, woollen stockings, the velvet frock, a winter coat, a brown straw hat and buttoned boots. Aunt Minnie stood in the bedroom, brushing the sand out of the creases of the dress, scooping it out of the coat pockets, shaking it out of the straw hat. Ellen could see the sand, falling away from her, drifting towards the floor and disappearing into the cracks between the wooden boards.

Father Scullion was waiting at the bottom of the stairs, a pyramid of black cassock topped by a small bald head.

'Am I not coming with you, Aunt Minnie?' asked Ellen, turning back to look at her.

Aunt Minnie's mouth tightened and twisted as she shook her

head. 'You see, Ellen, after the other night ... well, we can't be doing with ... and my husband ... he says ...'

'You need to learn,' said Father Scullion. He was using the voice he used for mass, booming and pious. It made the parlour door rattle. It made Da's scarf swing back and forth on its hook. 'You need training up, Ellen Pearson.'

She might have retorted, 'Training up for what?' but his voice was a sledgehammer, pounding and crushing.

'Come along now,' he said, taking her case and pulling her through the doorway. 'Say goodbye, say goodbye to your aunt.'

Outside, the wind scudded across the front garden making the Michaelmas daisies nod their heads. Then the sand in the air swirled up in a flurry, grazing her cheeks and stinging her eyes. It followed them all the way along the promenade and up the High Street and along Sidings Lane. But when they reached the station the wind dropped and the sand flopped down onto the street like a weary dog.

There was no sand on the platform while they waited for the train. The porter had swept it all away, along with the torn-up tickets and the lost handkerchiefs and the sweet papers. Ellen could see the clean stretch of the platform, and the railway that headed westwards, narrowing until the tracks merged and vanished into the horizon. She could smell the dry odour of steam coal and the stench of hot metal from the engineering works on the other side of the river. She could hear the flat rasp of the porter's voice, and the clunk of the station clock as its hand pushed forward from one minute to the next.

Sacred Heart

The train coughed and spluttered: 'Calm down and look at the view. Calm down and look at the view.' But the view was grey and soundless. Inch by inch the pale sea was disappearing out of sight.

It was almost dark when they arrived. The village was called Dinsdale, it was written on the board outside the railway station. When Ellen muttered the name under her breath it was a sad bell tolling in her throat. 'Dinsdale, Dinsdale.'

'What did you say?' Father Scullion was adjusting his cassock. It had got trapped between his legs; in the half-light their broad outline looked like massive tree trunks under the black gown.

'Does Henry know where I'm going?' she asked.

'I'll be seeing him at mass.'

'Yes, but will you explain, Father? Will you tell him exactly where I am?'

Father Scullion grasped her wrist with one hand and her suitcase with the other. 'I'll do what's best,' he said, leading her out of the village, slapping his large feet against the road: slap, slap, slap, slap. The noise he made was as grey as the view in front of them.

They climbed a slight hill. At the top was another board: *Convent of the Sacred Heart. Roman Catholic Home for Orphans and Necessitous Females.* There were gates, a flat lawn, a small tree and a large front door. Father Scullion dropped Ellen's wrist and pulled the bell. As the door swung open there was a squawk, followed by a scurry of black-clothed women from behind it.

'So good to see you again, Father.'

'Will you be wanting supper, Father?'

'A drop of the Irish, Father?'

'Good to see you, Sisters,' said Father Scullion, pushing his way through them and setting Ellen's suitcase down on the floor of the entrance hall. He followed the nuns into the darkness of the convent, and all that was left was his voice, lowing like a fat bull in a distant field. 'Is there any of that roast left from Sunday, Sister Matthew? I won't be saying no to that if you're offering.'

A young woman stepped forward out of the shadows. She was not much older than Ellen. She wore thick-lensed spectacles and a short white veil that covered her hair.

'You're to come with me and bring your suitcase.' She had a light nervous voice. As they made their way through the convent, she twitched and fluttered from one subject to another.

'There are rules in this house: no running in the corridors, and if you meet one of the sisters you're to stand back against the wall and let her pass. And no talking, no talking at all.'

They walked down a long white passageway lined with small plaster statues of the Apostles and the Blessed Virgin, set into niches or placed on plinths.

'I was a girl here once, then Our Lord called me to him. It doesn't happen to everyone. I'll be taking my vows in November. I'm to be Sister Mary Aloysius. The name was chosen for me.'

At the end of the passageway was a narrow staircase that twisted upwards.

'You'll get a good training here,' said the young nun as she climbed the stairs. 'You'll learn how to clean and mend. Our girls are sought after by the best families in Manchester and York: parlour maids, house maids, nurse maids.'

They reached a long low room on the second floor. There was a line of beds and between each bed was a wooden chair on which lay a neatly folded uniform. The heads resting on the pillows turned to look at Ellen as she passed.

'This is where you will sleep,' said the nun, pointing at an empty bed. 'And this is a new uniform for you to wear.' She gestured to a pile of clothes on the nearby chair. 'Tomorrow you're to give me your coat and dress and we'll put them away until you leave.'

'But where will they go, Sister?' Suddenly the velvet frock and the winter coat and the brown straw hat took on a new importance. They were her old self. They smelt of home, of seaweed and Da's tobacco and the damp wardrobe in which they had been stored. And despite Aunt Minnie's desperate shaking, Ellen could still feel the gritty sand inside the dress.

The nun did not reply, either she hadn't heard the question or she didn't think it was worth answering. 'Mass is at six thirty. You're to be washed and dressed and ready to go,' she said as she spun away.

In the dark, Ellen gently pulled off her coat and hat and lay them carefully on top of the new uniform. As she started to tug at the hooks at the side of her dress, a girl at the other end of the room sat up in her bed.

'You can't take your clothes off like that.'

'What do you mean?'

'You have to put your nightgown on first and take your clothes off underneath. It's a rule.'

'Why?'

'Modesty! You should know about that at your age.'

In her old life Ellen would have replied that she had nothing to be ashamed of, especially in the dark, that none of them had anything to be ashamed of. But the night was heavy. The darkness pushed her down, squeezed something out of her, the thing that made her Ellen. She had barely enough energy to open her mouth; better to say nothing at all. She took the nightgown from her suitcase, pulled it over her head then flailed under the white flannel for a while until her dress fell onto the floor.

She lay down in her new bed, but she didn't sleep.

When it was light again, she rolled over and peered out of the small square window beside her bed. The window overlooked the back of the convent. She could see a strip of yellow grass incised by a series of paths that led to a line of washing at the end of the garden. Sheets and pillowcases and tablecloths were swinging gently in the breeze: a long white undulating wall. It was almost impossible to see anything beyond them. Only occasionally was there a gust strong enough to lift up the corner of a sheet and reveal the view behind it, a fragment of ploughed field and stony track.

'We do all the washing and the mending for the nuns and the priest and the hotel in the village,' whispered the girl in the next bed. 'We have lessons as well, but not very many.'

She said her name was Bridget. She had red-rimmed eyes and a runny nose that she kept wiping with the back of her hand.

'I'm from Darlington. My father died last year and my mother couldn't keep me any more. I was the new girl before you, I'm glad you're here,' she said, unsmilingly.

The uniform on the chair beside Ellen's bed turned out to be a grey woollen tunic. The neck and hem were grimy and worn, and the pockets were misshapen. The tunic held the oniony odour of someone else's sweat, someone who was probably about to serve breakfast to a 'good family' in Manchester or York. When Ellen put the tunic on, it draped oddly over her chest and sat awkwardly on her hips.

Morning mass was followed by breakfast. Breakfast was followed by English and after that Arithmetic. She had never enjoyed school and had avoided it when she could, not because she was a bad student but because there was something about her that

23

the other children had taken a dislike to. She was always wrong in one way or another: what she said, how she looked, what she did. When Da was ill she had stayed at home and had read to him from Ma's old books. In the last few weeks she had been working her way through *Middlemarch*. It wasn't easy but there were things in it she had liked: 'If we had a keen vision and feeling of all ordinary human life, it would be like hearing the grass grow and the squirrel's heartbeat, and we should die of that roar which lies on the other side of silence.' That was the bit that had stuck. She had learnt it off by heart and had recited it to Da as he lay in bed the day before he died.

In the English class they were studying Butler's *Lives of the Saints*. Each girl took her turn to stand at the front of the schoolroom and recite a few lines. Ellen was instructed to read the story of Saint Agnes, whose head was cut off because she refused to get married. As Ellen worked her way through the tale, she could see the beautiful head rolling down a dusty Roman street, long locks winding themselves around the face until all that was left was a ball of golden hair.

Arithmetic was a sort of book-keeping lesson. The girls drew long columns on their slates and added up the prices of cream of tartar or cod liver oil then read out the answers to the nun standing at the blackboard. It was a bit like going shopping but for boring things. Ellen remembered the half-empty bottle of cod liver oil on the top shelf in the kitchen at home, and wondered what had happened to it, whether Aunt Minnie had slipped it into her Gladstone bag or whether the contents had been tipped out into the gutter and the bottle thrown away. She thought of the cod liver oil flowing down the gutter to the beach, then trickling through the sand to the sea.

'And what is the answer to the question, girl?' The nun's nose had pushed itself into Ellen's face. The nose was long and crooked and peppered with blackheads. 'What is the answer?'

'I don't—'

The nose twisted away and pointed towards the girl sitting at the next desk.

'What is the answer, Ernestine Smith?'

'Three shillings and twopence, Sister Bartholomew.'

'Three shillings and twopence is the answer,' said the nose, prodding itself into Ellen's face again. 'Do you hear me? Do you hear me?'

At midday the girls trooped in a long snaking line to the refectory. They all looked the same: straight, mouse-coloured hair, thin arms and legs, grey tunics, white blouses. Ellen followed behind, her mouth dry, her guts knotted.

Grace was said, then the room was filled with the sound of scraping spoons against dishes. The convent spoons weren't like the spoons in Teesby, they squealed and whined. The noise was so bad she wanted to put her hands over her ears and block it out. Instead, she breathed deeply and concentrated on making sure that her own spoon slid through the thin soup without touching the bottom.

Lunch was punctuated by whispers which scurried along the table, hissing and spitting at her.

'Tell the new girl that she can't . . .'

'Monica says to tell you that you're not to go anywhere near the nuns' parlour.'

'And outside, you're not to go beyond the washing lines.'

'And you can't go to the kitchen when . . .'

'And you have to tell Sister Bartholomew if you start to . . . well you know . . . She'll give you a rag if you need one.'

'Though we're not to mention it to anyone else.'

The girls stared at her, half-smiling: sneering, upholders of the rules. They were enjoying the discomfort of the new girl. They had all suffered once just as she was suffering now. They were gleefully getting their own back, for that was how the system worked.

In the afternoon, one of the older girls took her to the laundry room and showed her a pile of linen sheets that were covered in stains, overlapping circles of pale yellows and pinks. Ellen didn't want to think about how the stains had got onto the sheets. It was better to just grit her teeth and try and pretend they were only colours that needed to be white.

In the steamy heat, she scrubbed the linen in a tub of water then wrung it by hand, twisting and twisting it to coax the dirty water out. Even when she had wrung the sheet as dry as she could, it was too heavy for her to lift alone. It took two of them to heave it into a basket and carry it to the mangle – a hulking beast with a wooden bucket for a body and topped by a pair of rollers clamped together like a tight-lipped mouth.

'You have to keep your fingers out of the way,' said Bridget, as she turned the wheel. 'And your hair too … saw someone get themselves caught up in a mangle once. Horrible it was. She screamed and screamed and had to have all her hair cut off.'

Ellen kept her distance. She hovered behind Bridget, watching the mangle swallow the sheet then regurgitate it on the other side. The bloated, heavy linen was transformed into smooth unresisting folds that tumbled neatly from the rollers to the basket on the floor.

At the back of the room, overseeing the mangle, was an old woman.

Bridget said she was called Shirley. 'She doesn't talk. It's not because she can't, it's because she won't.'

'But why won't she?' asked Ellen.

Bridget shrugged her shoulders.

The woman must have been sixty or seventy. She was small and stooping and stony-faced. Once the linen had been wrung dry, she wandered stiffly into the garden and directed the girls like a policeman at a road junction, jabbing her finger at dropped pegs and trailing linen.

Ellen hauled the clean damp sheet over the washing line. She had been hoping to look at the view, the field and the stony track she had seen that morning. But Shirley had positioned herself at the edge of the hill where the land dipped down towards the valley, and all Ellen could see was the old woman's large red hands flapping at the washing lines and her sad, unblinking eyes.

At supper, when the whispering girls had run out of rules to relay, they whispered about Shirley.

'Came when she was seven.'

'Left when she was fourteen.'

'Scullery maid.'

'No, house maid. Lit the fires in the bedrooms.' Someone giggled at the word bedroom.

'But she had to come back again, didn't she?'

Heads dipped, eyes lowered, nodding and smirking. All of them understood except Ellen.

At the other end of the refectory, Sister Matthew stood at a lectern and read from a book called *True Devotion to the Blessed Virgin*.

'God the Father imparted to Mary his fruitfulness ... God-made-man found freedom in imprisoning himself in her womb.'

Old Ellen would have run away from the convent. New Ellen lay in her bed in the dormitory and realised there was nowhere to go. The thought made her feel like she was sinking.

'Tell the new girl that she has to fold her clothes not dump them on the chair.'

She pulled the covers over her head. It was like being underwater. She drifted for a while in the cold whiteness, hating it all. Hating the nuns – bad-tempered spirals of veils and habits and darned stockings. Hating the girls – the colour of spite and mockery, bright violet or vivid puce. Hating the statue of Jesus that stood on a pedestal in the schoolroom: his fingers ripping his tunic apart to reveal the hard dollop of scarlet plaster lodged inside his chest. Hating the stains and the creases and the bleak cry of the wind as it wrapped itself round Shirley and the washing lines. Hating the prayers at the end of the day.

Matthew, Mark, Luke and John

she had chanted with the rest of the girls.

Bless the bed that I lie on.
Four corners to my bed,
Four angels round my head;
One to watch and one to pray
And two to bear my soul away.

The Other Girls

As soon as Henry knew where she was he would come and get her. It was this thought alone that sustained Ellen through the long autumn and winter of her first year in the convent. Every afternoon, while she scrubbed the stains from the sheets, she imagined him like a detective clasping a notebook in his hand, like Sherlock Holmes in a deerstalker, scribbling down clues to her whereabouts. It was obvious that Father Scullion had not spoken to Henry, otherwise Henry would be here by now. Or he would have at least written to her to explain his plans to get her out.

Father Scullion visited the convent regularly. He dined with the nuns once a week and sometimes he took mass when the resident priest, old Father Hindmarsh, was ill. Ellen often saw the back of his gleaming head bobbing above the sea of black serge veils, as he swept down the corridor. He was always too far away to speak to.

Apart from her daydreams of Henry, Teesby was beginning to fade. She tried to recall the sounds of the fishermen on the quay and the foghorn on the ferryboat and the stuttering squeal of the terns. As the weeks passed, she could no longer remember what the parlour at home looked like, or the view from her bedroom window, or the Snook or the tower. She could no longer picture the colour of things or the shape of things.

*

At the end of November, young Sister Aloysius went to the Motherhouse to take her vows.

'She's to be a bride of Christ,' said Bridget, pulling a wet sheet onto the washing line.

As they pushed the pegs over the sheet, Bridget told Ellen that Sister Aloysius would wear a white wedding dress and that the priest and the nuns would cut off her hair. Then she would sit at the high table with an empty chair beside her because that was where Jesus was supposed to sit. And there would be a three-tiered wedding cake with icing on the top.

When Ellen traipsed back into the laundry with the empty washing basket, she imagined two tiny plaster figures perched on the top of the cake: bespectacled Sister Aloysius hand in hand with Jesus brandishing his dreadful sacred heart.

Ellen remembered what Sister Aloysius had said to her on her first night in the convent: 'Our Lord called me to him.'

And she wondered what it would be like to be called by Jesus. Would there be a thundering voice that obliterated every other sound in the universe, or would it be just a constant insinuating whisper? What if Jesus called her to him before Henry found out where she was. Would it be a sin to ignore him? Would she be punished? The thought terrified Ellen. At night she pulled the pillow round her head in case Christ came sneaking up and started muttering into her ear.

But Sister Aloysius was happy to be married to Jesus. When she returned to the convent, she kept self-consciously tweaking her new black veil. On her finger was a thick bright band of gold.

'I wish I was married,' said Bridget, gazing over at Sister Aloysius's ring. 'Then I could do what I liked.'

'Do you think Christ comes to her at night?' said Ellen, still worried by the strange shadows in the dormitory after the lights went out, by the night-sounds outside the window.

*

Advent came and went. Then Christmas.

Father Scullion took mass on Christmas Eve. He wore a gloriously embroidered chasuble which shimmered as he lifted the chalice to bless the wine. Ellen thought he looked like God. Not a kindly God but the sort of God who pointed his omnipotent finger at the earth and inflicted some awful terror upon it: a plague of frogs or locusts or fire. Father Scullion had a huge glowing head, giant limbs and torso, and a booming voice that made the nuns' rosary beads rattle at their waists.

On Christmas Day the girls were allowed to sit in the visitors' parlour where the fire burned in the grate. They played games or sewed, or they knitted baby clothes for the poor. Ellen sat in the corner of the room with Bridget and watched Sister Aloysius distributing Christmas gifts. The nun glided smugly from one girl to another, handing out oranges and small printed cards of Our Lady holding baby Jesus in her arms.

'Sister Aloysius is going to leave the convent after Christmas,' said Bridget as she dug her nails into the orange peel. 'She told me that the Reverend Mother has given her a special mission. I think she's going to Africa or China to teach little children. I wish I could go with her.'

Then the worst thing happened.

On the third of January Ellen turned thirteen. It had never been a good time to have a birthday because everyone was always fatigued from Christmas and the last thing they wanted to do was wrap presents again and eat more cake. It had been like that even when Ma and Da were alive. In the convent the girls' birthdays were marked by an announcement at breakfast and a brisk shake of Sister Matthew's cold dry hand. Then everyone stood up and sang 'Happy Birthday' before they cleared the dishes away.

At lunchtime, however, Ellen was handed a small blue envelope. She watched as it was passed along the table through soup-stained fingers, from one girl to another. She knew it was from Henry because she recognised the writing when it reached the girl sitting beside her. She could see his neat black copperplate: no smudges, no shiny splatters of ink. She could hardly breathe.

It was a card. Printed on the front were the words 'Birthday Greetings' surrounded by a wreath of roses and lily of the valley. Inside he had written, 'Dear Nell, Happy birthday, I hope you have a lovely day, with best wishes from your brother Henry.'

She turned the card over then opened it again. Henry knew where she was but he wasn't coming to get her. The neat words sniggered at her misery, first quietly then out loud. The N of Nell was laughing so hard she could see it wriggling on the white background.

'Who's the card from?' someone asked at the end of the table.

'My brother,' she mumbled, swallowing away a sob.

She shut the card and Teesby vanished. All of it, all at once. The card had left her breathless. It was the sort of feeling you have when you wade into the cold sea, and before the water reaches your chest you feel like you are drowning.

She may as well marry Jesus. She may as well serve breakfast and lunch and dinner to a good family in Manchester or York.

The walls crept closer. There was nothing to see from the windows but white washing. She belonged to the convent now.

She could have written to Henry of course. In exceptional circumstances the girls were allowed a piece of paper and an envelope. Although the letter had to be given to Sister Matthew unsealed before it was sent on. So what was the point? What was the point?

Time passed. The snow fell. She watched the flakes tumble outside the schoolroom window and bank up on the sill. It sat on top of the bare branches and the washing lines then dropped in great lumps to the ground. The snow lay over the grass for a week before it slunk away again, leaving small icy skims in the dips of the garden.

However bad the weather got, if it wasn't raining the washing was always hung out to dry. In February it was cold enough for the sheets to freeze to the line. The girls had to peel them off and carry them back to the convent like odd-shaped pieces of furniture, edging them carefully through doors and along corridors. Ellen didn't mind taking the washing off the line when it was that cold. It was easy to disappear behind the rigid sheets, slide in between them and hide from Shirley for a moment. She could inhale the cold air and stare at the view: the field and the stony track that led down the hill. Whenever she hid behind the sheets, she would try and imagine what was at the end of that track. There would be a valley, green and tree-lined. There would be flowers sprouting in the undergrowth: wild snowdrops and yellow aconites. There would be a cottage built of stone, painted pale blue or pink: somewhere she could be herself for an hour or two. Somewhere she could breathe.

Ellen chose the coldest day when no one wanted to bring in the washing. When even Shirley was reluctant to go outside.

'I'll get the sheets,' she called, snatching a basket from a shelf before anyone could stop her.

She ducked round the stiff washing and paused on the ridge. It was a bitter day, the grass was frosted and the puddles in the track had frozen. She began to struggle down the slope, holding out her arms to balance herself. As she stepped onto the puddles, the dark water slid under the ice then oozed out and seeped over the toes of her boots.

The track meandered down the hill. At each bend she thought she was almost at the bottom, but when she turned again she was faced with the same view, more field, more stony track. There were no trees, only scrappy bushes, and nothing was green, it was white or the palest of greys. The valley was as windswept as the plateau on which the convent stood.

When she finally reached the bottom she stopped. Ahead of her the track thinned and ended at a wooden gate. A few yards further on she could see a long stone farmhouse surrounded by a muddy yard. The mud had frozen into peaks and troughs, the peaks crested with frost.

She crouched low behind a bush and peered between the spiny branches. Strung across the farmyard were washing lines, and hanging from the lines were little square napkins and tiny sheets, miniature versions of the sheets that were hanging outside the convent. Beside the house, sitting on a bench, was a nun wrapped in a thick shawl. Trudging in and out of the house with baskets, just like the ones they used in the convent laundry, were girls just like Ellen. Except they moved slowly, labouring across the mud like old women. One of them lifted a sheet awkwardly over the line, then paused as if the effort was too much. Another moved towards her, said something and pulled the sheet straight over the cord. They all wore long smocks. Ellen could make out the form of their rounded breasts and stomachs underneath.

Without warning, a magpie shot out of the bush, making a loud scratchy noise as it soared across the washing. The nun sitting on the bench looked up. She stared at Ellen for a moment, the corner of her veil tapping like the tail of an angry cat. Then she pulled her shawl round her shoulders and scooted across the yard, her habit thrashing against her legs.

'Who said you could come down here?' It was Sister Aloysius, her eyes freakishly large behind her thick spectacles.

'I wanted to see—' Ellen started.

'But you can't see. You mustn't see!' She caught hold of Ellen's hand and tugged at it. 'Do you hear me? You mustn't see them. They are not fit to be seen!'

34

Sister Aloysius pulled Ellen back up the icy track to the convent, both of them tripping over the stones or sliding over the ice.

'They're wicked girls, Ellen Pearson.' Her voice grew higher and higher. 'You must pray for them. And you must pray for yourself.'

When they reached the back of the convent, Sister Aloysius dropped Ellen's hand. The black veil flapped around her face. She looked older than she had done in the convent, already there were faint furrows on her brow and her skin was grey and doughy. Being married to Christ must be difficult.

'You are to go to the dormitory,' she snapped before she turned on her heels and whisked away. 'Go to the dormitory immediately!'

Ellen lay down on her bed and closed her eyes. She must have dozed off because when she opened them again Father Scullion was standing in the doorway. He was cleaning his hands on a handkerchief, wiping each finger carefully one by one as he looked at her. When he had finished, he pushed the handkerchief into a pocket in his cassock and began to amble slowly towards her.

She scrambled off the bed and stood up.

'No,' he said, pressing her shoulders down so that she was perched on the edge of the mattress.

He took the chair from beside the bed, placed it in front of her and sat down. His enormous knees were wedged against hers. She could feel the warmth of them under her woollen stockings.

'I've been hearing about you, Ellen Pearson.' He sighed deeply; his breath smelt of meat, dark and bloody. 'I always knew you'd be one of those – a meddler, a troublemaker.' He spoke quietly; almost gently. If someone had been watching them from the doorway they might have thought he was consoling her.

Father Scullion leaned forward. She couldn't see his face, her own shadow fell across him.

'Women have an extra cross to bear, Ellen Pearson. A curse. They have to guard against it. They have to be trained.' He paused, then he sat back in the chair and his voice changed. 'What happened to Eve?'

'She ate something she shouldn't have done, Father.'

'That God instructed her not to eat,' he corrected. 'And Lot's wife?'

'She looked back when she was told not to.'

'Curiosity!' He spat out the word and it sounded like a threat. 'Curiosity!' he said again, this time slowly, quietly, relishing the sound of the word in his mouth. 'And what does Saint James say? What does he say, girl?'

'I don't know.' Despite the shadows she could see Father Scullion, she could see inside him. He was blazing red and yellow as bright as burning Hell. 'I don't know, Father.'

'Saint James said that curiosity leads to sin and that sin leads to death.'

She didn't know what he meant but she nodded.

'Let this be a warning to you, Ellen Pearson.' He pointed at the window where the track zig-zagged down the hill to the farmhouse. 'That's where curiosity will lead you.'

He sat staring at her in silence, rocking slightly backwards and forwards in his chair. After a minute or so he raised his hand towards her face and took a lock of her hair in his hand. She could feel a faint pressure on her scalp as his fingers ran down it, stroking it. When he reached the end of the lock he let it drop against her face then he stood up abruptly and left the room.

Ellen cried that night. She cried for the girls in the farmhouse, and for Da, and for herself. She cried for their empty house she could barely remember, for the spoons and knives that Aunt Minnie had taken away, for the dish with 'Souvenir' on the side that Henry had clasped in his hand the last time she had seen him. She cried for the forgotten bottle of cod liver oil on the kitchen shelf and for the joyful Michaelmas daisies in the front garden. She cried for every pebble, every shell, every grain of sand. She lay under the sheets, drowning. She lay under the sheets dying of that terrible roar from the other side of silence.

The grass near the washing lines grew green, and the crab apple at the front of the convent blossomed briefly. But for Ellen the world paled. Everything in the convent was white now apart from the statue of Jesus with his horrible heart. The walls were white and the floors were white. The washing that lay on the table in the laundry room was white. The pile of ironing in the baskets was white. The mending was white, the darning of shirts and socks and stockings. And the fancy work was white, too. All the monograms and flower borders were embroidered in white silk thread on white linen.

Occasionally, there were fleeting streaks of colours. Weekly confession with old Father Hindmarsh was a dull purple, and mass was a deep unpleasant brown. The sound of the blackberry bush tapping like an outcast against the chapel window was either tarnished silver or mottled gold. And at night, the waves of whispers that ran from one side of the dormitory to the other were shaded with a pale pink tint. All the girls were white, though, ghost white, like badly painted whitewash with just a hint of colour showing through.

Time passed. She sank down, focused on small things:

The glassy bubbles in the washing tub.

The small dot of dark blood on a pillowcase which flowered when she pushed it under the water.

The white embroidered altar cloth.

The tip of Father Scullion's fat pink tongue lightly sliding against his bottom lip as he slipped a communion wafer into her open mouth.

*

In the autumn Bridget left the convent. Her mother had married again and wanted her back. Ellen had no one to talk to.

There was a grey moth trapped in a cobweb in the corner of the dormitory window.

'I hate moths,' said the new girl in the next bed.

Ellen reached over and broke the web and the moth opened its wings, testing freedom. The wings were scalloped and edged with black. She watched the moth float upwards and disappear.

The Villa

The May sun was shining through the leaves of the tree outside the schoolroom window. The shadows dappled Sister Bartholomew's face, distorting her eyes and nose, making her monstrous.

'If a ball of wool weighing one and a half ounces costs threepence, how much would it cost to buy enough to make a—'

There was a gust of wind at the end of the corridor. A door opened. The sound was followed by a man's voice: 'I've come to see—' and a nun's anxious reply: 'But didn't Father explain to you that it was better—'

The girls in the schoolroom turned their heads, strained to listen to the conversation. Sister Bartholomew turned her head too then remembered who she was. She tapped at the blackboard with her long stick.

'If a ball of wool weighing one and a half ounces costs threepence . . .'

Ellen sat at her desk picturing balls of wool. She would choose pink wool, strawberry pink. She would knit a scarf so long it would trail behind her. She would have servants to pick up the ends.

The schoolroom door opened. There was a brief flustered exchange between Sister Bartholomew and Sister Matthew: 'But she's to come now . . . right now . . . the entrance hall . . .'

Ellen's pink scarf would have long fringes. She would

sew glass beads on the ends and every time she moved she would clatter.

'There's someone for you in the hall, Ellen Pearson.' Sister Bartholomew's nose had pushed itself into Ellen's face. 'Did you hear me? Did you hear me?'

Henry was standing against the sunshine in the open doorway to the convent. 'Nell!' he wheezed.

She made her way down the corridor. He was taller and thinner than she remembered. There was something tight about him too: his clothes looked like they were holding him together. When she reached him, she could see a red mark round his neck where his collar was rubbing and the button on his right cuff was pulling against the buttonhole. It was almost two years since she had seen him last.

'Where have you been?' she asked slowly. 'How could you leave me here? How could you do it?' The sobs bubbled up in her throat and she clenched her fists as if she was going to hit him.

He stepped forward, peered at her anxiously.

'But they kept telling me you weren't ready to come home. Father Scullion said you'd be better off staying a bit longer; he said it was good for you. And then,' he added quietly, 'I wasn't very well for a time.'

Henry didn't look very well. He was a cloudy yellow colour, like a sulphur sky before a thunderstorm. She could see the perspiration on his forehead. She could hear the breath rattling in his chest.

'I came today because Mrs Veasey's found you a job,' he said.

'A job, in Teesby?' Her voice was flat, unbelieving.

'Well, more or less. It's with an old woman. She wants you to look after her and to read to her. The pay's not very good, though, so if you'd rather ...' A lock of hair fell across Henry's damp face and he pushed it away. 'I mean, if you want to stay until we find you something better ... It's your life, Nell, your decision ...'

40

She unclenched her fists, moved towards him and gripped his sweating hand.

It was raining when the train pulled into the railway station. It was the sort of rain that only Teesby knew, rain that smelt of salt and seaweed, rain that was thick with sand. There were deposits of damp dark sand piled up by the ticket office and a dusting of paler finer sand on the pavement outside the station.

Henry and Ellen walked down Sidings Lane to the promenade. When they reached the sea front, she stood for a moment, her old coat flapping in the breeze – it was far too small for her now and she hadn't been able to fasten it across her chest. She held onto the railings and looked at the faint outline of the Snook in the drizzle. There was no hope of going there that afternoon: the tide was out and the ferryboat was leaning on its side by the quay wall. She gazed at the view expecting to feel something, relief or joy perhaps.

'You're to stay with Mrs Veasey tonight then tomorrow you're to go up to Mrs Tibbs in the villa,' said Henry, guiding Ellen away from the railings towards Marine Parade. 'I thought we'd go to evening mass before supper then you can tell Father Scullion about the job.'

'I'm not going to mass,' she said coldly, surprising Henry. Surprising herself. Her voice was an unfamiliar monotone: straight and steely. 'I won't be going to mass any more, Henry. You'll have to go on your own.'

She waited for Henry in his rooms on Marine Parade. When he returned from mass they went downstairs and ate tea in Mrs Veasey's dining room. Ellen sat opposite her brother at a round table that overlooked the street. Behind his head, she could see people scuttling past the window with umbrellas pressed against the wind.

'Father Scullion was upset that you didn't go to see him,' said Henry, picking his way across his plate of white fish and mashed potato. 'You'll have a day off soon, so you can go and see him then.'

She gazed out of the window as he rambled on: about Father Scullion and the repairs to the church porch and his new job at the Town Hall. Henry was second assistant to the chief clerk, for most of the day he sat on a stool in the back office and copied out letters and receipts in his best hand.

'It's interesting work, Nell.' He clutched Mrs Veasey's silent cutlery with his long fingers scrubbed clean of ink. His skin was red and in places quite raw, his nails were neatly bitten. 'Good prospects, plenty of opportunity for advancement.'

While they ate, Mrs Veasey's dining room slowly filled with men: businessmen and salesmen wearing white shirts and waistcoats festooned with gold-coloured watch chains. They spoke in low voices, a deep maroon hum so different from the high-pitched whispers of the girls at the Sacred Heart. When Ellen got up to fetch the brown sauce from the sideboard the men looked at her furtively – at her old dress that was too short for her now, at the bodice that was straining across her shoulders and the tops of her arms. She was relieved when she made it back to her seat again and could lower her head over her plate.

'Your sister's grown into a very nice-looking girl,' she heard Mrs Veasey say to Henry as she cleared away the dishes. 'But you need to keep an eye on her now. Keep her safe.'

Mrs Tibbs's villa was nearly a mile outside Teesby. The only way to get to it was by walking up the narrow lane that led to the Nab. There were no other houses, just fields and a few beech trees and dog roses growing in tumbles over the dry-stone wall that lined the path. At the top of the hill, the Nab stretched for about ten miles until it reached the next town. Apart from heather and gorse, nothing much would grow up there. In the summer, the thin grass was blackened by the heat, and in the winter the moor was covered in snow.

Henry paused to catch his breath and pointed up at the house. 'There it is, Nell. Huge isn't it, all roofs and chimneys.'

The villa was a long line of brick gables and bay windows that advanced and retreated across the ridge. Growing in the garden in front of the house were a heap of roses and a huge tree with dark crooked branches.

'Monkey Puzzle tree, I think,' said Henry. 'Great big ugly thing.'

But Ellen thought the ugliness made it beautiful in a strange way. She looked up at the tree as they turned off the lane into the villa garden; the leaves were shining and sharp as if they had been cut out of metal.

At the back of the house, sitting on the kitchen step, was a woman bent over a pile of potatoes. As Henry and Ellen approached, she snatched a muddy potato, spun it in her hand and a fine twist of brown peel fell into the lap of her apron.

'This is my sister, Miss Pearson,' said Henry, gesturing to Ellen. 'I think Mrs Veasey told you about her.'

The woman tossed the peeled potato into a bucket of water and stared up at Ellen. 'The missus wants to see you upstairs.' She waved her hand over her shoulder at the kitchen then picked up another potato, spun it clean of peel and dropped it into the bucket. 'And what do you think you're gawping at?' she said, turning to Henry.

'I'll leave your things here, Nell,' he mumbled, sliding Ellen's case beside the bucket of water. He lifted his hand slightly then crept away round the corner of the house and disappeared.

Ellen made her way through the kitchen into a long dim passageway that must have run the length of the villa. The house was dark:

43

she could see through half-opened doors into shadowy rooms. The shutters had been closed tight against the windows, although the sunshine was forcing its way through the cracks in the wood and sharp needles of light illuminated the dust sheets that covered the furniture. The villa smelt of old women, a sweet, stale dankness that turned her stomach. It might have been better if she had married Jesus after all, or found a position with a good clean family in Manchester or York.

At the end of the corridor was a wide staircase that swept up to the first floor. She climbed the stairs then hesitated in the gloom of the landing, unsure which way to go.

'Is that you?'

It was the faintest, thinnest of voices, almost transparent. It made Ellen think of spun sugar: the white glistening nests that sat on the fancy cakes in the window of the baker's on the High Street.

'Is that the girl? Is it? Is there someone there? I'm at the end of the house, in the drawing room. Yes, yes, that's right, keep going. The last door. The last one on the left.'

When Ellen turned into the room all she could see was a dark form lying on what she took to be a settee.

'Your name?' murmured the shape.

'Ellen Pearson, Miss ... Ma'am ... Mrs.' As her eyes adjusted to the greyness, she could make out a woman reclining on a chaise longue. She was as small as her tiny voice. She had thick pale hair, white glowing skin and tinted spectacles over her eyes.

'You can call me Mrs Tibbs and I shall call you Pearson,' said the woman, twisting round and placing her minute feet on the floor. 'I should tell you something about myself, perhaps.' She was sitting upright now with her hands neatly clasped in her lap. 'I am a widow, I have been for many years. And I am blind. Now it's your turn, Pearson.'

'I am an orphan,' Ellen replied. 'I have been for two years. And ... and ... I like reading ... Miss ... Mrs ...'

'Well, reading is something that I cannot do, Pearson,' said the old woman, nodding gently. 'So we complement each other rather well, don't you think?' She lay back down again and might have shut her eyes behind the spectacles but it was almost impossible to be sure.

'Listen to Beadie, Pearson.' Then Mrs Tibbs fluttered her fingers in the air and Ellen realised she had been dismissed.

Beadie, the woman who had been hunched over the pile of potatoes on the back step, was now sitting at the end of the kitchen table with a pot of tea and a cup and saucer in front of her.

'So you found her, then?' she said, lifting the lid of the teapot and inspecting the liquid inside. 'And did you talk to her?'

Ellen stood at the other end of the table and nodded.

'You listen to me,' said Beadie, slamming the lid down onto the pot. 'I were twelve year old when I came to this house. Mrs Tibbs came up to the village in a carriage to get me. I've been here forty years. Forty years, mark you.' Beadie poured the tea into the cup. 'There were a cook and a parlour maid and a boy to do the heavy work. All gone. All except me. And now she says I need someone to help me. Says I'm too old ... too old, mark you.' She tipped the cup and dribbled some tea into her saucer. 'So it's going to be your job to look after the missus, now. You're to serve her at table. You're to dress and undress her. You're to bathe her. You're to look after her clothes – she's very particular about them. And she carries a little bell with her, so you're to listen out for it at all times, at night as well as the day.' She took a long sip from the saucer and swished the tea round her mouth. 'You're to care for her like she were one of your own, do you understand me?'

Ellen, dry-mouthed and weary, nodded again.

'Now if you went and got yourself a cup from the dresser,' said Beadie gruffly, 'I could pour you out some tea.'

*

In the afternoon Ellen changed into a uniform supplied by Beadie, a pale pink dress several decades old and a white apron. Despite their age, the clothes were clean and pressed. As Ellen was passing a mirror in the entrance hall, she paused. She had forgotten what she looked like: she was tall with thick brown hair and a slightly surprised expression on her freckled face. Seeing herself in the mirror made her feel a little better.

In the evening Ellen served dinner to Mrs Tibbs at a small round table in the drawing room. She stood by the fireplace with her hands behind her back watching the old woman fumble her way through poached eggs on toast and a glass of claret. Later, she undressed Mrs Tibbs in her bedroom, carefully unhooking her clothes, the black silk blouse and the black silk skirt and all the cotton petticoats. Fully dressed, Mrs Tibbs was a slim woman, but as soon as her corset was removed, her body drooped and swagged and swung. It was a disturbing sight, even in the feeble light of the gas lamp.

Mrs Tibbs's white glowing complexion turned out to be a skim of iridescent powder across her face: it was called 'Poudre d'Amour' and sat in a glass dish on her dressing table. The thick pale hair that had been twisted into extravagant ringlets and dressed with silk flowers turned out to be a wig. Ellen peeled away the warm shabby hairpiece and found a single tuft growing from a shining scalp.

'You must brush it very gently,' said Mrs Tibbs, stroking the damp tuft with the palm of her hand. 'It does tend to fall out from time to time. Oh, and do be careful with the wig, Pearson. It was very expensive when I bought it, took weeks and weeks to make.'

The wig had begun to pill like an old woollen jumper and the yellow ringlets had grown fuzzy and lost their spring. Mrs Tibbs instructed Ellen to place it on the wooden block that sat on the dressing table and tweak the curls back into place.

'You must get it right, Pearson. I do like to look my best,' sighed the old woman.

After a restless night, Ellen reversed the process the next morning. She laced and she buttoned and she hooked. She dusted Mrs Tibbs's wrinkles with Poudre d'Amour, positioned the wig on her almost naked head and pinned the widow's cap into the artificial locks.

'Do I look nice, Pearson?' asked Mrs Tibbs, her hands raised towards her head, her tiny fingers feeling their way around the torn lace that edged the cap. 'I have to look my best in case there are visitors today.'

But no one came to the villa, and if they had they would barely have been able to see Mrs Tibbs's yellow locks in the dimness of the upstairs drawing room.

The air in the villa was thick with dust. It hung heavily in the rooms, in Mrs Tibbs's bedroom where the curtains were permanently drawn, in the drawing room and the pitch-black corridors. Even in the kitchen the air was still and brown although Beadie didn't seem to notice. She had been in the house so long she must have grown used to it.

Beadie was a sullen-looking woman with an unhappy mouth that pulled the rest of her face down with it. She rarely strayed from the kitchen; she stood at the table or the range growling and snapping at saucepans and mixing bowls and roasting tins. The meals she concocted, however, were delicious: exotic jellies and pies and cakes and syllabubs.

'If you're going to eat, you may as well eat as well as you can,' she said to the metal whisk as she beat the thick fresh cream into a gooseberry fool.

Beadie never said very much, but when she did speak she appeared to be talking to herself or to the kitchen utensils, or to the cat which, as soon as she settled herself in the chair by the range, grasped its chance and sprang into her lap.

'What's the cat called?' asked Ellen on that first evening after she had put Mrs Tibbs to bed. She thought it was an uncontentious question.

'Moggy!' replied Beadie to the snoring animal nestled in her apron.

'But doesn't he have a proper name?'

'You don't think Moggy's a proper name?'

The cat was mostly black with a collar of white fur circling his neck. When he wasn't curled up in Beadie's lap he strutted pompously round the kitchen, lurking in corners, staring unblinkingly at Ellen. She decided to call him The Reverend Casaubon after Dorothea's pious husband in *Middlemarch*.

Casaubon began to follow her through the house, into rooms she shouldn't have entered. She could make out the ghost-shapes of furniture, a piano, perhaps, a dining table, a credenza. In a room at the back of the house she found three glass-fronted bookcases. She spent a long time peering through the dust-mottled glass trying to decipher the titles: she managed to make out *David Copperfield* and *Great Expectations* and poems by Keats.

'Why are the shutters in all the rooms shut?' she asked at the end of her first week in the villa.

Beadie grunted at the bread dough she was kneading on the kitchen table.

'Because she wants it like that. Her house, isn't it?!'

A few days later, after Ellen had made a point of praising a particularly light coffee cake that Beadie had baked that morning, she asked the question a second time.

Beadie was bent double raking the ashes in the range. She flung the oven door shut and wiped her hands on her apron. 'Missus closed the rooms after Mr Tibbs and the little girl died.'

'What happened?'

'She got the measles, she gave it to their little girl and then to him. He and the little girl died and she went blind. I had to go and tell her they were dead. Missus was lying in her bed, so small, so still. Blamed herself for it all, of course. Likes to keep the house as it was before they went.'

Every afternoon, as the sun singed the grass of the lawn, Ellen read to Mrs Tibbs in the cold dark drawing room. She had hoped to read the poems and novels in the library. But on her first full day in the villa, Mrs Tibbs pointed towards the window seat, which was heaped with musty letters and old documents.

'We will start with these, Pearson,' said Mrs Tibbs. 'I would like to hear them all again, my dear friends, dear friends.'

Each day Ellen selected a handful of letters from the pile and read them aloud: short notes from long-dead relatives, contracts from lawyers, and agents' instructions concerning the state of tenanted properties sold years ago.

'My correspondents,' murmured Mrs Tibbs. 'I like to remember them, the way they wrote, their turn of phrase. Of course, they're all gone now but I do like to remember them, Pearson. I do miss them so.'

Ellen's eyes strained in the dimness of the room.

'Maybe I can open the shutters just a little so I can see better, Mrs Tibbs?' she suggested late one afternoon, having read ten pages of the last will and testament of Mr Ralph Parker, followed by a lengthy note written in 1852 by a Miss Carp, informing the recipient of the imminent arrival of a new governess.

'Oh no, we can't do that.' Mrs Tibbs waved her hand vaguely in the air. 'Carry on, carry on, Pearson.'

The letters were dull. There were no secrets, nothing untoward, nothing unusual at all. Occasionally, when picnics were mentioned, or when a writer referred to the 'promising bay filly' belonging to a certain Mr Cuthbert from Guisborough, Mrs Tibbs would say, 'So it was, just so, so long ago.' And the lace frill round her cap would shudder briefly. Then it would fall slowly back into place over the ragged wig with a little sigh.

She often repeated the lines that Ellen had just read aloud. She would whisper them to herself as if they were poetry or she would savour them as she might have savoured the sweetness of one of Beadie's sugar-crusted, soft-hearted meringues.

'Your ever-loving friend, Horace,' she would mutter, or 'I have not yet received the payment of fifteen pounds, three shillings and sixpence.' Or 'as to the matter concerning the state of the paint-work, I shall leave it entirely in your hands.'

When eventually the letter drew to a close, Mrs Tibbs would tap a long fingernail against the arm of the chaise longue and say, 'So nicely put, don't you think, Pearson? So beautifully phrased.'

Despite the shutters, the sun began to penetrate the house. It crept through the rooms almost unnoticed at first, lightly warm-ing the window seat and the wall against which Ellen leaned when she read the letters to Mrs Tibbs. Then it grew so hot that Beadie's pastry stuck to the table as she was rolling it out, and Casaubon abandoned the kitchen completely and hid in the washhouse next to the tub of soaking clothes, where the air was a little cooler.

The sweat ran down Ellen's arms and legs as she walked into Teesby on her first half day off. It was a Sunday afternoon, she was planning to visit Henry.

'But he's out, love,' said Mrs Veasey, standing on the doorstep of the boarding house.

'At church?'

'No, with his friend, on the Nab. They've gone for a walk. Although I can't imagine why they'd want to go marching around in this heat. I'll tell him you called when he gets back.'

Ellen was too hot to climb back up the hill to the villa, so she lingered for a while on the beach, wishing she could peel off her stockings and wade in the water. But people were watching her, young men lying on their stomachs on the sand, heads lazily resting on their hands, grinning, eyeing her up. She walked towards the waves feeling sticky and uneasy in her tight old velvet dress: her head throbbed from the bright sun.

She wanted to shout at the men: 'What do you think you're looking at?' She wanted to snap like Beadie when she scolded the sieve and the saucepan lids and the serving spoons.

She wanted to spin round and snarl, 'Leave me alone. I can do what I like!'

But she knew that she wouldn't.

She trudged along the shoreline, a lonely figure, dragging her heavy boots in the wet sand – hating the men and Henry's new friend and Mrs Tibbs and her dreary correspondence.

By the end of June they were still only halfway through the pile of letters on the window seat. She read Mr Cuthbert's accounts of his journey through the highlands of Scotland, the Reverend Potter's caustic opinion of Darwin's *Origin of Species* and several notes from a woman called Charlotte Biggs, of whom Mrs Tibbs had no recollection at all.

'You read very well, Pearson,' she said faintly.

'I like to read aloud,' Ellen replied. 'I like the words, how they fit together. I like the feel of them in my mouth.' This was true. She used different voices for the various authors of the letters, solemn and pompous for Reverend Potter, joyful for Mr Cuthbert, although the dullness of the phrases they had written infuriated her.

'Perhaps when we get to the end of the pile we could try something else?' she suggested tentatively. 'Maybe we could try Dickens or Keats.'

'What an interesting idea,' said Mrs Tibbs. 'When you reach the bottom of the pile, we shall have a think about it. Read on, Pearson, read on.'

*

It wasn't until the last week of July that the letters finally came to an end.

'There's no more correspondence, Mrs Tibbs,' Ellen said triumphantly one afternoon.

The old woman's small mouth opened into a little 'O', then it slowly closed again. She lay back on the chaise longue.

'So they've gone. They've all gone.'

'Yes, they're all finished now.' Ellen had slid off the window seat and was organising the letters into neat piles on the floor. 'We can put these away now and read something new. I could go and choose something from the library.'

'No, Pearson,' replied Mrs Tibbs with a little shake of her woolly ringlets. 'No. No. No. We must start again. You can begin with Mr Trantor's letter about the farm on Roseberry Topping . . . quite a peculiar turn of phrase he had. You do remember that letter, Pearson? You will be able to find it, won't you?'

Something rose up inside Ellen, something lurched. It could have been the cold pork and chutney that she had eaten for lunch, or the heat which now, in the height of summer, was torturous. Or it could have been something else, something less tangible. It could have been the old Ellen, the one that had shouted at Henry and the coats in the hallway, that had torn across the beach and searched for stones on the Snook, that had listened to the sand singing in the twilight.

'I can't do it again, Mrs Tibbs. No more letters. Life doesn't just stop. It doesn't go round and round in circles. Life goes on, Mrs Tibbs. Life goes on!'

'What on earth are you saying, Pearson?'

Ellen stood up from the window seat, grasped hold of one of the shutters and pulled it back. 'Look, Mrs Tibbs!'

Sunlight filled the drawing room. It was a lovely room with a white fireplace and a large mirror above it. There were paintings hanging on the blue walls – seascapes and landscapes. And on the table in the corner was a big bowl of dead flowers: the desiccated stems were still sticking out of the bowl but the petals were lying in a yellow cluster on the table.

'Look, Mrs Tibbs!' She tugged at the sash window and the breeze stirred the pile of letters on the floor. 'Look at the view!'

Ellen reached over, took the old woman's hand and led her to the window. Mrs Tibbs must have felt something. Maybe she could sense the bright light or feel the warmth of the sun through the open window. At first she shielded her face then slowly her hand dropped to her side.

The breeze was carrying the sound of Teesby into the drawing room, the starlings chattered on the telegraph wire, a horse was neighing in the field lower down the lane, and there were far-off shouts and crashes from the quayside.

Mrs Tibbs shuddered: her ringlets shivered and a fine dust of powder fell from her face. 'So much noise, Pearson.' But she stepped forward, clutched the sill and leaned out of the window. 'Tell me what you can see, Pearson,' she said quietly.

'I can see the Monkey Puzzle tree.'

'Ah, yes, the Monkey Puzzle tree. Tibbsy planted that tree the year we were married.'

'Its branches are all crooked, Mrs Tibbs. Like they've broken up the view. It's like looking through a cracked windowpane. I can see the stone balustrade at the end of the garden and the roses, they're all pink and yellow. I can see the church spire and the roofs of the houses, they look like they're falling down the hill. And right at the top of the tree, in the gap between branches, I can see a streak of sand and a triangle of sea and there's a ...' She paused, thinking she had said too much.

'Do carry on, Pearson,' said Mrs Tibbs. 'Do carry on.'

Henry

The war arrived at the villa on a sunny morning in August. It was slapped down onto the kitchen table by the paper boy. Yesterday's news screamed at them in tall black letters from the front pages.

'Germany declares war on Great Britain,' read Ellen from the *Northern Echo*. 'Momentous day in world's history. Nations are arrayed against nations.'

'What does arrayed mean?' asked Beadie through a mouthful of toast and marmalade.

'I think it's got something to do with lines but I'm not sure,' said Ellen. 'It can't be very good though.'

Upstairs in the drawing room, she read aloud to Mrs Tibbs from the *Daily Telegraph*.

'England defied by Germany. Warning disregarded. Stern British reply. Compliance demanded by Midnight yesterday.'

'Yesterday! Oh!' said Mrs Tibbs. 'You must stop, Pearson, stop! I don't like it at all. Read something nicer. Read one of the advertisements.'

Ellen scanned the page for something less contentious. 'Kutnow's Powder. The incomparable morning health invigorator. To banish acidity, indigestion, biliousness, constipation and sick headache.'

Mrs Tibbs's hand quivered in the air. 'No. Stop, Pearson. I never cared for that newspaper. Take it away, take it away.'

So that was it: Mrs Tibbs cancelled her subscription to the *Telegraph* and Beadie said they should do the same with the *Echo*. For a while the war was over in the villa.

Through the late summer and autumn, Beadie and Ellen opened the shutters in the abandoned rooms: the dining room and the morning room and the library. The wallpaper in the library was golden, birds shimmered in the sunlight and the strawberries hanging from their beaks were a rosy pink. Beneath Ellen's feet, the swirling pattern on the Oriental carpet was so bright it made her dizzy: the colours were rich and honest, deep reds and vivid blues and yellows all the way from Persia.

'Of course, if you hadn't gone and opened the drawing room window in the first place, we wouldn't have to be doing all this cleaning,' grumbled Beadie to the carpet sweeper.

As the evenings grew darker, Ellen read to Mrs Tibbs in the drawing room. They worked their way through *David Copperfield* and *Great Expectations*. Then at Christmas, Ellen found an old copy of *Middlemarch* on the library shelves and she clutched it excitedly to her chest as she ran up the stairs.

'*Middlemarch*, Mrs Tibbs,' she announced in the doorway to the drawing room.

'Oh yes, George Eliot,' replied Mrs Tibbs sleepily. 'I always found her a little dull. But if you wish to read it aloud, Pearson, I won't stop you.'

When Da died, Ellen had reached the point in the novel where the Reverend Casaubon forbids Will Ladislaw to visit Lowick Manor: she had to imagine the rest. In the convent she decided that Ladislaw would return to the house and rescue Dorothea and they would run away to Rome together. Ladislaw would become a painter while Dorothea would wear beautiful dresses and write stories in their ruined Roman palace.

But the real novel turned out to be a disappointment. Ellen was dismayed by Ladislaw's imperfections and Dorothea's quiet life.

Is that it? she thought, as she closed the cover and lay the book on the window seat. *Is that all we can hope for?*

Outside the villa, the war carried on without them. It wasn't until January that Ellen and Beadie were drawn back into it again. They had gone into Teesby together and were walking down the High Street to the market square when they saw a small group of cowed-looking men corralled by a cluster of women clasping little paper flags in their hands.

'England expects every man to do his duty!' they screeched, wiggling their flags in the faces of the passers-by. 'Every man! Every man!' The women were gleeful and loud, their teeth clenched into awful smiles.

'Bloody bunch of harpies,' said Beadie.

For a second or two she looked as if she was about to charge down the road and confront them. But she stopped herself, muttered under her breath, 'I don't like bullies.' Then she spun round and trudged back up the hill.

The war spread to the Snook too. When Ellen turned onto the causeway one morning in February, she found a roll of barbed wire blocking the path. In the distance, she could see a group of soldiers carrying things from the back of a cart. They waved at her, so she waved back. Then one of them came marching down the causeway towards her.

'You can't come any further, Miss.' He had a sharp shrill voice which fused with the cold wind and made her ears sting.

'Why not?' she shouted back.

'War Office, Miss. The land belongs to the War Office now.'

The soldier stood on the path with his hands behind his back and his legs slightly apart. 'We could have you arrested if you come any further.'

'But how long is it going to be like this?'

'For the duration, Miss,' he said proudly.

She turned away, smarting with anger. Da was on the other side of the barbed wire, so was the tower and the stones and the shells and the sand. She hated the war: the angry women in the market square and the barriers and the barbed wire and all the Union Jacks.

The following Sunday afternoon, Ellen asked Henry what the War Office had to do with the Snook. She had gone to look for him in the house on Marine Parade, but found him slouched on a bench on the promenade. He was wrapped in Da's old overcoat and was staring at the sea. He must have been sitting there for some time in the cold drizzle because there were little beads of water glistening in his hair.

'They're building a platform for the guns,' Henry wearily replied. 'So they can shoot them at the German ships. And there's talk that they're going to build a big disc out of concrete so they can hear the Germans coming. It picks up the vibrations in the air.'

He stuffed his hand into his pocket, pulled out a handkerchief and wiped the drops of rain from his face. 'My friend and I were going to join up together.'

'Your new friend?' She had assumed it was a woman.

'Yes, that's right. Thomas. They took him but they wouldn't have me. The doctor said there was a rattle in my chest, said I wouldn't last five minutes out there.'

'I'm glad you're not going.' She leaned into him and could feel his thin bony shoulder under the overcoat. 'I don't think anyone would last five minutes out there.'

'Doesn't make me feel any better, though.' He pushed his hand into his pocket again and stared straight ahead.

She looked up at Henry, at his long angular profile, his oddly crooked nose, his deep-set eyes. She tried to guess at the thoughts that were going through his head. Her own thoughts were knotting together: how the stray hair that lay across the collar of Da's old coat had a reddish tinge to it; how she could see the sea out of the corner of her left eye; how the waves that rolled onto the beach were green and blue; how she had hated the soldier on the Snook, how his sneering, high-pitched voice was like an arrow flying along the causeway towards her; how Da had told her that the fabric of his old overcoat was called dog's tooth, how she could smell Da on the tweed – oranges and lemons, Christmas with a splash of brandy; how little she knew her brother.

Ellen pulled away from him, straightened herself and looked at the sea. She felt weighed down suddenly: stiff and separate, as if the small gap between Henry and herself was solid.

'And then there's this,' Henry said quietly, pulling a small cardboard box from his pocket. 'It came today, delivered by hand the envelope said.'

He gave her the box and she opened the lid. Inside, wrapped in a piece of red silk – the way you might wrap a gift for someone you loved, a gold tie pin or a pair of cufflinks – was a single white feather. It was a horrible thing, lightly curled and nestling comfortably inside the silk.

'Do you know who sent it?'

Henry shook his head.

She tipped the box upside down and the feather swayed casually from to side to side towards the ground.

'I hate them,' wailed a gull above her head. 'Hate them all.'

And she could see the faces of the women in the market square again, and the busybody-bossing words on the recruitment posters stuck to the wall outside the Town Hall, and the newspaper headlines in the newsagent's window: 'Our brave boys!' 'England's spirit!' 'Great British grit!'

'Leave us alone,' cried the waves as they collapsed onto the sand. 'Leave us alone. Leave us alone. Leave us alone.'

The thin spring rain fell through the branches of the Monkey Puzzle tree; the daffodils beneath it waved limply in despair. In the villa, Ellen kept busy, sorting through Mrs Tibbs's wardrobe for clothes to be cleaned and mended. Mrs Tibbs didn't wear them any more, the fuchsia-coloured blouses and the sugar-pink tea gowns and the tea jackets, all of them dripping in Calais lace or satin ribbons or deep silk frills – but they were too beautiful to be left to rot. The clothes were proof of happier days when Mrs Tibbs and Tibbsy went dancing in Scarborough or dining in fine restaurants in York.

When the rain finally stopped, Ellen unpicked the lace collars and the cuffs in the kitchen, washed the dresses in the damp gloom of the washhouse, and pinned them on the line by the back door. There wasn't enough room for the trimmings so she slung another rope between the Monkey Puzzle tree and the wall of the villa and draped them over it. The ribbons and the lace spun and fluttered in the front garden like pastel-coloured streamers at a children's party.

At the end of the afternoon, as she was gathering up the trimmings and rolling them carefully into spirals, she heard a man's voice behind her.

'Girl!'

It was an incongruous sound in the villa garden, terrible and sharp like the teeth of a trap snapping shut.

'Girl!'

She turned round.

He was standing just inside the gateway. In his hand was a wooden case with a rough metal crucifix screwed to the lid.

'It is you isn't it? It is Ellen Pearson?'

'Yes, Father.'

Father Scullion nodded. 'I wasn't sure, it's been so long.' He moved towards her, his cassock flailing against his legs. 'Mrs Haines up at Easton Farm has just passed away. Did you know her?'

'No, Father.'

'Well, she's gone now. I thought I would come and see you on the way down from the Nab. Have a little talk.' He had lowered his voice, it had taken on a strangely conversational tone.

He looked expectantly at her, and she realised with horror that he was waiting for her to invite him into the house, into the warm kitchen where Beadie was making a shepherd's pie for supper. She didn't move. If she stayed still and upright, blocking his way, he wouldn't come any further into the garden.

He must have understood because he slammed the wooden case down on the drive by his feet and rubbed his sweating hands roughly on his cassock.

'Why haven't I seen you at mass?'

She paused, imagining a response: *Because I hate you, Father Scullion, because I hated your hand against my hair, because I hate your voice, it oozes out of you, thick and brown.*

'Because I didn't feel like it, Father,' she replied lightly.

'Didn't feel like it?' He was standing close to her now, so close that when the breeze stirred her skirt it became tangled in his cassock for a moment. 'Don't think I'm giving up on you,' he said quietly, calmly. 'It's my mission to guide you, to tell you where you're going wrong, to warn you. It's what I promised to God.' His face was round and puckered, a baby's face, his skin surprisingly smooth. He should have had a hard, flinty face: it was wrong that he didn't look the way he sounded. 'And what about your brother? Where has he disappeared to?'

She could smell Father Scullion's breath, it smelt of the tea that he must have drunk at Easton Farm while he was waiting for Mrs Haines to die. It was a drab, stale smell.

'I don't know,' she replied carefully.

'He doesn't feel like it either, I suppose?'

Ellen was confused. Henry went to mass every week and to Benediction on Thursday evenings. He had been an altar boy.

'It's been months since I last saw your brother,' said Father Scullion. 'I expect it of you but not of him. You can tell him that when you see him again.' He bent down and picked up the wooden case.

'You're a bad influence, Ellen Pearson,' he said, stepping out of the gates and onto the lane.

It wasn't long after Father Scullion's visit – a few days perhaps – that there was a knock at the kitchen door. Standing in the yard was a boy of about twelve, gripping the handlebars of his bicycle. It was raining again, but the boy didn't seem to care, he flicked his head and the water flew off him.

'Are you Ellen Pearson? Because if you are Mrs Veasey wants you to come down to Marine Parade straight away.'

'Why? What's wrong?' She remembered Da, his face lying on the pillow. She pictured Henry with a black smear of blood across his nightshirt. The thoughts made her dizzy. They made her ears boom, it was like the sound of a distant drum that blocked out everything else.

The boy shrugged his shoulders. 'Mrs Veasey says it's urgent, that's all.' He flicked his head again: he was growing impatient. 'You're to come right away,' he said, turning the bicycle round and wheeling it out of the yard.

In the hallway of the boarding house, Mrs Veasey grasped Ellen's arm. 'Henry's not ill. At least, I don't think he is. But he hasn't been out of his room for three days. He hasn't eaten, hasn't even gone to the bathroom as far as I know.'

One of the guests walked through the hall into the dining room and Mrs Veasey lowered her voice and pulled Ellen towards her: she smelt of cooking fat and peppermint.

'I tried to talk to him but he shouted at me and told me to go away – imagine your Henry shouting at me. I said if he wouldn't talk to you I'd have to get one of the guests to break the door down.'

Ellen could still hear the drumming in her ears as she climbed up the stairs but it was softer and steadier now. Her brother's room was on the second floor. She stood outside on the landing and called to him through the lock.

'Open the door, Henry! Open the door!'

She waited, listening for movement. But all she could hear beyond the gentle boom in her ears were the voices of the guests downstairs, and someone above her, padding across the floorboards in their socks.

'Henry!'

She had never known him to act like this before. He hated drama. He would slide away from it, clutching his handkerchief in his hand, wheezing slightly.

She leaned into the lock. 'If you won't talk to me, Mrs Veasey says she's going to get the police.' This wasn't true, of course, but the threat seemed to work. The door opened almost immediately.

Henry was wearing pyjamas, the front of the top was stained and the sleeves were damp. As she entered the room he collapsed into the armchair by the window. He wouldn't let her see his face. He turned away from her, hunched in the chair, his arms hugging his chest.

'What's the matter, Henry?' She knelt down on the floor in front of him.

He tried to say something but she couldn't make out what it was, his voice was thick with tears.

'Henry, tell me what's wrong.'

'You wouldn't understand.'

'I might do.' She touched his arm but he shrank away from her. 'You wouldn't. You couldn't.'

'Has someone sent you another feather?'

'No.'

'So what is it then?'

He pointed to a letter on the desk. Thinking he meant for her to read it she picked it up, but his hand sprang out and snatched it from her.

'No! I didn't say you could read it.'

'What does it say?'

'Thomas.' The name prompted another sob. 'He was knocked over by a van in Richmond, he was crossing the market place ...'

'A van?'

'A butcher's van.'

She reached out again and this time he let her take hold of his hand. 'I'm sorry, Henry,' she whispered.

On the desk, partly concealed by the letter, was a small photograph. She could make out a man's face. He wasn't smiling, although he possessed the sort of features that made him look like he was happy: large eyes and a wide straight mouth. She wondered briefly what it was like to be hit by a van. Did it swerve to avoid him then trap him under its wheels? Did it hit him face on? What did the driver do? And all the carcasses in the back swinging on their hooks, they must have smashed together when the van hit Thomas. And then what – a colourless oblivion, a void, or heaven? Heaven would be like the purple Nab. It would be like the Snook on a sunny day. It would be like the view from the tower.

'I'm so sorry, Henry,' she whispered again.

Ellen leaned over and tried to embrace him but Henry stiffened and waved his hand in the air, just like Mrs Tibbs when she wanted to be alone.

'You wouldn't understand, Nell,' he said. 'I can't talk about him, not to you, not to anyone.'

*

The following evening she went to Marine Parade to see how Henry was. She found him sitting at the table in the parlour playing cribbage with one of the older salesmen as if nothing was wrong. What was stranger yet was that Mrs Veasey had understood something that Ellen clearly hadn't.

'He's fine now,' she said as she washed the dishes in the scullery. 'We had a chat about it last night. Let's not trouble him with it, Ellen. It's over.'

The Lieutenant

'What can you see, Pearson?'

Mrs Tibbs lay on the chaise longue wrapped in a lilac-coloured blanket that Beadie had knitted her for Christmas. Ellen was on the window seat gazing at the view. It was early February, the villa garden was in the grip of a hard frost. Fingers of ice clung to the branches of the Monkey Puzzle tree and the stone balustrade at the end of the lawn, and the grass and the rose bushes were covered in feathery crystals.

'I think we might have snow later,' said Ellen. 'There's a heavy look about the sky, as if it hasn't got the energy to hold onto the snow any more and it's just about to let it all go and—'

At the edge of the window, a starling that had been pecking at a frozen pine cone flapped frantically into the air. And round the edge of one of the gates a figure appeared, a man gingerly stepping across the frost.

'What is it, Pearson? What can you see?'

'We've got a visitor, Mrs Tibbs.'

'Too early. Visitors should come in the afternoon, for tea.'

'He's wearing a uniform.' Ellen could see his cap and the khaki shoulders of his overcoat as he passed under the window.

'An officer?'

'I think so.'

'Is it my John?' Mrs Tibbs rose unsteadily to her feet. 'My little

Johnny?' The blanket slid off her back and dropped to the floor. 'Go and let him in, Pearson. Hurry, hurry.'

The man who was waiting at the front door was not little at all. He was tall and broad and blond.

'You're new. Who are you?'

'I'm Ellen, sir.'

The man raised his eyebrows slightly as he pushed past her into the hall. 'She's upstairs, I suppose?' he said, shrugging off his coat and thrusting it at her. 'Get Beadie to send up a sandwich and some tea. I'm famished.'

'Johnny Gargett.' Beadie was standing at the kitchen table, stirring batter in a mixing bowl. 'Don't see him from one year to the next, then he turns up and starts giving orders. Surprises me he's in uniform at all. Shiftless bugger.' She lifted the spoon and pointed it at Ellen; a little dollop of yellow mixture dripped onto the table. 'And you watch him, young lady. Make sure he keeps his distance.'

Ellen didn't see Lieutenant Gargett again until dinner time, but she could hear him. His voice was a low drone that vibrated round the house, and whenever he coughed or cleared his throat the noise reverberated through the floorboards. It was strange to have a man in the villa, it changed everything in small ways. It made her attentive to herself; she glanced at her face in the hall mirror as she passed it and changed into a clean uniform after lunch. Halfway through the afternoon, Lieutenant Gargett clomped down the stairs to the library in his boots, leaving muddy treads on the carpet that Beadie swore at when she discovered them a few hours later. And in the evening, when he was dressing for dinner, Ellen could smell him: a cold, browny-orange, peppery sort of colour that lingered in the passageway to the bedrooms. It was not an unpleasant smell, but there was something sad about it, like the first day of autumn.

That night Mrs Tibbs, who normally ate supper in the drawing room, asked for the dining room fire to be lit and the mahogany table to be set. It was a wonderful sight: the fire in the grate, the gleaming crystal and the shell-pink porcelain. Ellen stood by the dumb waiter and thought that even Mrs Tibbs in her frayed violet gown looked beautiful.

Lieutenant Gargett wasn't very talkative, but this didn't trouble Mrs Tibbs. She chirruped her way through the lamb cutlets and the junket, only pausing briefly when she upset half a glass of Sauternes over the tablecloth.

'Oh dearie me, Pearson, I can't be getting wine over John's uniform, can I?'

He gave Ellen a sly sideways glance as she dabbed the cloth and took the glass away, and another when she carried the cheese dome from the credenza to the table.

She wondered what he saw when he looked at her. She remembered the men on the beach and the salesmen in Mrs Veasey's dining room. At the time it had bothered her, their staring eyes, their silence, but Lieutenant Gargett's oblique gaze intrigued her.

She thought of him that night. He was not an attractive man. At the dining table his chest sagged and his belly slumped into his lap. He had light, bulbous eyes, like a deep-sea fish, and a wide thin mouth. But he had lovely hair, it was smooth and shiny: a swathe of thick blond satin. When Ellen had leaned across his shoulder with the cheese dome, it looked so soft she'd almost stroked it with the flat of her hand.

Ellen was scrubbing the sheets in the washhouse on the far side of the yard when she saw him again the following morning. He was ambling slowly across the garden, the way a plough horse might plod home at the end of the day – slow and swaying heavily from side to side. He lit a cigarette, smoked half of it then dropped the stub and squashed it into the gravel with his heel.

He must have seen her through the window because he

straightened himself and tugged the bottom of his tunic to neaten the buttons.

'I wondered where you were,' he said, leaning against the doorway.

'Saturdays are wash days,' she replied.

He edged his way into the room and propped himself against the wall. He hunched over, conscious of his size: his hands deep in his pockets and his head lowered. He sagged even more than the previous evening.

He watched her in silence as she turned the handle of the washing machine. Inside the tub the wet sheets were flung against the wooden slats – thwack, thwack, thwack.

'Who was it that opened all the shutters?' he said finally, still staring at the floor.

'It was us, Beadie and me.' She let go of the handle and leaned against the tub. Despite the cold of the washhouse she was sweating from the effort of spinning the wet sheets.

'After Uncle Harold died, Aunt Catherine shut the whole house,' he said. 'We used to sit together in the dark. It was a relief when I went to school.'

'You lived in the villa?'

'For a while. My parents were in Ceylon then they died and Aunt Catherine took me in. All pretty grim.'

Ellen would have liked to have said, 'Yes, I know, it was the same for me when Da died – pretty grim.' But she didn't. She didn't say anything. She opened the tub of the washing machine and the fragrance of the wet linen and the soap filled the room. The mood lightened for a moment.

'School was all right, though. Made a few chums. Used to stay with them in the holidays, better than coming back here.' He paused, tracing a pattern on the floor with the toe of his boot while Ellen pulled the sheets out of the tub and dropped them into a basket.

68

'And now this, of course ... my country, right or wrong.' He made a strange snorting noise, he was trying to laugh. Then he pulled out his pocket watch and peered down at it. 'Almost time for lunch,' he murmured, wandering into the yard.

In the evening, after Mrs Tibbs had gone to bed, Ellen could smell him again, the scent of dried grass and a musky damp odour that must have come from the oil in his yellow hair. He was waiting for her in the corridor that led from the hall to the kitchen. It was dark, she couldn't see his face.

'Do you need something, Mr Gargett?' She made her voice loud and clear and normal, like they were meeting in the daylight rather than the shadows.

He was weaving slightly, and he brushed his hands against the wall as he moved towards her. 'Do you like me, Ellen?' he whispered. 'Because I like you.'

It was difficult to know how to reply to this.

'Mr Gargett, is there anything I can do for you?' she asked, holding on to her brisk voice.

He laughed, a heavy laugh, as if he was dragging something out of himself. Then he stopped, grasped her shoulders and thrust his face into hers. Ellen could feel his tongue flap and fumble, warm and wet, against her lips. He managed to slip the tip of it inside her mouth then he pushed it hard against her gums. She clenched her teeth: she could taste salt and Rowland's macassar oil and bitter wine.

They didn't struggle together long. He soon gave up and let her go. Something had drained out of him, his body slumped again.

'I'm leaving for France on Tuesday. Can't you be nice?' He spoke in a high, petulant voice. 'I'm going to war for Christ's sake.'

'I'm not like that, Mr Gargett.' She pictured the track that led to curiosity, and the girls in the farmhouse. She thought about the story of Saint Agnes – the virgin martyr, in the *Lives of the Saints*.

She remembered Father Scullion's fingers in her hair. 'It's a sin, you see.' Although she didn't really believe that it was.

'Oh God!' John Gargett muttered, stumbling away from her. 'Oh God!' he cried, hitting the wall with his fat fist.

She managed to avoid Lieutenant Gargett the following day. It was a Sunday. She had the afternoon off and spent it with Henry as usual. Her brother was still taciturn and guarded. He looked at her strangely as if he thought she knew something important. He gave her small questioning glances as they played piquet in Mrs Veasey's parlour.

'How have you been, Henry?' she asked, setting down a card.

'I'm fine.'

'How's work?'

'It's fine.'

She was running out of questions. 'Have you been to church recently?'

He shook his head.

Later, when the sun came out, they went for a long walk up the cliff path to Bleaker's Hill. The exertion made Henry breathless and unable to speak.

Monday was the last day of Lieutenant Gargett's leave. Mrs Tibbs insisted that Beadie cook his favourite meal: roast lamb and duchesse potatoes followed by apple charlotte and custard. The dinner made both aunt and nephew sleepy. When it was over, Lieutenant Gargett sat back in the dining chair and shut his eyes while Mrs Tibbs's tiny head nodded over the tablecloth. They went to bed early leaving Ellen free to clear the table and wash the dishes without interruption.

That night, lying in bed in her room on the top floor, she heard doors being opened along the passageway. She knew who it was. She knew what he wanted. When he finally found her room, he pushed the door open and stood on the threshold breathing deeply.

'Ellen,' he whispered. 'Ellen, is that you? Are you awake?'

She shifted slightly under the covers. It was the smallest of movements, but it seemed to encourage him.

'Ellen?' He was beside her, his jowly face looming over hers.

She sat bolt upright. 'I don't want you to kiss me again, Mr Gargett. If you kiss me I will scream.'

He leaned away from her. 'I won't kiss you, Ellen. I promise.'

'So what do you want?' she said, tugging the sheet over her chest.

'I couldn't sleep.'

She could see his face in the moonlight. He wasn't looking at her, he was gazing at the floor and twisting one of the buttons on his pyjama top.

'I woke up, a touch of indigestion. Then I started to think about it all.'

'I don't understand.'

He paused, sighed deeply. 'All my life I've been made to do things I didn't want to do. Leave home, come here, go to school. And just when I thought I could do what I liked the war starts. I'll be in France the day after tomorrow and I'm supposed to be happy about it, excited.' He held out his fingers. They hovered over her hand which was still clutching the edge of the sheet. 'Ellen, are you listening? Say something, Ellen.'

She was thinking of her old home and the Sacred Heart and Father Scullion. She dropped the sheet and touched his palm lightly with her fingers. 'You can sit down if you want,' she said.

He perched on the edge of the bed, making the mattress sink. She rolled towards him slightly.

'Can I stay for a while? You don't mind, do you?'

'I don't mind,' she replied dozily.

She could hear him breathing in and out, until the slow rhythm

71

of his breath was broken abruptly by what sounded like a hiccup, followed by a muffled gulp. She held his warm damp hand in her own. Then she must have fallen asleep. When she woke in the morning he was gone.

He left the villa the next day without a word. She watched him from the window of the dining room when she was cleaning the candlesticks. This time he marched rather than lumbered along the drive, as if he knew she was standing at the window. As he walked through the gates and turned into the lane he was colourless.

The telegram arrived eight weeks later. She stood with her back to the fireplace in the upstairs drawing room and looked at the sheet of paper in her hand. Printed across the top of the page were four words. She read them aloud to Mrs Tibbs.

'Regret ... to ... inform ... you.'

Then she noticed that someone had thought to add in black ink the word 'Deeply'.

'Deeply regret to inform you,' she read.

'My John is dead?' asked Mrs Tibbs. 'Dead?' She held out her hand to take the telegram that she couldn't see. 'My poor John.'

The paper shivered between her fingers, and the lace on her cap shivered too. She lowered her head. Then the carriage clock chimed brightly on the mantelpiece, and she looked up again. Ellen could see tears seeping out from under her spectacles.

'Go away, Pearson,' she said, flapping her hands. 'Go away. Go away. Go away.'

'This'll be the death of her,' murmured Beadie into the mixing bowl as Ellen took refuge in the kitchen.

In the week that followed the telegram, Mrs Tibbs refused to eat. When Ellen carried up a bowl of soup or a piece of steamed fish to the drawing room, Mrs Tibbs would flail her hand in the air and cry weakly, 'Oh leave me alone, Pearson.'

She lay limply on the chaise longue and turned her face away, pressing it into the faded cushion, if Ellen tried to talk.

It wasn't until the letter from Private Walter Eales arrived at the villa a fortnight later that Mrs Tibbs began to rally. The envelope had been spotted with drops of rain, as had the letter inside. Although, in truth, it wasn't much of a letter at all, more of a note. Private Eales had written in minute words and thin ink, four lines like a scramble of barbed wire across the page.

Dear Mrs Tibbs,

Lieutenant Gargett was a brave man. He lost his life to save mine. I was trapped in a shell hole and he came running up with no regard for his own safety. He pulled me out and carried me back to the trench. I will always remember him. I will always be grateful for the sacrifice he made.

Yours,

Pte. Walter Eales

'What else does he say?' The lace on Mrs Tibbs's cap quivered. 'What else does he say, Pearson? There must be something else.'

But there was nothing else, apart from Private Eales's inky thumbprint at the top of the page, and a streak of gritty mud on the back of the letter where he had folded the paper in two and pressed the crease with a dirty fist.

A few days later Mrs Tibbs insisted that Ellen remove the carriage clock from the mantelpiece and replace it with Walter Eales's letter and John Gargett's pocket watch, which had arrived, along with his uniform, wrapped in a soggy package that morning.

'Is it all in place, Pearson?' asked Mrs Tibbs, tapping her fingers along the mantelpiece feeling for the watch. When she found it, she cradled it in her hand and stroked the silver case. 'Poor John. Poor John.'

*

Ellen didn't like to touch the watch. Whenever she picked it up to wind it or to dust the mantelpiece underneath, it trembled in her hand. From the first time she had seen him from the drawing room window, to the moment he lay dead in the trench somewhere near Arras, that watch had been inside his pocket, the silver case pressed against his chest. The watch was ticking against his chest the morning he had leaned against the wall in the washhouse, and the night he had sat on her bed, and on the boat to France, and when he had dragged Private Walter Eales from No Man's Land to the trench. Even when the bullet was piercing his forehead, then his skull, then the soft tissue of his brain, the second hand was making its way round the face of the watch. And now that John Gargett's body had stopped and was lying motionless in a grave somewhere in the French countryside, his pocket watch sitting on the drawing room mantelpiece was still ticking merrily away.

She remembered Henry in his sitting room on Marine Parade, hunched in the armchair weeping as the rain ran gently down the windowpane. She remembered the letter and the half-concealed photograph lying on his desk.

'You wouldn't understand, Nell,' he had said to her. But she did now. She was certain that she understood.

On Sunday afternoon, Ellen made her way down the hill to talk to Henry again, to talk to him properly. The day was warm and shadowless: the sun was high and the colours were vivid. The stone walls that edged the fields were yellow with lichen and in the distance the cattle were blazing red blots against the bright green grass. Growing in the verge were late violets and buttercups along with plumes of rye and wild carrot. She stopped to pick the flowers for Henry. As she pulled at the stems she could hear the bustle of creeping things through the long grass, and the rich, plum-coloured warble from the early swallows.

Mrs Veasey was out when she arrived at the house on Marine

Parade. One of the salesmen opened the front door to her and she climbed the stairs to the second floor, the floppy bouquet of wildflowers grasped in her hand. Henry's door was ajar. When she reached the landing, she could see the edge of the armchair, the small red and blue hooky rug that covered the lino and, oddly, the scuffed soles of her brother's shoes.

She crept forward and peered round the door frame. Henry was kneeling on the rug, his head lowered, between his fingers a set of rosary beads. Standing in front of him, his large hand clamped over her brother's shoulder, pressing him down, was Father Scullion.

Ellen sprang back so she wouldn't be noticed.

'And what does the Bible say about it, Henry?' asked Father Scullion.

'I ... I don't remember, Father,' he stuttered in reply.

'Oh Henry, how could you have forgotten!'

From her position on the landing, Ellen could see Father Scullion raising his eyes to heaven in disbelief.

'Our Lord told us that God made Eve for Adam, a woman and a man!' he shouted at the ceiling. 'You must study the Bible.' Father Scullion looked down at Henry and pressed him further towards the ground. Henry's head drooped, locks of his hair brushed against the rug. '"Know ye not that the unrighteous shall not inherit the kingdom of God?"' declared Father Scullion. '"Be not deceived: neither fornicators, nor idolaters, nor adulterers, nor effeminate, nor abusers of themselves with mankind." Corinthians, Henry, Corinthians, chapter 6 verse 9.'

She was back in the dormitory again, she could feel his warm knees against hers, his hot breath on her face, his fingers in her hair.

'Pray, Henry. Pray!' shouted Father Scullion.

'O my God, I am heartily sorry for having offended you,' cried Henry as if he really meant it.

'God the Father of mercies has sent the Holy Spirit among us for the forgiveness of sins,' said Father Scullion grimly, lowering his voice. 'Through the ministry of the Church may God give you pardon and peace. I absolve you from your sins, Henry Pearson, in the name of the Father, and of the Son, and of the Holy Spirit. Amen.'

'Amen, amen,' sobbed Henry.

Ellen crept back from the door and ran down the stairs.

The feeling came on slowly like a distant cloud over the waves, something spotted from the shoreline. She had been aware of it before at the Sacred Heart but never as badly as this. She hoped that the wind would blow the cloud back across the sea again, that the sun would come out. But the cloud grew thicker and she watched it tumble towards her across the waves. She ducked down, lay low, hoping it would pass over her and roll away. She realised how fragile things were, how things could fall apart so quickly, how they could be taken away. Da and Thomas and John Gargett: even Henry was distant now.

One minute she was holding Mrs Tibbs's blue Sevres milk jug in her hand and the next it was lying in pieces on the kitchen floor.

'Well, we'll never put that back together again,' said Beadie. 'Chuck it out! Throw it away.'

Ellen scooped up the pieces and wrapped them in newspaper, and the beautiful, complete, perfect blue jug was gone, forgotten, as if it had never existed. And the cloud descended further, white and heavy, and the colours seeped away.

The silver watch turned a pale, flat grey. It didn't shine any more, it stared at her when she swept the duster across the drawing room fireplace. Sometimes it squeaked when she wound it. Sometimes it whimpered. Sometimes it hiccuped and gulped.

'I'm sorry,' she whispered to the watch. 'I'm so sorry.'

Time moved slowly.

When she held the watch, she waited for the second hand to make its way around the face, but the white spaces in between the black marks were growing wider. The hand struggled. It trembled, shuffled back, advanced, trembled again, then stopped as if something were impeding it, as if the white space was a snowdrift that was impossible to cross.

Space shrank then stretched again.

Beadie was far away – on the other side of the ocean that was the kitchen table.

'Pull yourself together.' Her voice was distant, it sounded like the yelp of a farm dog on the Nab, or a child crying on the beach.

Henry's face appeared. It had shrunk to the size of a pea and was hidden in his handkerchief. 'You all right, Nell?'

Mrs Tibbs had almost vanished completely. She was a tiny speck, a sugar-pink grain lying on the blue chaise longue.

'I think you should lie down, Pearson,' sung a chaffinch somewhere in the Monkey Puzzle tree.

Everything lurched and spun, like twisting the sand clock upside down when Beadie boiled an egg. Then it started all over again, but in reverse.

Henry was so close that he was almost inside her own head. His voice was so loud that she had to cover her ears with her hands.

'You all right, Nell?' he screamed.

'Oh, pull yourself together,' boomed Beadie.

And black and white Casaubon sat on the kitchen table wailing like the siren at the works.

The breeze was like a storm at sea, and when the wet sheets

swung on the line they sounded like thunder overhead. She crouched down in the garden and covered the back of her head with her hands in case the sky was about to fall down.

You all right, Nell? Nell, you all right?

JACK

1931–40

The Starling

Jack was standing at the window in the back bedroom when they took his mother away. They led her out of the kitchen door and through the yard so the neighbours couldn't see. She was wearing the going-away dress that she had worn after the wedding. It was lilac coloured, with a dark flower print that scrambled across the fabric: from the bedroom window the pattern looked like a diamond-shaped net stretched across her back.

She must have known he was standing there because she twisted round and waved at him as if she was only going out for an hour or two. But he didn't wave back. He didn't move at all until long after she had gone, disappeared through the gate at the end of the yard and into the alley.

He asked only once, that first evening after tea. He was sitting at the kitchen table, tracing the knotted grain of the wood with his finger. The grain spiralled round and round and looped back and forth and folded in on itself.

'Where did they take my ma?'

Maurice was standing in the doorway to the backyard gazing at the potato plants. Granny Rush was at the sink, squeezing the last few drops of greasy liquid from a dishcloth.

'You going to tell the boy or am I?' she hissed at Maurice. But Maurice shook his head dolefully and ambled away into the yard.

'Your ma's gone to hospital,' said Granny Rush briskly, turning to Jack. 'And best place for her too, I'd say.'

Jack sighed – a short, sharp whistle. Then he breathed in again, filled his lungs until they hurt, and held his breath: one second, two seconds, three seconds, four seconds. But at eight seconds he had to let go, and the air burst out of his mouth.

He realised that the world, his world – the house on Invicta Road and all the things and people in it – had been holding its breath too. For most of the spring the world had held itself taut and tense, waiting in anticipation for him to do something or to say something. And now that the thing had finally happened, now she had gone, the world had let out a long sigh of relief.

Almost everything was calm that first summer. Upstairs, baby Cathy barely moved, barely made a sound. When he looked into her crib, he could see her lying on her back, staring blankly at the ceiling. Downstairs in the front room, the parrot in its cage was silent too. It clung to its perch, orange-ringed eyes fixed on the street outside. Only Granny Rush made any noise, banging buckets, splashing water and swearing at things as she scrubbed the kitchen floor and the table. She washed down the dresser, then cleaned away the black snippets of Maurice's moustache that had collected in the gap between the edge of the sink and the wall, for Maurice had a habit of trimming his moustache with a pair of nail scissors over the sink before he left for work.

'Dirty devil,' muttered Granny Rush, prodding at the gap with the tip of a potato knife. 'Mucky pup.'

In the front room she dragged the settee away from the wall and bundles of hair and feathers and fluff rolled over the linoleum, propelled by the draughts from the window. She chased the bundles round the room and cursed them as she swept them into the dustpan. Then she washed the floor and hung the hearthrug over the line in the backyard and beat it dustless.

When she had finished downstairs she trudged round the front bedroom, stuffing his mother's clothes and other belongings into an old suitcase.

'No point in cluttering up the place with stuff that no one's ever going to use,' Granny Rush said stonily, sliding the suitcase into the cubby hole under the stairs.

All that was left of his mother was the wedding photograph sitting on the mantelpiece in the front room, although someone had twisted the frame towards the window and the sunlight had faded the picture.

Maurice came home late. Most nights he reeled through the back door smelling of beer, the backside of his trousers covered in sand and his jacket rucked up as if he had slept in it. At the week-ends, he was out of the house for hours on end. When he returned again, he slouched through the front door and stared morosely at the photograph on the mantelpiece or leaned over the baby's crib in the bedroom.

Maurice was unusually quiet that summer. Before they took her away, he used to sing along with the radiogram: 'When the red, red robin comes bob bob bobbin' along'. Or he would re-tell jokes he had heard in the pub – 'I say, I say, I say . . .' But now he was calm, like the rest of the world.

That summer Jack stayed away from the house. It seemed the only thing to do, to keep a distance from Granny Rush's flailing duster and Maurice's miserable face. A week after his mother had left, he slipped past the dented pram in the hallway and slid out of the front door onto the street. It was a warm day, everyone was on the beach: he could hear the children squealing at the waves. When he reached the end of Invicta Road, he stood for a while, listening to their high-pitched voices carried inland on the wind. Then he turned the other way, resolutely: teeth gritted, fists clenched, out of the town and up the lane to the Nab. He kept to the shadows, skirted the garden walls and the hedges. He wanted no one to see him. He wanted to creep inside himself and retreat until there was nothing left of the real Jack. The sorry, sad, unhappy Jack. He wanted to grow a hard shell around himself so no one could see how bad he felt.

It was hot and airless on the moor. The wild carrot and the cornflowers had curled up and died, and the scrappy trees had already shed their leaves. He spread his jumper on the ground and lay down, sharp spikes of heather pricking his backside, the sun burning his arms and legs. The discomfort seemed appropriate, a retribution for the things he had said. He accepted it like a penitent, remembering the tales that Father Scullion had told them in Sunday School.

'Sackcloth! Flagellation! Mortification of the flesh, boys! Through suffering you'll be closer to Christ.'

Jack didn't believe he was any closer to Jesus, but for an hour or two, he did feel a small smug pleasure in the prickling pain.

Perhaps it was for a new sort of penance that a few days later he gave up on the moor and found a way into the garden of the villa below the Nab. The house was set on a narrow shelf of land that overlooked the town. From the moor, you could peer down at the peaks and valleys of shining slate and the dark square chasms of the chimneys. Beyond the house, if you looked carefully, you could see the faint traces of the formal garden, a knotted motif of box and lavender, now tangled and windswept. A few yards along the ridge, concealed in a mass of ivy, was a set of damp stone steps that led to the courtyard at the side of the house. He climbed down cautiously, and stood on the last step, trying to decide whether things had changed. A family of swifts had made a nest under the eaves of the washhouse and left a pile of bright white droppings on the cobbles, and puffy lumps of yellow moss had begun to grow on the kitchen step. But the washing line was still slung between

84

the washhouse and the wall of the villa, and the basket of greying clothes pegs was still hooked over the line.

In the garden at the front of the house, everything was yellow, all the colour had been scrubbed away. The shrubs had withered for lack of water, and the dried stems and twisted leaves were the same hue as Granny Rush's freshly scrubbed kitchen table. Only the Monkey Puzzle tree by the gates had prospered in the heat. At the ends of the topmost branches, held proudly aloft, were clutches of precious-looking golden-coloured cones.

Jack made the garden his den. He found the old invalid chair in the potting shed and sat under the shade of the Monkey Puzzle tree, just like Mrs Tibbs had done when she was waiting to die. In the afternoon, when it got really hot, he trudged into the chilly washhouse where the old Bradford washing machine still stood. He lifted the lid and peered into the barrel but the smell of stale water made him retch. He rotated the handle of the mangle once or twice, and remembered his mother doing the same, remembered the sound of the grating wheel and the water dripping from the sheet. Once, when she was in the yard hanging out the washing, he had tried to feed other things through the rollers: a slice of bread, a rasher of bacon, a whole banana. The banana was not a success, the pale yellow flesh smeared the rubber as it passed through the rollers and the rest of it plopped out of the other side and lay smashed on the cold stone floor. It was Beadie who caught him. She grabbed him tightly by the wrist and spanked him. 'You' – spank – 'do not' – spank – 'waste' – spank – 'food' – spank. 'You hear me, you little terror? And you could've trapped your fingers an' all.'

He was leaning against the mangle thinking about Beadie when he heard the sound of booted feet tramping down the steps. His own boots were outside in the middle of the yard, his socks stuffed into the tops. It was too hot to wear them, he had grown used to wandering round the garden barefoot. He couldn't hide his boots without being seen, but he knew that if he left them in the yard they would give him away. He waited, holding his breath, hoping that whoever it was would simply turn around before they reached the house.

'Hey, who's there? Jacky, is that you?'

Reluctantly, he stuck his head round the washhouse door. Standing on the steps just above him was Bob Marigold and a blond-haired boy called Lenny Grieve. Marigold was lean, long-limbed, with red, swollen-looking joints – elbows and knees – that he rubbed from time to time. Lenny Grieve was a year older than Marigold: a quiet boy, bronzed and curly headed, a stranger, an unknown.

'Look what I got for my birthday!' Marigold was waving a cata-pult in his hand. Jack could see the glint of the steel handle and the thick red rubber band that hung slackly from it.

'We're looking for ammunition,' said Marigold, bending down and selecting a stone from the ground. 'You want to play, Jacky?'

Jack did not want to play. He wanted them to leave him alone. The villa belonged to him, they had no right to be there. He wanted to stand in the middle of the yard and tell them to go away. He wanted to slide back into the cold of the washhouse and hide his head in the stinking barrel of the washing machine. He was certain they knew what had happened: everyone in Teesby knew.

'Are you going to play with us, or what, Jacky?'

He shrugged his shoulders. 'If you want,' he replied weakly.

Lenny Grieve drew a target on the washhouse door with a stub of white chalk that he pulled from his pocket. Then each boy in turn lodged a small stone into the leather pouch of the catapult and let it fly. Jack's attempts were inconsistent, sometimes he hit the chalky edge of the target, but mostly the stone was flung sideways and ricocheted off the wall. Bob Marigold had too little strength in his thin arms to pull the band far enough back, and every time he fired the stone, it fell short. But Lenny Grieve struck the target every time. When they paused to inspect the washhouse door, the bullseye was so pitted that the paint had begun to flake.

'How do you do it?' asked Marigold in frustration. 'Go on, show us. How do you do it?'

Lenny Grieve positioned himself in front of the target and placed the stone in the centre of the pouch.

'Watch what I do with my hands.'

He had rolled up his shirt sleeves, and Jack could see the taut swell of the muscle in his arm. But he didn't see the stone leave the catapult, he couldn't, it was far too fast. He only realised that it had gone when Lenny dropped his arms and said, 'See, see what I did with my hands, I flicked them,' and he lifted up his fingers and waved them in front of Marigold. 'Like this, you see?'

'Maybe it's the target,' grumbled Marigold. 'Maybe that's the problem.' And he plodded off towards the front of the house, looking for something more interesting to hit.

'We could try a window,' he shouted. 'Or what about them cones?' He was standing at the corner of the villa, pointing back at the Monkey Puzzle tree.

'No way,' said Lenny. 'If you can't hit the door, you'll never hit them. They're too small and too high up.'

'Give us it here.' Marigold snatched the catapult out of Lenny's hand, loaded it and fired. Jack and Lenny watched as the stone was propelled upwards, almost vertically, between the branches of the tree, then fell back again, landing at Marigold's feet.

Jack sniggered. He was beginning to enjoy the game, someone else's humiliation.

'Well, you try, then,' Marigold said, thrusting the catapult into Jack's hand. 'See if you can do any better.'

Jack took his time. He chose a sharp grey flint and placed it carefully in the pouch. Remembering what Lenny had done, he stood sideways to the target – a large yellow cone at the end of one of the branches. Then he pulled the rubber band back with his left hand until his knuckles were touching the side of his jaw. He was about to release the stone when a bird settled on the branch just beneath the cone. It was a starling. It sat awkwardly, gripping one of the sharp leaves with its feet. It hadn't noticed him, it was staring across the roofs of the town to the sea in the far distance. Jack shifted his boots in the gravel, thinking the bird would move. He shuffled again, hoping that it would look down and flutter its wings, that it would, at least, acknowledge he was there. He wanted to shout out: 'Hey, look at me. I could hurt you if I wanted.' But the bird didn't seem to care.

Jack stretched the rubber band as far as it would go and launched the stone wildly into the air. It was only when he heard the thud of the flint against the bird's chest, then a second, lighter thud when the bird hit the ground beneath the tree, that he knew he had hit it.

Marigold let out a long whistle and Lenny Grieve ran to the small black form lying on the moss. He prodded it gently with the toe of his boot then knelt down.

'It's dead.' His voice was flat. Jack couldn't tell whether Lenny was impressed or dismayed.

'You killed it, Jacky, you killed it dead!' Marigold shouted with delight. 'Go on, do it again. Look, there's another one up there.'

Jack looked up at a second bird, and the bird looked down at him.

'You shouldn't have killed it,' said Lenny Grieve softly as he turned the dead bird over with his fingers.

Jack dropped the catapult and crouched on the ground next to him. He touched the bird. It was still warm. He could feel the fragile skeleton underneath the feathers. The bird wasn't black at all, it was lustrous, shining green and purple in the sunlight. Its feet were red, its beak was bright yellow, and between its soft, short chest feathers was a thick clot of blood. The triumph ebbed away from him. What had felt like glory a minute ago was now dull and leaden.

Lenny took a handkerchief from his pocket and rolled the bird inside it. The black blood on its chest began to seep through the white cotton.

'Oh, chuck it away,' said Marigold. 'It's no good now.'

But Lenny carried the bird's shrouded corpse to the dead hydrangeas against the wall of the villa. Then he placed it carefully under the leaves, out of the glare of the sun.

The Colouring Book

The summer drew to a close. In September the villa garden was replaced by the classroom of Saint Ignatius School for Boys. They sat in rows, alphabetically. Jack stared at Bob Marigold's rounded back, and at the hole in Marigold's green pullover that grew larger and larger as the term went on. He learned the times tables. He learned how to parse a sentence. He learned that he did not want to be at school at all. There were whispers in the outside toilets, sly glances, a hastily written note shoved inside his desk: 'Your Mams a loony', like he didn't know already.

On Sunday mornings, Uncle Henry came to the house on Invicta Road and took Jack to mass at Saint Anthony's: Granny Rush and Maurice only went to church at Easter and Christmas.

Uncle Henry would stand in the doorway of the house smelling of breakfast: fried eggs and bacon with a touch of Mrs Veasey's lavender furniture polish. He never said much, but as they walked to church, he would smile down at Jack, a smile that he squeezed uncomfortably out of his long face.

In the front pew, Jack pressed close to his uncle so the other worshippers wouldn't see him, although Uncle Henry prayed so hard he never noticed. Sometimes when he said a Hail Mary or an Our Father he swayed and frowned as if he was thinking about the meaning of the words rather than just parroting them like everyone else. As Father Scullion berated the congregation from the pulpit, Uncle Henry's hands were pressed tightly together and his eyes screwed shut.

Jack always had vivid dreams on Sunday nights. Bad ones, memorable ones. He dreamt of impossible worlds where spaces stretched and retracted, where one object turned into another, where one person became someone else. He dreamt of the statue of Jesus standing in its dark alcove in Saint Anthony's. He hated the shabby, unkempt plaster Christ with his white toes poking out from his sandals and his badly painted beard. He dreamt he was walking down the cold aisle to tell Jesus to wash his dusty face, when the statue sprouted wings, huge black ones that unfurled like an angel's. As Jack approached, he could see that Jesus's chest was covered in short glossy feathers that were dripping with blood, though Jesus didn't seem to mind. He smiled and lifted his wing to hand Jack the stone that had killed him. Then he opened his beak and began to sing:

You can hear them sigh and wish to die, You can see them wink the other eye. At the man who broke the bank at Monte Carlo.'

In December, Maurice set up the Christmas tree in the corner of the front room. It was an artificial one, a skeletal metal structure covered with shiny green paper strips which were supposed to be leaves. Someone had switched on the radiogram and a child's voice wavered through the air all the way from London – 'sleep in heavenly peace, sleep in heavenly peace'. And drifting past the window were a few feeble flakes of snow. Teesby never had proper snow, all they got was a thin greasy covering that made the path outside the front door treacherous. Twice in the last few days Granny Rush had fallen over. And when no one was looking Jack had slid from the house to the street, propelling himself forward and grasping the top bar of the garden gate before he tumbled.

'So, what do you think, Jacky?' Uncle Henry was standing in the middle of the front room, biting his top lip. 'Did you hear what I said? Are you listening to me? I said your ma's asked to see you.'

Jack swallowed hard. There was something stuck in his throat. He swallowed again. The thing felt like it was expanding to fill the space.

'It'll be a tonic for her. An early Christmas present.' Uncle Henry tugged his handkerchief out of his pocket and wheezed into it.

'Why does she want to see me?' Jack's voice was thin. It shook like the chorister's on the radio.

'Why does she want to see you – ask a silly question. I thought you'd be pleased.' Uncle Henry patted him on the shoulder. 'Buck up, Jacky. It'll be a treat for you both.'

On Saturday afternoon they went to Williams and Son on the High Street and bought two Christmas presents: a box of handkerchiefs from Jack and a small brown diary from Uncle Henry. The handkerchiefs were white and embroidered with swags of daisies. The diary had a silk bookmark attached to the inside spine and a tiny pencil hanging from a string sewn into the binding. On the cover, stamped in gold, was the word *Appointments*, followed by the date *1932*.

'It's so she knows what day it is,' said Uncle Henry. 'So she can write things down in it if she wants. You know, her thoughts and such like.'

The following morning, Jack's suit was brought out of the upstairs cupboard, and Granny Rush made him polish his boots. Just before he left the house, she grabbed him roughly by the shoulder and rubbed his face with a dishcloth until his cheeks hurt.

'Can't say we don't look after you proper,' she called after him, as he made his way towards the bus stop.

It took them almost an hour to reach the hospital. The Winterfield County Asylum had been built eighty years ago on a stretch of flat land, close enough to the sea to be dusted by sand and for the grass to be tainted by salt, but too far away for anyone to be able to glimpse the sea or even smell it. The hospital formed part of Winterfield Village, although it was hardly a village at all, just a cluster of buildings divided by the main road. On one side were the high railings that enclosed the hospital grounds. On the other was a short terrace of brick houses that terminated at both ends in a shop.

What struck Jack first, after he had stepped off the bus and followed Uncle Henry along the road to the asylum gates, was the symmetry of the place. He stood at the gates and gazed up the drive. The right side of the garden and the right side of the hospital was a mirror image of the left. Until then, every building and every landscape he could recall seeing had been asymmetrical. There was the undulating muddle of the villa on the hill and the lopsided house on Invicta Road, its façade disturbed by the jutting bay window on the ground floor. Even the view from the beach was uneven: the Snook on the left curved gently across the estuary and the tower at its tip broke the horizontal line between the sea and the sky.

When they reached the entrance to the hospital – three shallow steps and a wide stone portico – Uncle Henry stopped. He put his hand on Jack's shoulder and said quietly, 'You have to remember, she might not be quite herself.'

It was as if he had only just thought of this. It was a hurried, slightly fearful remark.

'People change, Jacky. You do understand, don't you?'

Now Jack was dreading the visit even more. As they walked along the corridor, his heart was beating, pounding under his jumper: thump, thump, thump. He pressed his hand hard against it to try and make it stop.

She was sitting on a wooden bench in a long tiled room. She smiled faintly when she saw him in the doorway. She got up, stretched out her hand and held his limply for a moment. But Uncle Henry was right, she *had* changed. Like the hospital, his mother was symmetrical too. In Teesby she had worn a brooch on the left lapel of her frock, and her hair had been swept across her forehead and pinned on one side with a silver clip. In Winterfield, however, she sat straight in her hospital clothes. Her hair was parted in the centre and dressed evenly over each ear and, when she sat down again, she clasped her hands neatly in her lap. He waited, barely breathing, expecting her to say something about the day on the beach. But she was silent, as if she had forgotten it, or as if it had never happened at all.

Uncle Henry handed her the diary and Jack gave her the box of handkerchiefs. She lay the gifts carefully on the table beside her without looking at them.

'So, so kind,' she said.

'We thought they'd be useful,' replied Uncle Henry gruffly. He took off his coat and wiped the end of his nose with a handkerchief. 'So how are you feeling, Nell?'

'Very well, it's nice to have a good long rest.'

'They're looking after you then?'

'Very well.'

There was a long pause while they watched a group of visitors, bundled in coats and scarves, lean anxiously towards the nurse sitting at the desk near the doorway. Then Uncle Henry turned to Jack and touched his arm.

'Tell your mother about school. I'm sure she'd like to know how you're doing.'

Jack was doing badly, and there was nothing else to say about school except the fact that he hated it.

'We're reading *Robinson Crusoe*,' he said finally.

'How nice,' she replied.

She sounded like Mrs Tibbs. In the villa she used to call to him: 'Is that the little boy?' And his mother would make him go to her and stand close so that Mrs Tibbs could touch his face. Talking to Mrs Tibbs was like talking to someone far away. You had to keep the words simple and the sentences short.

'When we've finished that we're going to read *Gulliver's Travels*,' he said.

'Lovely.'

'And he's doing his catechisms with Father Scullion,' Henry chipped in.

'So nice,' she said, twisting her hands in her lap.

It was like she was acting. She was playing the part so well that his real mother had almost disappeared, buried deep underneath the fake one. He wanted to find her again, grasp hold of her hands and shake them. He wanted to shout: 'Ma, come back!'

The conversation stumbled on for a few minutes more. Then his mother stood up abruptly, held out her hand as if they were guests she hardly knew, and said, 'Do come again. I would very much like to see you both.'

Their second visit did not take place until long after Christmas. His mother was ill, Uncle Henry said. 'A touch of bronchitis, but nothing to worry about. Nothing at all.'

She wasn't well enough to receive a visit until the first week of February. By then, the snowdrops were blooming in the front gardens of Invicta Road, but Winterfield Village was still frozen and the hospital grounds were barren.

Jack's mother sat on the high-backed bench in the hospital parlour just as she had done before Christmas. And she was still symmetrical, apart from her right eye which wandered independently of her left. The dilated pupil kept drifting to the edge of her eye socket as if she could see something in the corner of the room beyond Jack and Uncle Henry, something invisible to them both.

She had been given a rosary, a clumsy chain of wooden beads

ending in a brown-stained cross, the sort that nuns wore hanging from a belt round their waists. She rubbed the beads between her thumb and finger and smiled at Jack, tentatively, uncertain of who he was.

'Baby Cathy's starting to walk now,' said Uncle Henry.

'Blessed is the fruit of thy womb, Jesus,' she replied, her fingers advancing along the beads.

'Your Maurice is working on the house near the villa again. You know the one, Nell, with the green railings, the house you used to like. He's wallpapering the hallway and the landing. They've chosen Anaglypta.'

'Holy Mary, Mother of God.'

Uncle Henry was struggling to find anything more to say. After several false starts he launched into: 'Old Mrs Rush is having all her teeth taken out. She's got a problem with the gums. Costing her a fortune.'

'Pray for us sinners, now and at the hour of our death. Amen.'

Jack clenched his hands and pressed his nails into his flesh. It was easier not to look at her, easier to gaze down at the floor, at the black and white tiles that looked like a draughts board. He stared at the chequerboard pattern, at the way it disappeared into the distance, at the way the squares turned into diamonds.

Uncle Henry twisted his head and peered down at him. Then he reached out and squeezed Jack's shoulder. Jack could feel the faint warmth of his uncle's hand all the way through his jacket and shirt to his shivery skin.

'I think we'd better be on our way,' said Uncle Henry suddenly. 'It's nice to see you doing well.' He was buttoning up his jacket and putting on his coat. 'We'll come back to see you soon, Nell, very soon.'

As they were about to leave, Uncle Henry paused to speak to the nurse who was sitting at the desk by the entrance to the room.

'Not so good today, then.'

'Oh, they can be quite changeable, Mr Pearson. It all depends.'

'On what?' asked Uncle Henry sternly. 'On what does it all depend?'

'The special treatment, Mr Pearson. The medication.'

'What are you giving her then?' He bent forward and placed his hands on the desk in front of the nurse. 'Because she looks quite strange to me. Not herself at all, not all there. She looks ...' he struggled for a word, 'cockeyed.'

The woman drew back from the table and sat straight. 'It's not for me to say exactly what the treatment is, you'll have to talk to Doctor. But I can tell you that Mrs Rush is a good patient. You mustn't worry, she's quite happy with us here. Look at her now.'

She nodded towards Jack's mother, who was sitting solidly on the bench, legs slightly apart, hands clenched together in her lap. She had worked her way to the end of the rosary beads and was murmuring a 'Glory Be' under her breath.

'Difficult day. Difficult day,' said Uncle Henry when they stood in the shelter waiting for the Teesby bus. He shuffled his feet once or twice, then inhaled the frosty air. Finally, without another word, he walked across the road to the shop at the end of the terrace and appeared a few minutes later carrying a paper bag of barley sugar and a small, soft-covered book.

He offered Jack a sweet and murmured, 'She was bit the worse for wear today, wasn't she?' Then he handed him the book. 'Something to make up for it.'

Jack held the book loosely by his side. He didn't want to look at the gift in the chill shadow of the bus shelter, in the strew of sand and sweet wrappers. He didn't want to look at it on the bus either, and he gripped it tightly in his hand as they accelerated out of the village. He didn't want to sully this book with the memory of his mother's dancing eye. He didn't want this book, whatever it was, to be tainted by its association with Winterfield Asylum.

He wanted it to belong somewhere else, beyond the limits of that dreadful, frozen afternoon, beyond Teesby, even.

Without knowing its contents, he began to believe in the book's power, its potential to catapult him out of Invicta Road, out of Teesby, far away from Winterfield. As he stared from the bus window and watched the landscape scroll behind his uncle's head, he transformed the poorly bound pages, clasped in his sweaty hand, into a talisman of sorts.

Sitting on the settee in the cold front room, he examined the book. It was called *The Modern World: A Colouring Book for Boys*. He had hoped for a story that might tell him something, that might help him forget the day. But this was just a book of drawings. There were no words, only black and white outlines: rough diagrammatic images of machines, buildings and objects, printed on thin, fawn-coloured newsprint. He turned over the pages. There was a bridge, an aeroplane, a telephone, a tractor, a doctor inspecting a syringe.

In the cubby hole under the stairs was a cardboard box that contained a few of his books and comics at the bottom was a tin of coloured pencils. Occasionally he had taken a pencil out of the tin and pondered what to draw while he chewed the end. Whenever he put pencil to paper, however, he was always disappointed by the results. He could not make his drawing of Uncle Henry look like the real Uncle Henry, or the parrot look like the parrot. And he could never make his picture of the sun resemble the huge boiling spot in the sky that it really was.

He unearthed the pencil tin and inspected the contents. There were only four: black, red, yellow and blue. He flicked through the book: there were forty-eight pictures in *The Modern World*.

The front cover showed a landscape, a wide river crossed by a railway bridge. A large ship was sailing underneath the bridge while a passenger train in the apple-green livery of the LNER steamed overhead. In the distance, in a gentle valley between two rounded hills, a car tilted as it cornered a bend. And flying high above the title, in the top left-hand corner of the cover, was a tiny glinting cross – a sleek, streamlined monoplane.

When he turned to the first page, he found the faint outline of a biplane. He gazed at the convex arc of the plane's body and wondered what colour it should be. On the cover, the monoplane was an unnameable shade: between pale blue and silver. In the hope of reproducing the same mechanical gleam, he coloured the entire picture using the blue pencil, careful not to escape the outlines. But when he held the book up and squinted at the page, the biplane was flat, just a silhouette of cobalt blue.

He moved wearily to the next outline, a rough drawing of a stocky driver in overalls, who was leaning against the door of his lorry. Overalls were brown, Jack knew this: khaki brown. Lorries were burgundy red, because he had seen one driving towards the engineering works. But how was he to reproduce that using only four colours?

In exasperation, he began to fill the voids lightly with all the colours in the tin, until the driver and the lorry cab were covered in an iridescent scribble. He paused briefly, examined the drawing, then added more blue to the driver's overalls, following the printed lines that suggested the creases and the seams. Once again, he held the book up to his half-closed eyes, and this time he was perplexed. The forms stood out from the rest of the page. They had been thrown into relief against the black outlines and the blank spaces he had yet to colour in. The driver's overalls appeared to ripple: he could see the folds and the wrinkles in the cloth. And the lorry cab shone like painted metal.

He had performed a trick. He had transformed the picture of the driver and the lorry into something almost real.

Fathers

It was Saturday morning, they had just finished breakfast. Granny Rush was clearing away the dishes while Maurice, who should have left for work ten minutes ago, was sitting beside Jack with Cathy on his lap. His arm was a tight band around his daughter's waist, and he was jigging her up and down as if he was a pony.

Jack was working on the last picture in the colouring book: a tractor with red wheels and a badge that said Fordson. The tractor was complicated, there were narrow pipes and gears, and the engine was a mass of strange shapes that bothered him because he was unsure what colour they should be.

'Clip-clop, clip-clop, clip-clop,' said Maurice to Cathy.

'Dada,' she squealed.

'Stop it,' hissed Jack under his breath, but no one heard him.

Granny Rush was standing by the sink with a dirty teacup in her hand. She was grinning at Cathy with her mouth wide open. Jack could see her yellowish gums and the dark space where her teeth used to be.

'Clip-clop, clip-clop, clip-clop.'

In irritation he ground his own teeth together and pressed the lead of the black pencil into the paper. When he lifted the pencil away again, there was a deep shiny scar along the tractor's side, a curving dent in the bodywork: even from a distance he could see it.

He sighed as loudly as he could. There was no point in carrying on now, he had ruined the tractor. And because of the heavy pressure of the pencil line he had spoilt the picture on the previous page too. He sighed a second time, slammed the cover shut and pushed the book away across the table.

'Clip-clop, clip-clop, clip-clop.'

The pony was trotting now, Cathy was pitching from side to side. She stretched out her arms to balance herself.

'Clip-clop, clip-clop, clip-clop.'

Then as Maurice lifted her up with his knee once more she lurched forward and her fat fist collided with the milk jug in the middle of the table.

If Jack hadn't pushed the book away there wouldn't have been a problem. But in an instant the jug was lying on its side, spewing milk over the cover of *The Modern World*. He stared at the mess in astonishment. Then he plucked the book from the pool of milk and began to dab at the cover with the sleeve of his jumper.

'Get up, you halfwit!' said Granny Rush. 'You're going to get milk all over you.'

He glared at his wet sleeve and the damp colouring book. 'Shite!' he said, letting the sound slide between his teeth and out of his mouth. It was the first time he had sworn in public and he was surprised at how the word made things better. The sound was exactly how he felt. He tried it again.

'Shite! Bloody shite!'

'Don't you speak like that in my house!' cried Maurice. He stood up and, clutching Cathy with one arm, he leaned over and deftly swiped Jack hard across the face.

The burning jolt of the slap took his breath away. It shook him out of himself, made him forget his milky sleeve and the sodden book. It reminded him of something else.

'You're not my dad,' he spat at Maurice. 'You're not my dad. My dad would never do that.' He reeled towards his stepfather with his fist clenched, but Cathy's head was in the way and when she saw her brother's face she began to sob.

He pulled back slowly and let his arm drop by his side. There was nothing he could do now. He swooped up the colouring book, still dripping with milk, and stalked out of the kitchen door into the backyard.

In time it became his catchphrase. Just as George Formby always used to say, 'It's turned out nice again, hasn't it?' Jack would say, 'You're not my dad. My dad would never do that!' Or 'You're not my gran!' Or 'You're not my sister!' Although this wasn't fair because Cathy *was* his sister, at least half of her was.

'You can't use my pencils because you're not my real sister,' he said one day, as Cathy, now two and a half, was sitting cross-legged in front of the *Northern Echo*, about to scribble over the empty squares in the crossword with the yellow pencil.

Granny Rush was on the other side of the room doing something with the parrot's cage. The parrot was perched on the edge of her hand, gazing at her face, its tiny claws piercing her liver-spotted skin.

'Give us the pencil back, you're not my real sister,' said Jack, snatching at it.

'Don't go talking to Cathy like that.' Granny Rush wagged her finger at him, which made the bird thrash its useless wings and squawk. 'You should watch yourself, young man,' she said. 'You're beginning to get a chip on your shoulder.'

Jack didn't know what having a chip on his shoulder meant. He was certain it was not the sort of thick-cut, under-cooked chip that Bakewells on the promenade served up for dinner and tea six days a week. On Saturdays, after the children's matinee at the Regent, Jack and Bob Marigold always asked for 'a penny-worth of chips and scraps, please.' Then they would lean against the promenade railings, picking at the pallid starchy mess while the pools of grease soaked into the Stock Reports and the Births, Marriages and Deaths and the advertisement for Mrs Prout's frock shop on Culver Road.

Nor did Jack think that Granny Rush was referring to the sort of chip that Maurice slid under the back door to stop it slamming shut when he was carrying his tins of paint into the house: a wedge of cheap yellow pine that Maurice was always losing.

'Where's the bloody chip?' he would cry.

And Granny Rush, nudging it out from under the dresser with her foot, would always reply, 'Where you bloody left it.'

When Jack asked Lenny Grieve about the chip, Lenny said: 'I think it means you're angry.' Then he paused and shook his head. 'No, I think it means you've got a grudge, like you think someone's done something bad to you a long time ago and you haven't forgotten about it.'

This made sense to Jack. If someone had done something bad to you it was right not to forgive them. In that case, having a chip on your shoulder was a good thing. Although he still couldn't understand what the chip had to do with Cathy not being his sister, or with Maurice not being his dad.

When Jack was small, his father's absence had rarely bothered him, after all no one else he knew had parents. Mrs Tibbs, Beadie, Uncle Henry and his mother seemed to have appeared from nowhere at all. He had tried to broach the question once, when he was about four years old, as he and his mother were walking across the Nab late one afternoon. They had been to the farm on Bleaker's Hill to collect the eggs so that Beadie could make a Christmas cake. He had been taken to the hen house and allowed to select the eggs from the nest boxes. While the hens clucked anxiously round his legs, he had picked the eggs out of the straw and noticed how warm the shells were. When he mentioned this to the farmer's wife, she told him that the hens sat on the eggs to make them crack open so a baby would appear. She took him across the farmyard to a small barn and showed him the chickens that would turn into hens that would lay more eggs that would become chickens if no one ate them.

'But you need a cock as well as hens to make babies,' she said pointedly. 'The hens can't do it on their own.'

He was still thinking about this conversation when he and his mother were walking home along the frozen ruts of the track that led to the villa.

He grasped her hand and wove his fingers between hers. 'So if a chicken comes out of an egg, Ma, where did I come from?'

She gazed down at him and smiled faintly. Then she twisted back to look over her shoulder at Bleaker's Hill as if she was going to point something out to him in the distance.

'You came from—' she began. But she stopped and turned to look down at him again. 'You came from the Snook,' she said, gesturing in the opposite direction. 'I went down there one day and saw your little head poking out of it, so I pulled you up and brought you home. That's where all the Pearsons come from, out of the sand on the Snook.'

He suspected the story wasn't true, although for a few minutes, as he traipsed along the track, he pictured himself emerging from the sea-spit, like the mole he had seen in Beadie's vegetable patch – the crest of a grey head and a pair of great pallid flopping hands pushing the soil away. Then he remembered what the farmer's wife had said about the cockerel and he was about to ask his mother if a woman needed a man to make a baby, like the hens had needed the cock, when they reached the back door of the villa and heard Beadie screaming at the cat. On the kitchen floor was a trail of sticky blood that led to the tiny corpse of yet another mouse abandoned under the table. Jack crouched down to inspect the stiff, half-chewed thing, and his question about the cockerel was forgotten.

*

When he started at Saint Ignatius the following year, after his mother had married Maurice, the inevitable question arose.

'What does your dad do?' asked an older boy in the playground.

After he had mentioned Maurice with his paint tins and his rolls of Lincrusta wallpaper, another boy retorted, 'But he's not your proper dad is he? Who's your proper dad?'

There was nothing he could say in reply. He had opened his mouth and flapped his lips together, pretending that he was about to say something important. But the boys had laughed at him, and they ran away across the playground shouting things about his mother.

It was then that the feeling began – like something was missing. Like an empty space, like the gap in your mouth when a milk tooth had fallen out, and without thinking you kept pushing your tongue into the space to make sure the gap was still there. When they took his mother away, he waited for his real father to barge through the front door and take him home. He assumed that if one parent left the other would eventually return.

Maurice was no substitute for a father. He was vain and preening. He fussed over collar studs and cufflinks and ties. Every morning he gazed at his reflection in the kitchen mirror before he smoothed down his hair with Brylcreem and fashioned his moustache into a thin glossy line that separated his wide nostrils from his fleshy lips. Maurice spent his days painting the panelling and wallpapering the walls of the big houses along the sea front, and he spent his nights dancing in the Zetland Club on the promenade or drinking in Hooper's Hotel on the High Street.

It was Uncle Henry who had taken on the role – awkwardly, hesitantly, as if someone had insisted that he should. It was Uncle Henry who organised Jack's confirmation at Saint Anthony's, who helped him with his homework, who read his school reports and admonished him for them, who bought him a new colouring book and more pencils, and a stamp album and his long-trousered

Sunday suit. And yet there was something not quite right. Jack could feel it. He could hear it in Uncle Henry's voice, the way his uncle spoke to him carefully, cautiously, giving nothing away.

When Jack was eleven, Uncle Henry organised a picnic on the beach. He spread a tartan blanket over the dry shingle near the snakestone cliffs and laid out a thermos of tea, a bottle of lemonade, a homemade pie and six fairy cakes. It was Cathy who had requested the picnic. She was nearly five years old now, with a round freckled face and long curling hair. She was standing on a ridge of pebbles, peering down at something by her feet.

For most of the morning, Jack had been lying on his stomach with his back to the sea, struggling to draw the shopfronts that lined the promenade: the bow-windowed tea rooms and Bakewells and the shabby stall with its red and yellow awning, that sold buckets and spades.

'Why don't you sketch the sea?' asked Uncle Henry, leaning over to look at the picture.

'It's too difficult,' he replied, which was true, because how was he supposed to draw something that was constantly moving, that was both transparent and opaque, that rose up and swelled into a solid mountain then exploded into nothing at all.

'What about the Snook then?' said Uncle Henry. 'At least it's prettier than those shops.'

But Jack hated the Snook. There was nothing to see except the flat salt marsh and the tower at the tip. Occasionally, he and Uncle Henry had taken the ferry across the river and walked along the road that edged the marsh: but they had never turned onto the causeway. The Air Ministry had fenced off the Snook five years ago, and from the beach, if the sun was strong, you could see the faint grey silhouettes of the new huts which, Uncle Henry said, housed radiograms that sent coded signals out to sea.

'Nothing's too difficult if you try hard enough,' said Uncle

Henry firmly. He took his penknife – the one he used to sharpen pencils and gouge out the dirt from under his nails – out of his pocket, and cut the pie into pieces and passed a slice to Jack.

The pie tasted of sea salt and wood shavings and margarine. Jack chewed through the wad of pastry and the sinewy apple, and watched Cathy, who was now nudging something with the edge of her spade. Cat-like, she crept forward and prodded the thing with her foot then sprang back in case it moved.

'What do you think it is, Jacky?' she asked, calling to her brother.

He got up from the blanket and inspected the shape at her feet. It looked like someone had tipped a bowl of translucent blanc-mange onto the pebbles. When he squatted down beside it, he could see a bulbous swollen head and stringy ribbons of watery flesh that seemed to be growing from it. It was difficult to work out where the edges of the thing ended and the pebbles began. How could something so ugly, so formless exist in the world?

'It's a monster,' whispered Cathy.

'No, it's a jellyfish, I think.'

'Leave it alone both of you, it's dead,' said Uncle Henry.

Jack sat down on the blanket again, while his sister dropped the spade and wandered along the line of pebbles humming to herself.

'Do you want pie or cake, Cathy?' Uncle Henry gestured to the food laid out on the blanket.

'Both.'

'Well, you can have a cake for now, but you have to sit down and eat it properly.'

She ran towards them, took the cake that was offered to her and pulled the cherry from the icing.

'You know how when you're dead and you go to heaven,' she said, putting the cherry into her mouth and swallowing it. 'Where are you before you're born?'

'I suppose you were with God then, too,' replied Uncle Henry.

'How did I get from being with God to being here?'

Jack knew how she got here. Last summer, Marigold had shown him a picture in a book that he had found in the library. The picture, more of a diagram really but enough to give a good idea of what happened, disgusted him and excited him all at the same time. He couldn't believe that such an appalling act was permitted, that people like Granny Rush and Maurice and his teachers and the librarian – who had adjusted her spectacles and was peering over the top of them at Marigold – could lie down and do something like that with someone else. The truth had astounded him and troubled him: 'You mean it goes in the pee-hole?' he had asked.

'Looks like it,' Marigold had replied, staring down at the book.

So what was Uncle Henry going to say?

'Your dad,' replied Henry, carefully wiping his penknife on his handkerchief, 'gave your mam a present and that present turned into you.'

'A present from God?'

This pleased Uncle Henry and he smiled at Cathy. 'Yes, that's right.' He slipped his knife back into his pocket and reached for a cake.

'But who gave our mam Jacky?'

'What do you mean?'

'Well, my dad isn't Jacky's dad.'

Uncle Henry stared obliquely at Jack. 'Who told you that?'

'Jacky did. He said I'm not his real sister.' Cathy looked down at her uncle and grinned. 'So who was Jacky's dad then?'

Jack rolled over onto his stomach again and gazed at the drawing of the shops. He wanted it to look like he didn't care, but he was barely breathing. He leaned his head towards his uncle so he didn't miss a word.

'He was a travelling man,' said Uncle Henry.

'Where did the travelling man go?'

'Oh, here and there, here and there. A very busy man. Travelled all over the world, I believe. Wasn't able to come home very often.'

Jack knew that this was just another story, almost as bad as his mother's story about the Snook. He shifted a little in the sand and focused on the drawing. It wasn't as good as he had thought, the lines were wobbly and the buildings tapered inwards as they reached the roofs.

'What was Jacky's dad called?' asked Cathy.

'John. He was called John.'

'So what happened to him – John, the travelling man?' She was whispering now as if she had sensed a scandal.

'He died, in his sleep.'

'On a train?'

'No, Cathy, in his bed.'

Jack took another piece of paper from the sketchpad and started again.

'So Jacky's dad weren't travelling, then?'

'Not when he died, love, no.'

'Oh,' said Cathy dully. She had lost interest. She placed the half-eaten cake on the blanket and sidled away towards a small girl with golden hair who was building a sandcastle near the waves. Normally Uncle Henry would have called her back, he was an anxious guardian, alert to every danger: drowning, abduction. But he turned away from the beach and looked at Jack. Then he lay his hand flat on the blanket as if he was about to pat Jack's fingers.

'I never met your dad but I'm sure he was a good man.'

This surprised Jack. Everyone knew everyone in Teesby, even if they were only passing through. How was it possible that Uncle Henry had never met his father? Did the travelling man sneak into the villa at night? Jack pictured the pink and yellow diagram in the library book, the labelled parts: vaginal orifice, glans penis, scrotum – a word that made Marigold snigger so much he had almost choked. Did Jack's mother invite the travelling man, with his foreskin and his testicles, into the house? Did she love him?

'You see,' said Uncle Henry, 'I wasn't very kind to your ma when you were born. I was upset for you ... I knew it was a cross you'd have to bear.'

The tip of Uncle Henry's index finger was almost touching Jack's thumb now, but Jack moved away. He was trying to picture the travelling man. Was he a gypsy or an acrobat with a circus, or a salesman in haberdashery or stationery? Or perhaps he was an explorer or a wandering journeyman or a pedlar with a basket of clothes pegs. Or perhaps he was a tramp. Perhaps he was looking for food and stumbled on his mother instead. He made her do the things in the diagram and he gave her a present that she didn't want. This was a terrible thought. It was a huge yawning hole opening up in front of him. It made perfect sense. She didn't want him either. No one did. He was the dead jellyfish lying on the pebbles, washed up, abandoned.

The Girl

As Jack grew older, he found there were advantages to Uncle Henry's detachment and Maurice's indifference. No one ever asked him where he was going or when he would be back. The inhabitants of the house on Invicta Road lived their lives apart. Granny Rush cleaned and cooked half-heartedly, running a dirty cloth over the china figurines in the front room, or stewing something indescribable in a saucepan on the stove. At the kitchen table, Cathy and her ringleted friends cut pictures out of the *Northern Echo* and stuck them into a scrapbook. Or they invented improbable lives for a pair of paper dolls called Delilah and Delphine. On Sunday mornings Uncle Henry appeared at the front door to take Jack and Cathy to mass. He wore glasses now, with thin metal frames, and the fluffy hair just above his ears had already turned grey. After mass, he would sprint down the hill to the High Street to catch the bus to Winterfield. Once a month Maurice went with him, steely-faced, gripping a small bouquet of yellow flowers: dahlias or chrysanthemums.

There was no space for Jack in the house on Invicta Road. He was twelve now, tall and clumsy, always inadvertently knocking things off shelves or dropping dishes. After school, he and Marigold made their way up the lane to the empty villa. In the spring, they tried to smoke roll-ups, leaning over the balustrade that edged the garden. In the summer, they sat under the Monkey

Puzzle tree and learned how to drink. Marigold, who was an altar boy at Saint Anthony's, had found half a bottle of rum in the vestry wrapped inside Father Scullion's spare cassock. In the villa garden, he pulled the bottle out of his pocket and swung it in front of Jack, just as he swung the belching thurible at the beginning of mass.

Marigold wisely sipped the rum but Jack gulped it like lemonade. At first it was sweet and he swished it confidently round his mouth. But when he finally swallowed it, the rum clawed at his throat, and after several minutes he vomited it up again. The foamy stream of syrupy liquid spewed from his mouth and formed a shallow puddle in the roots of the Monkey Puzzle tree. Marigold laughed, and Jack belched deeply and burst out laughing too.

When the weather changed, Marigold and Jack found a way into the villa through the coal cellar. He hadn't been inside the house since he left it with his mother when she married Maurice. All he could remember of that day was the wind and rain, flattening the flowers in the garden and beating against the windows.

In the villa kitchen, Beadie's copper pans were still hanging in a line above the range and the dresser was still loaded with mixing bowls and willow-pattern china. The long pine table stood in the centre of the room, although one of the chairs was skewed as if someone had just got up in a hurry.

The rest of the house had been cleared: the library was empty of books, and the bedrooms had been relieved of their dusty rugs and heavy furniture. The door to the drawing room had been taken off its hinges and was leaning against the wall. And nestled in the dining room grate were the feathery remains of a bird that must have been trapped inside the chimney.

As he wandered through the house, he thought he could hear her just ahead of him, along the corridor or round a bend.

'Jacky, is that you? I've got something for you.'

*

The autumn died, the mist fell over the town. Then the King gave a speech on the radio, and Jack thought about the word abdication: *ab* – away, *dicare* – declare. He didn't really like the King. He had seen a picture of him in the newsagent's: he had an alien face, huge eyes and tight, smooth skin. But as Jack sat next to Granny Rush on the settee in the front room and listened to the speech delivered in slightly sulky tones, he thought how good it must feel to give everything up and walk away.

A week later, Uncle Henry wheezed along the path to the house on Invicta Road. He seemed excited.

'Saw your ma yesterday, Jacky. She was looking very well. She'd made some of the decorations for the Christmas tree in the visitors' parlour. Beautiful they were, little paper birds and flowers.'

'Oh,' said Jack blankly. He was sitting on the floor in the front room, trying to stick the wings onto the body of a tiny wooden aeroplane.

'You could visit her with me if you like,' said Uncle Henry. 'What do you think? Next Sunday? You want to come along?'

Jack shook his head emphatically. Just like the King he had resolved to abdicate his filial duties. As if Uncle Henry had understood, he wiped his dripping nose and nodded. 'Righty-ho, Jack. Righty-ho.'

The following spring, Jack and Lenny Grieve planned a hiking trip across the moor. The trip was Lenny's idea. Lenny liked walking: he walked for miles to damp, eerie hollows in the woods where rare orchids grew, and to the steep escarpment by the railway line colonised by lizards and snakes. He said he wanted to be a biologist like someone called Huxley. Lenny was starting to imagine a future for himself.

They were standing in the Grieves' kitchen studying the map that lay across the table: the one-inch Ordnance Survey of Teesby-on-Sea and Outlying Districts.

'This is the path we'll take right across the top,' said Lenny, pushing out the creases in the map with his hand. 'And this is where we'll pitch the tent, here and here.' He tapped his finger authoritatively on the paper.

Jack gazed down at the map, at the sinuous contours that described the Nab, at the graduating colours. It surprised him that something as muddled as the countryside could be plotted to scale – all those woods and rocky coastlines and streams. He could see how it fitted together, how one thing related to another. He could see history in the map too. His hand hovered over the wispy symbols and the gothic lettering: 'Encampment', 'Tumulus', 'Fort'. It was all there in front of him, everything from the beginning of time to right now.

Jack and Lenny set off early in the morning a few weeks later, taking the track past the villa then trudging across the damp fields towards Bleaker's Hill. In the mist, the colours trembled – he could see the papery gold of the new grass, the purple-flecked heather, the chalky sky. Lenny walked ahead, pointing things out. He talked about the way the moor dipped and rolled, the way the cliff face had been shattered by the sea, the way that generations of sheep had forged the sandy paths across the Nab.

Jack, unused to walking so far, so fast, plodded behind him uncomfortably, feeling the burning swell of blisters on his toes. Because of the wind he could hear only snatches of what Lenny was saying, and after a while he didn't listen at all. As he walked, his thoughts stumbled just ahead of him: each time he managed to grasp hold of one it escaped him again. He picked up a feather caught in a nest of brambles and pictured his mother, her face in profile, as she stood on the edge of Bleaker's Hill looking out to sea.

Their first night on the moor was oddly solemn. Lenny crawled over the fern looking at birds through his monocular, while Jack took out his sketchpad and pencils and tried to draw the view – the

114

crooked trees against the pale sky, the shambles of an abandoned farm on the hillside. But there was something wrong with the view. He stared at the rounded forms of the dozing sheep and the bronzy yellow of the gorse in the twilight, and realised they had walked so far inland that he couldn't see the sea any more. He had always taken it for granted, had never understood why his mother spent so much time gazing at it. 'Look at all the colours, Jacky,' she used to say. 'Can't you see them, all those pinks and blues and greens in the water, rolling over and over.'

On the morning of the second day, his blisters burst. The pus oozed out of his skin and stained his socks. This relieved the pain a little and he was able to match the rhythm of Lenny's steps. He began to enjoy himself, although he wasn't sure why. For several hours he thought about nothing at all.

Their last morning on the moor was wet: the ground was sodden with dew. When they crawled out of the tent and stood up, their footprints filled with brownish-coloured water. The camp fire was dead. Lenny was hunched over a fragile pyramid of twigs and sticks, striking one damp match after another.

'Maybe you can go to the farm and get us some milk,' he said, looking up at Jack. Until now, it was Lenny who had gone to buy the milk or ask for fresh water. On both occasions he had returned with gifts: three apples, a slab of fruit cake, a pat of butter. People liked Lenny: his quiet politeness, his blond wavy hair, his open face. Jack walked reluctantly away from the camp, clutching the miniature milk pail, certain he would fail.

The farmyard was a muddy, messy place, guarded by a weary-looking sheepdog chained to a low stone wall. In one corner was a tumbledown woodpile half covered by a flapping tarpaulin. In the other was a heap of soggy straw and cow dung. A woman in a grey apron and heavy boots was making her way towards the farmhouse. When he called to her, she twisted her head lazily and said, 'She's in the milk shed, if you want her.'

The shed, on the far side of the yard, smelt of earth – damp and green and gloomy – an odour so strong it made his nostrils itch. He stood just inside the door and watched a girl pouring bluish milk from a group of buckets into a giant version of the pail he held in his hand. She was bending over, her back to him. Without looking at him, she said, 'You want to buy some milk?'

'Yes, please.'

'Be with you in a minute, then.'

When she had emptied the buckets, she straightened herself and turned round. She had a white face and bad teeth – an overbite. One tooth was set at a precarious angle and the tip of it peeped out of her mouth and rested heavily on the plump cushion of her lower lip.

She grinned at him. 'What's your name then?'

'Jack.'

'Mine's Dora.'

She was tall and wide. Her arms were muscled and her calves, already tanned by the sun, bulged out from under her woollen socks.

'You're a good-looking lad,' she said.

He was surprised by this remark, partly because it was a strange thing to say in a milk shed, and partly because he knew it wasn't true. He scowled and dug the heel of his boot into the earth floor.

'Tell you what,' she said, walking over to him. 'You can have the milk for free if you give us a kiss.'

Jack was clenching a penny between his finger and thumb; he thrust it at the girl. 'I'd rather pay, if it's all the same.'

She sighed deeply and he could see her breasts under her dress. 'Well, if you're going to be like that, you have to pay me the penny *and* give me a kiss.'

'Listen, Miss, just take it,' he said, holding the coin out to her. He couldn't return with the milk pail empty, not after Lenny's successes.

'What are you afraid of?' The kiss had become a matter of honour to Dora. She put her hands on her hips and swayed towards him.

'Nothing,' he replied.

'Well, it's simple, just give us a kiss and I'll give you the milk.'

He had rarely kissed anyone, never Granny Rush, once Cathy when she was a baby, and probably his mother when they lived in the villa. But what did the girl want – a peck on the cheek or the sort of kiss he had seen at the pictures: Robert Donat pressing his face into Madeleine Carroll's?

Dora was standing in front of him now.

'Come on, give us a kiss.'

She was taller than Jack: she hunched up her shoulders and spread her feet apart as she leaned over him. Her cold front tooth pushed against his lip and he felt the spongy softness of her breasts against his hard chest: it made him dizzy, his knees were giving way. He dropped the pail and raised his hand, gently sliding it down the front of her neck searching for the warm bulge.

'I said a kiss!' she cried, pulling away. 'A kiss, not a grope of my bloody tits.' She pushed him and he stumbled backwards. He grabbed hold of the door frame to stop himself from falling.

'Mam! Mam!' she called. 'Someone's trying to—'

He bolted across the yard, tripping over a stray log that had slipped out of the woodpile, then dodging the sheepdog, which leapt up and yelped at him. He arrived back at the camp breathless, with nothing but mud-splashed legs and a bloody arm that he must have grazed against the shed wall when he stumbled.

'What happened to you?' asked Lenny. The fire was burning well now: the flames were licking round the bottom of the frying pan. 'And where's my dad's pail?'

Jack couldn't tell Lenny about the girl. Lenny never talked about girls. If it had been Marigold sitting there by the camp fire

Jack would have told him everything and they would have laughed about it. But not Lenny.

'There was this dog,' he said. 'A really big sheepdog, it ran at me. Sorry Lenny, sorry about your dad's pail.'

He was relieved when Lenny smothered the fire and packed away the tent. As they walked down the track together, his thoughts hopped from the farmer's wife, who he suspected was just behind them with a policeman, to the girl's breast. He wondered what it looked like under her dress, imagined it, blue like the milk in the buckets, or pink and translucent like the jellyfish on the beach.

They climbed down the hill into the valley and the sun emerged from behind a cloud. The fields brightened and the shadows of the stone walls darkened for a second. He was beginning to learn how to be himself in the world: it wasn't easy.

The Envelopes

A grey voice in the grey front room.

'This morning the British Ambassador in Berlin handed the German Government a final Note ...'

In time, Jack would picture this moment like a painting, like a Vermeer.

Standing in the front room was Granny Rush, a dustpan in one hand, a dishcloth in the other. Maurice was sitting on an upright chair, his back to the door. He had taken off his jacket, and his shirt had parted company with the waistband of his trousers, revealing a roll of delicately freckled pale pink flesh.

The radiogram spat and crackled – an electronic sob – then Mr Chamberlain's funereal voice grew fainter as if he had turned away from the microphone to dab his eyes.

'I have to tell you now that no such undertaking has been received, and that consequently this country is at war with Germany.'

For Jack, slouching against the banister rail in the hallway, the words had little meaning. He didn't care about Germany or Mr Chamberlain or the final Note. He watched Maurice, who rose to his feet: 'Well, we knew it was coming.' And Granny Rush who flapped her dishcloth: 'Should I go and fetch Cathy from next door, Maurice? Should I go and—' She was interrupted by a shuddering cry from the police station on the High Street. 'It's the siren. We should get her home.'

'It's only a test, Ma. They won't be invading today.'

'But we should get her back all the same, shouldn't we, Maurice ... shouldn't we?'

Granny Rush was starting to crumble. Like a great cliff, she was collapsing under the weight of time, of the prospect of another war. Little bits of her had drifted away already, fragments of rock borne out on the tide.

She fluttered her dishcloth again, and the parrot in its cage, disturbed by the sudden movement, slapped its wings against the metal bars.

'But we should get her back, all the same,' said Granny Rush, repeating her refrain. 'Shouldn't we ... shouldn't we, Maurice?'

Jack stepped out of the house and strode along Invicta Road, though his outing had no purpose. Marigold was with his grandmother on the other side of town and Lenny Grieve was visiting relatives in Leeds. It was simply out of boredom that he made his way to the promenade and leaned against the railings. The beach was empty, apart from a few gulls skirmishing over a fish carcass and the waders strutting along the tideline. The sand was still smooth from the retreating tide and there was nothing to see but the sea – just a blue band of water and a paler band of sky. As he gazed at the view a thought entered his head – something about the way that things were just the same today when there was a war, as they had been yesterday when there wasn't. But it was the vaguest of thoughts, and before it was half formed he had turned away from the promenade and had started to walk back home.

Like the beach, Teesby was empty too, although the air was dense with the odour of Brussels sprouts and evaporating meat juices. As he made his way up the hill from the promenade, he could hear the sound of knives against porcelain. He could see the silhouettes of people through the windows of the larger houses, shoulders hunched over dining tables, heads bowed over plates.

He was turning onto Invicta Road again, thinking of his own dinner, when he heard a voice behind him.

'Jack? Jack Pearson?'

It was a woman's voice, high-pitched and rasping.

'It is you, isn't it?'

He twisted round. The woman was old, tiny, bent double. In one hand was a stick she was using to support herself. The other hand hung limp as if the arm above it was boneless. She was wearing a man's tweed jacket and a brown dress the colour of the dying heather on the Nab. On her head was a child's straw boater decorated with tattered orange ribbons.

'There was a time when you would have run up and hugged me, Jacky.'

'Beadie?'

The woman looked up from under the brim of her hat. She was grotesque, nothing like the Beadie he remembered. The old woman's eyes were dark and empty and the skin on her face had fallen into folds as if the bones had shrunk away behind it. She was shaking, her head trembled and her useless hand kept twitching by her side.

'How old are you now, Jacky?'

She shuffled towards him, studied his face.

'I'm fifteen.'

'Fifteen, eh. You're very tall. You look like your uncle.'

He stood still and stiff as she stared at him, afraid if he tried to step away she would simply move closer.

'I've been to see your ma in Winterfield,' said Beadie quietly. 'She wanted me to give you something.'

The word Winterfield made his heart pound. The stifling lump immediately swelled inside his gullet. He realised then that Beadie must have been waiting for him, hidden in the shadow of the wall, watching out for him.

She carefully propped her stick against the wall that edged the pavement, and with her good hand she pulled out a lilac-coloured envelope from the pocket of her jacket.

'It's a letter,' he said as she pushed it into his hand.

'Of course it's a letter.'

'What does it say?'

'How should I know.' She grasped the stick again and leaned her weight against it. 'Your ma wants to see you, Jacky.' Beadie was peering at him again, her head to one side, her eyes narrowed. 'She hasn't seen you for a long time, has she?'

'What's it to you?' he said sourly.

'What's it to me!' she snarled, her top lip lifting slightly like a dog showing its teeth. 'What did I say to you before I left?'

How could he remember what she had said? It was years and years ago, stupid old woman. Stupid, stupid woman.

He didn't reply and Beadie shook her trembling head at him. The bright orange ribbons on her hat swayed from side to side.

'You used to be such a nice lad.'

'What's that supposed to mean?' he spat.

But she had already begun to hobble away from him, and he watched her struggle along the pavement until she was out of sight.

When she had gone, he stood in the street, balancing the envelope in the palm of his hand. He could hardly bear to touch it. The paper was impregnated with the memories of all the things he had tried to forget: the cheap rosary beads, the whispered Hail Marys, the thick smell of Jeyes fluid that had been slopped across the floor of the hospital parlour. It would be better not to read the letter. He should tear it into pieces and slip them into someone else's dustbin. But as he reeled round looking for one, a thought struck him. Why hadn't she asked Uncle Henry to give him the letter, or just asked someone to put it in the post? There must be something wrong, something that even Uncle Henry didn't know about. He stuffed the envelope into his trouser pocket and sloped back past the Rushes' house into the narrow alley behind Invicta Road.

In the backyard, he went into the privy and locked the door. Bracing himself, he slit the top of the envelope with his finger and pulled the letter out. Except there was no letter, just a folded piece of paper torn from a notebook. When he opened the paper, lying in the fold were a small dead moth and a single buttercup petal. He let out a sigh, a whoosh of air that echoed back at him, bouncing off the wooden walls. He was relieved there wasn't a letter. He was annoyed there wasn't a letter.

He poured the contents of the envelope into the flat of his hand. Against his skin, the moth was velvety grey, huddled and cocoon-like, and the buttercup petal was the greasy yellow of cheap margarine. He looked for a coded message, the sort that spies sent – minute figures etched onto the petal, a tiny slip of paper rolled inside the moth. He nudged the moth's wings with his finger, turned the petal over, but there was nothing there. From his incomprehension grew anger. It rose in him. He could taste it. It tasted bitter: the lump in his throat had exploded into acid and the vapours had filled his mouth. He gazed down at the mess in his trembling palm, and with a brief sting of pity for the dead moth, he roughly rubbed his hands together and brushed the dust away.

In the following weeks, he saw Beadie everywhere, a lopsided scarecrow standing on the corners of roads and in the doorways of shops, waiting for him. He shied at people like a nervous horse, crossed the street, doubled back on himself. In the mornings, he left the house through the kitchen door then zig-zagged across the town, down alleys and ginnels, reaching Saint Ignatius long after prayers. For the return trip in the afternoon, he changed his route or he headed home with Lenny Grieve. He would arrive at Invicta Road in the dark, to be scolded by Granny Rush, who had been standing sentinel by the bay window, tweaking the blackout curtain as she checked the street outside.

In late October, he started to skip school altogether. He walked for miles, tramping over the sand to the southern end of the beach where a narrow path led up to Bleaker's Hill. He was comfortable on the hill; in the open countryside, he would be able to see her coming a long way off. When the weather was good, he paced over the heather, disturbing the game birds that shot up from the ground, beating their wings and making their awful choking cry. Sometimes he tried to draw them. Sometimes, if the drawings were good enough, he tried to colour them in using a watercolour set that Uncle Henry had given him for his last birthday. But the paints always ran into each other, and he was left with multicoloured blots and stains that resembled nothing at all.

In November, he discovered a decrepit-looking shepherd's hut near Robinson's farm. Something had happened to the wheel shaft, and the hut had lurched sharply to one side. The rotting wooden roof had been covered by a khaki tarpaulin and inside the floor was strewn with straw. It was dry and dark, a place to warm himself for a while, a place to rest his legs. The light was too weak to draw by so he sat listening to the silence: a field mouse gnawing at something beneath the wagon, a startled blackbird in the overgrown hedge at the edge of the field, the faint gush and suck of the sea as the waves were propelled forward then pulled back again.

He was soon found out. Just before the Christmas holiday there was a heated conversation across the kitchen table. Uncle Henry was holding Jack's end-of-term report and was waving it at Maurice.

'He's never going to get his school certificate at this rate.' Uncle Henry put on his spectacles and looked down at the card again. 'History!' He poked at the word with his finger. '"Does not apply himself to the task in hand. Mathematics, Absent! Latin, Absent!"' He wheezed, fumbled for his handkerchief and coughed away the phlegm. 'What on earth happened, Jacky?'

Jack sat at the table saying nothing, slouching, his head resting on his arms.

'I don't know, I don't know,' said Uncle Henry, his voice cracking and trailing away. 'I always knew it'd come to nothing. I always thought you'd come to ...'

Two weeks later – thanks to Maurice, not Uncle Henry – Jack was standing in the drawing office of Wilkie's Construction by the railway station. He was wearing a new suit that Maurice and Granny Rush had bought him for his sixteenth birthday, and he had tried to grow a moustache, although it was still just a dirty-looking smear above his top lip.

Jack was to be an apprentice with a T-square and a mapping pen, tracing the plans and elevations of factory buildings and hangars. He had been given a drawing board and a smock to wear over his suit. It was a yellow linen affair with large pockets and a belt which tied around his waist. When Bob Marigold saw him in it a few days later, he said, 'Hey Jacky, looks like you're wearing a dress.'

But Jack liked Wilkie's. No one in the drawing office seemed to be bothered about who he was. Some of the men remembered his mother of course, the ones who were too old to join up.

'So, you're the Pearson boy,' they said, with a slight nod of the head.

But no one really cared what she had done, as long as he traced the windows correctly and drew a double line for the pipework.

Jack leaned over the drawing board, copying the other men, sliding his T-square down the tracing paper, inking the plans. He was good at his job. The lines he drew were beautiful things, straight and shining, no smudges or blotches, no multicoloured stains, no random pools of colour.

It was late spring when he saw Beadie again. She was standing outside in Wilkie's yard, gazing at him through the drawing office window. She was wearing the same battered straw hat she had worn last autumn, her face was distorted by the light rain that ran down the glass. Jack froze. He was like a rabbit on the Nab who hoped it hadn't been noticed – his head was lifted halfway from the drawing board, his hand was riveted to his pen, his eyes were alert.

When he didn't move, Beadie knocked on the window – a light, frantic tapping that made everyone in the drawing office turn round.

'That your girlfriend, Pearson?' asked one of the men, laughing.

'Go and see what she wants. Can't leave a lady standing in the rain,' said someone else.

He managed to make his way out of the office and into the yard, a sandy wasteland dimpled with potholes and flecked with tufts of yellow grass. Beadie had limped away from the window and was now sheltering under the roof of the bicycle shed. She looked like something from a horror film at the Regent. Her face was pale yellow, the colour of a fading bruise, and there were deep black shadows under her eyes.

'What do you want?' he asked. He stood just outside the shed, at the edge of an oily puddle. Out of the corners of his eyes he could see the rainbow of colours floating on the water.

'I've got another letter for you, Jacky.'

She pulled an envelope from her jacket pocket. His name was written on the front, large looping letters in dark blue ink.

'I don't want it,' he snapped. 'It was rubbish last time.'

'She's written something,' said Beadie slowly, as if speaking were an effort. 'I saw her do it.'

The puddle between them was growing larger, the water slopped over the sandy rim and began to lap at Beadie's shoes. She looked down and shuffled round it, inching closer to him.

'Jacky, she's worried for you. She wants to see you before you go.'

'I'm not going anywhere.'

'You will be. Like the rest of them ... like the last time. Do it for me, Jacky. Do it for Beadie.'

She reached over and slid the envelope into the gap between his loosely curled fingers and his thumb.

'I'm not taking it!' he shouted as she trudged away. 'I'm not reading it.' And he let the envelope slip out of his hand and flutter into the puddle at his feet.

An hour or so later, one of the secretaries sashayed across the drawing office towards him.

'I found this outside, love, I think it's yours.'

She held up the wet envelope and pointed to his name. It was almost illegible now, blurred by the puddle and spotted by the rain.

'You should take the letter out so it can dry. If you don't, it'll all get stuck together and then you won't be able to read it at all,' she said, laying the envelope on top of the radiator beside him.

He managed to ignore the letter for an hour or two. He was working on a complicated drainage plan. He kept his head down and focused his eyes on the maze of pipes that led to the septic tank. But at the end of the afternoon, when he had returned from cleaning his pens at the sink, he saw the letter again. It had dried into a series of shallow undulations that followed the ridges of the radiator. There was something pitiful about it now, the small rectangle of lilac-coloured paper and his own half-erased name written on the front. He pictured his mother sitting at a desk, carefully forming the letters, a curling flourish on the J of Jack and another on the P of Pearson. He remembered her teaching him to write like that, at the kitchen table in the villa, both of them leaning over a piece of paper, her hand guiding his, her fingers gently pressing against his own: 'Look Jacky, you've written your name. Look at all those loops.' And he felt sorry for the envelope, sorry for the time it had taken her to shape the letters on the front, sorry for what she must have been thinking when she wrote his name, sorry for her, sorry for Beadie, sorry for himself.

He picked the envelope up and, expecting nothing more than dead insects and flower petals, he slid his finger quickly under the flap and pulled the paper out. But Beadie was right, this time his mother had written something. Although it was only one line addressed to no one at all.

'This is all there is,' he whispered under his breath. 'This is all there is?'

Because of the time they had spent in the puddle, the words looked like they had tried to float off the paper, each letter was surrounded by an aureole of pale indigo that rippled away into nothing.

He clutched the paper between his fingers, trying to comprehend what she meant. And the clock chimed six, and the men in the drawing office put on their coats and hats and began to lumber away.

'See you tomorrow, Pearson,' they called out as they passed him by.

The Airman

The war was real now.

In early June, Marigold's cousin returned from France with a stump instead of a hand.

'He can't talk about what happened, not one word,' Marigold said, pushing a Bakewells chip into his mouth.

Jack imagined the stump, rounded and bandaged. Then he pictured a beach, like the one they were looking at now, pinkish sand, but covered with mute khaki forms, each one cradling a severed limb. The limbs spewed blood that ran in channels across the beach and flowed towards the sea. He could see the bright red tendrils: fingers reaching into the water and turning it red.

In September, Lenny Grieve said he was joining the RAF. They were walking up the hill to the villa: it was evening, almost dusk. The day had been hot and the heat still lingered in pockets under trees and alongside walls and hedges.

'You have to go to Catterick first,' said Lenny. 'And if you're good enough they send you to Canada to become a pilot.'

Jack, who was learning to talk like a man, like a film actor in a trilby and raincoat, mumbled, 'Canada ... long way.'

Then he remembered Marigold's handless cousin and thought about asking Lenny whether he was scared of being hurt. But the question said more about his own fears than anything else, so he kept his mouth shut and marched ahead towards the villa, hands deep in his trouser pockets.

Jack and Lenny had spent the summer in the overgrown garden. The villa gates were wide open now. The padlock had rusted to nothing a year ago and no one had come to replace it. Most evenings when they weren't fire watching, Jack at Wilkie's, Lenny on the roof of the school, they leaned over the balustrade that edged the garden. Lenny watched the birds, the mewling, heavyset buzzards and the goshawks that scoured the town, while Jack rolled his cigarettes and smoked. Sometimes he took the pencil lodged behind his ear and the notebook he kept in his jacket pocket and sketched the view. But he had lost interest in the familiar curves of the coastline, and the hesitant colours of the Nab. He saw the world in black and white now, in bold horizontals and verticals, in plans and elevations.

That evening, the stone capping of the balustrade was hot from the sun, and the ground at its base was baked dry. Below the hill, Teesby was quiet, as if the breathless heat had exhausted the town and all it could do was to slump down into the shadows. Through Lenny's monocular, Jack could make out the faint contours of the gun battery on the cliffs, and the line of anti-tank cubes that ran from one side of the bay to the other. If he turned to his left and adjusted the focus, he could see the Snook on the far side of the river, and the new steel masts and the wooden huts inhabited by a gaggle of homely-looking WAAFs. He pointed the monocular skywards, but there were no hawks over the town, not even a late swift or a swallow. There were no birds in the Monkey Puzzle tree either, or hidden in the spindly hydrangeas or the rambling roses. There would be an air raid tonight – there had been raids every night for weeks – and as if they knew this, the birds had already disappeared.

Jack lowered the monocular and lay down on the grass.

'Wish I was going with you,' he muttered.

Lenny turned, and Jack could see his face silhouetted against the grey sky.

'I can't wait to go. But I'll miss being up here with you.'

How should the raincoated, trilby-hatted film actor reply to this? Lenny had already turned away, however, and like the garden and the roofs of the town he was beginning to dissolve into the dark.

The sirens started an hour later, a chorus of thin howls along the coastline that reached an unbearable crescendo then descended again. Jack hated the sound.

'Must be Hartlepool,' said Lenny, pointing at the bursts of light on the horizon.

Jack sat up and kneeled on the ground, his arms resting on the warm balustrade.

There was a faint boom from the north which shuddered in his guts, and the sky flickered – black, white, black, white – before it blushed and blossomed into a deep pink glow. The German bombers had probably passed over the roofs of Winterfield by now. He pictured his mother watching the gleam of the fires from one of the upstairs windows of the hospital, just as he was gazing at them from the garden.

'Look!' Lenny grasped Jack's shoulder and pointed at the sky. 'Look at that!'

Just above the sea, circling each other like small birds, were three planes: a German Heinkel and two stubby-nosed British Hurricanes. They shimmered in the rosy light. The first Hurricane twisted downwards, almost touching the waves before it swept into the air again. Then the second climbed above the German bomber and dived at it like a sparrowhawk catching its prey. Jack could see the flash of its guns like sparklers on Bonfire Night. The heavy bomber, trying to avoid the gunfire, pitched towards the surface of the water, but as it began to rise again it lurched into the sky.

Phut, phut, phut, it wheezed, *Phut, phut, phut*. Then it cork-screwed down again, smoke streaming from its engines as it burst apart.

It was as if the sun had suddenly risen in the northern sky. The explosion was so close that he could feel the warmth of it against his face. In the blast, the blackened fuselage was propelled sideways then shattered into pieces. At the edge of the fading flare, he saw a figure diving down amongst the fragments of burning metal. The man reeled for a second or two, before dissolving into ruby-coloured dust that was scattered across the surface of the sea.

'See that?' said Jack. He was leaning heavily on the balustrade, just as he knelt at the altar rail waiting for Father Scullion to slip a communion wafer into his mouth.

'Did you see that, it was ...'

He was going to say 'beautiful'. It was a word he rarely used, and yet it was the first one he had thought of. He was going to say that the sight of the burning plane and the dying man was beautiful.

'Did you see that, Lenny?' he whispered again.

Where did the German airman go? Where was he now, the man himself, the man's soul? Uncle Henry would say he was on his way to God, or at least to purgatory.

Jack sat back on his heels. Behind him, a second wave of Heinkels were targeting one of the RAF stations on the far side of the moor. From the villa garden, however, the raid looked and sounded like nothing more than a distant thunderstorm. Now the bombers were far away, he could hear an owl hissing from the roof of the villa. And by his feet, something small – a field mouse, perhaps – brushed past him through the long grass.

He lay down on the ground again and looked up at the sky. It was a clear night.

'Lenny,' he whispered. 'Do you believe in God?'

Lenny, who was still sitting on the edge of the balustrade,

turned. In the glimmer of the Hartlepool fires, his face and hair shone. He looked like he was made from copper.

'I don't think so.'

'So we're on our own?'

Lenny slid off the balustrade and sat on the grass beside Jack. 'Yes.'

'So you don't believe in heaven then?'

Lenny didn't reply. Jack could hear his faint shallow breathing as he sat beside him. On any other night they would have lain on their backs and Lenny would have traced the constellations with his finger.

'You don't believe in heaven, Lenny?' Jack whispered again.

'No.'

'So where do you go when you die?'

Lenny laughed gently. He reached towards the balustrade and thrust his hand into the ground where the brambles had overtaken Mrs Tibbs's Pierre Ronsard and Cécile Brunner.

'Here.' He opened his palm. Inside was a fistful of dark dry earth. Lenny shrugged his shoulders. 'This is where we go, like everything else.'

ELLEN

1922–24

The Railings

One of the fields on the other side of the lane had become a building site. Conical mountains of red earth were piled on the grass.

'There must be iron in the soil,' said Henry, as he and Ellen walked across the lane one Sunday afternoon.

They peered down at the straight clean trenches.

'It's going to be a house,' he said authoritatively. 'We've got the plans for it in the Town Hall. One day there'll be houses all the way down the hill until they reach the town.'

Ellen knelt on the grass and ran her fingers through the soil, picking out shards of pale grey pottery and tiny pieces of cloudy weathered glass. The colours had returned. In the palm of her hand she could see splinters of bottle green and deep Bristol blue. 'Look, Henry.' She held them out to him.

'Make sure you don't cut yourself,' he replied.

The old Henry, the uncertain boy with the ill-fitting clothes and the bitten fingernails, had disappeared. He had been replaced by an unyielding young man who walked with his hands behind his back, who kept *The Pocket Book of Catholic Novenas* on his bedside table, who went to mass every evening, who gave most of his money to the church and to a charity that sent orphan boys to Australia.

She never asked him about the day that Father Scullion had come to his rooms on Marine Parade. Nor did she ever mention

Thomas. Henry had carefully packed something of himself away, hidden it in his room on Marine Parade, folded it neatly and pushed it to the back of a drawer.

The walls of the new house on the other side of the lane emerged out of the red earth line by line. One neat brick was slotted against another. If she leaned out of the drawing room window, she could see the house growing. She could hear the faint calls of the workmen.

'Watch your head, Frank!'

'Get us another bucket, will you!'

The roof was clad with gleaming slate, the doors and windows were hung. A low stone wall was built to contain the garden and was topped with metal railings.

Then the snow began to fall. The workmen left and the house stood empty, waiting for the thaw.

In the spring, new workmen returned with brushes and buckets and dust sheets. One of the men stood at the railings and began to paint them green: at least, Henry called it green, as did Beadie. But for Ellen the colour wasn't just green, it was more than green. Whenever she looked at the paint on the railings the colour slid from one shade to another like lustrous velvet. Sometimes the railings were the green of a cooking apple or an oily puddle or the leather of the books in Mrs Tibbs's library. And sometimes they were the greeny-yellow of the lichen growing on the washhouse wall or they were bronze like the scales of the Monkey Puzzle tree.

The railings were long. It took a full minute to walk from one end to the other. The man who painted the railings was short and fine boned: he wore brown overalls and a red spotted neckerchief. He wielded the paintbrush as if it was part of a dance. He swooped and swayed from side to side, then he moved his feet back and forth as if he was dancing a foxtrot. There were days when he grinned at Ellen and his moustache grinned too. He would place the paint bucket on the ground and lay his paintbrush carefully across the rim and he would follow her on the other side of the railings as she walked into town. Sometimes he waddled like Charlie Chaplin. Sometimes he was a zoo animal pacing in a cage. Sometimes, without a word, he mimicked the way she walked. He held his head high, thrust his hands in his pockets and took determined strides to the end of the garden.

'What's your name?' he asked one day.

'Ellen Pearson. What's yours?'

'Maurice,' he grinned. 'Maurice Rush.' He wiped the paintbrush on a rag hanging from his trouser pocket. 'Want to come to the pictures, Ellen?' he called out, as she made her way down the lane into town.

On Saturday evening she put on her best clothes: a blue skirt and a blouse with lace edging round the collar and the sleeves. Over her shoulders she draped an opera cape borrowed from Mrs Tibbs's wardrobe. The cape was pink and embroidered with curlicues of flowers and leaves that clambered over the silk. Mrs Tibbs said it had last been worn at a performance of *Die Fledermaus* at the Alhambra in London.

'Tibbsy took me for a birthday treat,' she said. 'We stayed at the Langham, I think. But it was years and years ago so I can hardly remember.' She waved her hand limply in the air, then she fumbled with the cape lying in her lap and rubbed the silk between her fingers.

'Syllabub,' murmured Mrs Tibbs. 'My dear little Annabelle said the colour was raspberry syllabub. Such a fanciful child. God bless her soul.'

As Ellen made her way into Teesby, she thought about Maurice and felt something inside her. It was a feeling so deep and distant she couldn't exactly identify where it was in her body. She felt warm and calm. The calmness was a cool soft turquoise that made her want to lie down flat on her back on the grass verge, but the warmth, which was the colour of Mrs Tibbs's good Burgundy, made her want to sprint all the way to the cinema.

The picture at the Regent was a murder mystery about a woman who talked to the dead. There were shadows and a long séance scene with furniture that levitated and glasses that broke. In the shimmering light, Ellen could see Maurice clasping and unclasping his hands uneasily in his lap.

'It was a bit odd, don't you think?' he said later when they were sitting in the lounge bar of Hooper's Hotel. 'She could see things that weren't there. It wasn't very believable.'

'Oh, I don't know,' said Ellen.

Maurice was sipping his beer and he lifted his eyes over the rim. 'What do you mean?'

'Well, I can't see the dead or anything, but I can see colours.' She was nervous, the words rattled out of her. 'I mean, sometimes sounds have colour, and people. If I think of Beadie she's the colour of stewed prunes. And times of the day have colours too, like four o'clock is always purple and midnight is bright orange. You'd think it would be the other way round, wouldn't you? But it isn't.'

She had never talked to anyone about this before and as she came to a halt, she could see Maurice on the other side of the table shrinking back in his chair. He was growing smaller and smaller.

'It's a bit of a muddle really, there are so many things going on in my head.' She smiled at him apologetically and fiddled with the silky tassels of the opera cape.

'Very curious,' he replied, setting down his empty beer glass on the table.

On Monday morning, when Ellen looked out of the drawing room window at the railings on the other side of the lane, Maurice had been replaced by a stringy boy with ginger hair. The boy was whistling a few sad notes over and over again as he dipped the paintbrush into the bucket.

Maurice didn't appear all day, or the next, or for the rest of the week. It wasn't until the end of Friday afternoon that she saw him again, carrying a pile of dust sheets to the back of a van parked on the driveway of the house. He must have sensed that someone was watching him from the other side of the railings because he turned his head. When he saw it was Ellen standing at the gates he waved as if everything was perfectly normal. Then he turned away and hid himself behind the doors of the van.

For a month or so, things began to grow pale again. The green railings were the colour of uncooked cabbage and the new brick house was the colour of Beadie's strawberry fool.

Ellen felt the way you feel on the beach when the wind blows this way and that, first into your eyes then down the back of the neck. And you don't know what to do or which way to turn.

'Who are you? Who are you?' demanded the mangle in the washhouse as she fed the sheets through the rollers.

'What-do-you-want? What-do-you-want?' asked a bird sitting on a branch in the Monkey Puzzle tree.

'You should be thinking about moving on,' said Henry. 'Find yourself a better job.'

They were wandering along the promenade one Sunday afternoon. Henry had bought her an ice cream from a man with a barrow near the quay. The ice cream was lemon flavoured. The cold yellow taste went straight to her head and made her eyes pop. Everything was sharper and clearer for a minute or two.

'But I'm quite happy at the villa,' she replied.

'You can't stay there for ever, Nell. You should be more ambitious. You could be a lady's maid anywhere you wanted.'

'I'd hate to be a lady's maid for anyone but Mrs Tibbs,' she said, picturing someone else's dirty underwear and old skin.

'Well, a housekeeper then.' His voice brightened. 'Imagine being a housekeeper at the Hall, Nell.'

The Hall was a big brown place on the other side of Teesby. Mrs Tibbs had been sent an invitation to tea from Lady Gill last autumn. She said she wasn't going, but Ellen had managed to persuade her.

'You might enjoy it, Mrs Tibbs. It'll be like the old days, you could wear your Paris tea gown, the one that Mr Tibbs bought you at Le Bon Marché, and that lovely lilac toque.'

On the afternoon of the tea party they had taken a taxi that drove them across the Nab and down again, twisting and turning until they reached a large dark house at the end of a drive. While Mrs Tibbs was taking tea in the drawing room, Ellen was told to wait downstairs in the kitchen. It was like sitting in a railway station: maids scurried in and out as if they had important things to do, and the under-butler sat in a chair by the fireplace finishing a crossword in the *Daily Mail*. Except, after a while, Ellen realised that he wasn't doing the crossword at all, he was staring at her with the newspaper laid across his lap and the chewed end of a pencil in his mouth. She had looked down at the floor and had listened to the porcelain cups clattering on the tea tray and the maids' aprons thrashing against their skirts and the under-butler's teeth gnawing through the pencil. And the sounds had echoed up and down the kitchen and into the pantries and the sculleries and the wine cellars, until Ellen thought she was drowning in noise. Then one of the maids came to her and said, 'They want you upstairs, she's ready to leave.' And when Ellen had eventually found the entrance hall again, there was poor Mrs Tibbs, all on her own, bumbling around, muttering to herself.

'I would hate to work at the Hall,' Ellen said sullenly, kicking a stray pebble and watching it tumble ahead of her. 'Is that all you think I can do?'

'It's what you've been trained for.' Henry sounded like Father Scullion.

'I could have been a teacher if Da hadn't died and I'd carried on at school.'

'You hated school, Nell.'

'Or a writer,' she said, biting into the cold ice cream.

Henry made a face.

'Well, I like reading.'

She had just finished *The Portrait of a Lady* by Henry James, which was strange and good. And before that she had read a book called *The Voyage Out* by a woman writer whose name she had forgotten, which had made her cry.

'Reading isn't the same as writing, Nell,' Henry said stiffly. 'And the only thing I've ever seen you write are shopping lists.'

'I write things,' Ellen murmured weakly.

When she returned from her walk with Henry, she went straight to her room and took a notebook from the chest of drawers. Mrs Tibbs had given it to her on her twenty-second birthday.

'I sent Beadie all the way to Darlington to buy it from Dressers,' she had said when she handed it to Ellen.

The book had a peacock-blue cover and thick cream paper inside which smelt like clean washing hanging on the line. It was too good to use for ordinary things, so Ellen had placed it carefully in the top drawer ready for the day she had something special to write.

She pulled off her coat and hat and sat on the bed. But when she opened the cover and looked down at the blank page she knew immediately she had nothing to say. Every book she had read had something important to say, you could tell from the very first line: all that fog in *Bleak House* and the stuff about being born in *David Copperfield*. She sat on the bed waiting for something to happen, tapping the end of the pencil against her bottom lip, but her head had never been so empty.

She got up and looked through the window in the hope she could write about the view. The sun was setting behind the mist. There was a salmon-coloured glow surrounded by a halo of deep dark rose. Beyond the town, the sea was almost purple, and in the distance she could see the shadowy red line of the Snook. The view was beautiful, so beautiful there seemed little point in trying to write about it. Why should she spoil it with words? Why should she try and pin down something that was always changing when all she needed to do was to look?

'Beadie, what do you want out of life?' she asked the following afternoon. 'What do you dream about?'

As soon as she had said it, Ellen realised that this was a stupid question. Beadie was old. She was standing in the vegetable garden behind the washhouse, hunched over a spade. Her dress was the colour of damp moss and her wrinkled face was blotted by the pale green shadows of the fruit trees. She seemed to blend into the garden.

'What do I want out of life?' she said thoughtfully, running her rough fingers across the handle of the spade. 'What I always expected out of life, I suppose: nothing.'

She pressed down on the spade; as the metal slid against the soil it made a faint satisfying crunching noise. Ellen could smell the soil in the air, the quiet moist blackness.

Beadie worked her way along the line of potato plants, picking up the leaves and shaking the earth from the roots. Then she bent down and burrowed with her hands, picking out the pale pink potatoes which she dropped into a bucket by her feet. When she had reached the end of the bed, she gave the spade one final push into the soil then straightened herself and leaned against the handle to catch her breath. Casaubon, who had been stalking a chaffinch under one of the apple trees, sprang towards her and rubbed himself around her legs. He stared up at her face lovingly, his tail poker-straight in the air.

'Why should I expect anything more out of life?' said Beadie, almost to herself. 'This is it. This is all there is. It's enough, isn't it?'

The Stone Collector

Mrs Tibbs was ill. It began with a mild pain in her left side one morning in early April 1923.

'I'm a little stiff, Pearson,' she said, as Ellen was about to place the wig on top of her head, 'I think I will go and lie down again.'

She refused breakfast and slept for most of the morning. At lunchtime Beadie made her beef broth. But when Ellen carried the steaming bowl to her bedside, Mrs Tibbs raised her hand weakly and said, 'Oh Pearson, is that soup? No, no. A little warm milk will do.'

The doctor was summoned. He arrived in the late afternoon, brisk and breathless at the front door, smelling of damp tweed and cigarettes. In the bedroom he removed his jacket, rolled up his sleeves and fumbled with Mrs Tibbs's nightgown.

'Pearson, come here, undo this damn thing,' he called.

When she had unbuttoned the gown, the doctor slid his hand inside it. Ellen could hear the crisp sound of starched linen and Mrs Tibbs's faint whimpers as he pressed and prodded her stomach.

'Ah, yes,' he said. 'That's it, that's the problem.'

The doctor pulled his large hand away and murmured something to Mrs Tibbs. When he had buttoned his cuffs and put on his jacket again, he turned to Ellen.

'Nothing overly serious, Pearson. But it must be removed

as soon as possible. We'll take her to the infirmary tomorrow and after the operation she'll have to spend a few weeks in the nursing home.'

The following morning Mrs Tibbs was placed on a stretcher by a pair of orderlies. Ellen watched the white tuft on the top of Mrs Tibbs's wig-less head bobbing up and down as they carried her out of the front door.

'Don't worry about me, Pearson,' she called from the back of the ambulance. 'Just look after the villa while I'm gone.'

That same morning Beadie packed a few belongings into a carpet bag.

'High time I had a holiday. I'll be gone for a week or two,' she said, standing at the kitchen door with the bag in her hand. 'And don't forget to feed the moggy,' she shouted over her shoulder as she crossed the yard and climbed the steps that led to the Nab.

It was the first time that Ellen had been alone in the villa. Solitary days, she discovered, turned out to be far longer than the days she had shared with Beadie and Mrs Tibbs. The hands on the kitchen clock trailed slowly round its face, as she scrubbed at saucepan bottoms, the stained inside of the teapot, the gaps between the tiles on the floor.

She wandered from one grey room to another, lifting up ornaments and opening drawers then shutting them again. She sat in the library and tried to learn French from an old school book belonging to Mrs Tibbs.

'Un bag-wet see vouz plate.'

'Un bil-let pour Bordux.'

The villa was so quiet she could hear the Monkey Puzzle tree outside the window complaining about the breeze. She could hear the gleeful chatter of the bindweed as it wove itself around the rose bushes and the peonies. She could hear the groundsel and the dandelions talking in the drive.

Casaubon was as lonely as Ellen. At night he crept onto her bed and settled himself in the crook of her knees, or draped himself across her chest purring loudly. In the early morning he stood on her stomach pummelling it with his paws, mewing at her to get out of bed. She began to miss him when he slipped into the garden and disappeared, crouched, no doubt, under a dark bush somewhere snapping at birds.

At the end of the week, when she couldn't stand being in the villa alone any longer, she made her way into Teesby, smiling at passers-by, calling out 'Good afternoon' to faces she half knew. She chattered to the butcher's boy and the woman behind the counter at the haberdasher's and to a horse chomping at its bit outside Hooper's Hotel. She walked to the promenade and onto the beach, waving her hand at the ice cream seller and the man with the flea-bitten donkeys. She trudged across the sand to the southern end of Teesby bay, where the Nab met the cliffs, where the fossil hunters and the jet gatherers kneeled at the bottom of the rocks and turned over the stones, hoping to find something precious.

The fossil hunters were mostly elderly gentlemen, collectors who probably displayed the treasures they found on dusty shelves in their studies and their libraries. They moved in small groups, hailing each other when they had found something of interest.

'Hey, Jackson, come over here, have a look at this.'

Then they would stand for several minutes turning a stone over in their arthritic hands or staring down at the sand.

There was one man who appeared to be alone, younger than all the rest. He was thin with light brown hair that blew around his head. She watched him from the shoreline, intrigued by the intensity with which he worked: moving inch by inch as he scoured the cliff face for fossils.

She waited for one of her bold days, when it was windy and raining, when there was no one else on the beach but them.

He was tapping with a hammer and chisel at an outcrop just below the cliff.

'What are you doing?' she asked.

He turned and smiled briefly. 'Trying to detach this rather stubborn fossil from the cliff.' He pointed with his chisel to the ridged spiral nestled in the rock. 'It's an ammonite, you see, very old. Jurassic.'

'Oh, a snake stone,' she said. 'We get a lot of them here.'

'This one's particularly fine.' He pointed to the stone then started to chisel again.

There was something about the way he spoke that made her think he was a schoolmaster. Although a schoolmaster wouldn't be hammering at a rock in the rain on a Monday in April, dressed in a worn jacket with a tear in the lapel. And the man's face was gaunt and grey, he looked as battered and as lined as the rock he was trying to dislodge.

That evening, when she was making tea in the kitchen, she thought about the man again, the way his hands had shaken when he had shown her the snake stone, and how the small muscle on the left side of his face had made his cheek shiver.

The next morning, she filled a small cloth bag with two ham sandwiches and a couple of apples and made her way to the beach again. It wasn't long before she found him, wandering along the shoreline by the water's edge. He was stooping into the wind, looking down at the ground. She hadn't expected him to recognise her, but when she reached him, he lifted his head, tipped his hat and said something about the weather.

'Still hunting for fossils?' she asked.

'Jet and amber,' he replied. Out of his pocket he took a translucent yellow lump that lay in his palm like a hard drop of honey.

'What are you going to do with that?'

'I might sell it to a jeweller in Whitby.'

'And what about the snake stone?'

'I might sell that to someone in London, a dealer perhaps.'

'So it's your job, then?'

'More of a hobby, really.'

They walked along the beach together: the stone collector staring at the sand, Ellen gazing at the view ahead. In the distance she could see the Snook and the tower. The tower was dark blue that day, a small squat shape that appeared to be drifting on the sea.

'Look!' said the stone collector, bending down and picking something out of the sand. 'A piece of jet. It's a decent size.' He held it up for her to see.

From a distance the jet was pitch black, but when she looked more closely she could see other colours in the blackness, green and brown and purple. The colours were singing to her: a faint chorus drifted from his fingers.

'You wouldn't think it was just a stone,' she said.

'It's not a stone. It's a fossil too.'

He dropped the jet into her hand: it felt warm and alive.

'Millions of years ago there were pine trees all along the beach. When they died they fell onto the sand and mixed with the sea water and they gradually became fossils. Jet's made from carbon, you see.'

'Carbon?'

'It's an element. It's everywhere, in the sun, the stars, in human beings even.'

'So the stuff that the jet is made from is inside me too?'

'Yes.'

'And the sand?'

'Yes, beach sand has carbon in it.'

Things came together all at once, the things she could see. The old man on the quayside hunch-backed over his nets, the bird skull washed up on a bank of razor shells, the dust on the stone collector's hat brim caught in the weak sunlight, his bony hand still gripping the piece of jet. All of them were connected. A wave ran up her body to her head, filling her brain. So Da was right about the Pearsons coming out of the sand, they were the same as the sand, she was part of all this. Then the wave slowly descended again and the thought faded away.

They had reached the end of the beach where the river flowed out to sea. The stone collector stood at the edge of the water. Their conversation had drawn to a close and she wondered whether he was waiting for her to go. She knew it was what she should have done. She should have smiled at him and said, 'It was so nice to talk to you but I must be getting on now.' And he would have tipped his hat and replied, 'Goodbye, Miss, goodbye,' before he turned back to the beach and forgot her. But she didn't want to go. She didn't want to leave the stone collector. The warm calmness grew inside her.

Pulling an apple from the bag, she said quickly, 'Would you like one?'

He hesitated for a second, and she thought he might refuse out of politeness, but he took the fruit and rubbed it against his jacket.

The apple seemed to change something between them. In between bites, he told her his name was Edwin, that he came from Nottingham, that he was on a walking tour.

'Just felt like going off for a while. Thought I'd follow the coast. Started in Lincolnshire then worked my way up here.'

'Where are you staying?'

'I'm camping at Robinson's farm. They let me sleep in an old shepherd's hut on Bleaker's Hill. I'll probably move on in a few days' time. I'd like to get up to Scotland before the end of May.'

'So you don't have a job, then?'

He looked down at the half-eaten apple and turned it round in his hand. 'I was an engineer at a coal mine. Got a bit difficult, needed a break.'

They sat down on the quay and she took the sandwiches from the bag and handed him one. The ferryman's dog, chained to a metal ring set into the stone, strained against its lead. She watched the stone collector pull the crust from the bread and feed it to the dog.

When the sandwiches were gone, they sat in silence, the three of them: the satisfied dog licking its paws, the stone collector contemplating the river mud, and Ellen staring up at the man's face out of the corner of her eye. He was older than her, ten years older, maybe more. He had a high forehead, a long nose and deep lines that bracketed his wide mouth. It was a straightforward face, hiding nothing but revealing nothing either.

The tide was going out, the river water streamed past them into the sea. When she stood up again she could see the causeway raised above the watery salt marsh.

'We could carry on if you like,' she said hopefully. 'If we go over to the Snook, you might find some more jet, and I can show you the tower, as well.'

It was a long walk. They followed the river to the swing bridge, then took the coast road to the causeway. At the top of the causeway, she could see the wooden huts that the soldiers had built during the war, and the sound mirror – the huge concrete ear that had listened for vibrations in the air. Now that the war was over, the marram grass and seakale had grown through the causeway again, and the sea salt had stained the concrete mirror, and the sand had banked up against the walls of the huts.

She had expected the stone collector to ask about the mirror and the huts, but he didn't raise his head as they passed them. And when they reached the tower, he hesitated in the doorway, shuffling his feet in the shingle as if he was reluctant to go inside.

'It was a lookout once,' she said. 'You can go right to the top. We could go up if you like. It's beautiful up there.'

But the stone collector didn't move. He stood in the entrance peering into the room.

Leaning against the wall was a pile of empty crates that must have contained ammunition at some time. Beside the crates was a roll of chicken wire, and lying on the floor was a rusted metal helmet. The stone collector walked over to the wire and ran his hand across it: the metal sang out coldly as his nails hit the mesh.

'I've been in so many places like this,' he said wearily.

'Where?'

'In France.'

He prodded the helmet with the toe of his boot. It rolled backwards and forwards for a few seconds, and the grating noise echoed up the tower.

'So you were in the war?'

'Who wasn't?'

'You look too old.'

'Maybe the war made me old.'

He wouldn't go inside the tower, though it had started to rain. He pulled his jacket over his head, and marched across the Snook back towards the causeway. She stood outside the tower, as the raindrops pockmarked the sand, and watched him disappear into the drizzle. Until that afternoon, she hadn't noticed the crates and the helmet, nor the smell that rose up from the floor. After all this time, the tower still smelt of the war – of smoke and sweet cordite.

She found him leaning against a thin tree at the side of the road. He had his back to her and was bent forward, one hand pressed against the tree trunk for support, the other braced against his thigh. He was trembling, his whole body was shaking.

She touched his shoulder but he pulled away. 'What's the matter?'

'Leave me. It'll pass.'

He shifted away from the tree and stood looking at the marsh where the plumes of reeds growing in the black silt were buffeted by the rain and wind.

'Go home!' she heard him say suddenly. 'Leave me alone!' The words were barked like an order, something shouted at a subaltern in a muddy trench.

She didn't move. She waited on the road, thinking about Lieutenant Gargett. He would have been like this had he survived: thin and quivering, standing on the edge of things. A dull cold sadness swept over her.

The stone collector turned round slowly.

'I'm sorry, I get like that sometimes.' His face was blank, drained of colour. His wet hair was plastered onto his forehead and trickles of water were running down his face.

'If we go back to the bridge on the other side of the river, there's a bus that'll take us up the hill,' she said. 'You can come back to the villa with me, have some tea.'

It was strange to have a man in the house again. Apart from Henry's occasional visits their last male guest had been John Gargett. The stone collector asked her nothing about the villa, what she did there, why she was alone: he didn't seem to care. She handed him one of Mrs Tibbs's towels and he trudged away to the bathroom to wash.

She was boiling the kettle for tea when she heard the sound of a piano drifting along the long dark corridor. No one played the piano: it had belonged to Mr Tibbs. She had once lifted the lid and tried a few notes but Mrs Tibbs had called out straight away:

'Whoever that is, you must never touch the piano.'

She followed the music to the morning room and stood in the doorway. The piano was badly out of tune and sometimes instead of notes came the thud of a wooden hammer hitting air. The stone collector played on, however, running his hands from one end of the keyboard to the other. The music sounded like a prayer, not the sort of prayer she knew, an Our Father, a Glory Be. The music was a proper prayer, soft and solemn, a long gentle sigh.

He stopped abruptly. He must have sensed that she was standing at the door.

'That was lovely,' she said.

'I saw the piano when I came downstairs. I should have asked.'

'It's all right. Please carry on.'

'No.' He took his hands off the keyboard and lay them in his lap. 'But it was so good.'

'Yes. Brahms, an intermezzo.'

He swivelled round on the stool, stood up and took his jacket that was lying on a side table.

'I'm sorry about this afternoon,' he said.

'Don't worry.'

Without thinking, she moved towards him and took his hand. It was cold, she could feel the bones under the skin. 'Come and have some tea, we can talk about it.'

'I'm not sure why I would want to talk about it,' he said softly, pulling on his jacket.

'It might help.'

He gazed at her for a while as if he half-believed her, then he shook his head. 'You weren't there, you couldn't understand.' He picked up his hat from the table. 'I'm sorry Ellen, I have to go.'

He wasn't on the beach the following day. She walked from one end to the other under a thunderous sky. As she was making her way back to the villa, the wind spiralled up. When it finally began to rain, she stood at the morning room window and watched the storm-lashed garden.

She waited for the storm to end, then she packed a basket of food – eggs and bacon, a twist of tea – and climbed up the lane to the Nab. It was early evening, but the last of the sun had managed to force its way through the thick cloud, and the tiny droplets of water sparkled in the distance.

Bleaker's Hill was right at the edge of the moor. On one side were the cliffs that led down to the beach, and on the other was a line of stunted elms that hid the stone collector's hut from Robinson's farm. She could see him in the distance, crouching in front of a fire.

'I've brought you something to eat,' she called as she walked across the meadow.

He hadn't seen her and he scrambled to his feet, brushing down his clothes. He was embarrassed. His face shivered and his hands hovered over the basket, unsure about accepting it.

'You really shouldn't have come,' he said quietly.

'Would you like me to go?'

He was silent for a while, and she could hear a child shouting far away on the beach, calling to a brother or sister, or to his mother, perhaps. Then the wind changed direction, and the child's voice died away, and all she could hear were the farm dogs barking as if they were just behind her.

'No,' he replied finally. 'I think I would like you to stay.'

He brought out a rug from the hut and lay it on the grass. She sat down and watched him break the eggs into a frying pan smeared with bacon fat. His hands were clumsy. He fumbled with the pan as he set it on the flames, and the eggs slid in the slick of fat towards the metal lip.

'Damn!'

'I can do it if you like,' she said.

'No, no. I'm fine.'

He balanced the frying pan carefully across two logs and the fat began to spit. Then the charred wood underneath it crumbled a little, and the pan lurched sideways again. He thrust his hand into the flames to steady the handle, but it was too hot. As he pulled back from the heat, the pan slipped and the four eggs fell into the fire.

'Damn! Damn!'

He held his hand limply, then shook it so the cold air would ease the pain of the burn.

'Let me look.'

She leaned over. She could see that one of his fingers was swollen and red. Without thinking she kissed it, as she might have done to a child. Then she slipped the tip of his finger inside her mouth, and with her tongue she could feel the ridges of dry skin and the blister that was beginning to form. It tasted of ash and bacon fat. It tasted metallic – of iron, of the blood beneath the burnt skin.

'I have a wife, Ellen,' he said quietly, pulling his hand away. 'I should have told you.'

She sat back on the rug. She couldn't really see his face, it was too dark now, but the flames lit up his hands: they were clenched.

'What's her name, your wife?'

'Madeleine. I haven't seen her for a while. We found it difficult to get along. I was difficult . . .'

She reached out and took his clenched fist. She began to unpick each finger until his palm lay flat in her own. She could hear Robinson's dogs barking in one of the outhouses, and the fat, still cooking in the pan.

The stone collector shifted slightly, moved closer. She could hear him breathing now, short low breaths. He was gazing at her, she could feel his eyes, they were soft and light, scanning her face in the firelight.

'Ellen, I can't—'

She reached out and touched his lips with the tip of her finger.

'It doesn't matter about your wife,' she whispered. 'I don't mind.'

'Ellen. *Ellen*.' His voice was soft, insistent, urgent. No one had ever said her name like that before: it was as if he was trying to grasp it, hold on to it – as if he needed her.

That night, she lay with him in the hut as the rain beat down on the wooden roof. She could hear the horse snorting at the edge of the field and Robinson's dogs growling gently in the dark. And when the wind began to blow, a small branch from one of the elm trees broke and fell against the side of the hut, then a fox screamed in the gorse thicket on the edge of the bluff.

What they did together was black. Soft black. Black so deep you could fall into it. Black like the night sea. Black like the wet sheen on his boots. Black like the buttons on his shirt, and like the black of his eyes. Black full of colour.

What they did together was as black as the circle of charred ground where the fire had burned outside the hut when she returned the following evening. She opened the door of the hut but he wasn't there.

What they did together was as black as the ink drop that must have fallen from his pen after he had signed his name at the bottom of the letter she received two days later. As black as the small round piece of jet that fell into her lap when she pulled the letter from the envelope: a piece of jet engraved with a flying fish, and the word 'Forward' carved beneath the waves.

Teesby-on–Sea, April 14th, 1923.

    My dearest Ellen,

    By now you will probably have guessed that I have had to leave Teesby quite suddenly. My father is very ill and my wife thought it best that I come home for a while.

    Over the short time that I have known you, Ellen, I have grown very fond of you. I wish you luck in whatever you choose to do, and I enclose a small trinket for you to remember me by.

    Your friend,

    Edwin Forward

The Blue Baby

She pictured the baby as a tiny worm curled up in a hollow of velvet: it was bright blue and shimmering, like the blue enamelled lid of the powder pot on Mrs Tibbs's dressing table. As the weeks passed and the worm grew, she could feel it coiling into the shape of a snake stone. Now it was the blue of a kingfisher's wing, or the blue of the jay's feather she had found on the lane outside the villa, or the blue of the cornflowers in the rain.

The baby was swelling inside her and there was nothing she could do. The stone collector had gone, he was on his way up the coast to Scotland, or on his way home to Nottingham. He had only existed for one long afternoon and a single night. All she had left was the baby inside her and the piece of jet, the beginning of something and the end of something, a solidified fragment of time clutched inside her hand.

'Bugger me!' said Beadie. She was standing at the kitchen table, slicing bread for Mrs Tibbs's teatime sandwiches. 'Bugger me! You're either getting very fat or you're in the club!'

Ellen was in the armchair by the range, sewing a button onto a pair of combinations. She couldn't really sit upright any more and had slumped against the cushion. She didn't reply.

Beadie lay the bread knife on the table and said quietly, 'When did it happen?'

Ellen stared down at her sewing. 'April,' she mumbled.

'April? When Mrs Tibbs was ill, when I was away.' It was a statement not a question and Beadie shook her head and began to butter the bread. 'You should make him marry you.'

'He can't.'

'Why not?'

'He just can't.'

Beadie scraped the knife across the pat of butter, and smacked the butter onto a slice of bread. 'And how many times were you with him?'

'Just the once.'

'Bugger me! Unlucky, that's what you are.' She slapped the thin, wet shavings of cucumber onto the bread and butter, then slammed another slice of bread on top.

'So what are you going to do about it?'

'I don't know.'

'Well you're going to have to do something, young lady, because you're going to be a mother, like it or not. You'll have to tell her upstairs, and what's that brother of yours going to say?'

In the end it was Beadie who told Mrs Tibbs about the baby. She stood beside Ellen in the drawing room with the plate of sandwiches in her hand and said, 'Pearson's going to have a baba.'

When Mrs Tibbs heard Beadie's voice she looked up from the chaise longue and smiled vaguely at her, but she could barely understand what Beadie had said. Since her return from the nursing home, Mrs Tibbs was losing her mind. She lived mostly in the past now, in memories as fragile and flimsy as the yellowed lace on her widow's cap. She could remember the name of her dog when she was six years old, and the layout of the formal garden of her childhood home. She could remember John Gargett and would fumble along the mantelpiece for his watch from time to time. But she seemed to have forgotten everything else.

'Oh, how nice,' she said, as her crablike hand reached out to take a sandwich from the tea plate. 'What shall we call it, Beadie?'

She asked about the name again, later that evening, as Ellen was peeling away the wig from her head.

'What are you planning to name the child, Pearson?'

'Edwin,' she replied. 'Or Sidney, maybe.'

'Sidney?'

'It was my da's name.'

'No, no. Neither of those will do, Pearson.' Mrs Tibbs spoke slowly and with unusual firmness. 'He shall be called John. And if it's a little girl you may call her Catherine, after me. But it won't be a girl, it will be a boy, and you shall call him John.'

The summer passed. Ellen let out her clothes, moved the buttons on her skirts and unpicked the seams of her blouses, adding wide strips of cotton to accommodate her growing breasts. Henry hadn't noticed yet. He came to the villa on Sunday afternoons and sat in the armchair by the range while Beadie made the tea and cut the cake. Ellen didn't shift from the hard kitchen chair, carefully concealing her belly under the table.

'When are you going to tell him?' asked Beadie after he had left one evening in late September.

'I'll tell him soon,' she replied. Although she was certain what would happen once he knew. It was inevitable. She remembered the frozen track down the hill, the sharp shuddering screech of the magpie, Sister Aloysius's cold grip and Father Scullion's face in the half-light of a winter's afternoon.

She planned her announcement so that Henry couldn't make a scene. She invited him to the Victoria Tearooms on the promenade the following Saturday afternoon. It was a warm day: through the salt-stained windows, she could see children with buckets and spades propelled along the pavement by the wind, she could hear squeals of delight as they stepped onto the sand and ran towards the sea.

Henry ordered a plain scone and butter. Ellen ordered a slice of Battenberg cake: yellow and pink chequerboard like the tiles on the washhouse floor. She stared down at her plate, feeling the awful words in her mouth. *I'm pregnant, Henry. You're going to be an uncle, Henry.*

'You should watch yourself with all that cake, Nell,' said Henry, patting his waistcoat and pointing at her across the table.

'I'm not getting fat,' she replied quietly. 'It's a baby, Henry.'

He stopped dead, knife in one hand, plate of butter in the other. Then he dropped everything onto the tablecloth and threw himself back in his chair as if she had struck him.

'What? How?'

He began to wheeze, swayed backwards and forwards with a napkin clamped over his mouth. Heads turned, and a waitress who was standing by the counter hurried over and asked if she could help. He waved her away. 'I'm fine, I'm fine,' he croaked. But when she had gone and the heads had returned to their own tables, he lunged at Ellen, his face inches from her own.

'Who was it?' he hissed between his teeth.

'You don't know him, Henry. He came and went. He was a travelling man, here one minute, gone the next.'

'One of Mrs Veasey's salesmen?'

'No.'

'Did he force you?'

It would have been easy to say yes, but she shook her head.

Henry sat back in his chair again, his fingers clutching the napkin. For several minutes he said nothing at all. She knew what he was thinking, she could see it in his eyes. He was picturing her lying on the beach or in the tower on the Snook, her blouse unbuttoned and her skirt hitched up around her thighs. She turned away, listened to the polite clatter of the tearoom: the sound of cup against saucer, of teaspoon against porcelain. Hats bobbed up and down in gentle conversation, silk flowers and feathers nodded in agreement.

He leaned forward again. 'Every day, I try not to sin. Every day I pray to Our Lady, I pray to God.' With the word God, he hit the table with his fist and the scone on his plate bounced up and down. 'And then you go and do this. And it's not just any old sin, a normal sin that no one knows about, it's a sin that everyone can see. It's a sin that's going to be born and that's going to grow up, and that's going to be with you for the rest of your life.'

'But it's a baby, Henry, not a sin.'

'Well whatever it is, you'll have to get rid of it!'

The café was silent. The women in the hats gaped at Henry. The waitresses turned to one another and Ellen was sure that someone giggled. But Henry didn't care, he pushed his plate away, got up from the table, pulled out a few coins from his pocket and threw them down next to the bill.

'You're going to have to sort something out, Nell,' he said, gazing down at the half-eaten scone and shaking his head. 'You can't keep it, you must know that.'

She watched him go. The little bell tinkled joyously as he swung the tearoom door open and slammed it shut again. Then he stooped up the road, struggling against the current of small children running down it to the sunny beach.

She knew what would happen next. She was waiting for him. She waited for him at night in the kitchen after Beadie had gone to bed, and early in the morning when she was lighting the fire in Mrs Tibbs's drawing room. She expected to see him on the Nab, fluttering in the distance, or as she walked into Teesby. He would step out from behind a bush or a doorway and grasp her hair. *Curiosity, Ellen Pearson. Look where it got you.*

She waited a week, then another. Then the first frost came,

clutching the edges of the leaves in the garden, forcing the late flowers to collapse. And she began to wonder if she was safe after all, if Henry was so disgusted by her that he hadn't even dared tell Father Scullion. She was wrong of course. A few days later, he rounded the corner of the villa when she was pulling the washing from the line. Beadie was visiting a cousin in Yarm, she had taken the bus that morning.

'Don't do anything stupid,' she had called as she left.

If only Beadie were here now, thought Ellen, as he walked towards her, slowly, calmly, ducking his bald head as he passed under the washing line.

'I always knew it would come to this, Ellen Pearson. It was only a matter of time.' He spoke gently, sounding the way a priest should, slightly tired but caring, a faint warmth to his voice. He had nothing to lose by being kind, not now she had proved him right.

Ellen stood by the washhouse door, a sheet bundled in her arms.

'You've been a bad girl,' he said quietly. 'Wilful, sinful.'

He was standing in front of her now, close – too close. He looked directly at her, into her eyes. He looked at her in a way that no one would dare to look at anyone else. He was the terrible omnipotent God again. He could see everything. He could see John Gargett in her bedroom, and Maurice Rush in Hooper's Hotel. He could see the stone collector lying on the mattress in the shepherd's hut.

He nodded, moved closer. He didn't need to tell her what he thought of her. He was breathing quickly: disgusted, excited.

'I said to your brother we would sort it out. I told him not to worry.'

'Yes, Father.'

She was a child again. He was pulling her up the road to the station, tugging her up the path to the Sacred Heart. She felt the heaviness pushing her down. She felt the whiteness again.

'You're to write a letter to your Mrs Tibbs. You're to tell her you have to go away for a while.'

'But she can't read, Father.'

'Well, read it to her, child. Read it to her.'

The sheets flapped on the line, and the cassock twisted round his legs. He took her by the arm and she could feel the soft pressure of his hand on her skin. He led her to a corner of the yard that was sheltered from the breeze.

'After you've read your letter to her, you're to pack your bag.'

'Yes, Father.'

'Then tomorrow morning at half past six, you'll be waiting for me at the gates. Do you hear me? Do you hear what I say, Ellen Pearson?'

She was trapped against the wall of the washhouse. All she could do was to nod.

When he had gone, she went to her room and wrote the letter to Mrs Tibbs. She left it on the top of the chest of drawers, knowing that Beadie would find it eventually.

She pulled out her case from the wardrobe and folded up her clothes: the pink dresses, the skirt and blouse. On the top she placed the peacock-coloured notebook and the piece of jet the stone collector had given her.

She didn't sleep that night. She could feel the baby. He curled and uncurled inside her like a sickly kitten. She lay on her back, put her hand over her stomach and sang him songs, the songs that Da used to sing to her when they walked across the beach together:

> *You can hear them sigh and wish to die,*
> *You can see them wink the other eye*
> *At the man who broke the bank at Monte Carlo.*

In the morning he was waiting for her in the lane, standing next to a small car with its engine running.

The sky was dove grey. The moon was a ghostly disc just above the sea.

'Get in child, hurry yourself.'

He guided her into the passenger seat and slid her bag into the back. As he leaned across her she could smell him, a faint fragrance of oxtail soup on his cassock and the violent odour of strong coffee on his breath.

He got into the driver's seat and let off the handbrake: the car started to roll down the hill. She could feel her mind slipping away from her, she had left it behind in the sleeping villa. She was already one of the girls in the farmyard. She was already sour-faced Shirley in the laundry. She would lose him as soon as he was born. He would be handed over, one of the boys that the church sent to Canada or Australia. Canada was too cold to imagine, Australia was too far away. Australia was a strange pink shape in the middle of the sea. She would have to dig a hole to get him back. She would have to dig down through the black soil and the stones and the rock and the fiery-molten core. And she would fall out of the earth on the other side – upwards or downwards, she wasn't sure which – and he would be sitting there waiting for her to take him home.

Now she was splitting, dividing into two. She was someone calmly sitting in the car next to Father Scullion with her hands clasped in her lap. She was someone else, clenching her fists, about to beat the dashboard. A scream shot out of her mouth so loud, so piercing that it hit the tower on the Snook and bounced right back at her.

Father Scullion slapped his large foot hard on the brake then both of them lurched forward, hitting their heads on the windscreen.

And there was Beadie, standing on the brow of the hill, a giant woman in a brown frock and apron, hands on hips, shouting at them.

'What do you think you're doing?' She opened the passenger door and pulled Ellen roughly by the shoulder. 'Get out! Get out this instant!'

Ellen hauled herself out of the seat and stood dazed on the lane as Beadie leaned into the car again.

'And you!' Beadie snarled at Father Scullion. 'I don't ever want to see you here again, you hear me! The baby's hers, not yours! Call yourself a Christian stealing other people's bairns!'

The Tower

The baby arrived late. For several days she could feel it shuffling its hands inside her looking for a way out. She was so large now she couldn't sit down any more. She had taken to wandering through the villa with her hand underneath her belly in case the weight of the child tore her apart.

She went to bed early and watched the snow tumbling against the black sky, it banked up on the sill and turned the window white. What if she hated the baby? What if the baby died? What if Father Scullion came back and took the baby away? What if she decided to let him?

She dreamt she was in the washhouse doing the laundry. She had lifted a wet tablecloth out of the tub and was pushing the edge of it into the mangle. As the cloth started to glide through the rubber rollers she cried out in shock: it wasn't her hand that was turning the handle, it was Henry's, it was Father Scullion's. Ellen wasn't Ellen any more, she was the white tablecloth that was stretched and flattened and wrung dry between the rollers.

She dreamt of the clothes in the ironing basket in the kitchen. She dreamt of holding up the dresses and the skirts, and shaking out the creases ready to spread them flat on the board. She took the hot iron from the range and slapped it down on a petticoat and could hear the piping squeal of the petticoat's frills as the heat burned through the fibres.

'Push, for Christ's sake! Push!'

She dreamt of Mrs Tibbs in a grey silk dress. She could see the line of hooks and eyes at the back of the bodice. She eased the first hook out of its metal eye, and Mrs Tibbs started to inflate as if someone had attached her to a bicycle pump. The old woman expanded slowly at first, then she swelled to twice her size. Her chest and arms ballooned, and the stitches that had held the gown together split wide apart.

'Push harder!' shouted Beadie. And another woman leaned across the bed and wiped Ellen's brow.

She dreamt of openings: the lock in the parlour door through which she had peered when she was a child; the doorway to her bedroom where John Gargett had stood; the entrance to the hut on Bleaker's Hill. She dreamt of a pair of unlaced boots, an unbuttoned shirt, his unbuttoned trousers. She dreamt of the circle of black earth on the damp ground where the camp fire had burned, and the fragment of jet lying in the hollow of her palm.

When the baby was born he was blue – bright blue and silent. Someone grasped his ankles and held him upside down. And someone else smacked him, the way you smack your clothes to get rid of the Teesby sand. She heard the baby gasp, a deep intake of breath: astonishment at the cold white world he had just entered, the attic bedroom, the snow outside the window, Beadie's determined face scowling down at him.

Then he began to wail, a long screech that made Beadie and the midwife smile.

They placed him in Ellen's arms and something unexpected overcame her. She had been seized by a great force, the birth had imbued her with a power so strong it was like steel running through her.

In the spring she took him for trips into town in an old pram that Beadie had found in the box room. She didn't care about the glances from the Teesby women, she didn't care about the things they whispered as she passed them by. She flicked her head at them, and she smiled down at the baby lying in the pram. He had a small alert face and round dark eyes. He was always looking at things, and she thought how wonderful it must be to be seeing those things for the very first time, shapes and colours, the sea and the sky. She would park the pram on the promenade and hold him up so he could look at the Snook. He would lift his arm and reach out to grasp the tower in his hand and turn to her and chuckle.

She was sitting on the bench outside the tearooms one afternoon when she saw Henry. He was sloping along the pavement in Da's old overcoat with his hands pushed into his pockets. He didn't look well. There was something green about him: the grey-green of the damp seaweed that had piled up just below the promenade. She assumed that he would duck away into one of the shadowed side streets when he saw her, but he carried on plodding straight towards the bench.

'Nell.' His voice was small: tentative, as if he was gently prodding something to test its reaction. 'I saw you from my window. I've seen you a couple of times in the last few weeks.'

'The baby likes looking at the sea,' she said coolly.

Henry peered under the hood of the pram. 'What did you decide to name him?'

'John,' she replied. 'But I call him Jack.'

'Good name, John – John the Baptist, John the Apostle.'

The baby burbled and kicked his foot under the blanket. Henry pulled away. He retreated a few steps and leaned against the railings of the promenade.

'But have you thought about how you're going to manage with the baby?'

The steel hardened inside her. 'I'm managing very well.'

'For now, Nell.'

'What do you mean?'

'What if Mrs Tibbs changes her mind about letting you stay. What happens when she passes on?'

Ellen would not think about that now, not on a sunny day with the sand spread out in front of her and the sea swaying gently from one shade of green to another. Not with the baby lying in the pram, grinning at her. The blue baby, her perfect baby.

'Look at me, Nell. Have you thought about it? Have you?'

'I'll find a way. It'll sort itself out,' she replied cheerfully.

Henry took his hands out of his pockets and began to pull at a torn nail. 'I really wanted to talk to you about having him baptised.'

'Baptised, in the church?' She turned on him. 'So that's it. You haven't spoken to me for months and months then you come out here and start talking about christenings.'

'But Nell . . .'

'I won't have Father Scullion touching my baby! I won't have him touching his hair!'

Henry looked confused for a second. 'But Nell, if the baby dies he'll be stuck in limbo for eternity and you'll never see him again.'

'Limbo doesn't exist!' she snapped. And yet as soon as she had said this she could see limbo just ahead of her: vast, watery, white. The unchristened children floated inside bubbles unable to speak to one another, unable to reach out and touch one another.

'I honestly can't imagine why God would be so cruel,' she muttered, turning her hands over in her lap, weaving her fingers together.

'It's not cruel, Nell, it's how it is.'

'I don't understand him, your God. I don't understand him, cruel, cruel man.'

Henry was gazing at her strangely, as if there was something wrong. She gave out a deep sigh then turned away to look at the beach.

'You can't expect to understand God, Nell.' Henry had lowered

171

his voice. He was speaking gently, almost in a whisper. 'You have to have faith. And faith doesn't just come to you, you have to work at it.'

Now that he had changed his tone, she twisted round to look at him. 'I don't think I believe in any of it any more.'

'But what if you're wrong?'

'I can't be wrong.' She leaned over to make sure the baby was comfortable. As she tucked the blanket back round him he lifted up his hand and flexed it open and shut. She slid her finger inside his curled palm and he burbled at her. She could not bear the thought of never seeing him again.

'Nell, what if you're wrong?'

'I'll think about it, Henry,' she replied dully.

He seemed satisfied with this.

It was Henry who organised everything, who bought the christening gown and persuaded the reluctant Father Scullion to officiate. It was Henry who wheeled the pram down the hill from the villa in the sunshine. Ellen trudged behind in a new green frock and hat, with Beadie walking close beside her. Beadie hadn't wanted to come, she had said she didn't believe in all that mumbo-jumbo. But Henry had cajoled her in the kitchen. Ellen had heard them whispering together over a bowl of rising bread dough.

Despite the sunshine, it was cold and damp inside Saint Anthony's. The walls of the church had been painted brown, but the humidity had lifted the paintwork and great patches of chalky white plaster had been revealed beneath the Stations of the Cross. Everything was brown or white, thought Ellen: Jack's gown was white, Father Scullion's vestment was white, the handkerchief that Henry gripped in his hand was almost white, and Beadie in her woollen coat and flea-bitten fox fur stole, borrowed from Mrs Tibbs's wardrobe, was as dull and as brown as the Nab on a wet winter's day.

'I baptise you in the name of the Father, and of the Son, and of the Holy Ghost,' mumbled Father Scullion in a flat voice. He scooped up the freezing holy water and poured it over the baby's brow. Jack squealed with shock, then the squeal echoed round the church making the Stations of the Cross tremble against the clammy walls.

'As Christ was anointed Priest, Prophet, and King,' said Father Scullion, raising his voice above the baby's screams, 'so may you live always as a member of his body, sharing everlasting life.'

'Amen,' murmured Henry.

'Amen,' muttered Beadie at the fox's head lying on her chest.

'Amen,' said Ellen through gritted teeth.

Henry had told her that the baby would be reborn after the baptism. He had said that Jack would be filled with the grace of God. But if there was a God he certainly wasn't in Saint Anthony's that sunny afternoon. He was outside blowing round the heather on the Nab, or on the beach, rolling in the sand.

She was wheeling the pram out of the church after the christening when Father Scullion called her back.

'I'd like a word, Ellen, before you go.'

His voice was a lasso around her neck, drawing her backwards. Henry gently prised the handle of the pram from her and pushed it into the porch, and Beadie, who narrowed her eyes at the priest, turned away and trudged up the aisle behind him.

'Come here, child.' Father Scullion slid into the front pew and patted the seat beside him. His voice had a soft brown lilt to it: it was a voice that knew it held all the power. 'Come here, I just want a quick word.'

But she would not move. She stood straight and still, gripping the wooden back of the pew, glaring down at him.

'I think I should warn you, Ellen.'

She could smell him: today he smelt of sweat and wine and

tobacco. There were deep lines around his eyes and his mouth. There were clods of mud on the heels of his shoes. Behind him, Jesus was ripping his robe apart. The sacred heart beat at her: thump, thump, thump.

'Are you listening to me, Ellen? Look at me, Ellen.'

She fixed her eyes on him, unblinking.

'This will be difficult for you to hear, but I think it's important to warn you.' She held her breath, Jesus's heart stopped beating, the church was silent.

'You see, I don't believe that you are capable of looking after that child, Ellen, I don't believe that you will be a fit mother.' He paused. 'If I ever have my doubts proved, I will take him away. I will make sure he is safe. Do you hear me, Ellen? Do you hear me?'

She ran. She ran up the aisle and out of the church. She grasped the handle of the pram from Henry who was standing with Beadie in the porch, and she propelled it as fast as she could out of the graveyard and down the road. The baby bounced: she could see him flailing underneath the sheets. The baby squealed, squealed so loud the whole of Teesby turned and looked: mothers and children with mouths wide open; the ice cream salesmen, cornets aloft; even the weary donkeys turned their heads.

On the ferryboat, the passengers stared at her too. They were sitting on a long bench, old men and women, with baskets and string bags, one with a cockerel in a cage, another with a dog on her lap. They gawped at her.

'Looks can kill, you know!' she snapped.

And the passengers gazed down at their hands or their handbags or the toes of their shoes. And the ferryman holding the rudder raised his hefty eyebrows to the sky.

On the other side of the river, she didn't have to run any more. Ahead was the thin red line of the Snook, at the end was the tower. It looked like glass today: it had taken on the calm blue tone of the sky. She pushed the pram over the causeway, then ploughed it through the sand. When it became too heavy to push she abandoned it on a bank of pebbles and carried the baby the rest of the way to the tower.

Inside, the ground floor was just as it had been a year ago when she had stood there with the stone collector. The helmet that he had nudged with the toe of his boot was probably exactly where he had left it. She didn't miss him. She didn't even think about him any more: she didn't need to.

The baby struggled in her arms, he was damp and heavy. She carried him through the room, past the chicken wire and the wooden crates, then climbed the twisting staircase to the second floor.

'One, two, three, four.' She counted the steps, jigging the baby up and down in her arms. She was going to replace Henry's useless sacrament with something better. She was going to erase Father Scullion's evil words.

The top floor room was small and dark, so dark that it took her eyes a few seconds to adjust to the brightness from the window. She held the baby up and he pressed his plump hands against the glass. She remembered standing here with Da, waiting for the picture to appear. The room was silent, there was no noise inside her head – no chattering, no humming, no songs – no confusion between colour and sound. Everything came together, slipped into place. Nothing was anything other than itself.

'Look,' she whispered. 'Look, Jacky. Beautiful.'

JACK

1943–49

Iris

Aircraftman Jack Pearson was leaning against the sink washing brushes. He watched the paint, an eddy of viridian green and yellow ochre, disappear down the plughole. The sink was in the basement of Danesfield House, a white castellated mansion built on a rise above the Thames, near Henley. In the rooms above him sat men and women scrutinising aerial photographs of unnamed parcels of land somewhere in Europe. In the basement, the model makers created small-scale versions of the sites, fashioning hills and valleys out of layers of card and plaster of Paris, destined for Bomber Command and the Army.

Jack was responsible for colouring the models. He painted the fields and beaches, then filled in the hedgerows and the trees with a green substance made from glue and tinted sawdust. There was something incongruous about it all, he thought: an entire unit of men working day and night to reproduce perfect scale models of bits of the world so the real thing could be flattened.

The war was elsewhere for Jack, far away from the topiary and fountains of Danesfield House. He was out of it – safe – embarrassingly, annoyingly so. The war was happening to other people: to Lenny on an air base in Lincolnshire, to Bob Marigold in Burma, to Cathy and Uncle Henry in Teesby where the bombs had begun to fall, plunging into the sand of the Snook, and the salt marsh and the works.

Twelve-year-old Cathy sent him telegram-like messages on the back of cheap pre-war postcards that showed the old ferryboat crossing the river, or the angry-looking sea. A few days after he had arrived at Danesfield House, she wrote: 'Dear Jack, your old villa's been taken over by the WAAFs, love Cathy.' A month later she sent a second card: 'There was an air raid last night and Granny had a heart attack under the kitchen table. They took her to the hospital but she passed away in the ambulance. Then this afternoon the parrot went and died like he knew that she'd gone.'

Cathy didn't write again until just before Christmas. He wandered wearily into the barracks one evening after a long shift and found a picture of the snowy Nab lying on top of his locker. 'Lenny Grieve's mam got hit by a bomb yesterday,' Cathy had scribbled on the back of the card. At the bottom, she had added darkly, 'They haven't found the body yet. I don't suppose they ever will.'

Unlike Cathy's laconic messages, Uncle Henry's missives were long and meandering, one topic seamlessly merged into another. He wrote as he spoke, in breathless sentences.

'It's a shame you couldn't get home for the funeral – poor Mrs Rush,' he wrote after Granny Rush had died. 'You might not think it now, Jack, but she did a lot for you – Cathy was with her when she went – and the next day the poor parrot passed on – I've had a mass said for her – Looks like Mrs Veasey's cat's got the influenza – sleeps all day on my bed – Your stepfather's an ARP Warden now – he's shaved off his moustache.'

After the air raid that killed Lenny's mother, Uncle Henry wrote: 'Mrs Grieve was at the station going into Darlington for something or other – and then she was gone – twelve killed, don't know how many injured – Your young friend, Lenny, came to see me when he was home for the burial – poor lady – not much of a show – no priest or vicar anything – just someone reading a poem, Mrs Veasey said – All very odd – Lenny asked about you – he's

180

grown very tall – asked if you'd got some leave coming up – have you? Be nice to see you, Jacky.'

Jack thought about Lenny as he painted the handkerchief squares of meadowland which he guessed were somewhere in northern Germany, near Bremen or Hamburg. Lenny was a bomb aimer in a Lancaster. He lay on his stomach inside a metal tube below the gun turret, staring out of the Perspex nose at the landscape below. Jack remembered him standing with the catapult in front of the washhouse door, and wondered how Lenny felt when he was just above the target, over Hamburg or Cologne; above all those intricate patterns of houses and hospitals and railway stations. He wondered if Lenny would soon be flying over the ground that he was smothering in ochre-coloured oil paint, whether the meadows were on the bombing run. What did Lenny think when he let the bomb go and saw the burst of light beneath him? And afterwards, as he listened to the rear gunner describing the fires, he could see when they had turned tail and flown away.

In the New Year, one of the model makers, a part-time teacher at the Slade before the war, lent Jack a book about landscape painting. After his shift, he lay on his bed in the barracks trying to understand the fluffy, pastel-coloured Renoirs, which he was beginning to dislike, and the Cézannes, which confused him. He flicked through page after page of studies of Mont Sainte-Victoire, each one more awkward than the last, until he reached the final painting, a mass of green and blue blocks into which the mountain had dissolved. It was hardly a landscape at all, and yet there was something more real, more honest about it than all the other pictures in the book. Looking at the Cézanne painting in the dim light of the Nissen hut was like looking at the Nab on a rainy day.

'They're not bad reproductions,' the teacher said casually, when Jack handed him the book the following morning. 'Nothing like seeing them in the flesh though.'

Jack had never seen an oil painting before, at least, not a proper one. Hanging above the bar in Hooper's Hotel was a buckled canvas of an arch-necked horse that had won the Derby a century ago, but he had never been to a museum or a gallery to see a work of art. That was how the teacher from the Slade described the pictures in the book, in a reverential tone, like the voice Father Scullion used when he blessed the wine on Sunday mornings.

'Of course, looking at reproductions is a way of getting to know the great works of art,' said the teacher, patting the cover of the book. 'But if you're really interested in painting, Pearson, you should try and see them for real, nothing like it. You should go up to London, see what's left in the National Gallery.'

A few weeks later, on a grey day in January 1943, as Lenny was preparing to bomb Berlin again and Marigold was struggling through a Burmese jungle, Jack was sitting on a train to London – a map in his pocket, money in his wallet – on his way to see a painting in the flesh. The train was a stopping train: it lurched from Henley to Shiplake to Wargrave to Twyford. At Slough, a girl got into his carriage and sat directly opposite him. She looked like a woman in one of the Renoir pictures: fuzzy-haired and buxom, with dark blue eyes and a roundish nose. As the train started to move again, she took a magazine and a packet of sand-wiches from her bag.

'Always get peckish on the train,' she said, smiling at him. She held out a wedge-shaped sandwich. 'Want one?'

He shook his head.

'Suit yourself.'

He pretended to look through the window, but managed to tilt his head in such a way that he could peer slyly at the girl. Her head was lowered over the magazine and all he could see of her face beneath the mass of red hair was her dimpled chin, which moved – cow-like – gently up and down as she chewed. Around her neck was a pale green scarf that looked like silk but was probably rayon, and hanging from her wrist was a pair of narrow silver-coloured bangles that jingled like alarm bells each time she turned a page.

He was able to stare at her for almost a minute before she lifted her head.

'Caught you looking.' She smiled again as if she didn't mind. Then she closed the magazine and placed it on the seat beside her.

'You going to London?'

'Yes, I've got a day pass.'

'That's nice,' she said, stuffing the half-eaten sandwich back into its wrapper. 'So what are you going to do?'

'I want to see the National Gallery – the picture of the month.'

'The what?'

'The painting they show in the National Gallery.'

'Not much fun on your own.'

'I'll be all right.'

She paused, gazing at him, as if she was in the process of calculating something. 'We could meet up later if you want. I could show you around.'

He would have liked that, but he shook his head politely. 'I'm sure you're busy.'

'Don't be silly, it's no bother. I could meet you in the Kardomah on Piccadilly.'

She marked the café on his map with a blunt eyebrow pencil that she found in the bottom of her bag, and on the corner in the margin, she wrote in large smudgy letters: 'Iris. 4 o'clock'.

The picture of the month was a Turner. It was hanging on a panel in one of the galleries that still had glass in its windows. He stared at it, first from a distance, then close up. Unlike the bright, glossy reproductions in the teacher's book, it was muddy and unfinished. All he could see was the coarseness of the canvas and the seemingly random flicks of dull paint that hardly covered the surface.

The painting was a seascape, just water and sky and sand. It was almost impossible to work out where one thing ended and the next began, all three had blended together. In the foreground was a boy with a shrimping net, accompanied by a small, pale dog. In the centre of the canvas was a thick, white vertical smear of paint, which he took to be a figure wading in the water.

The teacher from the Slade had told him that looking at a work of art could be a transformative experience. When Jack had replied that he wasn't sure what that meant, the teacher had said that the colours and forms might stir something in him if he let them. But the only thing that stirred in him now was a memory: his boots sinking into the sodden, silty sand, a boy pointing his metal spade at the sea, and a windowpane check coat swaying gently from side to side in the distance.

He gazed at the painting obliquely, hoping that the memory would be overtaken by something better, when he noticed a typewritten text pinned to the wall beside it. The picture, he discovered, was called *The Evening Star*, and the short, impasto line in the middle of the scene wasn't a figure at all. It was simply the reflection in the water of a star that was barely visible in the sky. He turned away from the painting and walked through the dusty gallery, hating Turner, hating the deceit.

Iris was late. He managed to secure a small table by the window on the first floor of the café and from there he scanned the pavement. Just as he was beginning to think that she wouldn't come and that the day would turn out to be a disaster, he finally noticed her at the corner of the road. She was strutting along the pavement, followed by a nervous-looking naval rating in a sailor suit. As she reached the entrance to the café, the sailor appeared to pluck up courage. He bent forward and tugged at the belt of her coat, but Iris swivelled on her heels and waved her hand at him as if she was trying to shoo away an irritating dog.

'He's my ex,' she said when she arrived at the table. 'Bit of a brute, to be honest. Glad to be shot of him.'

When she sat down, he noticed she had lost the green scarf that had been draped round her neck that morning and her skirt was twisted.

'Order us a couple of rock cakes and a pot of tea, will you,' she said, glancing at the menu.

When the cakes arrived, Iris consumed them delicately, giving the impression she was hardly eating at all. She broke the cakes into pieces on her plate and picked at the crumbs. And each time she raised a fragment to her mouth the silver bangles on her wrist rang their faint alarm.

There was something troubling about Iris. She talked loudly and laughed with her mouth wide open and her head thrown back. People at nearby tables turned and grimaced, it seemed to irritate them that she was enjoying herself so much.

'So where shall we go now?' she asked when she had finished the cakes.

He had planned to see Westminster Abbey and Big Ben, but when he suggested this, Iris made a face.

'It's a long way, and it's what everyone does when they come here.' She put on a posh strangulated voice: 'We're goin' up to tyne to see the Abbey.'

This made him laugh, and she grinned broadly, pleased with herself.

'I've got something better to do.' She leaned over the table and he could feel her warm cakey breath on his face. 'There's this street of fancy houses in Saint James's that's just been bombed. You can see all the stuff inside, all the furniture and bits and bobs – much better than a stupid old church.'

She was right. The terrace with its missing façade was like a row of full-size dolls' houses. Some of the interiors were unscathed: tables and chairs stood in the rooms as if the occupants had left momentarily and would, at any minute, return to continue their afternoon tea or their rubber of bridge. Other houses had been cleared completely and were merely a shell. Several were listing, and their floors sagged like cardboard.

Iris walked along the street and stared up at it as if she was window shopping.

'Would never have chosen that paper, myself,' she said, gesturing to a first floor room, its three remaining walls covered by a Regency stripe. 'And that settee's hideous.'

One of the houses in the middle of the terrace had been demolished completely, all that was left were the stone steps that once led to the front door. Jack climbed them and stood in what must have been the entrance hall. The back wall had gone and he could see the remains of an ornamental garden. Part of a balustrade and fragments of a statue lay like shattered bones in the yellow grass. Beside the statue's head was an old tin bath that must have fallen from one of the upper floors when the house was bombed and was now entangled in brambles.

At the end of the garden, banked against the back wall, was a pile of rubble. On top of it, pawing the stones, was a rangy-looking dog. It was so thin that even in the dull light, he could see the shadows in between its ribs. As he made his way towards it, the dog's back legs trembled as if they couldn't support the weight of its body any more.

'Here, doggy,' called Iris, stepping into the gap and opening the palm of her hand as if she had something to offer it. 'Here, doggy, here!'

The animal raised its head and glanced at her doubtfully. Then it heaved its quivering body over the rubble and clambered through the undergrowth into the neighbouring garden.

Suddenly the bombed-out houses were no longer an amusement. He knew they shouldn't be standing there, in the twilit ruin, amongst the scattered limbs of the statue: he remembered the

German airman falling into the sea, and Lenny's mother, disappeared in the rubble of the railway station.

'We should go,' he murmured.

'We could go get a drink,' Iris said brightly, leaning into him. 'I know somewhere that opens early.'

As she turned back to the street, she brushed gently against his arm and he could feel her damp warm breath on the side of his face again.

The air raid siren began to scream as they reached the pub door.

'You don't want to go to a shelter, do you?' asked Iris, challenging him.

He shook his head, dizzy from excitement or trepidation, he wasn't sure which.

The pub was called The French House. It was packed with men in uniform and women with bright hair lacquered into tight curls. He fought his way to the bar and ordered the drinks: half a pint of beer for himself and a port for Iris. There was nowhere to sit down, so they slouched against a wall clutching their glasses.

He didn't hear the bombers approach. It was only when the wall began to vibrate against his spine that he knew they were close. He could hear a piercing sound like the whistle of a frantic kettle which was followed by the wail of a plane overhead. As the bomb struck its target, the whole room rattled. He pressed himself against the wall and watched the pub door bulge in then out again.

He must have flinched because Iris turned to look at him.

'Don't worry,' she said. 'It's miles away.'

There was a second thump and his stomach shuddered, it was like being punched from the inside.

'Honestly, Jack, it's miles away.' She took his empty glass and placed it on the edge of the table beside her. 'You don't need to worry,' she said, lifting her finger and stroking his face.

She slid her hand round the back of his neck, the touch of the bangles was icy against his bare skin. As she bent towards him, he could smell her: cake and port and the sharp metallic odour of the bangles. Since Dora in the milk shed, he had kissed other girls, had clutched their shoulders or their waists and pushed his lips onto theirs. Sometimes his fingers had found their way inside a blouse or along the warm skin of an inner thigh. Although the girls had always pulled away from him then, saying, 'Not now, Jacky. Not now.'

He had expected to meet the same reluctant tight-lipped pout from Iris. But her mouth was wide open: his face melted into hers. As his tongue stumbled into the sickly-sweet void, he forgot everything: the bombers, the drinkers, the shivering wall. His tongue fumbled round hers, brushed against her teeth, found its way into deep port-rinsed corners. Then she slid away from him, kissed his cheek lightly.

'Let's go,' she said, grasping his hand. 'Let's go right now.'

'Now, in the middle of the raid?'

'Yes, right now.'

Suddenly she was tugging him through the groups of drinkers, disappearing for a moment behind khaki-clad shoulders and navy-blue backs, then appearing again, her frizzy red hair a beacon ahead of him. He followed her out onto the street and they ran down the darkened road like they were dodging a rainstorm. He could hear her laughing, and he wondered briefly if he was going to die and decided that he didn't care.

They took the Underground to Paddington Station, then she led him down the platform to the head of the Henley train. In an empty compartment, she wedged the door shut with a folded piece of cardboard. And as the train jolted forward, halted, then jolted again, she pulled away her blouse and his jacket and his shirt.

They grappled together, rolling with the movement of the train, his trousers caught around his ankles, her pink skirt rucked around her waist. In a feverish moment she let out a sharp gasp

188

and pushed him away. He lay there for a moment, jerking limply over her leg and the horsehair seat.

'Can't take any risks,' she giggled, pulling a handkerchief out of her bag and wiping her thighs with it.

Iris got off at Slough with a smirk on her face and a promise to meet him the following week. But he would never see her again, nor his wallet, which was secreted in her bag, between the half-eaten sandwich and last week's copy of *Woman's Own*. When the train finally arrived at Henley, he collected his bicycle, which was hidden behind the men's lavatories, and cycled the five miles back to Danesfield. The moon was high, and he could see his faint shadow on the tarmac – a rounded form hunched over the bicycle and the brisk movement of the pedals. He thought about Iris, her pink mottled thighs and her large mouth opened slightly, and he let a wave of triumph wash over him.

It was not until the morning that he saw the postcard of Teesby lying on his locker. It showed a black and white picture of the tower on the Snook and the dark grey sea behind it. Cathy's message was slightly longer than usual.

'Dear Jacky, Dad fell over in the blackout. He slipped on Mrs Veasey's basement steps and ended up at the bottom with a broken leg. He's in hospital now and I have to stay with Mrs Peters next door. Can't you come home and look after me? Love Cathy.'

At the end of the card, as a sort of postscript, she had added in small, neat capital letters, 'REALLY SAD ABOUT LENNY.'

Uncle Henry's letter arrived later that morning. 'Dear Jack – I'm writing with some bad news – Lenny Grieve's plane didn't come home the other night – someone in another bomber thought the crew had parachuted – although he couldn't be sure – I thought you should know. Say a prayer for him, light a candle.'

Jack pictured the reeling airman over the sea again and Lenny's golden face in the burst of light from Hartlepool. He pictured the map of Teesby and Outlying Districts, and Lenny pointing up at a bird and saying something about Huxley; and the perfect pyramid of twigs outside the tent and the rattling milk churn as it rolled over the floor in the cowshed.

He wanted to feel something. He wanted to make sure he remembered this moment, this precise moment: standing in the studio with the letter in his hand, the paper quivering slightly, the grey light from the window above the sink falling in a wide beam across the dark blue slanting words. And yet it slid away from him like any other, as the present gently slipped towards the past.

The war would not bother Jack again. The night that Corporal Bob Marigold was ambushed by a group of Japanese soldiers on the edge of a Burmese jungle, Jack was sweating in the basement studio, modelling the Normandy beaches out of cardboard. When the head draughtsman from Wilkie's Construction was staggering across that same beach to Ouistreham on the sixth of June 1944, Jack was packing away the paints and brushes, rolling up the maps and photographs.

Once the air force no longer needed topographical models, he trailed from one airfield to another: posted to bases in the east of England he would instantly forget once he left them again. They were all the same, a flat strip of low land and too much sky: sky that always vacillated between heavy cloud and thick fog. His task in those nameless places was to make inventories of things to be removed from the sites when the airfields were shut. In reality there was little to do. He stood in drab offices, filling in dockets or filing irritatingly small pieces of paper that slid between the cardboard folders and lost themselves in the dust at the bottom of the metal drawers. Unlike the other men, he was not eager to go home now the war was coming to an end.

Teesby Again

'I've been to see your mother,' wrote Uncle Henry inside the Christmas card he sent to Jack in December 1946. 'Now don't go getting excited – but she seems a little better to me – quite cheery and chatty – I thought we could talk to the doctors when you got back – see what can be done – Why don't you stay with me when you come home in the spring – your stepdad's got a lodger now and Mrs Veasey said she'd put a camp bed in my sitting room – Have a think about it – God bless you and Merry Christmas – Uncle Henry.'

It had been a long, hard winter. The snow was heaped along the edge of the pavement like a miniature mountain range, it was an unusual sight in Teesby. But the sky was just as he remembered it, shifting slowly from dull Payne's grey to a threatening Prussian blue. And the sea: he could taste the sea long before he saw it. It tasted of home, of somewhere half-forgotten, of somewhere he wasn't sure he wanted to be. When he turned onto the High Street and finally saw the huge expanse of bright, cold water framed by Barclays Bank on one side and Boots on the other, it was as if there was nothing there. He had to pause for a moment as the sight of the empty space ripped the air from his lungs.

*

Mrs Veasey took her time opening the front door to the house on Marine Parade. He knocked twice and waited for almost a minute before he heard footsteps. They echoed down the stairs.

'Oh, it's you, Jack. I wasn't expecting you, love.'

She pulled the door wide open and stood outside on the step. Her milky-coloured cat slid between her ankles, shuttling anxiously back and forth.

'You did get Cathy's letter, didn't you? She sent it at the end of February.'

He shook his head. 'What letter?'

'Your uncle had a stroke. Didn't you know?' A sudden gust tugged at Mrs Veasey's hair, and she patted the curls back into place. 'It was almost a month ago now. It was very quick. He didn't suffer.'

'Almost a month?' The words splintered in his dry throat.

Mrs Veasey reached out and gripped his shoulder but all he could feel was the sand in the cold breeze stinging the side of his face.

It was Maurice who opened the door to the house on Invicta Road.

'So you've heard then? Cathy sent you one of her postcards after he passed away. She tried to ring you and all, but the lines were down because of the snow. I told her not to worry. I said you'd find out soon enough. We knew you'd never be able to get back for the funeral anyway.'

Maurice was half dressed. He must have been in the process of washing himself when Jack rang the doorbell. His shirt was unbuttoned and his braces were swinging loosely against his legs. On either side of his waist was a swag of fat that hung over the top of his trousers. The hair on his chest was grey, and his face was lined. Only the pale moustache-less gap between his nose and his top lip was smooth and white.

'Come in then. I suppose you'll want to sleep here for a night or two.'

In the kitchen, Maurice took off his shirt again, cupped his hands under the tap and threw the water onto his face and under his armpits.

'So how've you been?' he asked, reaching for a towel.

'All right.'

Jack sat down at the table. Things had changed. The parrot's cage was on the floor by the sink, and draped from the hook on the back door was a long pink scarf with daisies printed on it. There was something else too: the house smelt different. It had always reeked of Granny Rush, a blend of liquorice and sweat and coal fires, a smell so strong it hit you as soon as you stepped inside the front door. But now he could detect a hint of paraffin in the air, the sort that Maurice used to clean the paint from his hands, and there was the thick, murky whiff of the pie heating in the oven. There were more exotic perfumes too: a waft of Imperial Leather from a bottle by the kitchen sink, and the faint fragrance of scented geraniums or roses perhaps.

There was someone else in the house. Jack could hear a woman singing to herself upstairs in one of the bedrooms. He could hear the soft tread of her feet against the linoleum.

'Joyce is staying for a while,' said Maurice, buttoning his shirt. He looked warily at Jack. 'You remember Joyce? Clarence's daughter. You must remember her from the wedding.'

Jack ignored the question. 'Where's Cathy?'

'At some Labour League of Youth jamboree. Then she's off on a school field trip, she'll be back in a couple of weeks.'

'And what about my mother?' he said stiffly. 'Uncle Henry told me she was getting better.'

Maurice gave a short sharp sigh as if he had been waiting for this question. He removed the pie from the oven, set it on the table and cut himself a slice. 'Your mother's got worse since Henry

193

passed away,' he said finally, breaking the grey pie crust into pieces with the side of his fork.

'Worse? What does that mean?'

Maurice leaned across the table and lowered his voice. 'If you'd made an effort to visit her more often you'd know what it meant.' He took a large mouthful of pie, chewed it thoughtfully and sat back in his chair. 'I used to see her every month when you were a kid and you never asked to come once. Your uncle was always trying to get you to go to the hospital with him. He said he thought it would help her to get better. She was always asking for you, "Tell Jacky to come," she used to say. You didn't even bother to see her before you left for the RAF.' Maurice tussled with a piece of gristle that had caught between his teeth. When he managed to extract it, he placed it delicately on the side of his plate. 'You're too late, Jacky,' he said. 'Go and take a look for yourself if you don't believe me.'

Jack should have left then. He thought about it as he watched Maurice rinsing his dirty plate in the sink. He should catch a train to Darlington, take the main line to Newcastle or York. And yet he couldn't bring himself to pick up the suitcase that he had left in the hallway or put on the raincoat that he had hung over the banister rail. After Maurice and Joyce had left for the Regent, he sat in the kitchen reading old copies of the *Evening Gazette* that had been piled on one of the chairs. Later he pulled out the blankets from the cubby hole under the stairs and made up the bed on the settee in the front room, just as he had done when he was a boy.

In the morning he visited Uncle Henry's grave. The stone was hidden by a pillow of greying snow and he crouched down and brushed it away. As he gazed at the inscription, the absurdity of it struck him. Henry, a living, wheezing, complex mass of thoughts and desires, was reduced to this: a small slab of dark brown granite, a name etched in gold, two dates bracketing his existence.

He remembered Henry standing in the graveyard pulling at the weeds around his parents' graves.

'Come and have a look, Jacky. Come and say a prayer for your grandparents.'

Together they had stood side by side: Jack's hands loosely knotted together, Uncle Henry's eyes tightly shut.

Eternal Rest grant unto them, O Lord,
And let perpetual light shine upon them,
May they rest in peace.
Amen.

When Uncle Henry opened his eyes again, he turned to Jack. 'Each time we say one of those prayers, Jacky, it helps them make their way through purgatory, it washes away their sins.'

And Jack had imagined an elderly couple inside the Bradford washing machine in the washhouse of the villa: Sidney and Sarah Pearson hand in hand tumbling amongst Mrs Tibbs's underwear, being cleansed of their sins.

Jack left the churchyard and made his way up the lane to the villa. The gates were locked and the new padlock glinted in the sunshine. The garden was being used as a store for broken-down vehicles. Parked over the rose beds was a pair of military vans that had been used as balloon winches during the war, and under the Monkey Puzzle tree was an old Austin 10 with its bonnet up. He had hoped he might find Lenny in the garden – a ghost, a presence, a sign of some sort. But Lenny was ashes on a bombsite somewhere in Berlin, blowing about the city, carried by the breeze or caught in the rain.

By the end of the day Jack had managed to get his old job back at Wilkie's, although he promised himself that he wouldn't stay long. At the weekend he moved out of Invicta Road into

Henry's rooms on Marine Parade: it seemed appropriate, a legacy of sorts.

Mrs Veasey's house was empty now. When he was a child the sign on the front door had always read NO VACANCIES, and the parlour and the dining room had been a flurry of salesmen clutching cases of stockings or paper samples.

Now with nothing much to do, Mrs Veasey traipsed up to his room in the evening with a tray of tea and biscuits and sat in Uncle Henry's armchair.

'Such a lovely man, your uncle, I do miss him Jack. Did so much for the church. Did you know that Father Scullion's retired now? He must be almost eighty. Gone to the Sacred Heart, looked after by the nuns. There's a young priest at Saint Anthony's now, not to everyone's liking, I hear.' She stirred the tea and tapped the teaspoon on the side of the cup.

'You could give him your uncle's clothes, Jack. I know they're old but they might be useful for someone.'

Mrs Veasey had sorted through Uncle Henry's possessions after he had died. She had piled them in the corner of his bedroom: his suit, his shirts, his sweaters which had been carefully darned, a bone-backed set of hair brushes, a ceramic dish with the word 'Souvenir' painted on the side, the penknife, a quantity of handkerchiefs, a few letters and a creased photograph of a young man in uniform that at some time Henry must have carried in his pocket or folded inside his wallet.

'You will do something with his things, Jack, won't you?' said Mrs Veasey. 'I'll find you a box to put them in.'

But Jack couldn't bring himself to touch them. It seemed wrong to give them away, and he knew he would never use them himself. He left the pyramid of possessions untouched in the corner of the room, leaning slightly to the right: a small shrine to Uncle Henry.

Jack had arranged his own belongings round the rooms: two second-hand books on the history of art, a few postcards and three prints of paintings by Cézanne and Picasso, a Penguin copy of *David Copperfield* and his old colouring book, *The Modern World*, which he had found in a box in the house on Invicta Road. He was going to throw it away, but something about the pictures had made him stop. After the milk had dried all those years ago it had acted like glue, melding the pages together. When he prised them apart again fragments of one image had merged with another on the opposite page. The arm of the doctor holding a syringe had become attached to the seat of the Fordson tractor, and the wing of the monoplane had sliced through the driver and his lorry. Jack wanted to make paintings like this, pictures where traces of the past fused with the present.

The snow melted. At the end of the month, he bought himself a large pad of paper and a new tin of pencils. On the first warm Saturday in April, he climbed up the cliff path to Bleaker's Hill and began to draw. Perching on an old upturned bucket he had found, he studied the view. The shepherd's hut that he had sat in when he was hiding from Beadie had gone now, and the field was overgrown with thistles: in front of him were tall spikes of steel blue, sprouting unruly heads of last year's fluff. In the distance was a low ridge of pollarded trees, a small ramshackle cottage belonging to Robinson's farm, and a washing line. The rest of the view was sky: smears of vivid cobalt blue were beginning to break through the dark grey cloud.

He had been working on the drawing for an hour or so when he saw a girl walking along the track at the bottom of the field. Her head bobbed just above the thistles, her long thick curly hair bounced with every step. She was scanning the horizon: she raised her hand to shield her eyes from the sunlight.

'I thought it was you,' she called out. 'Mrs Veasey said you were here.'

He scrambled up.

'Don't you recognise me, Jacky?' Cathy waded through the field, pushing away the thistles with her clenched fists. Her face was bright, illuminated by the spring sunshine. Her hair was black with flecks of copper, her smile was broad. She caught hold of him, hugged him uncomfortably to her.

'Aren't you pleased to see me?'

He was. He was pleased to see her. He laughed. 'You came all the way up here just for me?'

'Of course I did. Earliest opportunity. I got back on Monday, but then there was school and you were at work.' Cathy collapsed onto the ground. 'It's a long walk, though.'

He sat down beside her. There were clusters of freckles on her red cheeks, a small dimple in her chin. He wasn't sure what to say to her. 'How have you been?'

She gave a deep sigh and shrugged her shoulders. 'All right, I suppose. School's good. We went to the Lake District, a field trip. We went on Lake Windermere in a boat, it was freezing.' She plucked a strand of grass and chewed on it. 'Have you met Joyce yet?'

'Yes, briefly.'

'She's awful, isn't she. She's only twelve years older than me. Uncle Henry hated her.' Cathy paused, the piece of grass still between her teeth, and stared blankly into the distance. 'Can I come and live with you, Jacky?' She turned and grinned at him, knowing the response.

'I'm sure Mrs Veasey has a spare room if you can afford it.'

Cathy rolled her eyes at him. 'Did Dad tell you I'm going to teacher training college in York in September?'

He shook his head. She didn't look old enough. She still looked like a child: restless and fidgeting. She wore a yellow skirt and an oversized jumper that had probably belonged to Maurice and ankle socks and brown and white saddle shoes.

'I honestly didn't think you'd come home, Jacky.'

'I didn't think so either, but to be honest I didn't know where else to go. I don't think I'll be here for long.'

She lay down on her back and put her hands behind her head. 'So what do you think about Teesby after all those years away?'

'Not too bad, I suppose.'

'If I were you, I would never have come back. But I'm really glad you have.'

He was surprised by his sister, pleased by the easiness of their conversation, by her warmth.

'Did you hear about Father Scullion?' Cathy sat up again all of a sudden and brushed away an ant from the back of her leg.

'Yes, Mrs Veasey told me.'

'I'm glad he's gone,' she said, inspecting the ant bite on her shin. 'He stroked my head once, it was really strange. The new priest's handsome, he looks a bit like Gregory Peck if you squint your eyes.' She gazed over at the sketchpad that was lying open on the grass. 'So what are you drawing, Jacky?'

'Just the view.'

He showed her the page covered in cross-hatched meshes of colour and accumulations of overlapping shapes. He had wanted to draw something lasting, something universal like Cézanne's *Mont Sainte-Victoire*: not just an impression but a swathe of time contained within a single image. His drawing was a failure, however: it said more about him than it did about the view. The colours were drab and there was something disjointed and uneasy about the composition.

'Oh, that's good.' Cathy stood up and surveyed the field then looked down at his drawing again. 'But you should put a person in there, it would be better with a person. I can pose for you if you like.' She placed her hand on her hip like a second-rate film star. The pose was ugly, awkward.

'No, don't do that, honestly it's not ...'

She dropped her arm sulkily and kicked at something on the

ground. 'Why don't you ever draw the sea, Jacky? It's just over there.' She pointed at the sharp edge of the field and the cliffs below it. 'You've never painted the sea or the beach.'

'I'm not interested in the sea.'

'Too difficult to draw you mean, all those waves moving all the time.' Cathy slumped onto the grass again. There was a long silence. She was breathing, short shallow breaths, as if she was about to say something important but wasn't sure how. When she finally spoke, her head lowered, a strand of hair coiled around her finger, the question was unexpected.

'So when are you going to visit Mam?'

'I don't know, why?' he replied carefully, coaxingly.

'Uncle Henry said she was getting better.'

'Your dad said she was getting worse.'

Cathy drew up her legs and curled them under the yellow skirt. 'What was she like?' she asked cautiously.

'Didn't you ever talk to Uncle Henry about her?'

'Yes, but he's not here now and he never really wanted to talk to me about her, no one did.'

He looked down at his sister. She had dropped the coil of hair and it had fallen across her face, all he could see was the tip of her long nose. He remembered his mother like this, sitting in the armchair in the villa kitchen reading a book or sewing. For the first time, he realised she was something shared, a shadow over both Cathy and himself. What if he were to tell his sister what had happened that day, what he had said to Father Scullion? He pictured his mother's swollen fingers rubbing the rosary beads, her blue eyes peering up at him, that strange lopsided gaze: all-seeing, or seeing nothing at all.

'I don't really remember her, Cathy. If you really want to know what she looks like there's the wedding photograph on the mantelpiece.'

'You can't see her any more, it's all faded. Was she pretty?'

'I suppose so.' He pictured her scrubbing the step outside the house on Invicta Road, red hands, brown apron, blue cardigan, dark wet step. Now she was raising her arms to peg a sheet onto the washing line in the courtyard of the villa, her fingers gripping the linen over the cord, and her body, a pale blue silhouette, coming and going as the sheet swayed gently in the breeze.

'But was she nice?'

'Sometimes. Then sometimes it was like she wasn't there at all.'

'Don't you miss her?'

'No.' He shook his head.

'If you go and see her and she's all right, I'll come with you the next time.'

'You want to go to the hospital?'

Cathy shrugged her shoulders. 'Maybe. Then if she's well enough, she can come home and we can get rid of Joyce.'

'So that's your plan,' he said laughing gently.

But Cathy wasn't laughing. 'Do you think ... do you think ...' She was looking down at her hands lying in the lap of her yellow skirt. 'Do you think it's a family thing, what she's got, why she's ill? Do you think it's hereditary?'

This had never occurred to him. 'No, of course not.'

'It's just sometimes I think if I stay here too long I'll be like her,' said Cathy, still staring at her lap.

'You think Teesby makes you go mad?'

She looked up and grinned briefly. 'It's all that sea and sand, enough to drive anyone mad. I don't blame you for not wanting to draw it.'

The sun was strong now. Cathy got up and wandered towards the side of the field where the forget-me-nots and the buttercups were growing. She watched a butterfly hovering over the flowers while she hummed 'We're in the Money' gently to herself.

He picked up the sketchpad and started a new drawing, measuring the distance between the cottage and the washing line with a pencil. Somewhere in the sky there was a lark singing, and from a faraway field he could hear the faint gentle rumble of a tractor.

He went to Winterfield for Cathy and for Uncle Henry. He caught the Sunday bus and watched the landscape scroll past the window as it had done sixteen years ago: flat bands of rough pasture interrupted by flashes of dark grey sea. The asylum was not as he remembered it, however. The building wasn't symmetrical at all, and the drive wavered round the misshapen bushes as if it was reluctant to reach its destination. The mismatch between his memory and the reality in front of him made him feel a little better as he climbed the steps to the front door. Although, as soon as he walked into the entrance hall, and smelt the bleach rising from the floors, and the deep, dull stink of cheap meat and turnips wafting along the corridor from the kitchens, his stomach turned and the lump in his throat swelled again just as it had when he was a boy.

'I've come to see Ellen Rush.'

The nurse was sitting at the desk in the visitors' parlour. 'And you are?'

'Her son.'

She looked at a ledger lying on the desk. 'And you've spoken to Matron?'

'Was I supposed to?'

She ran her finger down the list of names. When she reached the bottom of the page she looked up at him again. 'You'll have to wait here.'

After the nurse had bustled past him into the hall, he leaned against the doorway to the parlour. The room was just as he remembered it. On one side were windows that overlooked the grounds, on the other were low wooden benches pushed against the walls. At the far end of the parlour, several huddles of anxious-faced men and women were stooping over their relatives, whispering in a futile attempt at privacy. For every sound, even the shuffling of feet or the unbuttoning of a jacket, reverberated round the room.

Jack turned away. He did not want to overhear the faltering conversations. He wandered into the entrance hall again and gazed out at the grounds: at the bright green grass and the flower beds filled with vivid tulips. He was thinking of slipping out of the dark hall into the sunshine, when a draught of cold air struck his back – a sharp biting gust, as if a window had just been thrown wide open behind him. He twisted round and saw an orderly careering along the first floor landing, heading for one of the wards. As he moved forward and looked up, he could see a spiral of greying hair and grey striped dress in the gap of a half-opened door. A light flashed, followed by the crystal sound of something shattering on the floor.

The door to the room was pulled shut briskly. Then a few seconds later it opened again.

The matron appeared at the top of the landing.

'Mr Rush? Are you Mr Rush?'

She was short and bulky with thick auburn hair, some of which had slipped out of the bun at the back of her head. Her cuffs were crooked and there was a tiny splatter of blood across her apron. She climbed down the stairs towards him, her pink hand gripping the banister rail, her knuckles white.

'We're having some trouble with your mother, Mr Rush.'

'Pearson. My name's Pearson.'

'There'll be no visit today.' The matron was breathless, agitated.

'What's wrong with her?'

'You'll have to speak to the doctors.' The matron lowered her head, and she must have noticed the drops of blood on her apron because she clasped her hands across them. 'I suggest you speak to the doctors about your mother, they can explain better than I can.' She shook her head slowly. 'I'm very sorry, Mr Rush.'

Hannë

It was late summer. Bob Marigold was sitting on a stool in the bar of Hooper's Hotel. He was hunched and unbelievably thin. The skin was stretched tight over his cheekbones and his wrists looked like knotted wire. Every part of his body twitched and trembled. His foot tapped against the floor as his fingers, in syncopated rhythm, tapped against his beer glass.

'It made sense being in the camp. It was like I was being punished.' He took a sip of his beer and the liquid shivered at the edge of the glass. 'I was a bad kid, Jacky.'

'I don't remember you being that bad.'

'I was always nicking things, just never got caught. I used to take stuff from shops and people's houses and Saint Anthony's. Even in the army I lifted a couple of things. Then the Japs got me, and the only way I could cope with it was to think that I deserved it. It helped, it made sense somehow. Divine retribution and all that stuff that Father Scullion used to go on about. I think that's why I'm still here.'

Marigold's foot was now banging against the side of the bar. He gripped his knee to make it stop. 'But you can see what happens whenever I start to talk about it.'

Jack looked down at his glass.

Marigold let go of his knee and grasped his beer glass again. 'You remember Jimmy, my cousin?'

'The one at Dunkirk?'

Marigold nodded. 'When Jimmy lost his hand he couldn't talk about it. Every time he tried to tell us what had happened his voice just disappeared. And now when I try to talk about Burma I start to shake.' He lifted up his hand and his fingers trembled. 'Moira says I should go and see someone, a doctor, a trick-cyclist, so I can talk about it even more. What good's that going to do?' He squinted into the beery froth then pushed his glass away. 'You can't let your whole life be about a year and a half in a prison camp in Burma. It's got to be better than that, hasn't it?'

'It's definitely better than that,' said Jack firmly.

A few days later Cathy left for York. She had asked Jack to wave her off at the railway station.

'Come and visit,' she shouted as the train slid out of the station.

Jack was walking back along the promenade to Marine Parade when he saw Marigold on the beach, accompanied by two women wearing raincoats and headscarves. Marigold was wavering over the women, bending this way and that in the Teesby breeze. When he saw Jack, he lifted his hand and beckoned to him.

'This is Moira,' he said, draping his long arm proprietorially round the shoulder of one of the women. 'And this is her friend, Anna. They work in the same office.'

'It's Hannë,' said the second woman, stretching out her hand for Jack to shake. 'Hannë Hájková.'

They walked along the tideline – Jack and Hannë, Marigold and Moira – and as the sun came out and their shadows darkened on the sand, Hannë's face gleamed gold for a second or two. Then the sun went in again.

Hannë was wearing a beige raincoat and a blue headscarf that had slipped back off her head. Loose strands of blonde hair blew in the breeze, so fine they were almost invisible against the clouds. She was older than him. Faint lines had already begun to set under

205

her eyes and at the corners of her mouth, and she walked with a slight limp. She dipped and rose like one of the small wading birds that pecked at the edge of the shore.

They made their way across the sand, Hannë laughing at Marigold's jokes and nodding in agreement with Moira. But she was different with Jack. She looked at him for a second too long for it to be polite. She looked at him as if she was searching for something.

Jack and Hannë slowed, walked side by side, and she told him how she came to be in Teesby. Her voice was light, each syllable pronounced with the same careful emphasis. She spoke English as if she was walking a tightrope, faltering from time to time, but always continuing courageously to the end of the phrase.

The sun came out again and the four of them sat together by the snakestone cliffs, two couples, slightly apart. He watched her bend down and trace her name in a patch of damp sand – 'Hannë'.

'Han,' he read aloud.

'No, Hann-a, the ë says a.'

He wrote his own name – 'John' – 'But everyone calls me Jack.' Then he added his surname – 'Pearson'.

'Pear-son,' she said. 'Pear – like the fruit?'

'No Pearson, as in peer, like looking at something.'

Hannë smiled at him, then turned and gazed at the sea.

'So what do they call that island over there?'

'It's not an island, it's a sea-spit. It's called the Snook.'

'And what's that?' She lifted her finger and pointed at the tower.

'Nothing. A watchtower. It's nothing at all.'

She asked him about the tower again when he met her the following Saturday in the Victoria Tearooms on the promenade.

'There's nothing to see,' he said. 'Honestly, you can't go there. The air force blocked it off years ago.'

Instead they took the bus to Robin Hood's Bay and walked

206

along the beach, gazing into the rock pools at the sea sponges and the spider crabs. Hannë removed her shoes and paddled in the tide. He could see her on the horizon, a small figure backed by a strip of sea, stepping amongst the shells. She was so far away she seemed to ripple behind the haze of sea mist which separated them. From where he stood, it looked as if she was dancing.

Hannë came and went all autumn. He wouldn't see her for several weeks then she would turn up on the doorstep of the house on Marine Parade, and Mrs Veasey would shout up the stairs, 'Your Miss Hájková's here to see you, Jack.'

Except she wasn't *his* Miss Hájková. Hannë belonged somewhere else, to some other time, not to a dingy seaside town that smelt of seaweed and battered fish.

He knew almost nothing about her, other than facts. She worked as a trilingual secretary to the Assistant Manager of Brentwood Engineering on Scarborough Road. She was almost eight years older than him. She had been born in a town with an unpronounceable name. She had been a displaced person, a refugee. Like Marigold, Hannë had buried the rest. There were times, as they walked along the High Street or the beach, when he thought she was about to tell him something. He could see the words forming in her mouth and he braced himself for some dreadful story. But she always cleared her throat and coughed a little, stifling whatever it was she'd been about to say.

In November he showed her his drawings of Bleaker's Hill and the Nab. Since the spring he had completed four large pencil sketches of the thistle field, a dried-up dew pond, the ramshackle cottage, and a sharp outcrop of lichen-covered granite that resembled the fang of a prehistoric beast. He unrolled the drawings and lay them on the floor of his room. Hannë knelt down and examined them.

'You make things look like they really are,' she said, pointing to the cottage. 'You should think about going to art school, Jack. You should go to Newcastle or to London.'

'I don't want to go anywhere right now.' He smiled as broadly as he could, hoping she would understand what he was trying to say.

She ignored the remark, however. 'You shouldn't stay here, Jack, it really is a waste.'

A few days later, she sent him a large package containing a book about a Renaissance painter called Benozzo Gozzoli. There was no accompanying letter, but on the flyleaf she had written a short message:

'Dear Jack, I wanted to give you this as a gift. I saw the fresco of the Three Wise Men in Florence just before the war. I think you are going to be a great artist. With love, Hannë.'

The book was a limited edition: vellum covered, with a title inlaid in gold leaf. He had never owned anything as beautiful, it was an astonishing present. He turned it over in his hands, imagining Hannë shimmering in a light-filled foreign city before the war.

In the centre of the book, spread across two pages, was a colour reproduction of the fresco. A procession of richly clothed riders were descending a vertiginous hill topped by a castle. The colours were startling, bright lustrous reds and blues and greens. He leaned over the picture and studied the details: the misted landscape in the distance, the thin hunting dog sniffing a rabbit trail, the blond boy in the foreground on the back of a white horse. The boy must have been a prince because he was wearing a crown of sorts. He had yellow curling hair and large radiant eyes. There was something knowing in his gaze, something wistful and wary, something that reminded Jack of Hannë.

He wrote to her and thanked her for the book, but he didn't hear from her again until three weeks later when she appeared on the doorstep of Marine Parade.

'Let's go for a walk,' she said brightly.

They wandered along the beach together and he talked about

the fragments of jet that were buried in the sand. He told Hannë what someone had once told him – Henry or his mother or a teacher at school. He explained that jet was the fossilised wood of the Monkey Puzzle tree and that millions of years ago there was a black jungle of trees where the town now stood. When the trees had died they had collapsed onto the beach and lain there for centuries – great lumps of wood, washed over and over by the waves until somehow or other they turned into fossils.

Hannë crouched down in the sand and began to dig like a hungry dog looking for a bone. She searched for some time but only found two bottle tops, a glass marble, and a scratched lens that must have fallen out of a pair of wire-rimmed spectacles. She held the lens up to her eye and stared across the sand at the Snook.

'And what about the tower, Jack? Tell me about the tower.'

'I don't understand why you're so obsessed with it.'

'I'm not obsessed with it. It just looks somewhere quiet over there, somewhere not like here.'

'There's nothing to see,' he replied sharply. 'The tower's falling down, it's dangerous. And it's too far to walk there, anyway.'

'It doesn't look far from here. We could just walk across the sand,' she said.

It was true, the Snook didn't seem so far away. The tide was out and the wide gulf of water that separated the sea-spit from the beach was barely visible: from where they stood it was just a shallow stream of blue water between banks of red sand. It was as if the lens that Hannë had placed across her eye had magnified the Snook, narrowed the distance between one shoreline and the other.

'But you can't walk across there,' he insisted. 'You'd have to swim across. It's much deeper than it looks.'

'Well, in that case, if you don't show me another way, I'll have to start swimming, won't I,' said Hannë, smiling at him.

He walked slowly, reluctantly. She limped ahead, the heavy heels of her shoes kicking clumps of wet sand into the air.

When they reached the swing bridge that crossed the river, they stopped for a moment and leaned over the railings. He could see the sea-spit in between the thin trees that grew at the edge of the marsh. The wooden huts and the sound mirror from the first war were still standing, so were the steel masts of the radar from the second. But when they finally arrived at the head of the causeway twenty minutes later, he noticed that the old red and white barrier had been replaced by a flimsy-looking padlocked gate.

'Let's go on.' Hannë was gripping the top rail of the gate, about to climb over it.

'We can't go on any further than this.' He pointed at the old sign planted in the sand: 'Property of the Air Ministry. Trespassers will be Prosecuted'. Although the raised metal letters were rusting away and the words no longer possessed the authority they once had.

'But there's no one here,' she said, clambering onto the gate and perching on the top bar. 'I can't see anyone.' She slid clumsily down onto the other side.

He stood motionless, just as he had done once before. He watched her step, at first cautiously then more confidently, over the causeway. The gap between them, in reality a distance of about a hundred feet, was suddenly immense. He waited, hoping that she would at least turn and wave, but she carried on towards the Snook without looking back. He kicked at the shells that had piled up beside the concrete gatepost. She had reminded him of things he had tried to forget: the blue felt hat with the feather pinned to the band, the shadow on the pavement, his mother's cold white fingers.

'I'm going back,' he called over the gate. But the words were blown sideways by the wind and Hannë didn't hear him. He turned and started to walk slowly towards the coast road. The tide was coming in and the waves were spilling over the marsh.

'If you don't come now, you'll be stuck there all day,' he shouted over his shoulder. But Hannë had already disappeared.

He waited for her back at the bridge. It was over an hour before he finally saw her, walking uncomfortably up the road.

She called to him. 'Why didn't you come with me?'

'It's dangerous, I told you.'

She shook her head. 'It's beautiful.'

'What is?'

'The view from the tower, it's beautiful, Jack.'

Just before Christmas he was standing at his bedroom window when he saw Hannë making her way along the promenade with another man. She was wearing a cherry-coloured scarf and a coat he hadn't seen before. She walked unsteadily beside the man, grasping his arm for support as they were buffeted by the squalls of wind and sand from the beach. Because of the force of the wind, her companion had removed his hat. From the window Jack could see a shimmer of light on his scalp and a few sparse strands of grey hair growing from his crown. They rose and fell with every gust, and the man, aware of the spectacle above his head, clamped his hand over his scalp to hold the hair in place. Jack watched the couple for several minutes before they turned away from the sea front and got into a large green car parked in front of the Victoria Tearooms.

Christmas started festively then descended quickly into gloom. On Christmas Eve he went drinking with Marigold and forgot he had promised Cathy, who was home for the holiday, that he would accompany her to midnight mass. The following day, after a quiet lunch with Mrs Veasey in the empty dining room, he took Cathy's present, a silver-plated bracelet, to Invicta Road.

'She's gone out with one of her friends,' said Maurice in the doorway. 'And she's not very happy with you for standing her up.'

When he went to Invicta Road again on Boxing Day Cathy had already left for York.

The winter of 1948 was neither as long nor as severe as the year before. The snow still fell, however, and it lay for some weeks, a thin greying sheet across the beach and the town. It was too cold to draw on the Nab. At weekends Jack sat in his room and painted the scenes he had sketched in the spring and summer. He removed the trees and the buildings, and bathed the skies in stains of pink or pale green, until the once-familiar places appeared strange to him. As he waited for the watercolour washes to soak into the paper, he lay on the bed. He cushioned his back with one of Mrs Veasey's thin pillows folded in two and thought about Hannë.

It wasn't until the end of February that he saw Hannë again, in the blue-lit basement of the Zetland Club.

'Look what we found for you!' said Marigold, gesturing towards her with his beer glass.

She was standing at the edge of the dance floor, illuminated now and then by a spotlight that swung across the room. She wore an evening gown that must have been made in the thirties. He remembered seeing pictures of film stars wearing clothes like it. It was pale turquoise, the colour of the sea when the sun came out. Under the iridescence of the Zetland's mirror ball, there was something tragic about that dress. It hinted at the sort of woman Hannë might have become had the war not taken place, a woman who would never have expected to find herself in the Zetland Club on Teesby promenade, tentatively courted by a man like Jack.

They danced uneasily in the aquatic gloom. Her shoulders were stiff and her spine rigid. She was holding herself back, determined to keep a small sliver of space between them.

'I haven't seen you for a long time,' he said.

'I wasn't very well,' she replied.

'Flu or something?'

'Yes, flu,' she said quickly.

They danced on in silence and he pictured the man on the promenade, the way she had clutched his arm.

'I saw you with someone before Christmas. I wondered who it was,' he said as casually he could.

'Saw me with someone?' She repeated the phrase slowly as if she hadn't understood.

'I saw you getting into a green Riley with someone, just before Christmas. No law against it, of course,' he added awkwardly.

'Mr Latimer.'

'Who?'

'Someone who helped me when I first arrived.'

'In Teesby?'

'In England. He lives in London.'

'He's a friend of yours?'

She laughed and nodded. 'Yes, he's a friend, but he lives in London and I don't see him very often.'

After the second dance, Hannë said she was tired. She sat at the table with her head bowed slightly. He gazed at her over the rim of his beer glass. She had rolled her thin hair into a chignon that rested on the nape of her neck. He could see the sharp, high slant of her cheekbones and the jutting line of her jaw. She was cold and still: untouchable.

He looked away from her, glanced at a group of women by the entrance. And as he turned back to Hannë again, the lights over the dance floor dimmed for a second or two, then faded completely. In the dark, the music stopped. There was a hush followed by a frantic rustling of hands in jacket pockets. In the flash of cigarette lighters and matches, he could see Hannë's face. She was staring directly at him as if she was about to ask him a question. Then the band started up, playing blindly, 'When the Lights Go On Again', and everyone laughed and began to sing. Only Hannë was silent. Without a word, she took her coat from the back of the chair, grasped his hand and led him slowly up the narrow staircase to the street.

In his bedroom on Marine Parade, he lit two candles. Hannë removed her coat and sat on the edge of the bed. She was almost invisible in the weak glow: vaporous, like steam in a cold room. He sat down beside her and took her hand, he could hardly feel the touch of her fingers in his palm. They sat listening to the seagulls outside the window and the Whitby bus, which slowed down at the stop in front of the house then accelerated again up the hill. In the lull that followed, he could hear Mrs Veasey calling to her cat from the kitchen window, and someone peeing in the toilet on the landing above them – the heavy sound of liquid hitting the pan, the flush and thunder of the water along the pipes, then the shrill whistle of air from the cistern. It was only after Mrs Veasey had shut the kitchen door and climbed the stairs to her room, that Hannë moved towards Jack and kissed him lightly on the mouth.

Jack loved Hannë. He loved her solemn face, the sound of her voice, her rare laughter, like the light ripple of the narrow stream that crossed the Nab and trickled over the cliffs into the sea.

He loved her, but he didn't know what to do next, what was expected of him: in Teesby people got married. He sat in the drawing office at Wilkie's trying to imagine Hannë standing outside one of the new houses on Nab Lane with a baby in her arms. It was a predictable picture, but it was the only one he had.

One lunchtime, he went to Trotmans on the High Street and bought an engagement ring, a diamond chip set on a thin grey band of silver.

'It's very unique, sir,' said the sales assistant as he slipped it inside the box. 'I'm certain the lady will like it.'

But Jack wasn't sure.

He kept the ring loose in his trouser pocket and clutched it every so often, feeling the cold metal between his fingers. He almost proposed when they were walking beside the river one afternoon, and again when they were lying together in his bed in the house on Marine Parade.

The ring was in his pocket when they climbed the hill to the Nab on the first frost-free morning since autumn. It was a mild day, although the breeze soon brought a rain shower that swept across the moor like a thin curtain drawn over the pale blue sky. They sheltered in a barn filled with old feed sacks and dishevelled bales of hay. He pulled at one of the bales, flattening it into a bed, and they made love as the rain fell against the metal roof.

Afterwards, she lay on her back, her hands clasped tight across her stomach.

He lay beside her. He had pulled the ring out of his pocket and was gripping it inside his hand.

'You're very quiet. Are you all right?' he asked.

'Yes. It's just, sometimes I get . . .' She searched for a word. 'I get homesick. It's like an illness.' She rolled over on her side towards him. 'You're lucky to be at home, where you've always lived.'

'Teesby's never really felt like home.'

Hannë wasn't listening. 'I had a daughter, Jack, a family.'

He was not expecting this, not now, not here in the barn. 'You were married?'

'Yes,' she replied lightly, as if she had almost forgotten her husband. 'Yes, I was married.'

He pictured Hannë sitting at a table beside a child in a high-chair, beside a suited and upright man. The room was like the dining room in the villa, filled with objects they had collected together, precious glass and china, pictures and books.

'My daughter was called Erika.' The lines around Hannë's mouth had deepened and her eyes were colourless. 'I thought she was safe. I'd found someone to look after her. But in the end I was safer in the camp than she was.'

The sunshine broke through a gap in the rafters. He could see the sheen of a scar on her forehead.

'Erika was in Dresden,' she said quietly.

'Dresden.' The name made him shudder. He remembered the models in the basement studio at Danesfield House, all those tiny fragile walls and roofs carefully fashioned from linoleum. He saw Lenny in the Lancaster again.

'The bombing was so bad that when I went back I couldn't even find the street. Nothing left. Everything flattened. I was standing where the street had been and there was nothing there.'

It was as if she had opened a door onto a vast dark space and was inviting him to step inside with her, and yet he could barely cross the threshold. The suited, upright husband would have taken her in his arms, would have held her for as long as she needed, would have known what to say. All Jack could manage was: 'I'm so sorry.' He reached over and tried to touch her face, but Hannë was too far away.

'It makes me ill sometimes.' As she said the words she looked old. Her eyes had sunk into her face, her mouth drooped strangely on one side.

She smiled weakly at him. 'I wanted you to know so that you could understand.'

The rain had stopped, but there were intermittent drops still falling from the rafters onto the sacks below. He could hear a sheep bleating outside on the moor. He put his hand in his pocket and let the ring go.

Spring turned into summer again. He was standing at his board in Wilkie's drawing office, tracing plans and elevations. Mr Wilkie and his son had purchased a stretch of flat wetland on the other side of the river and were planning an estate, a complicated operation of crescents and cul-de-sacs with patriotic names like Windsor Drive and Buckingham Close. The draughting was dull work. The houses were all the same: semi-detached with bow windows, brickwork on the ground floor and a dismal-coloured render above.

He inked in the lines and thought about Hannë, remembered her small hands holding a bunch of frosted snowdrops, the flower pattern on her dress in the sombre light of the Regent, her shadowed face as they climbed the stairs to his room, her light, pale clothes lying on the chair beneath his.

Hannë had gone. She had told him she was leaving as they sat in the Victoria Tearooms one rainy afternoon in May. He realised then that their conversation in the barn had been a prelude to this. When he reached out to take her hand, she had pulled it away from him.

She gave him a gift. *The Complete Works of Samuel Palmer*, a perceptive choice. On the flyleaf she had written: 'To Jack, I won't forget you. With all my love, Hannë.'

She left a few days later, driven away in a dark green Riley Continental.

But Jack saw Hannë time and time again. He saw her in the faces of the women he passed on the promenade and in the shops on the High Street. He saw her surrounded by a group of soldiers slouched against the bar in the Zetland Club. He saw her at the window of the Whitby bus, and on the beach, looking at the ground, as if she was searching for something in the sand. He wanted to run towards her and tell her he had made a mistake. He wanted to push his hand into his pocket, give her the ring and say, 'I love you, Hannë'.

'Oh, for God's sake, give it up,' muttered Marigold, clutching his trembling glass of beer in the bar of Hooper's Hotel. 'She wasn't for you. Not your type. I was surprised you got together in the first place.'

'What do you mean?' asked Jack coolly.

'She had her problems.' Marigold shifted uncomfortably on

the bar stool. 'Anyway she left weeks ago, went back to London. Moira told me she got married.'

Everyone was leaving Teesby. In the autumn, Marigold got a job with a printer in Sunderland. Mrs Veasey said she was thinking of selling the house and moving in with her sister in Withernsea. Then just before Christmas, Cathy turned up at Marine Parade and told him she was getting married.

'Look,' she said, thrusting the ring in front of him.

It was just like the one he had bought Hannë, the ring that was sitting in its box at the back of one of the pigeonholes in Uncle Henry's roll-top desk.

'I'm going to Tubac, Arizona,' she announced proudly.

'What?'

'America.' Cathy inched into the room, eyed the armchair as if she was about to sit down then appeared to change her mind. 'I met Rickie in York, at a dance.' She gazed down at the ring and rubbed the tiny stone with her thumb.

'I don't understand. What about being a teacher?'

'I didn't like it,' she muttered. 'I wanted to talk to you about it, but you never came to visit.'

He ignored this. 'You're only eighteen, Cathy. Can't you wait?'

In fact she looked a lot younger than eighteen. Her face was still rounded and pouting. She had done something different with her hair, pinned a bit of it off her forehead with a star-headed clip, and she was wearing lipstick, but it didn't make her look any older.

'I knew you'd say that.' She stuffed her hands into her skirt pockets. 'That's why I waited until now to tell you. Dad says it's all right. He likes Rickie.'

Jack cut across her. 'And where the hell's Arizona, anyway?'

'It's the desert, almost in Mexico.'

'You're going all that way, on your own?'

'I'll be with Rickie.' She sighed. 'You're not going to change my mind. It's all sorted. I knew you'd never understand.' She turned away from him and he thought the conversation was over. Then she spun back again, breathing fast, short breaths. 'I wanted to talk to you about it all, about teaching, about me, about Mam. I asked you to come to York but you never did. I was going to talk to you at Christmas but you never turned up. You're always avoiding things. You're not the only one who hasn't got a mother, you know.'

The words stunned him. If he could have done, he would have stuttered, but you don't understand *me*. You don't know what it was like being with her. You don't know what happened.

Cathy turned away from him again. He watched her stalk out of the room and slam the door behind her.

He told no one that he was planning to leave Teesby too. It was surprisingly easy. He wrote to the teacher at the Slade who he had worked with during the war. A few weeks later he received an invitation to an interview at the school. He took the suitcase down from the top of the wardrobe, and made a portfolio from two sheets of cardboard to contain the drawings and the paintings of the Nab.

A week before he left for London, Jack caught the bus to Winterfield again. He had no intention of visiting his mother, no intention of even stepping inside the gates. When he got off the bus, he wasn't certain why he had bothered to make the journey at all.

He walked to the entrance and looked up the drive. It was a warm day, Winterfield was unusually leafy and green. Five or six patients were sitting in wheelchairs under the shade of one of a pair of lime trees. Several others were pacing along the paths, some frantically, others shuffling, hardly lifting their feet at all. In the distance, a woman in a grey dress was raking the gravel by the doorway to the hospital, and a second woman was bending down, picking out groundsel shoots and dandelions from the drive.

His mother could have been one of the patients working in the garden. She might have been the tall woman stamping down the path, waving her arms from side to side, or she might have been the gaunt figure slumped in the wheelchair. As he stood at the entrance, clutching the sun-warmed bars of the asylum gates, he decided that he did not need to know. He only needed to know that she was safe, filed away like a document that he had to keep but would rather forget about.

ELLEN

1928–29

Beadie

Mrs Tibbs died on a Thursday in early April. She must have fallen out of bed in the night. When Ellen opened the curtains that morning, she found her lying face down on the Persian rug like a doll that had been flung on the floor by an angry child.

Ellen called to Beadie from the top of the stairs and together they placed her carefully back on the bed, though it hardly needed two of them to lift her.

'Fill a basin with warm water,' murmured Beadie softly, as if she hoped the old lady was still asleep. 'And I'll go and fetch some towels.'

That morning was just the same as the morning before. A soft mist dissolved outside the window: a veil lifting on the lilac bushes and the bright new grass pinpricked with violets so dark they were almost black. It was the beginning of another hopeful spring day, and yet everything had changed, would keep on changing. And the change was the sound of something breaking – glass shattering as it hit the ground.

They washed Mrs Tibbs gently. Then they dressed her in her wedding gown. Beadie arranged the flounces and the frills and the wide lace collar round her face, and Ellen dabbed Violette Précieuse onto Mrs Tibbs's wrinkled wrists and over the folds of the thin skin around her neck.

'And don't forget the wig,' said Beadie. 'Give it a bit of a clean and a brush and we'll pin it on her.'

They chose a mauve lining for the coffin. And in Mrs Tibbs's hands they placed a bouquet of violets that Jack had picked from the garden. It was only after she was ready and they had closed the shutters in all the rooms that both women sat down and cried.

Two days before the funeral Ellen went into town to buy some black ribbon for her hat. She had just stepped out of the haberdasher's when she ran headlong into Maurice Rush, carrying three rolls of wallpaper under his arm.

'Watch yourself, Miss!' He reached out to stop her tripping over, and the wallpaper tumbled onto the pavement. Together they crouched down and picked the rolls up, then Maurice straightened himself and said, 'Haven't seen you for a long while, Miss Pearson.'

'I've been busy,' she replied uncomfortably, remembering the sticky table in Hooper's Hotel at which they had sat and the half pint of mild that Maurice had gazed into when she had talked about the colours. Then she pictured Jack, back at the villa, helping Beadie make the bread, coaxing the flour and water with his fingers until it turned into dough. She was certain that Maurice knew about Jack, everyone in Teesby knew about Jack. Was that what he was thinking about when he smiled at her, the rolls of wallpaper safely lodged under his arm again?

'I was sorry to hear about Mrs Tibbs,' he said. 'A nice lady by all accounts.'

'She was always very kind,' replied Ellen.

Since the last time she had seen him, Maurice Rush had slipped from youth into middle age. He was solid, broad chested with thick arms and short legs. His face, which used to be oval, had a fleshy squareness to it, and there were little bits of white wiry hair in his moustache.

'I suppose you'll be moving on now.' There was an odd look in his eyes.

'I've got plans,' she said as brightly as she could.

She thought he was going to ask her what those plans were. He opened his mouth then closed it again, looked at her a little longer with that strange glazed expression, and said, 'Well, I'd better be getting on, Miss Pearson.'

Mrs Tibbs was buried in the cemetery next to the Quaker Meeting House on the side of a hill that overlooked the sea. The grass was dotted with buttercups and daisies, and thick twists of brambles covered the stone walls. As Mrs Tibbs's coffin was lowered into the grave all Ellen could hear was the humming of the bees inside the flowers and the soft hissing of the waves.

After the funeral, they sat round the dining room table in the villa, while Mr Boothby, the notary, read Mrs Tibbs's will. There were several bequests: to the Society of Friends, to the Cats' Protection League, and to a large family called Hodge, who no one had heard of. Mrs Tibbs had left fifty pounds each to Ellen and Beadie, and between them they had inherited the contents of her wardrobe: the moth-holed silk pelisses and the opera cloaks and the fur collars.

The villa and the grounds had been willed to a distant relative in the Indian Civil Service, a second cousin of Lieutenant John Gargett.

'Mr Quinlan has a number of commitments and won't be able to return to England until the middle of next year,' said Mr Boothby gravely. 'It's been decided that Miss Pearson will take care of the property until his arrival.' He pointed at Ellen across the table. 'But don't imagine you'll be staying on afterwards, Mr Quinlan will be organising his own staff.'

'And what about me?' cried Beadie from the other end of the table.

'There's no need for the two of you,' said Mr Boothby, peering over the top of his spectacles. 'If you ask me, there wasn't enough work for you both when she was alive, let alone now. Mr Quinlan's made himself clear, one servant. You're to go back wherever you came from, Miss ...' He stared down at the will again and made a face. 'Miss Beadie.'

After Mr Boothby had left, Beadie sat in the kitchen staring glumly ahead. Ellen made her a cup of tea and placed it beside her on the table, but Beadie didn't move. A grey milky skim grew across the liquid.

'I were twelve years old when I came here,' she muttered finally. 'Nearly my whole life. Mrs Tibbs came to get me from the Nab. She came specially for me. "I'd like you to come down to the villa and look after me, Beadie," that's what she said. She called me by my name like we were friends. She was pregnant with little Annabelle then. I saw the baby born. I saw Mr Tibbs weep after I'd told him they were both safe.'

Beadie peered down at the cup and pushed it away.

'I looked after her when she had the measles. I had to tell her that the child was gone and Mr Tibbs too. And she said to me, "Close all the shutters, Beadie, and don't you ever leave me."'

Ellen reached across to take her hand. 'You don't have to go. You can stay here. No one will ever know.' She looked at Jack standing uncomfortably by the dresser watching them both. She glanced at the sink and the copper pans hanging in a line above it, and Casaubon curled in the armchair by the range. She tried to imagine the kitchen without Beadie, then she gripped Beadie's hand as hard as she could. 'I don't want you to go, if you go it'll all fall apart.'

But Beadie wasn't listening. 'Thought I'd be the one to leave here first, not her. She were kinder than my ma. This were my home.'

*

Beadie went to bed early that evening. She spent most of the night pacing across her room. Ellen could hear the faint thump of her feet on the floorboards.

In the morning, however, she was up before anyone else, frying bacon on the range.

'I'll be off tomorrow morning, if that's all right with you.'

'But where are you going to go?'

Beadie flipped the bacon over. 'Don't fuss me, Ellen,' she said.

All day Beadie worked at the kitchen table, making cakes and biscuits and pies. Jack stood beside her on a tomato crate and watched her weigh the ingredients then beat the butter into the sugar and add the eggs. She made coffee cake with walnuts on the top, and choux buns filled with sweetened cream, and saffron-coloured gingerbread, and fruit cake, and parkin to be kept for later. She rolled out pale yellow pastry and made bite-size apple pies and Bakewell tarts.

'We're going to have a party,' declared Beadie, as she slid the pies into the oven.

In the late afternoon, they carried the round table from the morning room onto the lawn. Then Ellen went to the shed and pulled out half a dozen old Japanese lanterns which she hung from the lower branches of the Monkey Puzzle tree.

'What's happening, Ma?' asked Jack.

'It's a party for Beadie.'

'Why?'

Ellen wasn't sure how to reply. 'Because it's the end of things, my love. And it'll soon be the beginning of something new.'

He didn't catch the sadness in her voice. He skipped away across the garden and began to pull at the long-stemmed buttercups that had taken over the rose beds. He selected the flowers carefully as if it was the most important task in the world, and when he had collected a fistful, he ran towards her, the yellow heads bobbing up and down.

'They're for the table, Ma,' he said, handing her the bunch.

As she placed them in the vase, she wondered how much he would remember of that day: the sweet smell of the baking cakes from the kitchen, the sound of the squawking starling babies in their nest in a hole in the wall, her own face, pale blue, under the branches of the Monkey Puzzle tree.

In the evening, after they had eaten, Beadie and Ellen watched Jack dancing after the moths that fluttered round the lanterns. They were like flakes of silver spinning above his head. He stretched out his hand and they rose up in gentle waves then fell again.

'Look, Ma,' he called to her.

'Beautiful, Jacky.'

Then Beadie sang a song:

> *The water is wide, I cannot get over*
> *And neither have I wings to fly*
> *Bring me a boat that will carry two*
> *And both shall row, my love and I.*

The world halted when Beadie sang: the owl perched on the roof above them, the mice creeping through the long grass by the stone wall, the small scratching beetles under the bark of the Monkey Puzzle. And the sea: even the sea stopped for Beadie.

'That was the best day, Ma,' Jack said, when she put him to bed.

'Yes, it was, Jacky.' Ellen sat on the edge of the mattress and pulled the covers over his narrow shoulders. 'You mustn't forget it. You must hold onto the good memories.'

She watched him as he sank into sleep, he must have been thinking of the grey moths and the buttercup petals glowing in the moonlight. His face relaxed then slumped. His mouth was open slightly, his eyes shut tight. This was what he would look like when he was old, she thought, brushing her hand across his forehead.

And where would she be then? Long gone, buried next to Da and Ma in Saint Anthony's, buried in the sand on the Snook.

'The best day,' Jack mumbled again before he finally slept.

The following morning, Beadie stood in the kitchen wearing Mr Tibbs's brown tweed jacket and a straw boater with orange ribbons that must have belonged to Annabelle. At her feet was a large wicker basket containing Casaubon. He was old now, he could hardly move, just twisted and turned stiffly in an attempt to relieve his aching bones.

Beadie was crying silently. Ellen could see the watery surface of her eyes wobble slightly and bulge as the teardrops began to form. A tear slipped over the edge of her eye socket and ran down the long channel between her nose and her cheek.

She looked round the kitchen, at her stone sink, at her mixing bowls standing on the dresser. Then her weepy eyes settled on Jack. She reached out and grasped his shoulder with her bony hand.

'You look after your ma. You promise me that, young man. You look after her.'

They followed Beadie out of the front door and stood on the drive as she walked through the villa gates.

'Where's she going, Ma?' Jack pulled on his mother's hand. 'Where's Beadie going?'

When Ellen didn't answer, he dashed after Beadie, out of the gate and up the hill. He ran so fast that the dust from the gravel rose up in clouds. And as he turned into the lane, a small flock of finches flew out of the hedge and scattered across the fields.

He returned about ten minutes later. Ellen heard him before she saw him, feet trudging across the gravel, the heavy laboured walk of an elderly man.

'I don't know where she went,' he said, panting. 'She was going up the hill and then she just . . . she just disappeared.'

Maurice

Henry had come for tea. He was sitting at Beadie's end of the kitchen table finishing the last piece of coffee cake.

'At least you've got a year's grace, Nell,' he said, pulling out the walnuts from the sponge and laying them on the side of his plate. 'Enough time to find yourself another job.'

Ellen was looking out of the window at Jack, who was thrashing the yellow grass growing by the gate with a long stick. She had already searched through the Situations Vacant in the *Echo*, but there was little she could do with a child in tow.

Without turning round she said tentatively, 'I could look after you, Henry. If you got a little house, we could all live together.'

She heard his cup rattle in the saucer, followed by the chime of a teaspoon when it hit the tiled floor. Henry groaned as he bent down to pick it up.

'I'm a town clerk, they don't pay us that much. And you don't want to rely on me, Nell, do you? I told you when he was born that you'd have to plan ahead.'

She hated Henry then, just as she had hated him all those years ago after Da had died. He always shrugged her off, sloped away from her, back to his precious rooms in Marine Parade with his desk full of secrets, old letters that he wouldn't let her read and half-hidden photographs he didn't let her see. This time she didn't shout at him. Instead she opened the window

230

and called to Jack, 'You be careful with that stick or you'll have your eye out!'

Henry poured himself another cup of tea. 'I'm sure Mrs Veasey would let you stay at Marine Parade for a few weeks if you still hadn't got anything by then.' He pushed the plate of walnuts away from him. 'Although maybe in the end you're going to have to think about finding somewhere for Jack to go.'

Father Scullion's face loomed up at her, she could see him sitting on the pew, the white chasuble, the muddy shoes. 'Like the Sacred Heart, I suppose?' She made a faint snorting noise in her nostrils as if Henry had made a bad joke.

'Well, you must have some savings, and there's the fifty pounds that Mrs Tibbs left you. And I might be able to find a little bit to help you out.'

So that was it, Henry would find a little bit to send Jack away but not to help them live together.

She stood at the window and watched the branches of the Monkey Puzzle tree shudder in the breeze. Jack was standing underneath in the shadow, the stick loosely in his hand, gazing at her sullenly.

Life in the villa was quiet now. Time stretched again. Ellen tried to fill the lengthening hours with dull tasks, cleaning and sorting and packing away. She went through the clothes in Mrs Tibbs's wardrobe, pulling out the bustled evening gowns made in Paris and the velvet cloaks and jackets labelled Harrods or Liberty and Co. Beadie had refused to take any of the clothes apart from the tweed jacket and the boater. 'You have them, Ellen, they're not my style,' she had said before she left. Sometimes Ellen tried on the dresses that now belonged to her, but most of them were far too small.

When she had emptied the wardrobe, she wandered through the rooms, glancing at the discoloured spines of the books in the library and the dull blue gleam of the salt cellar in the dining room, eyeing John Gargett's pocket watch on the drawing room mantelpiece, which she had stopped winding now that Mrs Tibbs was gone. She missed Beadie's clatter, and the high-pitched ring of Mrs Tibbs's bell, and the rhythmic popping of Casaubon's claws tearing through the seat of one of the upholstered chairs.

Jack kept to himself. She watched him from the morning room window as he stalked round the edges of the garden, kicking at things: stones and snail shells and birds' eggs that had fallen from their nests. At meal times he was taciturn and sulky, refusing to eat the food that Ellen cooked.

'This isn't like Beadie's shepherd's pie,' he muttered.

No one came to the villa except Mr Thurrock, the notary's assistant, who had been given the task of making an inventory of Mrs Tibbs's possessions. Every Wednesday he sat in an armchair with his long legs crossed, notebook on his lap, while Ellen pulled out drawers of linen or silver cutlery, and called out the name of every object.

'Crumb scoop, plated and engraved with stag handle. One pair of grape scissors in Morocco case. One fluted sugar basin, gilt inside.'

Mr Thurrock complained. He complained about the steepness of the hill up to the villa, about Jack's muddy boots in the hallway, about the dryness of the cake or the strength of the tea that Ellen had made him; about the dust in the bedrooms and the spring that had dislodged itself in the seat of the armchair in Mrs Tibbs's drawing room. He had an inquisitive face, like a squirrel or a stoat, always shifting and twitching. She wondered briefly if he didn't trust her. Often she would catch him fumbling in the backs of cupboards they had already been through as if he was checking that the objects were still there.

And yet she began to look forward to his visits. She liked the smell of the Brilliantine that rose up from the collar of his jacket. She liked the way that he stood square and pushed his hands deep into his pockets when he talked to her. And she liked the faint trace of the blond moustache above his narrow lips. She smiled at him. She changed her hair for him. She dusted her face with Mrs Tibbs's Poudre d'Amour. Mr Thurrock didn't seem to notice.

In the summer, when it was warm enough, Ellen took a pair of dining room chairs and a small card table out onto the lawn. She and Jack ate their breakfast and lunch there listening to the creak of the gates in the breeze. The novelty of eating outside distracted Jack, and for a few weeks he forgot to be miserable. He carried a box of wooden bricks onto the lawn and built castles and mansions while Ellen sewed buttons back onto his shirts or tried to make something of the dresses that Mrs Tibbs had left her.

Jack didn't mention either Beadie or Casaubon any more, he must have realised there wasn't any point. He was a quiet, self-contained child. When he grew bored of the bricks he traipsed round the flower beds, crouching down and digging holes in the dry earth in a hunt for treasure. She looked at him over her sewing, watched him as he scooped up the loose earth and let it trickle out of his hands and over his shorts. He was unaware of anything but the feel of the soil running through his fingers.

It was from the garden after lunch one afternoon that Ellen saw a figure climbing up the path from the town. It wasn't Henry because the man was neither tall enough nor hunched enough to be her brother. It wasn't Mr Thurrock either, because it wasn't a Wednesday morning, it was a Saturday afternoon. The man wore a tweed cap and carried a walking cane. As he climbed the hill, he swung the cane from side to side, then he kicked something in the road – a stone or a bottle – and did a little sidestep as if he was dancing the Black Bottom.

Halfway up the hill at the bend in the lane, the man vanished from sight. Either he had changed his mind and turned back or he had paused at the five-bar gate hidden from view by the line of poplars at the edge of the road. She stood for a while peering over the balustrade. But when he didn't appear again, she gave up and collected the glasses and the jug and carried them back to the kitchen.

By the time she had returned to the garden for the dirty plates, the man was already standing at the villa gates.

'Come to see the Duchess in her fancy house,' said Maurice Rush when he saw her on the drive. He thrust his moustachioed face between the bars of the gate and grinned at her.

She knew then that she would marry him, that it was only a question of time. This small square man with his neat clothes, shiny shoes and thin lank hair, was the man who would be her husband: the thought provoked neither joy nor dismay. As she crossed the lawn to open the gates, she practised her new name under her breath: 'Ellen Rush, Mrs Rush, Mrs Maurice Rush.'

She showed Maurice round the house that afternoon. She opened the shutters as they went from room to room, Maurice running his hands along the paintwork. He was knowledgeable about the different types of wallpaper and how they were made, and the names of all the colours.

In the library he stroked the walls and said, 'Now this is a good paper, William Morris if I'm not mistaken. Hand printed, wooden blocks, a lot of work.' In Mrs Tibbs's drawing room he gazed up and said, 'Ah, yes, Nile Blue, lovely colour, pity she couldn't see it.'

'She could feel it though,' Ellen replied. 'Colours vibrate like sound. You can feel them in the air.'

Maurice laughed uneasily. 'You and your colours, Miss Pearson. You've got some funny ideas.'

She took him downstairs and boiled the kettle on the range. He stood close to her. She could feel the rough tweed of his jacket against her bare arm, and she remembered the stone collector's

234

cold hand in hers. Maurice had leaned his cane against one of the chairs and had laid his cap on the kitchen table. It was an incongruous sight, the tweed cap on the pine table, quite ordinary and yet intimate. As she put the teapot down beside it, she could see a single brown hair that had loosely woven itself into the tweed.

'Oh, my mistake, Miss Pearson,' said Maurice snatching up the cap. 'Should never leave a hat on a table, brings bad luck.'

He hung it from a hook on the back of the kitchen door, then helped her with the cups and saucers. She could smell him faintly: turpentine and the sweet leathery fragrance of his cologne. It floated towards her as he carried the tea plates to the table. When he looked at her, he wore the same expression on his face that he had worn when she had met him on the High Street, a quiet unfocused look as if he was trying to make a decision about something difficult.

Maurice Rush returned the following Saturday afternoon. Maurice Rush returned every Saturday until long after Christmas.

On Saturday afternoons, she did what she could. She put on her best dress, and looped up her hair with diamante clips or with ribbons that she had found in Mrs Tibbs's dressing table drawers. She dusted her face with Poudre d'Amour, dotted spots of rouge on her cheeks and dabbed her wrists with Yardley's April Violets.

She thought the proposal might come sooner than it did. It wasn't until late January that he finally stretched his hand over the kitchen table and grasped her fingers.

'I think you know what I'm going to ask you.'

It was difficult to reply to this, so she smiled and tried to look confused.

'I should have asked you a long time ago.' He coughed and cleared his throat. 'Would you like to marry me, Ellen?'

Before she could respond, he started off again, the words tumbling out of his mouth.

'You see, I've always thought ... well, I've always liked you very much. And when I saw you on the High Street that time last year ... well ... well. I know people say things about you ... but ... well. And of course I'd be happy to be a father to Jack. And I thought we could use your little nest egg from Mrs Tibbs to get ourselves a house ... not with Ma, of course ... I thought maybe we could get ourselves a cottage, one of the fishermen's cottages with a nice garden and a view of the sea ... thought you'd like that.' He paused, 'Oh and there's this ...'

He pulled a piece of paper out of his jacket pocket. Printed at the top of the page in black gothic script were the words: 'Rush and Company. Decorative Painters and Paper-Hangers. All estimates speedily delivered. All work speedily completed.'

'Starting my own business.' He pointed at the letter heading. 'Do you like it? Made it up myself. Rush, you see, like in a hurry.'

It was the best offer she was likely to get.

'Of course I'll marry you, Maurice,' she said, smiling as sweetly as she could.

After Maurice had left, she searched for Jack. He had got into the habit of disappearing on Saturday afternoons. Often she would discover him in the washhouse playing with the mangle or in the shed sitting in Mrs Tibbs's invalid chair, pushing it backwards and forwards, his hands gripping the tops of the wheels. That evening, however, he was neither in the washhouse nor in the shed, he didn't appear to be in the garden either. She returned to the villa, and worked her way through the house from his bedroom and hers to the drawing room and the dining room then back to the kitchen again.

'Jacky, I've got something to tell you. Good news, Jacky.' She really did think it was good news. It sparkled round her like a halo.

The house was silent and empty. She walked across the yard a second time and peered into the washhouse again, then scoured the edges of the grounds, the thickets of brambles and the old raspberry canes. It was dark now, she could see the street lights glimmering in the cold mist and the white glow from the chimneys of the works. She called Jack again and again, but he didn't appear.

Her calmness began to fizzle away. All her thoughts, which until then she had managed to keep in straight logical lines, coiled up and tangled into knots.

'Jacky! Jacky, where are you!'

In desperation she marched up the lane and onto the moor. There was only a sliver of a moon that night, and when she reached the edge of the Nab she could barely move for fear of falling over or twisting her ankle on the pitted path. She struggled onward, certain she could hear someone breathing gently just ahead of her. But when she reached the source of the noise there were half a dozen sheep standing on the heather, staring at her, their bulging eyes gleaming faintly in the dark. As she stumbled back towards the lane, they careered away, their hooves thundering across the moor.

She found Jack standing in the kitchen doorway, clutching the door frame with his small hand.

'Didn't you hear me calling?' By then she was frantic. Her fear of losing him had collided with the relief of seeing him again. She grasped his shoulders. 'You must have heard me! You must have known I was worried!'

'You're going to marry Maurice Rush and we're going to leave here and never come back.'

She paused, hands still gripping his shoulders. 'You were listening?'

He lowered his head.

'Where were you, Jacky?'

'In the corridor, outside the kitchen door.'

The bright halo of good news faded. She saw it for what it was. She saw it through Jack's eyes, the scene at the kitchen table: a stocky middle-aged man in a Fair Isle pullover clutching the fingers of his no-hope mother.

'You know it's wrong to listen to people's private conversations.' She tried to take his hand, but he wouldn't let her. He pulled it away and hid it tight behind his back.

'Listen Jacky, we're going to have our own home. I know it won't be like this one but it'll be almost as nice. You'll get used to it and very soon you'll forget being here.'

He shook his head.

'Honest, Jacky. We'll have a home of our own.'

Suddenly he capitulated, from tiredness rather than submission. His stiffness melted away and he plunged towards her and pressed his face into her arm. She reached over and stroked his head. He was saying something but his voice was muffled against the sleeve of her dress.

'What is it, Jacky?' She lifted his chin gently and gazed down at him.

'Why do things have to end, Ma?'

She thought of Da and John Gargett and Mrs Tibbs. She pictured the empty hut on Bleaker's Hill. She imagined the villa after they were gone, the slowly changing lives of things – the dust breeding along shelves and dado rails, the tarnish spreading over Beadie's copper pans, the pages of the books in the library crumbling, the rugs unravelling, the colours dimming.

'I don't know why things have to end, Jacky.' She held him in her arms and rocked him slowly. 'I don't know. I don't know. I don't know.'

The Wedding

A storm came spinning over the town the night before the wedding. It sank two fishing boats in the harbour, wrenched out the roots of the old oak on the Filey Road, and carried off a large wooden chicken coop: the hens were found a week later, strutting amongst the Brent geese on the salt marsh. The storm was still going strong the following morning. The wind reeled round the villa garden, thrashing against the kitchen door and worrying the metal roof of the washhouse, rattling it so fast it sounded like gunfire.

Ellen was certain it was a portent. She sat at Mrs Tibbs's dressing table and thought about grabbing Jack's hand and running away, stuffing the skirt of her wedding dress into her knickers and bolting to the Snook. In the mirror, she could see her narrow face framed by the rigid waves the hairdresser had laboriously curled the day before. Then she pictured the guests in the church, and the tables in the Memorial Hall decorated with loops of lilac and pots of primroses. And she felt sorry for them, not the people, but for all those flowers, abandoned then thrown away.

They were waiting for her in the kitchen: Henry and Jack and a bridesmaid, a girl called Joyce who was the daughter of an old friend of Maurice. They made their way along the drive to the hired car, Henry battling the squally rain with his small umbrella. In the sky was a flock of starlings: tiny black scraps against the white clouds. They were trying to head towards the sea but the wind forced them backwards and the birds scattered like soot.

Inside the church, Father Scullion was standing at the altar. She noticed him long before she saw Maurice. He was blazing white and gold in his cassock and his stole. When she reached the end of the aisle, he held out his arms, welcoming her: a small, tight smile on his face. She could feel the weight of his hands on her shoulders, pressing her down. She could hear his voice, thick like gravy, over the screams of the wind outside. The vows knotted round her, binding her to Maurice, who stood beside her smelling of roses and hair oil, his moustache quivering.

As soon as the ceremony was over the wind gave up. It turned tail and slouched away to the sea. By the time Ellen and Maurice had walked out of the church together, there was hardly a breeze at all. The day had become the sort of day it should have been, a proper wedding day: a pale blue break in the clouds, cherry-pink blossom swaying in the churchyard, cowslips growing in the long grass. For a moment she thought she had broken the spell.

In the Memorial Hall there were salmon sandwiches followed by sherry trifle. Maurice's mother had sprinkled hundreds and thousands over the custard earlier that day, and they had lain so long on the surface that all the colour had seeped into the yellow of the topping. The sugar strands were tiny bones washed up on a sandy beach.

Ellen carried a bowl of trifle to Jack. He was sitting at a table with his head bowed, his shoulders sagging like an old wire coat-hanger.

'We're going to have a lovely time in Invicta Road,' she said, placing the trifle in front of him and ruffling his hair. 'And soon we'll get a home of our own.'

He nodded politely as if he only half believed her. Then he picked up a teaspoon and dipped it cautiously into the grainy custard.

When the trifle was finished, Ellen and Maurice cut the wedding cake. His hand enveloped hers, pushing the knife down through the icing, the marzipan, the currants and the cherries, cutting through the dark layers to the bottom where the blade hit a white paper doily and the white porcelain plate. Everyone clapped, and Maurice's mother seized the knife from them and chipped away at the cake, handing out tiny portions to the guests and the children outside.

Later, when Ellen changed her clothes in the cloakroom, she watched the pastel-coloured day ebbing away. Through the cloakroom window, the sky had taken on a green tinge, it was about to rain again. She pulled off her wedding dress and stepped into the going-away frock she had made out of one of Mrs Tibbs's old tea gowns. It was silk, patterned with pink rosebuds clambering over a dark brown trellis. When she had tried the dress on in the villa she had been pleased, but there was something wrong with it now: the way it hung, the colour. Or perhaps it was just because it was a going-away frock, a dress to mark the end of things.

On the pavement outside the Hall, she said goodbye to Jack, surrounded by people she barely knew: Maurice's friends clasping handfuls of confetti, excited children, their mouths smeared with icing.

'It's only for a few days and then I'll be back. Things will be just the same, I promise.'

She was kneeling in front of him, her hands clutching the top of his arms. He was so small that afternoon, she could feel him shrinking away from her.

Maurice must have noticed there was something wrong. He gripped her hand in the back of the car on the way to the station, and he squeezed it again as they sat on the train.

'Happy?' he asked. His mouth had puckered slightly, a little boy's mouth in a man's face, uncertain, pouting.

'Lovely,' she replied.

But she didn't like the hotel in Scarborough. The entrance hall was damp and muffled, like a doctor's waiting room or a funeral parlour. And on the landing outside the room was a grandfather clock which mumbled and wheezed and chimed every quarter. Even with the bedroom door shut she could hear it ticking.

When Maurice was in the bathroom, she perched on the end of the bed and ran her finger over the new wedding ring. The ring was tight and hot red springy cushions of flesh had spilled over the gold band. She tried to twist it, but her finger had swollen and the band would not move.

In the evening they sat in the dining room, at a table by a large bay window that overlooked the sea. While they were waiting to be served, Maurice grinned at her and said, 'Well, it's been a long day, Mrs Rush.'

'Yes, long,' she replied, but the words hovered in the air without reaching him. He smiled at her and she turned to the window and watched the streaks of rain run down the glass. Then Maurice filled the silence with his plans for the following day. And she peered beyond the rain and gazed at the white glowing tide, sliding backwards and forwards across the sand.

After the waiter served them, she watched Maurice bone the baked trout lying on his plate. He slipped the tip of his knife under the flesh and lifted the fillet away from the bones. It was a tricky operation: he grimaced and his thin moustache disappeared for a second into the fold of skin above his lip.

This was it. This was to be her life, this man in front of her and his moustache. At every meal she would watch it moving gently up and down as he chewed, she would follow the progress of the beads of fishy grease and the breadcrumbs caught in the hairs, dabbed away with the corner of a napkin or licked away with his tongue.

She was certain that he loved her and she had believed that she could love him too. How fickle love was, she thought, sliding the potatoes round her plate. It came in waves, advanced briefly then retreated again, like the tide going out.

That night, as the clock muttered to itself on the landing, Maurice made love to her. He rocked gently backwards and for-wards on top of her, coughed – a strange little cough – then pulled away from her.

'Didn't hurt you did I?' He rolled onto his back and stared at the ceiling with his hands behind his head.

'No,' she whispered beside him. 'Don't worry. I didn't feel a thing.'

JACK

1957–61

Private View

Jack spent his first year at the Slade mixing paints to fill the segments of an enormous colour wheel, and reproducing the tonal values of a top-heavy cheese plant that stood on a pedestal in the centre of the studio. He completed the exercises and the assignments reluctantly and often carelessly, dismissing it all as child's play.

In his second year he fell in with a group of male students, mostly ex-servicemen, who stumbled through the yellow fog to the bars of Soho. Every evening they would weave from Jimmy's or The French to the Colony Room. Jack had never been much of a drinker, but he began to enjoy the sweet, sour waves of beer washing around his mouth and down his throat, or the bitter shock of Scotch. He was a bad drunk, however: after an initial burst of good humour, he would turn sulky and sad. He would sit over his glass, squinting into the beer, and see Hannë's face again, or his mother's blue felt hat floating on the surf. In the morning he would always wake in a rage. Dry-mouthed and brain-fogged, he would spill tea over his clothes, trip over his shoelaces when he climbed down the stairs, then curse the wind as it battered the cumbersome portfolio which he carried under his sweating arm to the studios of the Slade.

Towards the end of his third year, Jack bought a small reproduction of a painting by Caspar David Friedrich from a second-hand shop on Brewer Street. He pinned the picture to the wall at the end of his bed and lay against his musty pillow contemplating it. The painting showed a frock-coated figure standing precariously on a rocky mountaintop, staring at the view: a pale, grey peak in the distance, and the pale, grey sky beyond. Jack wanted to paint that view, not as it was pictured in the print on the wall: he wanted to paint what he thought the figure saw, what the figure was thinking and feeling. From time to time, he tried to reproduce what was in his mind, a brief faraway flicker – light blue, dark blue – which shimmered for a second before it disappeared into the fog again.

When he left the Slade, Jack rented a studio above the Duke of York on Poland Street. The studio was large. Out of the back window was a view of a brick wall. Out of the front, Jack could see the steamy tussle of a damp summer's night in Soho: the tarts and the punters, the transvestites and the tramps. Beneath his feet, on the ground floor, the Duke of York pumped out a constant smog of stale beer and tobacco, waves of laughter and singing and shouting. Jack didn't sleep. He worked at night on two paintings at a time, twisting from one to the other on a typist's chair. He mixed the colours on a sheet of glass that served as a palette, and applied thick streaks to the canvases with a decorator's brush, the sort that Maurice used to use for painting cornices and panelling.

His belongings were ranged around the room: a rack full of finished paintings and rolls of drawings, the books Hannë had given him, Henry's penknife and the dish with 'Souvenir' written on the side. Pinned to the wall were the Cézanne and Picasso reproductions, the Friedrich print, a detail from the Gozzoli fresco, the only likeness of Hannë he possessed, and a postcard from Cathy that he had carried with him from his student digs on Tottenham Court Road. It showed a vivid hand-coloured picture of a desert: a red mountain framed by giant spears of cacti. There was a caption underneath, 'Central and Southern Arizona is renowned for the

Beauties of its Desert.' On the back Cathy had written, 'Come and visit one day, I think you'll like it.' But Jack hadn't replied.

In front of him, propped against the table, was a small portrait of a woman. She was sitting on a bed, wearing a loosely knotted dressing gown. One hand was pressed against her right breast, the other was twisted awkwardly by her side. She looked like the barmaid in *The Bar at the Folies Bergère*. She had the same amber-coloured hair and pouchy, melancholic face. The painting was called *Christina*. It was signed T. Leeming.

Tony Leeming lived on the floor above. He was a lean, devilish-looking man with black hair and black circles under his eyes. Pinned to his walls were pictures of the victims of Dachau and Auschwitz, and photographs that must have been taken in Normandy: bodies on a beach, and the contorted corpses of plough horses and milk cows lying in a shallow ditch.

Leeming painted nudes, women splayed over the ripped settee that stood at the end of his studio. One of the settee's flimsy legs had snapped off some time ago, and he had replaced it with an ancient copy of *War and Peace*. The cover of the book appeared in every painting, peeping out from under the torn pink valance.

Leeming chose his models carefully: startled-looking shrew-faced shop assistants or secretaries, and a housewife or two. They crept up the stairs to his studio on Sunday afternoons and posed uncomfortably while he painted. He usually had sex with them once the painting was finished, then sent them down to Jack to be consoled.

Thanks to Leeming, Jack had acquired several girlfriends: Wanda, a receptionist from a large hotel in Bloomsbury, and Hilary, who worked in a pet shop on Charing Cross Road. But he hadn't forgotten Hannë. He still saw her, glimpses of her among crowds, in galleries and exhibitions, or waiting tables at Wheelers, or standing in the hat department of Dickins and Jones, and in the shadows of the Colony Room, a bar that Hannë would never have frequented. He saw her at work too, in the photographs he printed for Brights Photographers on Wardour Street. As he slid the paper into the developer, there she was, materialising under the rippling liquid.

Jack had a new girlfriend, the woman in the portrait on his table: Christina Balmforth, daughter of a Tory MP and granddaughter of a Sheffield businessman. He had met her on the stairs to Leeming's studio. She was crouching on the top step, wrapped in a striped dressing gown, sobbing gently to herself. Her lipstick was smudged and her mascara lay in sooty clumps beneath her eyelids. He had seen it all before. He told her to dress and wash her face, then he took her to tea at Lyons on Coventry Street.

He liked Christina. She smiled a lot, was pretty enough. She hung off his arm at parties and openings, gauzy in ice-blue or sugar-pink cocktail dresses, her face powdered and rouged. She took him to the races and to rowdy dinners in the Chinese Room at Mirabelle's. Sometimes she turned up at the studio in an evening dress, boozy on champagne, her hair heavy with cigar smoke and the sulphurous London air.

'I do love you, Jacko,' she gushed, her arms wrapped tightly round his neck.

'And I love you too,' he replied easily, vaguely, stroking her face and eyeing the half-finished paintings behind her head.

It was mid-summer 1957, the end of a hot Saturday afternoon. London smelt of piss and beer and petrol. Jack had spent most of the day south of the river, sketching the bombsites: wastelands of tall weeds and buddleia scattered with trembling butterflies. He was on his way home when he stopped at an abandoned street in Battersea. There was something about the shapes of the collapsed buildings that intrigued him, something in the shadows. The roof of one of the houses had fallen in completely and all that was left were the timbers that spanned the empty space. He lay down on a patch of singed linoleum and looked up at the beams. Between the gaps, he could see the sky.

Jack had been drawing for almost an hour when a man, carrying an umbrella and wearing a bowler hat, appeared on the pavement in front of the house. Without a word, he stepped carefully over the rubble and gazed down at a small crater in the backyard. With the tip of his umbrella he poked at the beer bottles and sodden magazines that had collected in the hollow, and after a few minutes he turned back to the house again.

'You always lie down on the job?' The man had a faint London accent.

'I'm drawing the roof,' Jack replied. 'The beams.'

'You do know this place belongs to someone, don't you? You do know it's not yours to go wandering into whenever you like?' He spoke slowly and deliberately, punctuating his questions with long chilling pauses.

Jack sat up. 'Do you want me to go?'

The man didn't reply. Instead he took out a handkerchief from his trouser pocket, dusted a flat block of masonry and sat down.

'My sister used to live here. That was her room.' He pointed to the space above Jack's head. There was another long pause while the man gazed up at the sky.

'I own the whole street. We're going to get rid of all this soon.' He gestured to the rubble and his voice brightened a little. 'We're going to build something really nice.'

He removed his bowler hat and scratched his head. He had dark, waving hair tamed by Brylcreem, and a surprising, almost feminine face. His eyes were wide, his nose retroussé. Without the hat, he seemed smaller, more vulnerable.

'You're an artist?' He pulled a slim silver case from his jacket, offered Jack a cigarette then lit one himself.

'Yes. I'm a painter.'

251

'You got a dealer?' The man inhaled the smoke and his eyes grew small and pinched.

'A gallery? No, not yet.'

'Sell much?'

'Not much.'

'How much?'

'A few paintings.' That was a lie. He had sold one painting to the landlord of the Duke of York, and given another to Leeming in exchange for the portrait of Christina. There had been a small group exhibition in a coffee bar last year, but no one had bought anything.

'So what do you do for cash?'

'I work for a photographer, in Soho.'

'And what are you going to do with the drawings?'

'Make a painting.'

The man stood up and ambled over to Jack. He smelt of tobacco and lavender.

'Like to see it when it's finished, your painting.' He took a business card from his wallet. 'Give us a tinkle when it's done.'

The man's name was Ernie Green. He owned two restaurants and a nightclub near Shepherd Market on the edge of Mayfair.

'You lucky bugger,' said Leeming when he looked at the card that evening. 'I've heard of him, he's a collector. You'd better bloody make sure he comes and sees me as well.'

When the painting was finished, Jack rang Ernie Green from the telephone in the hallway. Green came the following day when Leeming happened to be out. He stood in front of the painting for several minutes, breathing deeply, while Jack leaned against the table, watching his reaction. The surface of the canvas glowed in the low autumn light and the colours seemed brighter than they had done when he had mixed them.

He had wanted to make a resolutely abstract work, a painting about painting, not about a bombed and burning building. The abstract shapes were still there – the thick, dark lines edged with scarlet that ran diagonally across the blue background. But in the same forms, he could make out the roof timbers of the house, and the heavy wooden beams that had probably carried on smouldering long after the fire was extinguished.

'I'll call it *Milly's Room*,' muttered Green. 'Twenty-five seems fair, don't you think?' He pulled the notes from a wedge of money clasped in a silver clip. 'I'd like to have a look at the other stuff when I've got more time,' he said, waving his hand towards the paintings in the rack.

When Ernie Green left the studio that afternoon, Jack was still naive enough to think that it was talent and not luck that had led to him selling the painting. He lay on his bed with his hands behind his head, dreaming for a while. Then he pulled out the rolls of drawings and selected new pictures to paint. As he started to work again, Soho dissolved outside the window. Even Leeming, who was now home and playing Mahler at full volume on his Dansette, didn't bother Jack.

He had felt like this once before. He remembered sitting on the settee in the house on Invicta Road, filling in the picture of the driver and his lorry in the colouring book. He remembered the way that the lines had pulled together to make the picture right, while everything around him slowly vanished, the pricking horsehair against his legs, the hissing gas fire, the muttering parrot in its cage.

Jack used some of Green's money to buy Christina a brooch from a jeweller on Regent Street: it was a swirling silver knot of flowers and leaves. In the shop, the jeweller placed the brooch in a small leather box. It was not much bigger than a ring box, Jack realised when he handed it to Christina later that day. He watched her face light up for a moment then compose itself again when she opened the lid.

'This is so lovely,' she said in her husky voice. 'Pin it on me, Jacko.'

In the evening, Jack took Leeming out for dinner at Wheelers. They drank Chablis and ate oysters, and Leeming grew surly and sorry for himself.

'I'm a far better fucking painter than you are, Pearson,' he moaned when they stumbled back to Poland Street. 'Far fucking better painter.'

Ernie Green bought three more paintings before he introduced Jack to Margo Peters, a gaunt, grey-haired woman who ran a gallery called l'Oeil near Berkeley Square. Peters was tall, with an unusually long jutting jaw as if her teeth were permanently gritted, and there were deep lines engraved on her forehead and round her mouth. She arrived at the studio one morning, flanked by a pale assistant, Tim or Tom or Terry. Together, they pulled the paintings from the rack and peered at them suspiciously then whispered to each other.

Peters would lift her head every now and then and ask, 'What were you trying to do here?'

But as soon as he replied she turned away and carried on her hushed conversation with the assistant.

'Now there's something about this one,' said Peters, pointing to a small canvas that he had painted just after leaving the Slade. She passed it to the assistant and he nodded obediently. It was a scrappy, soupy-coloured picture of a pair of cranes on the south bank of the Thames.

'But this is much better,' said Jack helpfully, holding up another canvas of the same scene.

'No, too abstract,' said Peters briskly, turning her back on him again.

He watched her riffle through the rest of his paintings. The assistant mumbled something and she laughed briefly. 'Yes, yes, that's right,' she said. Then she held a drawing up to the light, shrugged her shoulders, made a face and put it to one side.

It was as if his work did not belong to him, existed without him, he did not matter any more. He was tempted to tell her to leave. The words bubbled into his mouth and he tightened his lips to stop them escaping. He sat down on the typist's chair, clamped his hands together and stared out of the window. He could see a brewery cart on the other side of the street: the dray horse shook its head. There was the heavy rattle of beer barrels being rolled across the road, and someone shouted from the Duke of York. Then Leeming thudded across the floor above them and put a record on the Dansette: '*She's putting on the agony, putting on the style,*' bellowed Lonnie Donegan through the ceiling.

Suddenly Margo Peters was standing behind him. 'I'm thinking of offering you a show.' He twisted round. The assistant – beige hair, beige suit – was beside her, smiling feebly. Peters looked down at Jack dubiously, like a mother bribing a difficult child.

'What do you think, Jack? Would you like that?'

After they left, he collected up the drawings and sketchbooks and piled them on the bed. In the far corner of the studio, the paintings had been arranged into two groups. He had been instructed not to touch them: tomorrow the assistant would return to make notes.

Margo Peters had given him what he had wanted: what he had hoped for when he sat in the drawing classes at the Slade, and when he had hung the paintings above the coffee-stained tables in the Soho bar. He should have been happy. But happiness, he had learned, was found in ordinary things, the extraordinary was far too fragile and fleeting to be trusted with joy. Happiness was a muted trace running through memories he could barely recall: talking to Cathy in the thistle field on Bleaker's Hill, Hanne standing on Mrs Veasey's doorstep smiling at him, the smell of baking cakes and a long-legged bunch of buttercups clutched inside his small fist.

He called the exhibition 'The Modern World'. Margo Peters appeared to like the title, which was a relief. She had selected eighteen paintings of bombsites, building sites and wastelands: ten large canvases hung downstairs in the gallery, eight smaller ones hung on the mezzanine.

On the evening of the private view, the rain was gently falling. The critics arrived promptly. Clutches of middle-aged men in tweed scanned the work, while Peters swept from one group to another in a black turtleneck and slacks. Jack stood as far away from the paintings as he could get. He could not bear to look at them. He could only see their defects: a line too thick, a colour too vivid, all of them heightened under the gallery lights.

For a short while, Christina was beside him. She was wearing a new dress of frosted tulle which was far too grand for the occasion. He should have told her that she looked nice. She *did* look nice: but he was uncomfortable, unsure of himself. He wished she was wearing what Peters was wearing, or the woman in the corner of the gallery with the glasses and the grey sack dress. Christina clung to him, her voice growing louder with every glass of wine she drank. She reached out to touch him, just the tip of her finger against the back of his hand, but he moved slightly. Then she was on the other side of the gallery talking animatedly to the assistant. And after a minute or two she disappeared from sight and someone guided him towards a critic who wrote for *The Times*.

Jack spent the rest of the evening in conversations with huddles of tall men. They were serious people with beards and knitted ties. They didn't smile very much, but they rubbed their chins a lot with their long fingers. He could hear himself as he spoke: his voice was thin and reedy, his northern vowels slowly stretched and strained transforming themselves into more acceptable sounds. There was a sharp pain above his eyes like something metallic clattering against his skull every time he opened his mouth. Someone started to talk about Greenberg and someone else mentioned Rothko and Pollock. Then he remembered the teacher at Danesfield House.

'Art should be a transformative experience,' he piped. 'The colours and forms should stir something in the viewer.'

The men appeared to like this. They all nodded, and he began to relax.

It was two o'clock in the morning when he returned to Poland Street. He had drunk far too much, acid was rising in his throat. Thankfully, the clattering in his head was more of a velvety thud now, dulled by tiredness and alcohol. In the entrance he fumbled for his studio keys then started to climb the stairs, wheeling a little, hauling himself up by the banister rail. When he reached the half-landing he heard a faint noise echoing down the stairwell. It was unmistakably human, rhythmic. He managed to scramble up the next flight then craned his head back far enough to look at the landing above. He could see Christina. She was lying on the floor, pinned there, her face hidden behind Tony Leeming's lurching body. He recognised the tulle, rucked and crumpled like sheets of old tissue paper, and her elegantly gloved hand, gripping one of the spindles of the stair rail.

He shouted, involuntarily. And there was the thrash and flail of the evening dress. Then Leeming got to his feet and smirked down at Jack. He knew what he was doing: he thought he was stealing something precious, out of spite, out of childish jealousy, out of boredom, perhaps.

A few minutes later Christina was standing in Jack's studio, sobbing.

'I don't know what happened. I didn't want to …' She was gasping, gulping the air. 'I came back here and I was waiting for you and you didn't come and Tony told me to come up and have a drink … and I tried to leave … and …'

A wide smear of lipstick ran obliquely across her mouth, from her philtrum to the dimple in her chin. The left strap of her dress had torn, he could see the delicately frayed fringe of silk that hung limply across the top of her breast. He noticed that she was wearing the brooch he had given her. It was pinned to the opposite strap, glinting.

'Jacko, it was a mistake, he ... I didn't want to ...'

Of course, he should have held her in his arms, or at the very least he should have sat her on the bed, taken off his jacket and covered her shoulders with it. But he blamed her, not Leeming. It was Christina who had willingly gone upstairs, it was Christina who had allowed Leeming to touch her. It was Christina's fault.

Later he would despise himself.

'Just go,' he said, pushing her out of the door and onto the landing. 'Just leave me alone.'

Connie

There was a piece about him in the *New Statesman* titled 'Painter of the Modern World'. It was headed by a black and white photograph taken in his new studio. He was standing by the window, a paintbrush in one hand, a turpentine-soaked rag in the other. His face was slightly blurred, and the left side was overexposed, almost white, apart from the grey hollow of his eye socket.

The article was written by a man called Nigel Bedford. He had come to the studio one morning clutching a notebook and a Montblanc pen. He hadn't stayed long; the interview was an uneasy experience for them both.

'When you look at his paintings,' Bedford wrote, 'you might be forgiven for thinking that Jack Pearson is an angry young man, the Jimmy Porter of the art world. Like Auerbach and Kossoff, Mr Pearson's canvases are heavily impastoed, and the colours are either viciously vivid or menacingly dark. He paints the bombsites of London as if they are the stumps of amputated limbs, and the pitted ground as if an organ, something vital, has been ripped away and the wounds have been hastily stitched. And yet there is a disarming stillness about the artist himself. One might be tempted to read this as quiet self-confidence, although I suspect it is probably timidity. Mr Pearson says little about his paintings, and when I change the subject and ask him about his childhood in northern England, hoping he will feel more comfortable with this line of enquiry, he offers me a cup of tea in an attempt to evade my questions.'

Jack's new studio was in a mews, over a garage near Chalk Farm tube station: it had a separate kitchen and a small narrow bathroom. At the back of the building was a square yard and a strip of muddy grass which was permanently overshadowed by a plane tree. In the winter when the fog lifted, he painted small, austere pictures of the view by superimposing glazes of glacial blues and greys until each surface glinted like the feathered frost on the studio window. In the spring and summer, the back gardens were obscured by washing lines. Rows of sagging cords, covered in towels and shirts, were slung from the walls of the houses or from wooden posts cemented in the ground. As he sketched, he remembered the bed linen that used to hang from the line in the courtyard of the villa, and the thin cotton sheets that used to flap in the backyard of the house on Invicta Road.

He enjoyed the solitude of the studio. It was the first time in his life he had been quite so alone, quite so quiet. He relished it: no cursing Granny Rush, no parrot, no Mrs Veasey with trays of tea and biscuits, no Leeming with his clomping feet and Dansette. Jack worked long hours. He was happy: things were going well.

In the spring, Margo Peters had managed to get him included in a group exhibition at the Institute of Contemporary Arts. He had been to the gallery to talk to her about it, and was crossing Berkeley Square on his way back home when he noticed a woman just ahead of him. She had thin blonde hair coiled into a French pleat and was wearing a light blue suit, the colour of a faint shadow. But it wasn't the hair or the suit that made him stop. It was the way she dipped and rose as she walked. With every other step, the woman swivelled her left ankle as if she was grinding a cigarette butt into the ground.

He accelerated, was almost a half-length behind her, so close he could reach out and touch her shoulder. But there was nothing he could think of to say, no words apart from her name that he could conjure into his mouth. He hesitated, stepped back and watched her turn onto Bruton Street. She stood in front of a shop, gazing at the window. He didn't move again until she had pushed the door open and walked inside.

The shop sold antique clocks. The bow window was filled with bracket clocks and carriage clocks arranged on a sweep of shelves. Between the ornate handles and the brass curlicues and finials, he could see the woman. She had picked up a small clock from a round table in the centre of the room and was talking to an assistant. She turned slightly, and for a second he could see her profile silhouetted against the pale back wall: long forehead, long nose, receding chin. Then she moved into the shadows and all that remained was his own distorted reflection in the convex glass: an elongated hollow-cheeked man in an old Harris tweed jacket and a pair of slacks.

'Can I help you?' A girl's head appeared from around the door, she was leaning out into the road.

'I was looking ...' He gazed at the window. 'I was looking at ...' He eyed the clocks: he didn't like them. 'I was looking at that one.' He gestured to a large bracket clock at the back of the window display.

The girl had stepped into the street and was standing next to him. She could have been sixteen, she could have been thirty-six. She was very short and her honey-coloured hair had been backcombed in a futile attempt to give her more height.

'You mean the Robert Seignior. Lovely, isn't it? I can show it to you if you come inside.'

'I don't think so.'

But the girl was insistent. 'Honestly, I can show it to you.' She lowered her voice. 'You don't have to buy it. You can just look. Come on,' she said, pulling the door wide open.

There was something about her enthusiasm that made him follow her: she had taken charge so quickly. He stood on the threshold and gazed into the shop. The woman in the blue suit had disappeared with the assistant, there must have been a back room or an upper floor.

'Come over here,' said the girl, taking the clock from the shelf and placing it on the table. 'Look, it's beautiful, isn't it?'

She showed him the back plate engraved with garlands and winged cherubs. Then she twisted the clock round and pointed to the workings through the side glass.

'This is called the conical spool, and this is the mainspring and the gut line.'

In between her naming of parts, he listened to the faint drift of another conversation coming from the room behind the shop. But the voice of the woman in the blue suit could never have belonged to Hannë. There was no struggle for the right word or the correct verb ending, no upward questioning swing at the end of a sentence.

'And this is what's called the mainspring barrel,' said the girl. 'Magical isn't it, how it all fits together, how it all works.'

'Magical,' he replied, gazing down at her.

He went back and asked Connie out to lunch the following day. She was ebullient, like a small child who had just been given a toy she had always wanted: she was excited and rather pleased with herself. In the restaurant, she spoke to the waiter in French and was charming to the diners on the next table, one of whom spilled wine over her dress. Connie went to the kitchen and asked for a damp cloth, then helped the woman clean the stain from the skirt. Her self-assurance impressed him.

'Why were you looking at the clocks yesterday?' she asked. 'I knew straight away you couldn't afford them. Did you want to paint them or steal them?'

He laughed. 'Steal them, of course.'

262

'I thought you were a private detective and you were following Mrs Craven.'

'Who?' He moved his plate to one side and managed to knock the wine glass with his dirty knife: the sound rang out.

'The lady in the suit. I saw you looking at her through the window.' Connie sat back in her chair and grinned at him challengingly. 'You weren't following her, were you?'

'No, I was only interested in stealing the clocks.' He replied as flatly as he could.

'Well that's all right then. I'd hate to think she'd done something wrong.'

'Who is she, Mrs Craven?'

'So you *were* following her then?' Connie smiled knowingly.

'No, I'm just curious.'

'She's a collector, loves clocks, or hubby loves clocks, something like that.' Connie looked at him with her head on one side, assessing his reaction. 'It's such a treat being taken out to lunch,' she said, grasping his hand and holding it tightly. 'Such a lovely treat, Jack.'

A week later, Connie came to the studio one evening carrying a large wicker basket containing half a dozen eggs, some bacon and a Battenberg cake. Jack had suggested she could visit whenever she liked, but had assumed by then that she wouldn't bother coming. When she knocked on the door, he was sitting on the typist's chair looking at a canvas propped against the wall. He had spent the day consumed by soft glazes of colour: sea blue, moss green and a brownish, rusty pink.

He opened the door and she was standing in the entrance, swinging the basket self-consciously backwards and forwards. He showed her in and watched her gaze around the room. There was a damp towel draped across the back of a chair and several books lying open on the floor. The bed was made, although there was a heap of unironed clothes on the top of it. He wondered what she was thinking, what she was thinking about him, what she saw in him: the tall thin man in a paint-clotted sweater, stooping over her, trying to grasp the handles of the basket.

'It's very nice, your studio,' said Connie. 'It's quite big really, and light.' She put down the basket and turned to look at the canvas that he had been struggling with all day. She considered it carefully, her hands behind her back, as she rocked gently on the balls of her feet.

'So what does it mean?' she asked, finally.

'It's about seeing things differently, seeing the world differently. Trying to see the truth in it. What it really looks like.'

'Oh.' Connie was perplexed.

'I mean the starting point is the view out of the window, obviously. But it's also about colour and form.'

He was fumbling. The words sounded trite and unconvincing. He was used to people nodding wisely when he talked about his work, but Connie's face was blank.

'It's not a metaphor for anything,' he continued. 'The painting just stands for itself. It doesn't have to mean anything really. The marks are just marks, the colours are just colours. There's no symbolism.'

'Yes, I see.' Connie smiled as if she had understood. 'Are you hungry, Jack?' she asked brightly, picking up the basket.

She fried the eggs and bacon on the gas stove in the tiny kitchen. Then she carried the plates and the frying pan to the table. As they began to eat, she looked round the room again.

'I thought you'd paint pictures of nudes, of your girlfriends.'

He laughed. 'I don't have any girlfriends.'

'I thought all artists were supposed to be promiscuous. Aren't you supposed to love them and leave them?'

'They always leave me in the end.'

His answer pleased Connie, she smiled broadly. 'Now you're

trying to make me feel sorry for you.' She stared at the canvas propped against the wall behind him. 'But do you make much money from it, art, I mean?'

He was surprised and a little annoyed by the question.

'I have a gallery. I sell work,' he replied gruffly. 'I used to have a job at a photographer's but I stopped because I needed the time to paint.'

Sensing that his tone had changed, Connie made a faint babbling noise in the back of her throat, an embarrassed chuckle, and said, 'You're so lucky you can do what you want, Jack. I've never told anyone, but I really hate antique clocks.'

After they had eaten she insisted on clearing the table and doing the washing up. It was a performance just for him, the way she bustled back and forth from the kitchen to the studio with a cloth slung over her shoulder.

It irritated him slightly. 'Why don't you sit down, I'll do it later.'

'I'll just finish the table,' she said, bending over it and wiping the surface with the cloth. For once she wasn't looking at him, but concentrated on scooping the crumbs into her cupped hand. She was small and clean and pretty. There was something delicate about her.

'Let me finish it.' He moved towards her. He was close enough to smell her perfume: lilies or lilac. It was the villa garden on a spring afternoon.

When he took the cloth, she looked up at him, forgetting the crumbs in her hand. They showered over the table and the floor – pink and yellow cake crumbs and scraps of bread. She giggled faintly, then leaned towards him and kissed him on the mouth. It seemed inevitable. It was what she had come for.

Connie was eight years younger than Jack. She had been only nine when he was running down the platform to the Henley train with Iris, fifteen when he was dancing with Hannë in the

265

Zetland Club. He was older than he had thought, life was sneaking away from him.

They lay in bed together, he with his hands behind his head, she on her side, gazing at his face. She shot questions at him: 'So where were you born, Jack? Where did you grow up?'

He managed to weave a story of sorts, making it as dull as he could. He referred to his 'parents' vaguely, saying, 'They were away a lot.' He mentioned Cathy and Henry and, oddly, the parrot in its cage. But he didn't tell Connie about Ellen or the travelling man or Winterfield Asylum.

She tried to measure her own life against what little he had told her about his. She searched for small coincidences and similarities, for something they held in common.

'When I was little we lived in Pimlico. Then Daddy went into the Navy and I was evacuated to Kent. But the place I was sent to was so dirty that Mummy brought me home again. Then we moved to Twickenham.'

What a smooth life Connie had led, from school to secretarial college and Lucie Clayton, to a florist's in Chelsea, then the shop on Bruton Street.

'You know, Jack, I was about to go for lunch when you turned up that morning.' She looked up at him, solemnly. 'Just imagine, if you'd been a minute or two later we would never have met.'

'Yes,' he said. 'It must have been fate.'

He held her hand, which was as small as a child's. Her fingers were short and thick, her neat nails carefully painted. The varnish, she told him, was called Coquille-d'oeuf. 'The same colour the Queen wears,' she said proudly. This was apparently important to her.

One afternoon, he took Connie to the National Portrait Gallery and tried to explain the paintings. He waved his hands around a lot and talked about colour and how the gesso and the paints were made. She listened for a while then drifted towards the Gainsboroughs and the Reynolds: she liked the dresses, she said. After a while, he suggested they search for the portrait that most resembled them. They raced through the rooms together, he pointing up at double chins and hooded eyes, she giggling at his suggestions.

For himself, he chose a picture of Captain Cook, not so much for the shape of the face or the blunt ruddy features, but for the Captain's dubious expression. In the painting he appeared to be pulling back from the artist, as if an unpleasant operation was about to be performed. He looked like a wary patient in a doctor's surgery waiting for a boil to be lanced.

Connie selected a portrait of Elizabeth the First holding an orb and sceptre. Jack thought it was an astute choice, although he didn't tell her. They looked up at the chalky-faced queen, who glared back at them disdainfully.

'She isn't beautiful,' said Connie, leaning her head to one side as she always did when she was being thoughtful. 'But she does look brave, don't you think, Jack?' The queen was clothed in a dress of gold encrusted with pearls and gleaming rubies: a tiny woman ready to do battle in an armour of jewels.

Connie liked a routine. She visited the studio two or three evenings a week. At first he worried that she would disturb him, that she would clatter round the kitchen, banging saucepans or cupboard doors. But she was surprisingly discreet. Even if she hadn't understood his paintings, she seemed to respect them. He rewarded her with a spare key to the studio. 'You can come whenever you like,' he said.

Usually, she arrived with a basket of shopping and busied herself with recipes she was learning from a book called *The Cordon Bleu Cookery Course*. One Monday night, after a weekend with her parents in Twickenham, she appeared at the door with a chicken wrapped in pink butcher's paper, a garlic bulb and half a pound of butter.

'I thought I'd try Chicken Kiev,' she said, carrying the ingredients to the kitchen.

She was quiet that evening. She spent most of her time struggling to bone the chicken then pound the garlic into the cold butter. When he went to the kitchen for a glass of water, he found her peering grimly down at the recipe, muttering instructions to herself while she stirred something glue-like in a saucepan. It was only when the meat was frying in the pan that she finally emerged, standing in the doorway with a spatula in her hand.

'You know, I was thinking, Jack,' she said, in what sounded to him like a carefully rehearsed off-hand tone. 'I don't really understand about your family at all. None of what you've told me makes much sense.'

He was in the process of stretching a canvas: he had pulled the fabric tight over the frame and was nailing it to the wood. He put down the hammer and turned to look at her, but didn't reply.

'I mean, I don't understand about your parents,' Connie continued. 'You've never really mentioned them at all. I can't believe they were always away. It seems very strange.'

'You think it's important for you to know?'

'Yes, of course. Family's important, isn't it.'

He had never talked to anyone about his mother, apart from Cathy and Henry. He had shrugged away the few questions that Marigold had posed with a gruff, 'It's none of your business.' Hannë never asked him about his parents, nor Christina. Leeming didn't care.

'Families are important, they're where you come from, they're who you are,' Connie said.

'I don't think that's true at all.' He shook his head, picked up the hammer and banged a nail home into the wood.

'Well, to be honest with you, Jack, the very fact that you don't

268

want to talk about it makes it very odd.' And Connie turned calmly back to the kitchen again.

Through the doorway he could see her lift the frying pan from the heat of the gas ring and roll the chicken pieces over with the spatula. She strained the potatoes and the peas, and pulled out the plates from the cupboard under the sink. Reluctantly, he cleared the table of nails and shreds of canvas. Then Connie swept into the studio with the food and sat primly on the typist's chair without another word.

She was a master at this, at long cold silences. He watched her slip a piece of chicken into her mouth and chew it slowly – contentedly almost – as if she was enjoying herself. He looked down at his own plate and moved the potatoes around, sliding them into the pool of yellow butter: some were overcooked and dry, others were still hard. But he couldn't eat. He couldn't stand the silence. It was almost tangible: sharp and shrill and steely. It was better not to prevaricate, easier to tell her the truth.

'I didn't know my father. My mother went into hospital when I was young. Is that enough for you?'

Connie lay her cutlery gently down on the side of her plate and looked up at him. 'She went into hospital?' Her eyes grew large and strangely luminous. 'But what was wrong with her?'

'It was a mental asylum,' he replied bluntly.

'Oh!' She shrank back from the table. 'Well, I can see why you wouldn't want to talk about it.'

He didn't respond. Instead he sorted through the potatoes, prodding them with his fork.

'So where is she now, your mother?' Connie whispered the question.

'Still there, I think.'

'Do you ever go and see her?'

He pictured the matron standing in the hallway of the hospital: he pictured the splatter of blood on her apron. 'Not any more. They told me not to.'

269

'Oh, how awful! Awful for you, I mean.' She reached over the table and touched the back of his hand.

He had expected her to pursue the topic, to berate him for not visiting Ellen, to suggest a trip north. He was surprised, relieved.

'I promise we won't talk about it any more, to anyone,' said Connie. As if to reinforce the fact that the conversation was over, she speared a piece of chicken with her fork and began to eat, smiling reassuringly at him as she chewed.

The Taxi

After Christmas he saw less of Connie. She had moved from her bedsit in Earl's Court to a top floor flat in Pimlico.

'Daddy's helping me with the rent,' she told Jack. 'And Pimlico's much more convenient for work.'

She was busy choosing curtains and cushion covers. Whenever they went to the cinema or to a restaurant, she lingered in front of shops selling furnishing fabric and dining room sets. She still visited the studio once a week, bringing something she had baked in her kitchen: a sponge cake or an apple pie, although she seemed weary and quiet, had lost a little of her brightness. He wondered if Connie had met someone else, someone younger, and he couldn't decide whether the thought bothered him or not.

Jack was busy too. In January he was asked to teach a class in one of the cold drawing studios at Saint Martin's School of Art. Every Monday afternoon at four o'clock, the first-year students trailed through the door and spent the next three hours sketching the elderly life model who posed naked on the dais in the centre of the room.

The students stood in front of their drawing boards, while Jack moved from one to another, tripping over easel legs and bags and feet, entreating the class to look closer, measure more accurately.

He gestured at the model, posed like Dürer's melancholic angel:

the old man's head leaning heavily in his hand, his withered genitals nestling in the shadow of his belly.

'Don't just look at his body, look at the spaces in between.' Jack pointed to the model's quivering arm, 'Positive space,' then he directed his finger towards the crooked triangle between the man's fleshy torso and his armpit. 'And negative space. It's just as important.'

Sometimes he urged the students to move round the room, to stand on a chair and look down at the model, or lie on their backs and look up.

'Look at things differently,' Jack implored. 'Try and see them from another point of view.'

The finished drawings clipped to the easels were always the same, despite his pleading: clusters of hesitant feathered lines, or tiny misshapen figures floating in the middle of the page. And teaching was exhausting, Jack discovered. In the last hour of the class, he was often so tired that all he could do was to sit on a stool and watch the rain fall against the window, or listen to the gentle brush of charcoal against paper and the whir of the electric heater as it warmed the model's swollen feet.

That spring the rain fell for weeks. First it was torrential, then it turned into thick drizzle that tasted of petrol and caught in his throat. In late April, there was day after day of hailstorms. He stood in the drawing studio one evening and watched the icy chippings hurl themselves against the window and collect on the sill, before they melted away. When the class was over, he had to wait in the lobby for the hail to ease before he could trot up the road, the brim of his hat turned downwards and the collar of his coat turned up.

He was almost at the bus stop when a taxi just ahead of him slowed to let an elderly woman cross the street. When he reached the side of the cab something made him turn and look: perhaps it was simply because the passenger was looking at him. He hunched his shoulders to get a better view and peered into the window. But before he noticed her white face and her blonde hair, he knew it was Hannë. She was staring at him, her hand pressed against the glass in a frozen wave. He gazed back, frozen too. Then the old woman stepped onto the pavement and the taxi moved forward again. He waited, assuming that Hannë would tell the driver to pull over and stop, expecting at any minute to see the brake lights turn red. But the taxi carried on up the road, accelerating with the traffic.

He began to follow it, first walking then jogging along the pavement. As he ran, in the back window two more heads twisted round to look at him: a man and a boy with dark hair and dark eyes. Jack slackened his pace and stopped. He stood on the edge of the pavement, dizzy from the effort of running. The three faces continued to stare at him, then the car swerved right onto Tottenham Court Road, and the reflection of a street light in the gleaming paintwork flashed and blinded him for a second. When he looked again the taxi had gone.

The hail had turned to rain, thick drops patted on his hat brim and the shoulders of his coat. He made his way down the pavement to a pub: he needed to steady himself. At the bar he ordered a whisky, then another. He was drinking just as he used to drink when he was a student, gulping it down, although it had no effect, did nothing to stop the cascade of thoughts. He could not believe he had just seen her, not a shadow or a ghost, but the real Hannë. And the man had looked no older than he had done on the promenade. And the boy's face, framed between his mother and his father, the boy's face looked like his own.

It was almost ten o'clock as he turned into the mews. There was a light in the window, which surprised him. When he opened the front door, he could see Connie standing at the top of the stairs. She was wearing her coat and scarf and was clutching an umbrella.

'I was just about to leave,' she said sharply. 'Your dinner is on the table if you want it.'

'I'm sorry, Con, I didn't know you were here.' He had climbed the stairs, was trying to guide her back into the studio. He put his hand on her shoulder but she shrugged it away. 'Honestly, Connie, I didn't know you were coming tonight.'

'I told you last week. I said I'd be here on Monday. Don't you listen?'

'Connie, I'm sorry.' He was too tired for this.

'I suppose it was one of your students.' Her lips were tight and thin.

'What do you mean?'

'You went drinking with one of your female students.' She said this as if it was a fact rather than an accusation.

'No, I didn't,' though he realised that his breath must stink of cheap whisky.

'So what were you doing then?'

'Nothing. I wasn't doing anything.' What else could he say?

'You see, this is the problem, Jack.' Connie was remarkably calm, remarkably cold. 'I never know what you're doing, what you're thinking, you're so ...' She shook her head as she searched for a word. 'You're so remote.' She was pleased with her choice. 'Yes, remote. In your own little world. Completely wrapped up in yourself. It's like I'm not here, or only here to cook or—'

'You should have said something.' He was still trying to coax her back into the studio. 'You should have told me.'

'I'm telling you now.' She managed to slide away from him towards the stairs. 'You've clearly no idea what you're like, which frankly makes me wonder ...'

She paused deliberately, waiting.

'Wonder about what?' he snapped.

Her thin lips turned upwards, she smiled smugly. She was completely in control of the argument. 'It makes me wonder about your mental state, Jack.'

274

'My mental state.' He repeated the phrase slowly.

'Well, I'm sure these things run in families.' And she spun on her kitten heels and climbed down the stairs.

In the studio, Connie's pie was sitting on the table. It was shrivelled and dry. Across the top were flakes of carbonised pastry and blackened blisters where the meat juices had bubbled up then evaporated with the heat. Lying next to the pie was the spare key that he had given her last autumn. He pushed it away.

These things run in families. He pictured Ellen sitting on the doorstep of the Rushes' house, a bucket of steaming water on one side of her, a scrubbing brush on the other. She was wearing Granny Rush's brown apron and a blue cardigan, the sleeves rolled up to her elbows so they wouldn't get wet. He remembered skimming past her, knocking her arm as he ran out of the front door and into the street. She should have shouted at him, asked him where he was going and when he would be back: that was what mothers were supposed to do. But she didn't say a word, she didn't even look up at him.

He remembered wandering up the lane to the empty villa and pressing his face against the bars of the wrought-iron gates. The garden was green and damp. Tufts of grass had sprouted between the gravel and there were buttercups and clover growing in the lawn. A group of baby rabbits were squatting in the weeds. He picked up a handful of stones from the lane and hurled them through the gate, watching the animals scatter across the garden. When they were gone, he found a long stick in the ditch and ran it along the railings of the house next door, scratching the paintwork and making a satisfying rattling noise until the stick broke in two.

He must have been messing around on the lane for over an hour before he trailed back to Invicta Road. But his mother was still there, in a world of her own, sitting on the doorstep, the water now cold in the bucket beside her, the scrubbing brush dry.

*

In the morning Jack threw Connie's pie into the rubbish and slid the spare key into his trouser pocket. He half-heartedly tidied the studio, cleared away old drawings and paint tubes and overused brushes, then swept the floor. When he pulled the covers over the bed, he noticed that Connie had left a bottle of nail varnish on the bedside table. And on the rug beside the bed, splayed open, was a library book: Jean Plaidy, *The Scarlet Cloak*. He lifted it up and looked at the docket inside, tomorrow it would be overdue.

In the afternoon, he went to Saint Martin's and gave the door-man a piece of paper with his address written on it.

'There may be a woman who comes asking for me: blonde, foreign.'

'Oh yes, Mr Pearson,' grinned the doorman wryly.

'She's just an old friend, no one special.'

But he knew now she wouldn't come back, it was better that she didn't. The whole thing had happened in a split second, just a glimpse through a rain-stained window, distorted by the reflected street lights on Charing Cross Road.

He pictured himself standing alone on the pavement staring at the family in the back of the taxi that was speeding away from him. He pictured himself as a small boy again, sitting on the settee in the front room, Granny Rush shouting at Maurice in the kitchen, the parrot beating its wings against the cage.

He needed another drink.

He sought out Tony Leeming in Soho. Leeming was doing well now. He had rented a tall narrow building on Wardour Street, with small bare rooms that were filled with nothing but his paintings. Jack and Leeming spent the evening in the Colony Room, ordering glass after glass of whisky, each drink making Jack thirsty for another. By the end of the night he could barely walk: his legs propelled him forward, his body followed but his head didn't seem to move at all.

He was standing on the edge of the road searching hopelessly for a taxi when a woman appeared at the end of the street. She was as drunk as he was, wheeling and muttering and giggling. When she saw him, her face lit up and she staggered along the pavement.

'I've been looking for you, son,' she shouted.

She tried to swing her arm round his waist and he managed to push her away. But she gripped the sleeve of his jacket and leaned in towards him. She reeked of Scotch. He could smell it on her breath and on her clothes. He could smell it on himself.

'Why didn't you come and see me,' she wailed. 'I've got something for you, son.'

The following morning he woke in a panic. He could not be sure if he had imagined the woman or if she was real. He couldn't remember getting home last night.

Never again, he promised himself, his head thumping, his stomach churning. Never, never again.

The days rolled on. He tidied the studio a second time. As he swept the floor he found a torn cinema ticket to *Room at the Top*, a film that Connie had hated.

'It was just so bleak, Jack, and so northern.'

'What's wrong with being northern, Con?' he had asked with a smile on his face.

And she had giggled. 'I know, I know, I'm such a snob.'

Jack bent down, picked the ticket up and slid it inside his sketchbook.

The next morning, when he was pushing a painting into the rack, he managed to knock a bottle of turpentine off the table with his elbow. The smell was unbearable, it stuck in his throat and made him retch. He mopped up the turps then rubbed the linoleum furiously with a damp cloth, although it didn't make any difference.

He opened all the windows and abandoned the studio, he couldn't bear to stay there any longer. In the rain, he walked to a café he knew near Regent's Park and sat at a table watching the steam rising from the tea urn. The dampness muffled the voices of the waitresses behind the counter and the couple who were holding hands across a small table in the corner. The clammy hush was disturbed only by the clatter of a fork hitting the tiles, and by Perry Como's gentle voice from the radio sitting on a shelf next to the bottles of lemonade. '*Catch a falling star and put it in your pocket, save it for a rainy day.*'

When he finally returned to the studio, the silence was thick and cold and the smell of turps was still strong. He stood by the open window and watched the rain, it was so dark it appeared to be dragging the clouds down with it.

The Scarlet Cloak was eight days overdue now. On the front cover was a sinister-looking figure dressed in a bright red robe. He opened the book and began to read: 'At the window Señorita Isabella de Ariz sat fanning herself.'

He remembered Connie lying in bed next to him reading the novel. She was the sort of person who fell asleep easily, often when she was halfway through a chapter. He would have to unhook the book from her fingers and move it gently away so she didn't wake.

He should have taken the book back to Connie days ago. Now, as he stood in the gloom of the studio, he wondered why he hadn't: it was the obvious thing to do. It was almost a relief to put on his coat again and slide *The Scarlet Cloak* under his arm.

Connie's flat was at the top of a shabby building on Lupus Street. As he climbed the stairs, he could hear the other tenants. It was tea time: there was the gentle to and fro of a conversation between a man and a woman, a child's laughter, something frying in a pan.

'Oh, it's you,' said Connie softly when she opened the door to him. She had been baking a cake, he could smell it on the landing: warm vanilla.

'I brought you this. I'm sorry, I should have given it to you sooner. I'll pay the fine, Con.'

She took the book from him and he wavered outside the door: he had planned nothing more.

But she already knew why he was there. She only needed to nudge him along a bit, show him the way. 'I hoped you might come back,' she said finally.

'Really?'

'Yes, really, Jack.' She wasn't wearing any makeup, her eyes were small, her face was pale. She looked so young.

He stretched out his hand to her and said something which surprised him. 'I love you, Connie.'

The Painting

The wedding took place in the Kensington and Chelsea Register Office on an October afternoon. Jack had bought a new shirt and tie for the occasion and Connie wore a peach-coloured dress. It was a hue that Jack normally disliked, but it suited Connie rather well.

On her head was a pillbox hat that she had bought from Harrods the week before.

'It's the sort of thing that Jackie Kennedy wears,' she informed him proudly, patting the top of it as the cab halted in front of the old town hall.

Connie had invited a school friend called Wendy to the wedding and Jack had invited Leeming, although he didn't turn up. Bob Marigold and Moira had come all the way from Sunderland to be witnesses. Marigold trudged up the steps, leaning heavily on a stick. All that was left of his haggard face was a beaming smile.

'You'll love it,' he said. 'Getting married, being a husband. Good for you, Jacky.'

When Marigold was out of earshot, Moira shook her head. 'They say it's something he caught in Burma, but they have no idea how to treat it. He won't talk about it, of course.'

Connie's parents were waiting for them in the lobby, sitting side by side on a wooden bench. He hadn't met them before, Connie had been careful to keep them all apart.

'So this is Jack!' said Ralph Meakin, rising to his feet.

He was strangely shrunken, as if he had once been a much larger man. The sleeves of his jacket hung over the top of his hands and his trousers bagged around his shoes. Muriel Meakin towered over her husband, though she wasn't much taller than he was. She had a long face and thin lips. Pinned to the top of her head was an elaborate bun, so thick and lustrous it must have been a hairpiece. And clinging to her dress was a three-clawed silver-tipped rabbit's foot brooch that trembled when she spoke.

'It's such a shame about your family,' she said, taking Jack aside after the ceremony. 'Constance tells me they've passed away. It's a shame, for you, I mean. Families are important, they're where you come from, they're who you are.'

'Yes,' he said quietly, remembering Connie standing in the kitchen door with the spatula in her hand. 'It's a cross I have to bear.'

At Christmas Connie told Jack she was pregnant. They were lying in bed in Lupus Street surrounded by discarded wrapping paper. Jack had bought Connie a small bottle of perfume, Chanel No. 5, and a French cookery book. She had overwhelmed him with gifts: a new shaving set, a record of Brahms intermezzi, a novel by Evelyn Waugh, and a V-neck sweater. When she handed him the last present, she leaned against him and watched him pull at the Sellotape. Nestling inside the paper was a pair of blue bootees.

'Surprise!' she cried. 'I know it's going to be a boy, Jack.'

He kissed her and told her how pleased he was. He *was* pleased but he felt something else too, an emotion that was entirely new to him. He couldn't name it, and later he would think of it as a deep sense of compassion, for Connie and the baby, for himself. The feeling took his breath away. How alone they all were, he thought, as Connie collected up the wrapping paper and threw it away, how vulnerable, how small.

*

281

In the early spring Connie left her job at the shop and spent her days knitting clothes for the baby. She bent over patterns for cardigans and tiny sweaters, whispering 'Knit one, purl one,' just as she had muttered the recipes to herself in the studio. He watched her, fumbling along the knitting needle for a dropped stitch, deep in concentration.

The baby was growing. A few weeks ago it had been just a cluster of cells, but now he could see the slight curve of her stomach under her dress. It was becoming real: there would soon be a child, his child, flexing its tiny fingers and toes, kicking its chubby legs. He could barely imagine what it would be like to be a father. He had a faint memory of Maurice cooing over Cathy in her crib, then jigging her up and down on his knee at the kitchen table. But Maurice had soon lost interest, had slid away to Hooper's Hotel.

That spring Jack was overtaken by worries about money. The class at Saint Martin's would soon come to an end and Margo Peters had only sold two paintings in over a year. He was paying the rent for both the studio and the flat, and Connie had spent a fortune on a large pram from Selfridges. It was too big for their hallway and had to stand on the communal landing outside the flat. The other tenants on the top floor had begun to complain.

Connie had mentioned the possibility of giving up the studio and finding a bigger flat, or moving out of London altogether. She had started to search the newspaper for job advertisements. When she found something suitable she tore it out and left it on the table in the kitchen for him to read. They were things he could never have done – art master in a minor public school, assistant in an auction house. He began to resent her for this, began to resent the baby for it.

'There'll be three of us soon,' she said one evening, her arms folded across her stomach. 'We have responsibilities, we need to think ahead.'

'Of course I'm thinking ahead,' Jack replied.

*

When April turned into May, Connie grew listless and unusually quiet. She gave up on knitting and lay on the bed for most of the day, reading magazines. In the evening, when he got home from the studio, he washed the breakfast and lunch dishes then cooked the supper. The stale odour of fried bacon and the crust of burnt scrambled egg on the bottom of the saucepan lying in the sink depressed him. As the days grew warmer, he stayed in the studio, working late.

Connie didn't seem to mind, however. She said she could watch the television without him complaining. Ralph Meakin had bought the television set as a wedding present. It stood in a teak cabinet, taking up most of the left-hand corner of the sitting room. Jack hated the thing – the great, grey screen that stared blankly at him when he was trying to sketch an idea or read a book – but Connie loved it.

'It's company when you're not around,' she said.

On those balmy nights he found her curled up in the armchair in her creased nightdress, watching *Double Your Money* or *Come Dancing*.

He began to take long diversions when he left the studio in the evening. He would trail through Regent's Park or sit in cafés in Marylebone listening to the thin transistor jangle of Elvis Presley or the Shadows.

He visited Tony Leeming in his empty building in Soho. They sat in his studio at the top of the house and knocked back Glenmorangie from tumblers that Leeming had always forgotten to wash. Jack enjoyed the drink, welcomed the numbness in his legs and the slight buzzing in his head that stopped him from having to think for an hour or two.

Connie didn't mention the drinking, though she must have noticed. She would pull away from him when he got into bed at night. Things had grown silent between them. Their conversations revolved around food and shopping. She left notes for him on the kitchen table: 'Remember the tomatoes and get some ham.'

She was large, beached on the bed for most of the day, heavy and unhappy.

'You think it's comfortable being like this?' he heard her mutter one morning, to him or to the baby, or to herself. 'And it's so hot, so bloody hot.'

The days grew hotter still. In the studio he pulled down the blinds and worked in the gloom. Or he sat in the typist's chair and listened to the radio, his damp shirt sticking to the vinyl backrest. Sometimes it was so stifling that he lay on the bed and dozed late into the afternoon. He closed his eyes and saw brightly coloured pictures, part random thoughts and part dreams.

Connie was on Teesby beach, making her way towards the sea. When she reached the tideline, she turned back to look at him and he noticed she was clutching the baby to her chest. As she stepped into the water the force of the waves whipped her off her feet and the child flew out of her arms. He ran towards her, following her into the sea. The grey, viscid liquid seeped down his throat and into his lungs, weighing him down. He gulped and wheezed, sinking towards the bottom. But he could still see her in the distance, a small gleaming form, waltzing in the waves.

At the end of the month, Tony Leeming had a private view in a gallery in Kensington. It was so warm that the gallery owner flung the doors open and all the critics and students flooded onto the pavement with their drinks and cigarettes. Someone had found a record player, and Jack stood outside watching the girls in tight dresses doing the Twist, while Leeming, glass in hand, spun, smirking, from one to another.

It was late when Jack left, well after midnight. The streets were empty and the houses dark. He had reached Kensington High Street and was skirting the edge of Kensington Gardens when he heard a sharp whistle from one of the trees. It reminded him of the villa garden at night. Those wild nocturnal noises had terrified him as a small child, he used to pull the sheets over his head and hide there until he fell asleep. Even now, as he ambled boozily along the road, the sound made him shiver. He didn't look back, he didn't dare. He carried on, his head pounding from the whisky.

Connie must have been awake for hours, listening for the sound of the front door. She was already on the landing by the time he had climbed the stairs to the flat. She looked flimsy, almost transparent in her pale cotton nightdress. Her right hand was gripping the edge of the pram for support. Her left was clutching the corners of a bath towel which she had draped round her waist and hips. In the moonlight that shone through the window, he could see the perspiration glinting on her face.

When he reached the landing, she stumbled forward. 'I don't know what's happening, Jack.'

He moved towards her to take her in his arms and noticed a dark stain on the skirt of her nightdress, a stain so dark it was almost black.

Time stopped. Then it started again, slowly.

Connie was lying on her back in a hospital bed, weeping. He was sitting beside her.

Everything was white: white walls, white sheets, white nightgown. The whiteness was so thick it was almost opaque.

'He was a little boy,' she whispered.

Jack saw the child's face out of the back window of the taxi growing smaller and smaller.

'Did I do something wrong, Jack? Was it my fault?' She was reaching over the bed, trying to grasp his fingers.

He leaned forward, took her hand in his. 'Of course it wasn't your fault, Con.'

It was easy to say because he knew it was his fault. His resentment had forced the child to vanish. He hated himself.

The day before Connie came home from hospital, he asked Ralph Meakin to take the pram back to Twickenham. They carried it down the stairs together and Ralph mumbled gently, 'For next time, eh Jack.'

When he was alone again, he stuffed the blue booties and the half-knitted cardigan into a drawer in the bedroom. In the sitting room, he switched on the television and watched the flat grey ghosts move across the screen.

In the summer Connie took a part-time job in a florist not far from the flat. She wore a headscarf like a Russian peasant and a pink gingham apron over her dress. In the evening she came home clutching bunches of anemones with black velvet stamens and petals the colour of sweet wrappers.

Her brightness had returned, although there was something fragile about it now. On her days off she went to Twickenham to see her mother, or she bustled round the flat cleaning things with a big smile on her face, pretending to enjoy it. She started to cook again, complicated desserts, multi-layered cakes filled with mousses that neither she nor Jack could stomach.

Moira had written to Jack to tell him Bob Marigold had died. 'Bobby was cremated. I scattered his ashes in the sea. He said he didn't want any fuss.'

Jack took several days to reply. In the end it was a long letter, the longest he had ever written. Marigold had been with him since his first day of school, a lean, awkward boy standing slightly away from the group of taunters, biting his bottom lip. He had never defended Jack, but he was always there: a witness, an observer.

When Jack put the letter into the envelope and sealed it, he wished he could cry. He had watched Connie cry about the baby, easy tears that welled up in her eyes and tumbled down her face.

286

He had held her tight and rocked her as she sobbed. She always appeared to feel better in the end.

Jack had a full day of teaching at Saint Martin's now, which helped. In the autumn term he showed the first-year students how to mix paints in order to fill the segments of a colour wheel. In the winter term they reproduced the tonal values of a large yucca that stood on a stool in the centre of the room.

When he wasn't teaching he started to take the Underground to the end of the line, to places that were merely names in Johnston typeface until he arrived in them: Edgware, High Barnet, Cockfosters. He was looking for the edge of the city, searching for the point where the countryside began. He was beginning to detest London for all the reasons he had enjoyed it when he arrived as a student: the noise, the people, the parties.

He walked for miles through ragged suburbs separated by thistly paddocks and lines of pylons. He wandered along semi-rural tracks dotted with oily puddles and patches of black mud. There was always something troubling along those paths: a broken-down car, metal canisters half buried in a ploughed field, oddly formed bundles of wet sacking hidden in the undergrowth.

He sketched the scrappy paddocks and the overgrown gardens and the unpruned trees that reached through rusting railings and over high walls. He drew the passers-by bundled in their winter coats, children on their way home from school, old women peering down at him from upstairs windows.

In the studio, with the sketchbook open, he began to work across the canvas creating fragmented pictures: half invented, half real. They were just shards at first, a shattered mirror reflecting a faraway scene. He added figures, the people he had sketched in the suburbs: a child standing at the entrance to a garden, a woman on a path, a featureless face like a silvery disc gazing out of a top floor window.

'Oh, this is a good painting. It looks so real,' said Connie on one of her rare visits to the studio. She was standing in front of the canvas. It was the largest painting he had ever made. It took up the entire end wall of the studio. 'So what does it represent? What does it mean?' she asked, tipping her head to one side.

'It doesn't really represent anything,' he replied.

'Well, where is it then?'

'Nowhere really, a mix of lots of places. Edgware, Barnet.'

'But it has to be somewhere specific, Jack, it looks so real. You could almost walk into the garden. And you've never painted people before.' She smiled at him, she was trying to be helpful.

A few weeks later, when he showed the painting to Margo Peters, she asked the same question.

'Is it somewhere you know, somewhere you've been?'

She was standing with her back to him, motionless, as if she was studying the painting intensely. Although he began to suspect that she was just desperately trying to think of something else to say.

'Listen, Jack.' She turned to face him. 'I've been meaning to tell you this for a while. The work isn't selling as well as it did. Ernie Green has moved on to the This Is Tomorrow crowd. And the other collectors ... well, they've lost interest too. I think they find the work a bit passé. I mean, look at it.' She waved her hand at the new canvases. 'This is so ... dated, so impressionistic, Jack. Nostalgic, not your sort of thing at all.'

He didn't know what she meant. It must have shown in his face.

'Look at Blake. Look at Hamilton. You need to take more risks. Where's the irony and the grit? It *is* 1961, Jack.'

After she had gone he left the studio, slamming the door behind him: he couldn't bear to look at the painting any more. He went to the pub at the end of the road and stood at the bar gripping his glass, sipping the whisky slowly through clenched teeth.

It was only when he returned to the studio that afternoon that he realised she was right. As he walked through the door, the picture instantly came into focus, it was like turning the lens of Lenny's old monocular and seeing something shockingly familiar. There were long lilac shadows striped across an unkempt lawn, the faint sun-projected pattern of gates on gravel. There were clusters of leggy-stemmed buttercups growing against a wall. There was a sliver of a woman creeping out of the picture, a child under the branches of a tree, reaching up to a glistening ripple just above his head.

Some things should not be pinned down, not made visible.

He turned the canvas over and levered out the nails from the stretchers with a screwdriver, then he peeled away the fabric from the wood. He carried the picture down the stairs and left it in the yard, and returned to the studio for his rubbish bin and the stretchers. Outside on a patch of earth, he built the bonfire, just as he remembered Lenny building the camp fires on the Nab: a conical pyramid composed of twists of paper and kindling. When the fire was burning well, he threw the canvas into the centre of the flames and watched the images slowly curl and disappear. After a while, the bonfire started to spit: it kept advancing towards the building whenever Jack's back was turned. Every so often he had to kick the paper and the fragments of burning canvas back into the centre of the flames, then he fussed and fidgeted with a long stick at the ashy edges, picking out nails and staples. All afternoon, particles of carbonised paper and canvas floated round the yard, wafting into the air, stinging his eyes.

ELLEN

1929–31

The Red Baby

Maurice always called her the Duchess.

'How's the Duchess been today?' he would ask when he got home from work, sliding his short arm round her waist and brushing his moustache gently against her cheek. 'So what's the Duchess made for tea tonight?' he would murmur, as he lifted the lids of the saucepans that were sitting on the range.

Since the wedding things had grown pale again. There were days, if she was in the kitchen with Maurice's mother or upstairs in the bedroom with Maurice, when she thought it would be easier just to let the whiteness obliterate her.

She didn't like the house on Invicta Road. She didn't like the kitchen: it was small and it wasn't hers. She didn't like the front room either, the parrot always spat at her when she sat on the settee by the gas fire. She didn't like the bedroom with the yellow paper on the walls, or the lithograph of Our Lady and Saint Anne above the bed.

But most of all, she didn't like the bed. The bed, which she thought she would enjoy, which she thought would make up for the loss of the villa, turned out to be a terrible disappointment. When Maurice made love to her, he shut his eyes and furrowed his brows as if he was concentrating hard on something, calculating wall surfaces and tins of paint or rolls of paper.

Maurice was different in the house on Invicta Road. He was torn between Ellen and his mother. He would say one thing to Ellen in the bedroom, muttered under his moustache, and exactly the opposite to Mrs Rush in the kitchen, his face twitching, his hands fluttering by his sides.

One evening after tea, he said, 'Went down to the quayside to look at those cottages I've been talking about.'

Ellen was clearing away the dishes. Maurice's mother was at the sink.

'What cottages?' snarled Mrs Rush.

Maurice realised he had made a mistake: he stuttered and stumbled, flicked his eyes across the table at Ellen. 'I . . . we were thinking about getting our own place. Not right now, of course, but soon . . . maybe.'

Mrs Rush moved from the sink and stood over him.

'You can't go getting yourself fancy houses now. There's a slump on, you great lummox. You've a business to run.'

'It wasn't a fancy house, Ma, just a cottage.' He glanced at Ellen again: his moustache lurched uncomfortably above his top lip. 'But you've got a point, Ma, you've got a good point.'

Ellen lifted the serving dish slopping with cold meat juices and tiny discs of congealed fat from the table, and she could feel the hope drifting away from her. She could see it, like a feeble coil of smoke rising up from a fire that wouldn't burn.

Jack hated Invicta Road. He didn't say anything to her but his unhappiness was evident from his pinched face and his dark eyes. He loafed around the house, knocking into walls and furniture as if the rooms were too small for him.

'Watch the paintwork, Jacky!'

'He can paint it again, can't he?' was the surly reply.

The house was full of ornaments: clumsily moulded, glossily glazed vases and figurines of milkmaids and dancers – factory seconds, slightly deformed – spread along mantelpieces and corner shelves. She watched Jack slide his hand lazily over them.

'Watch the china lady, Jacky!'

He slunk away from her. He curled up on the settee and bit his nails.

She wanted to say: 'I'm sorry, Jacky. What could I have done? I had no choice.' But she scolded him instead. 'Now don't go getting all sulky on me, Jacky. Go out into the yard and play.'

He was supposed to share a bedroom with Mrs Rush. But halfway through his fourth night in the house he pulled the sheets and blankets off the bed and dragged them down the stairs to the front room. Ellen found him in the morning, lying on the settee. He had buried his face into his pillow and all she could see was his thick black hair.

She stroked his head. 'What are you doing here?'

He slowly twisted round so that she could see his pallid face.

'I can't sleep with her, Ma, she farts and she snores.'

'But you can't sleep here,' she said, brushing the hair from his eyes. And she told him to carry the sheets up to Mrs Rush's room and make the bed again.

The following night was just the same. Except this time Maurice's mother stood in the doorway to the front room in her vast grey nightgown and said, 'Oh, leave the boy alone, if that's what he wants. Can't say I wanted to share a room with him either.'

One afternoon Ellen walked up to the villa and looked through the newly padlocked gates. The grass in the garden was long now and there were dandelions growing in the drive.

Maurice had told her that Mr Quinlan wasn't coming back to Teesby after all, he said that the house was probably going to be sold. Ellen clutched the wrought-iron bars and felt the unfairness of it all. The villa was their home, hers and Beadie's and Jack's. It would be sold to someone with money from York or Darlington: a country home for a factory owner or a businessman. One day other people would sit in the dining room and the drawing room and in the kitchen. Other people's children would sprint along the passageways into the garden and play in the shade of the Monkey Puzzle tree.

In the house on Invicta Road, she thought about the tower on the Snook. They were brief thoughts, glimpses of colour when she was peeling potatoes or basting the meat, or at night, when she lay beside Maurice in the yellow bedroom. It was more of a dream than anything else: Jack smiling in a sand garden of samphire and driftwood. Ellen sitting on a bench looking at the blue shadows on the sea-rippled shingle and the terns twisting in the sky.

The months grew paler. Autumn arrived. She took Jack for his first day of school. He clasped her hand as they walked up the street, his small cold fingers knotted round hers. She stood at the school gate and watched him trudge across the playground without turning back. But when she returned in the afternoon, he was waiting for her on the pavement outside.

'Do I have to go back tomorrow?'

'Yes, Jacky.'

'And the next day?'

She nodded.

'How many days altogether?'

'Quite a few.' She must have made a face because he flinched and edged away from her.

She wanted to tell him that this was what the real world was like. Days and months and years of it: multiplication tables and Latin verb tables and dates learned by rote – 1066, 1659, 1707, 1815, 1914 repeated over and over again until they turned into a meaningless white noise.

'Try and make the best of it, Jacky,' she said cheerfully, as they made their way along the pavement in the sunshine towards Invicta Road.

Just before Christmas, Henry came marching into the house, tugging Jack behind him.

'They rang me at work, Nell. I've never been so appalled.' He swung Jack round so the boy was facing Ellen. 'You need to get a grip on him right now. Because if you don't there'll be worse trouble later on.'

'What on earth happened?'

'He went and hid himself in a cupboard. The teachers were looking for him all afternoon. And you know what he did when they found him?'

She looked down at Jack. He was small and cowering.

'When they opened the cupboard door, he went and bit Mr Armstrong on the wrist.'

'Why did you do it, Jacky?' she asked him later.

They were sitting in the backyard on the bench, both of them gazing at the vegetable bed: the frosted floppy leeks and the Brussels sprout stalks.

'Because I hate it here.'

'It'll get better.'

'You said that before. You keep saying that.'

'I promise you, Jacky, it'll sort itself out.' She took his hand and held it as hard as she could so he would believe her. But he tugged his fingers out of her clutch.

'You're hurting me, Ma!'

'I'm only trying to help.'

She wanted words of colour to come spinning out of her mouth. She wanted to take his hand and tell him that one day soon they would live in the tower, they would barricade the door so no one could find them and they would be hidden and happy: 'Hidden and happy. Hidden and happy,' cried the squeaking leeks and the baritone Brussels sprouts.

'I hate you, Ma,' said Jack, kicking the leg of the bench with the heel of his boot. 'I hate you! I hate you! I hate you!'

Ellen didn't feel the baby straight away. In fact, she didn't feel much at all. It was only when she started to be sick – in the afternoon not the morning – that she went to see the doctor. The queasiness hung heavily in those long dark hours before tea. She lay on the bed and listened to Jack in the yard, kicking a ball against the back wall – boom against the render, bang against the paving stones. She could feel the vibrations in the bedroom, great tremors oscillating through her body, making the nausea rise, making the tiny fish-form inside her flip and squirm.

The baby grew slowly, so slowly. The doctor cupped his hands round her stomach and pummelled it gently, feeling for life. He took the horn out of his bag and pressed it into her flesh.

'Don't worry,' he said, raising his head above her great white moon-belly, 'I can still hear it. The baby's hanging on. But you mustn't move now. It's bed rest for you until it arrives.'

She lay upstairs, far away from Jack, listening to Mrs Rush and the nattering parrot in the front room, and Maurice singing, 'The red, red robin comes bob, bob, bobbin' along,' as he washed his hands at the kitchen sink. And in the picture hanging on the wall above her head, Our Lady and Saint Anne were singing too, a trembling, tuneless duet: 'Immaculate Mary, thy praises we sing.'

The noise was too much for her. She turned to the alarm clock on the bedside table, and crawled into the wide white space between one minute and another.

When the baby was born, she was the colour of glistening sand. She shone brightly in the drab rooms of the house on Invicta Road.

Maurice's anxious face appeared in the doorway. 'I've come to see the baby, love.'

'Leave us alone! Don't touch her!' she snapped.

She growled at them, bared her teeth at Mrs Rush, whined and howled at Jack. She lay on her side guarding the child, sleeping with one eye open. The baby lay in the cradle next to the bed, shining pink then red then pink again. She was pink like the Pierre Ronsard roses in the villa garden.

'Cut me a bunch, Pearson, put them in a vase and bring them to the drawing room.'

She was red, like the purple red of the Persian carpet in the library.

'Oh yes, Pearson, such a beautiful colour. Tibbsy told me they dyed the wool with madder root.'

'Madder! Madder! Madder!'

They were sitting in the front room. Ellen was holding Catherine in her arms. Maurice was next to her, gazing down at the baby he was not allowed to touch. Sitting opposite them, in Granny Rush's armchair, was Father Scullion. Ellen could smell him. Old age was inside him, breeding in the warm and the wet, creeping out of his mouth like bad breath.

The front room was filled with men's words. Father Scullion's deep voice coiled itself round Maurice's. She looked down at the baby, buried herself in the baby's scarlet gleam.

'We were hoping to choose a date for Cathy to be christened, Father,' said Maurice.

'Catherine, not Cathy!' she barked.

Maurice gave a shudder beside her. 'Catherine,' he repeated quietly.

'What about May?' said Father Scullion, lowering his nose into a small black book clutched in his hand. 'The twenty-ninth?'

*

The twenty-ninth was a Thursday or a Friday. She wasn't sure which because the days were running away without her. She stood at the top of the stairs in her dressing gown, holding the baby to her chest.

Maurice was in the hall in his best suit. Behind him, Mrs Rush filled the doorway. She was wearing a bright purple coat and a hat with a bunch of artificial daisies stuck into the band. Jack was nowhere to be seen.

'I'm not going!' Ellen shouted down the stairs. 'God's not in Saint Anthony's and the christening's a spell that doesn't work.'

'But Father Scullion and Henry will be waiting. And we bought a cake.' Maurice's moustache drooped down glumly on either side of his mouth.

They sent for Father Scullion again. He came to the house and spoke to her in a dark voice about duty and motherhood. His words lingered in the air like stale grey clouds of incense. She could smell the communion wine and the roast dinner he had eaten for lunch, and the coffee he had drunk afterwards. She could smell the devil on his breath.

He made her kneel on the rug.

'Put the baby down, Ellen. Put her in the basket.'

His voice pinned Ellen to the floor. His words were as heavy as Beadie's weights, the ones she used to measure the flour, the black cast-iron ones. One pound, two pounds, three pounds piled up on Ellen's shoulders.

'Pray, Ellen, pray. Repeat after me: Hail Mary full of Grace. The Lord is with thee. Blessed art thou amongst women, and blessed is the fruit of thy womb, Jesus.'

It was summer now. It was cold. She wore her new felt cloche hat pulled down over her ears, and her windowpane check coat buttoned to the collar. The church was airless. When she walked towards the font, she thought she had slipped into the sea.

Father Scullion poured the holy water over the baby's head and Ellen felt the waves hit her and push her down. She couldn't save herself. She could hardly lift her arms or move her feet. All she could do was to let the current take her, drag her down towards the sea bed.

'In the name of the Father, and of the Son, and of the Holy Ghost,' murmured Father Scullion. Then the baby howled like an animal in pain, and the scream reverberated through the church, twisting round the pillars, circling the plaster statues, lifting the flakes of dark brown paint from the humid walls.

Father Scullion had promised her baby salvation. He had promised her sanctifying grace. But after the blessing things were just the same, except that Catherine remained above the waves, while Ellen was beneath them, sinking slowly towards the bottom of the sea.

JACK

1967–68

The Beach

The house was pale pink. It had bay windows set on either side of the green front door and a dormer in the roof. Against the backdrop of fields and farms it was an odd-looking building. It should have belonged by the sea, on the south-west coast, not in the East Midlands countryside.

Connie said she didn't like it. She muttered to him as they followed the agent, a young man with a tight suit and a Beatles haircut, into the entrance hall.

'It's too small,' she whispered. Although, when the agent pushed the doors open and they stepped inside, the rooms were surprisingly large. There were wide fireplaces and dado rails and panelling. And set into the tops of the windows were tiny motifs made from stained glass. The reflected colours gleamed on the wooden floors.

'And this is the kitchen, Mrs Pearson.'

Connie sailed past the agent and inspected the ancient sink. 'Of course this would have to go. And this,' she said, pointing to the gas cooker.

Jack left her to it, slid out of the kitchen and into the garden. He stood in the long grass beside a crop of nodding poppies. Through the open door he could still hear her fluty voice, the one she used for shop assistants and waiters.

'My husband's a lecturer at the art college in Nottingham ... a painter ... quite well known.'

This made him smile. He could see them through the kitchen window: the agent stifling a yawn and Connie gesturing at light switches and cupboards. 'Yes, this will all have to go.' She swept her arm around the room, then moved out of view. 'You see we're expecting a baby. It's due in December, which is why we're looking for something now.'

He turned away, began to walk through the garden. The grass was so long he had to wade through it like water. Growing amongst the rye grass and the wild oats was a mass of overgrown roses that had flopped over, heavy with buds, their stems arching under the weight. One or two of them had managed to clamber up the trunk of an arthritic apple tree. He could see sprays of pink and white flowers peeping through the spotted leaves and in between the wormy fruit.

At the far end of the garden was a small wrought-iron gate which had rusted open. He pushed through the nettles and brambles and stood at the top of a meadow that slipped away towards a shallow valley. It was a surprise. The view was wide and open, uninterrupted by roads and telephone lines and farm buildings. He could see broad bands of green and yellow fields that faded to blue in the distance. On the left was a silver birch straining against the breeze, on the right a line of shivering willows that edged a narrow stream. Somewhere in the sky a lark was singing, and from a faraway field he could hear the rumble of a tractor. He remembered feeling like this before, a faint unexpected sense of contentment.

Jack had become a surprisingly good teacher. He taught drawing: life drawing and observational drawing – the fat naked model or the cheese plant positioned in the centre of the room. When the weather was good, however, he sent the students out of the school and into the city.

'Everything's worth looking at,' he told them, as they slipped their sketchbooks under their arms. 'Look closely. Even the small-est, the most banal things are worth drawing.'

On Wednesday afternoons he gave lectures on contemporary painting. He stood in the warm glow of the projector, his voice accompanied by the scrape and clunk of the carousel while it made its circular journey from the first slide to the last. He showed the students paintings by Freud and Auerbach, Bacon and Leeming.

The students loved Leeming's work: the overweight figures reclining on the settee, the ubiquitous copy of *War and Peace*, the viscous paint – the phlegm-coloured greens, the semen-coloured creams and pale yellows.

'And what about your work, Jack?' they sometimes asked.

But he had stopped painting. He had put away the tubes of paint, and rolled up the canvas. He made drawings and prints now: fine-lined semi-abstract landscapes on sheets of deckle-edged, hot press paper. At weekends and in the holidays, he drove into the hills with a sketchbook and a bundle of pencils. When he arrived at his destination – an outcrop of rocks, or a damp gully, or a dry-stone wall – he positioned the car so the view was perfectly composed, framed by the thin metal edge of the windscreen. The scene in front of him was always partially obscured by the wipers, and the glass was speckled with traces of rain and the corpses of small flies that had collided with the car during the journey. These accretions had become important to him; each layer was essential. He blocked in the landscape then overlaid it with the spots and stains of the squashed insects on the screen.

In term time, he worked on monochrome engravings of the sketches. He sat at the table in the printmaking studio and pre-pared the copper plate, making narrow furrows with an etching needle. He relished the slowness of the process, the way it filled the time. He was meticulous. He inked the plate carefully, placed it in the press, then turned the wheel, just as his mother used to turn the handle of the mangle in the washhouse of the villa.

Jack and Connie moved into the pink house in early August. A month later he started to repair an old potting shed that had been built against the boundary wall. He replaced windows, fitted skylights and laid a concrete floor. When the floor was dry he carried in his bookcase, a new plan chest and a trestle table. On the wall, he pinned the old reproductions of Cézanne and Picasso, the detail from the Gozzoli fresco and a photograph he had cut from a Sunday supplement last year – the first picture of the earth taken from the moon: a grainy dimpled surface in the foreground and a brilliant white crescent beyond, emerging from the dark. He added two new pictures to the collection, Polaroids, one of himself, the other of Connie, taken when the sun was bright – except the colours had paled since then and the surface of the photographs was strangely milky. In the first picture, Jack was leaning in the doorway of the studio gazing down at something on the floor. He was just a silhouette, a jutting brow, an aquiline nose, a pointed chin – a profile like the outline of a rocky coast, all promontories and inlets. In the second picture, Connie was standing in the middle of the long grass in a beige maternity dress with a white Peter Pan collar. Her arms were folded across her chest and her eyes were looking skywards, out of boredom or irritation perhaps.

Early on Christmas Eve morning, Connie woke him.

She gripped his hand. 'It's happening, Jack. It's on its way.'

He bundled her into the car and drove her to the hospital, but was told by the midwife not to wait.

'It's going to be a while,' she said. 'We'll telephone you when we've got some news.'

He returned to the cold house and tried to fix the Christmas lights. Then he made himself a sandwich and ate it standing over

308

the kitchen sink while he looked out of the window at the glint of frost across the garden. He prayed briefly. Not to God, that would have been impertinent after all this time, but to Saint Anthony, patron saint of lost things: after all, he didn't want to lose this baby. He remembered the statue in the church in Teesby, the dour figure in monk's garb, clutching a lily in his hand.

'Make it all right,' Jack whispered, as he waited for the kettle to boil. 'Look after her, look after the baby.'

It wasn't until half past nine in the evening that the hospital finally rang to tell him that the child was born.

'Congratulations, Mr Pearson, it's a little girl,' said the voice on the other end of the line.

Connie was already asleep when he arrived in the doorway to the maternity ward. As he began to make his way towards her, the nurse sitting at the end of the ward twisted round and frowned at him.

'Your baby's in the nursery, Mr Pearson. Down the corridor and turn left,' she hissed.

In the nursery he was allowed to hold his daughter. He clutched her awkwardly, his left hand cupped against her head, his right against her lower back. She whimpered, then she let out a wail that started somewhere in her belly and vibrated upwards to her open mouth.

He remembered Cathy's cry all those years ago: the cat-squall when Father Scullion had dabbed her forehead with holy water. Cathy's shriek had sounded like a refusal, like a long drawn out *Noooo* – piercing and pagan. Even after it had stopped, its echo bounced from pillar to pillar down the aisle and out of the church door. He remembered leaning back against his mother's legs and pulling her coat around him to cover his ears. That was the coat she would dance in later, the blue windowpane check coat, its hem drenched with salt water.

'You should hold her closer, Mr Pearson,' said the nurse, who was standing beside him. 'Like this,' and she nudged the new baby into the crook of his arms. 'That's better, isn't it,' she whispered to the child as she stroked its cheek with her forefinger.

The baby was warm against his chest. He had tried to hold Cathy like this outside the church after the christening. They had sat on a bench and someone had taken a photograph, while he'd attempted to cradle the baby in his arms. Cathy had flopped around like a large fish: her hands and legs had flailed as if she was trying to swim. Maurice, seeing the struggle, had taken hold of his daughter, and had said, just like the nurse, 'Now, that's better, isn't it?'

He remembered holding his sister when he carried her across the beach a few months later. He had gripped Cathy then, like a voluminous package or a bundle of damp washing pulled quickly from the line.

Jack lowered his head and drew closer to his daughter. When he had held Cathy she had smelt of soap flakes and sweet curdled vomit. Sometimes she smelt of Granny Rush, a flat, burnt odour like charcoal. Sometimes she smelt like Beadie's cat. On the day he had carried her back from the beach, she had smelt of seaweed and that oozy dark miasma that rose up from the greasy rock pools below the quay – the reek of dead molluscs rotting inside their shells.

But this baby, the baby he held in his arms now, his baby, smelt of nothing at all. She was odourless, as if she didn't yet belong to the world, as if she didn't yet belong to him.

He handed the child back to the nurse.

'Have you decided on a name?' she asked, placing the baby in the crib.

'Rosie,' he replied quickly. It was the first name he could think of. He wanted to end the conversation. Easier to supply a name, any name, than to stand there turning over the possibilities with the weary nurse.

He stopped for a drink in a pub, a street away from the hospital. He wasn't sure what else to do. He hadn't expected to feel like this, the exhaustion, the relief, the faint anti-climax. He could not untangle the extraordinary from the banal: the birth of a child, her first night in the world, his dry mouth, his stale breath, his need for a drink. The creature, who this morning he had only been able to picture as a curl of soft bone and pale flesh inside Connie's watery womb, was now the baby who lay sleepily in her cot, who breathed just as he did, who, immediately after her entrance into the world, knew how to move her limbs, knew how to cry. He was disappointed at his inability to take it all in, to understand it, to celebrate it. Already the magic had drifted away. Already he was thinking of other things: whether he should have another drink, whether he should ring the Meakins tonight or wait until tomorrow.

When they brought the baby home, he gazed at her lying in the cradle, and vowed to be a good father. He vowed to love her beyond his initial raw, instinctive desire to protect her. In the weeks that followed, he manoeuvred her into clean nappies and clean clothes. He dabbed her mouth with a damp cloth and wiped her runny nose. And yet, he still did not feel she belonged to him.

Connie behaved as if their daughter was immutably connected to them both, merely an extension of themselves. But he was certain that the baby was separate, a distinct and complete entity, a being whom he could not entirely fathom. He sensed this most strongly when he bathed her, when he clutched her slippery body and watched her wild kicking in the water. At such moments an extraordinary force, like a sinewy cable, pulsated through her body.

The baby remained nameless for several weeks. His suggestion of Rosie was dismissed straight away. Connie favoured longer names – Vanessa, Victoria, Cressida – while Jack preferred something shorter and more modern. There were times when they agreed, when they settled on Jemima or Sarah. But as soon as they had whispered the name over the sleeping baby, he shook his head. He saw the name slipping away from the child, a gap suddenly opening up between the sound of the syllables he and Connie had just enunciated, and the small human form in the cradle.

'How about Hannah?' asked Connie one morning, standing in the doorway to the studio. As always, when she posed a question she suspected was contentious, she held her head on one side, waiting for his reaction.

'What about Hannah, Jack?'

'Hannë?' When he repeated the name it was a sharp, short sigh.

'Yes, Hannah. It's nice, isn't it. Or Anna, if you want, but I prefer Hannah.'

He didn't know what to say. He pictured Connie rifling through the studio when he was at work. He was tempted to glance at the bookcase to see whether Hannë's books had been disturbed.

'Hannë,' he muttered again, testing the shape of the name in his mouth. He could not decide if Connie was playing a game with him, or if her choice was just a horrible coincidence.

He could have said that the name didn't suit the baby, or that he didn't like its indecisive sound – the unnecessary 'ah' of the second syllable. Or he could have just told Connie the truth. He could have said: 'Hannë was an old girlfriend, didn't I ever say?' Although he knew that once he had mentioned Hannë the questions would begin. Then Connie would hang onto every answer he gave.

'Hannah or Anna? It's one or the other,' she said sharply. 'Time's running out, Jack, we have to register her tomorrow.'

'Anna,' he replied. 'I prefer Anna.'

*

312

The baby had stirred something. The present and the past had begun to collide. The small child lying in her cot in the upstairs bedroom was propelling him backwards, to Hannë dancing in the sea mist at the edge of the Snook, to Cathy in the pram, kicking the warm damp sheets, to Ellen in her windowpane check coat marching down Invicta Road.

He saw the river again, a dark mark in the sand; the ice cream salesman on the beach lifting up a cornet as they passed by; the sad donkey shaking its head at the flies; and the boy who had wandered towards him with a spade in his hand. Everything was turning in circles or shuffling back and forth like his small booted feet in the Teesby sand.

Jack planned the trip carefully, imagining it as a doctor's prescription, a list of medication to be taken only once. He would start with the villa at the top of the town, descend to Invicta Road, drive past Mrs Veasey's boarding house, and end his journey at the sea. It was time to find out whether it would hurt as much as he thought, like biting down on a bad tooth in the hope of discovering that the ache had faded at last.

He didn't tell Connie where he was going, and Connie didn't ask.

He was standing in the bedroom doorway in his car coat.

'I'm going out for the day, if that's all right. I'll be back quite late.'

Connie was feeding the baby. She didn't look up.

'Yes, of course, that's fine,' she said, brushing away a dribble of milk from Anna's mouth with her finger.

It was raining when he left. As he turned onto the motorway, it became a downpour. Even when the rain was flung away by the wipers all he could see ahead of him was wave after wave of water. He stopped at a service station near Wetherby and drank a beige-coloured cup of tea while he waited for the weather to change. He sat for an hour watching the lorry drivers and the families traipsing across the wet floor to the self-service counter while he listened to Marianne Faithfull's mournful voice piped through the speakers above his head.

By the time he reached the junction for Teesby, the rain had thinned into a wet film across the windscreen. He flicked the wipers on and listened to the whine of the rubber against the glass, then flicked them off again. Ahead of him, the landscape had started to take on a familiar shape and the sky possessed that misty brightness that suggested the sea was not so far away.

He turned off the main road into a twist of roundabouts and one-way systems, and found himself heading into Teesby from a direction he hadn't anticipated. Once-familiar landmarks – the spire of Saint Anthony's, the tower of the Protestant church, the works chimneys – were aligned in such a way that, for a second or two, he could not identify them at all. He slipped down into a narrow street that must have been a sheep track when he was a boy, then followed the edge of the hill that flanked the town. He had already driven past the villa before the view in front of him fused into the landscape he remembered.

He parked crookedly by the old green railings that bordered the garden of the neighbouring house. He had expected things to have changed. But when he reached the gates, the villa was just as he remembered it: deep red brick and flaking white paintwork. To one side of the entrance, planted in the ground, was a large sign: 'Teesby Borough Council', and part of the front garden had disappeared under a small square car park.

The Monkey Puzzle tree was still standing, the base of its trunk cocooned in thick black tarmac. He remembered wandering under the tree as a child, stroking the trunk. The bark looked like old skin rippling all the way down to the roots, like the dimpled fat that used to wobble on Mrs Tibbs's arms. He remembered Henry, standing at the gates telling him that the Monkey Puzzle tree was the only tree that would grow properly in Teesby, because of the salt in the soil, and the salt in the air. *Araucaria araucana*, he had called it, and Jack had repeated the name. Saying *Araucaria araucana* was like rolling a sweet between his tongue and his palate. It sounded like a prayer, like something Father Scullion might have said to him in the confessional box: 'You must say three Hail Marys and an *Araucaria araucana*.'

'*Araucaria araucana*,' he muttered to himself, waiting for an emotion – nostalgia, regret, relief that nothing had changed. But as he stood in front of the villa, gazing at the green Anglia and the red Hillman Imp parked in the shadow of the tree, he felt nothing at all. He didn't care that the front garden had gone, Mrs Tibbs's precious Sarah Bernhardt peonies and the lupins and the lavender bushes swallowed up. He didn't really care that the Monkey Puzzle tree had been saved.

He was just as indifferent when he stopped in front of 33 Invicta Road, its front door boarded with a panel of plywood on which someone had daubed, in electric blue paint, the word 'Scab'. And again, nothing when he sat in the car, with the engine still running, outside the house on Marine Parade.

He drove along the promenade and parked opposite what had once been the Victoria Tearooms, and was now a café called Fred's. It was raining again. He put on his coat, crossed the road and leaned over the railings. From this position, slightly elevated above the empty beach, he could see all the way from the snake-stone cliffs to the mouth of the river. In front of him was a wide sweep of sand and a narrow shimmer of sea, broken in the distance by the tower on the Snook. The rain was a soft veil over the scene. Looking at the beach and the sea was like looking at an unfinished painting. The first glazes had been applied and now all he needed to do was to block in the figures.

His mother was standing near the estuary, at the point where the river met the sea. She was wearing her windowpane check coat, but she had lost her hat, and her hair was blowing wildly in the breeze. A few feet away, next to the empty pram, was a policeman, and beside the policeman, head lowered, hoping he wouldn't be noticed, was a small boy clutching a baby to his chest.

The Duchess: July 1931

From the doorway of the front room, he watched her carry the baby down the stairs and place her in the old pram in the hallway. She was wearing her new check coat and her blue felt hat, despite the heat.

'Where are you going?' he asked.

He was half dressed. He had pulled on his shorts but was still wearing his pyjama top.

'The Snook,' she replied. 'Come on. Get a move on, Jacky. Tidy your bed and put your shirt on.'

'Why are we going to the Snook?'

She ignored him or she didn't hear him. She released the brake of the pram with her foot and wheeled it along the hallway to the front door.

'Hurry up, Jacky. I'm not waiting for you.' She opened the door and bumped the pram down the step and onto the street.

She was already at the end of Invicta Road by the time he had left the house. She was marching along the pavement, the feather in her cloche hat bouncing up and down. The sun was low and her shadow was long, it trailed behind her rippling over the uneven paving stones. When he reached her, she stretched out her hand and waved it at him, but didn't wait. He had to jog for a few steps before he could finally grasp her cold, damp fingers in his own.

They made their way through the quiet town, down the High

Street and along the promenade to the quay. The ferryboat was about to leave. There were half a dozen passengers hunched on the benches and a pair of hens squatting nervously in a lopsided cage. The ferryman and his mate picked up the pram and lifted it over the side of the boat as if it weighed nothing at all. The baby cried out in surprise, and the passengers turned and looked at them, at the old pram, the overdressed woman in her winter coat and the small sleepy boy. His stomach lurched as he stepped from solid ground to the gently rocking boat.

The ferry turned in the water and the skyline he knew so well began to slide away from him: the church spire and the roofs of Marine Parade merged for a moment then stretched apart again. He looked over the edge of the boat at the marbled oil puddles floating on the surface. On any other day it would have been a treat to cross the river, but he felt sick, from hunger or from anticipation.

When they reached the other side, the ferryman's dog, tied to a post, barked excitedly, and the baby whined as the pram was lifted back out of the boat onto the quay. While his mother fussed with the baby's blanket, he looked at the view. From this side of the river, the sea was the colour of soot-flecked glass, and the sky was flat and white. In the far distance, behind the heat haze, the tower had almost vanished.

She pushed the pram briskly down the coast road. He ambled behind, pulling at the clumps of grass that grew on the verge. At the bend in the road, he paused to inspect a coin lying in the dust. When he kicked it with the toe of his boot, it turned out to be a bottle top, and he had to run for a few yards to keep her in his sight.

He saw her haul the heavy pram off the tarmac and disappear down the muddy lane that led to the marsh. It wasn't until he had passed several thickets of tall reeds that he finally caught up with her. The pram was standing in the shadow of a thin willow and she was looking at a metal sign which had been screwed to a stake planted in the sand. 'Air Ministry. Trespassers will be Prosecuted,' he read aloud. Beyond the sign was a barrier, a long wooden pole freshly painted in red and white bands. It was suspended horizontally from a post like a gate at a level crossing. She bent over it, inspecting the mechanism: the pole was counterweighted on one side.

'We have to push that down,' she said, pointing to the counterweight. 'Then the pole lifts up. If I lift it up a bit, you can push the pram through.'

He hadn't completely understood the words on the sign, but he could guess what they meant. He could guess what the barrier meant too.

'Jacky, are you listening to me? Come on, I'm doing this for you. I'll lift it up and you can wheel the pram through.'

She pushed down on the weight and the pole, in a wide satisfying arc, swung up into the sky. He gripped the handle of the pram and forced it forwards over the causeway. It was difficult to steer. The track was rutted and there were deep puddles of sea water and piles of stones and shells that had been swept onto the causeway by the high tide. He pushed blindly. He was too small to see anything beyond the pram's leather hood, and the breeze kept blowing his hair into his eyes. The sun had disappeared behind the sea mist now, but it was still hot. He was sweating underneath his shirt, and the baby was kicking at the sheets. He stopped for a moment to catch his breath, then forced the pram forward again. It groaned and rattled over the track as the baby muttered gently to herself.

When he was halfway along the causeway, the wind changed direction. Over the noise of the straining pram and the gurgles from the baby, he could hear a faint voice in the distance. Someone was calling to him. A man was shouting from the Snook.

'Can't you read the sign? The sign, didn't you see it?'

Jack stopped pushing and peered round the side of the pram.

At the end of the track was a man in a blue-grey uniform. He was standing at the point where the rubble of the causeway met the sand of the Snook. Behind him, parked near the old huts, was a lorry. Beside the lorry was a group of soldiers, five or six of them. They appeared to be unloading something heavy from the back.

The man on the track, more of a boy really, was shaking his head.

'Can't you read the sign?' he called again, gesturing frantically towards the barrier.

Jack looked over his shoulder at his mother. She had lowered the pole and was marching across the causeway. When she reached him, she grasped the handle of the pram and began to push it stubbornly towards the Snook.

'Didn't you hear me, didn't you hear what I said?' shouted the man. 'This is government property, Missus.' He took a step towards her – his legs apart, his arms folded – in an attempt to block her path with his body. 'It's Air Ministry land, Missus. It's dangerous.'

'I have to get to the tower,' she said, trying to thrust the pram forward again.

The man was nervous. He twisted and turned, looked over his shoulder at the Snook then jabbed his finger at her. 'If you don't turn back, I'll have to get the others.' The soldiers had stopped what they were doing and were leaning against the lorry staring at Jack's mother.

'I'm warning you, Missus.'

'Don't call me Missus,' she said sharply. There was a silence, she must have been thinking about what to say next. Then, quite calmly, quite reasonably, she said, 'I'm not called Missus. I'm a Duchess. You have to call me Duchess.'

The men standing by the lorry were laughing. He could hear them above the sound of the sea and the sea birds and the scuttling crabs and his own small feet shuffling in the rubble of the

320

causeway. He wished she would disappear. He prayed to God that she would disappear. He wanted to wake up and find himself lying on the settee in the front room so the morning could start all over again.

She turned and called to him. 'Jacky! Jacky!'

But he wouldn't move. He stood in the middle of the causeway and gazed down at the track. If he stared at the track he could ignore what was happening ahead of him, and he pushed the toe of his boot into the stones and the shells, then he crouched down and examined the pebbles.

'Jacky!'

He slowly lifted his head again, thinking that by now she would have forced her way onto the Snook and that he would have to make a decision. He would have to choose who was right, his mother or the man in the uniform. But when he finally looked up, he could see that the soldier was walking away towards the lorry and that his mother was pulling the pram backwards along the causeway.

'Don't fret,' she said when she reached him. 'Don't worry, I know another way round. We'll get there in the end.'

It was late morning. The tide was out. The ferryboat sat low in the estuary mud, and the ferryman was sitting beside his dog on the quayside, smoking a cigarette. To get to the town now they had to cross the metal bridge upstream, another half a mile or so up the road. His shirt was wet with sweat and his stomach grumbled from hunger. The baby was wide awake and was fidgeting under the sheets. His mother was calm, however, almost serene.

When they finally arrived at the bridge, she halted. She looked down the muddy river channel towards the estuary and said, 'We can get to the tower from the beach. We can walk right across the sand.'

She was right. He peered between the railings and could see that the deep river had disappeared, it was just a dark stain in the middle of the muddy bed. The wide gulf of water that usually separated the Snook from the town appeared to have drained away.

It was a long walk: down the road to the promenade, then down the ramp and across the shore. His mother ploughed the pram diagonally over the beach, past the donkeys and the ice cream salesman and the children hunting for cockles. The pram creaked and moaned over the undulating sand, splashed through the rivulets of clear salt water.

When the wheels began to sink into the wet beach, she said, 'We'll leave it here. We'll come back for it later. It'll be all right.'

He watched her lift the baby from the pram and wrap it in a shawl. Then she began to trudge across the beach again with the child held tight against her body. He followed a few feet behind. He could see the baby's head above his mother's shoulder, she was looking back at him with round eyes and a round open mouth.

They drew close to where the river had run, and he paused and looked back to see how far they had walked. He could trace the journey they had made from the dry sand to the wet. He could see the empty pram silhouetted against the sunlight, and the two sets of footprints, his mother's and his own. In the distance, the prints were shallow, hardly visible at all, but those closest to him were deep and were starting to fill with water.

'Ma, I think we're sinking.'

But she continued to tramp forward with the baby in her arms.

'We're sinking, Ma.' He ran towards her, up a steep ridge of sand, kicking up clods of silt that spun into the air then shattered into fragments. He could smell the estuary now, the thick odour of rotting seaweed and dead fish.

When he reached her, she was standing at the edge of the channel, at the point where the river met the sea. The wide gulf which divided the northern end of the beach from the coastline of the Snook had not vanished after all. It was simply hidden behind a bank of sand.

He gazed down at the water. 'Can we go home now?'

'Oh, come on, Jacky, it's not that deep. We're almost there.'

He stood at the edge of the slopping, sickening river, and watched her take a step forward from the muddy sand into the silty water.

Far away on the quay, the ferryman's dog was barking, and the sound came and went, looping in and out of the soft breeze. Now his mother was wading shin-deep with the baby in her arms, her windowpane check coat trailing in the water behind her. She lurched sideways as the sand gave way under her feet, and when she tried to steady herself the baby in her arms cried out – a shrill yelp like a frightened puppy.

Further down the channel, a dark-haired boy who had been digging a moat in the sand looked up.

'She your mam?' he called, casually swinging his small spade at the figure in the water.

Jack shook his head.

The boy sauntered over. 'Is she mad, your mam?' he asked, just as her blue felt hat was knocked sideways off her head by the breeze.

Jack and the boy watched the hat as it began to bob up and down, appearing then disappearing like a resolute seabird in the peaks and troughs of the waves.

'She must be mad, looks like a flipping loony to me,' continued the boy.

Jack ignored him. He moved his feet, shifted them back as the tide crawled over the sand towards the toes of his boots. The boy shuffled too. Then he pointed with the edge of his metal spade at the waves.

'Is she drowning the baby, like what you do with kittens?' He grinned a toothless grin at Jack, and without waiting for an answer he wandered back to his ditch, now brimming with sea water.

Jack's mother had almost made it to the middle of the channel. But the water was deep and the waves were reaching up to touch the baby's shawl. He knew he should wade into the river and try and drag them out, but he could not move. He stood with the toe of his boot as close to the tide as he dared, but each time a small silt-coloured wave approached he drew his foot away.

'Come on, Jacky!' His mother twisted round, held out her hand and fluttered her fingers at him. 'Come on, come with us. We're going home.'

As she turned back again, a policeman appeared over the ridge of sand. He was tall and burly with a luxuriant handlebar moustache. He hurled himself into the river and grasped her hand, like a footman helping an elderly lady to alight from a carriage. But once they were on dry land again, he pushed her towards the sand bank. And with a great sweep – the way a bird of prey might pluck a tiny rodent from the ground – he snatched the baby out of her arms and thrust her into Jack's. In Jack's small hands, his sister was just a swaddle of wet shawl. She didn't move, and as far as he could see she wasn't breathing either.

They walked across the beach to the promenade, the small boy, the woman in the wet windowpane check coat, and the policeman who had taken the baby back from Jack and was cradling her in his arms. They walked up the High Street, past Hooper's Hotel, past the Town Hall, past the big houses and the shops. Jack could see the women's faces at the windows, watching as they passed. There were shadows in the gaps between the neatly hemmed curtains, behind the stacked boxes of Lux and cakes of Knights Castile, between the dress shop mannequins.

Someone must have told Maurice; he was staring out of the bay window of the house on Invicta Road as they walked up the path. He had pulled the curtain away from the glass and was leaning awkwardly, the palm of his right hand against the windowpane, his left hand clinging to the curtain. He was biting his lip, and his moustache, a thin black line above his mouth, contorted with every movement of his face.

Inside the house, the policeman guided his mother into the front room. But Jack was pushed straight through the hallway and into the kitchen by Granny Rush. She had seized the baby from the policeman, and was holding it in the crook of her arm. With her other hand she propelled Jack past the dresser and the sink towards the back door.

He watched her lay the baby carefully on the table and pull away the wet clothes. She filled a kettle with water and set it on the range.

'You all right?' she asked, turning to Jack.

He nodded. And she puckered her lips into a brief, cold smile and nodded too. From the jug on the windowsill, she poured some milk into a cup and handed it to him. Then she gave him one last shove, out of the kitchen and into the yard, before she locked the door behind him.

He sat on the bench near the back wall, next to the potato plants that had begun to wither in the heat. Through the kitchen window, he could see Granny Rush turning from the range, where the kettle was beginning to boil, to the baby lying on the table. She stripped the child of its damp clothes and washed it carefully. After she had dried the baby, she wrapped it in a bundle of blankets and, without a look towards Jack, she left the kitchen with the child in her arms.

When she had gone, he got up from the bench and tried the door. But before he turned the handle he knew it would still be locked. He trailed back to the end of the yard, picked up the cup and started to drink the milk. It tasted sour, and when he took the cup away from his mouth he noticed that a cluster of small black flies had flown into the liquid and were floating on the surface. A few of them had become stranded on the edge of the cup, so he tipped it from side to side and watched the wave of milk lick at the beached flies, lifting them up then depositing them on the opposite edge. He played like this for a while, until the sour milk slopped onto his shorts and dribbled down his bare leg. He poured the rest of the milk into a hollow that he made with a long stick in the dry yellow soil of the potato bed. Standing over the hole, his hands on his knees, he watched the liquid soak into the earth.

When the milk was gone he made his way to the bench again and sat down slowly. His body felt heavy. His arms ached from pushing the pram along the causeway. The crooks of his elbows, the muscles in his forearms, and even the joints between his fingers were stiff. His boots had acquired leaden heels, and his thin shirt lay uncomfortably over his shoulders and his chest. But it was his insides that felt really bad – his gut, his belly. He had always imagined his body as a deep, uncharted sea full of dark spaces where spongy forms drifted like jellyfish, or waved their tentacles like sea anemones. Now, sitting on the bench in front of the dying potato plants, he was aware of his insides as he had never been before. It was like they were being pulled down by Maurice's lead sinkers and all the jellyfish and the sea anemones were descending rapidly to the soles of his feet.

It was late afternoon when Granny Rush finally unlocked the back door again and led him through the kitchen and into the hallway. He was cold, his arms were covered in goose-bumps. Uncle Henry, who was hovering by the staircase, handed him a jumper that Jack had left that morning draped over the banister rail. The jumper was inside out. He managed clumsily to turn it the right way round, but when he pulled it over his head, he discovered that one of the sleeves was still caught inside the body. He struggled with it, tried to thrust his clenched fist through the tangled armhole and push against the tight weave of the wool, but nothing gave way. If his mother had been there, she would have knelt down in front of him and pulled out the sleeve. But no one in the hallway had noticed his struggle, not Uncle Henry, lodged uncomfortably in the angle between the staircase and the kitchen wall, nor Granny Rush who, with the air of a prison guard, was leaning against the front door with her arms folded. Jack pulled the jumper back over his head, and returned it to the banister rail.

Someone opened the door to the front room, perhaps it was Maurice. Someone else led him to the settee that faced the bay window. Jack sat on the hard edge, the rough horsehair seat pressed against the backs of his bare legs, and looked round the room. Standing next to the parrot's cage was the doctor. Jack knew the doctor, he remembered the ear syringes and the tongue depressors and the smell of the Bunsen burner. The doctor's moustache was untrimmed. Stiff white hairs overhung his wide mouth, like the uneven bristles in the cheap brushes that Maurice had used when he had repainted the front gate last summer.

Next to the doctor, sitting in Granny Rush's armchair beside the gas fire, was Father Scullion. Father Scullion was old. His face was creased and crinkled: his cassock smelt of the damp prayer books piled on a shelf at the back of Saint Anthony's. Father Scullion was leaning forward slightly, his hands clasped in his lap. He was smiling gently at Jack.

'Now tell us what you saw,' he asked quietly, calmly. 'Tell us what happened, Jack.'

He wanted to tell Father Scullion that the world was unjust, unkind and cruel. It was filled with sneering boys, angry policemen, sour milk, locked doors, inside-out jumpers. She should have been there with him, holding his hand, brushing the hair back from his damp forehead.

'Where's my ma?' he whined.

'She's in bed, Jack. Now tell us what happened. Did your mother do something bad? You shouldn't be afraid to tell us, it's not your fault if she did something wrong. We know what she can be like, Jack. You can tell us the truth.'

Father Scullion reached out and patted Jack's bare knee, his hand was large and warm.

'Don't be afraid to tell us, Jack,' he murmured, still smiling. 'Your mother was trying to hurt the baby, wasn't she?'

It was easy now. Father Scullion had made it easy.

He pictured the scene on the beach, not as he remembered it but as it suited him. He could blame her for his heavy, queasy body; for sending him to Saint Ignatius, for bringing him to Invicta Road. Father Scullion was right.

'She tried to drown the baba in the sea.'

As soon as he had uttered the words, he made it true. He was certain that he *had* seen the baby's head sliding under the surface of the water, and his mother drawing the waves over the baby's face like a sheet over a corpse. And now he hated her even more because he believed his story. He hated her because of the barrier at the causeway, and the uniformed man shouting at him, and the long walk back to town over the metal bridge, and his own chilly goose-bumped arms, and his aching stomach. So he said it again, clearly this time, just to make sure that Father Scullion and the doctor had heard.

'My ma wanted to drown the baba like a kitten in the sea, she told me so.'

Ellen

The Villa that isn't the Villa

There was sand in her mouth, under her nails, in the curls of her ears, in the creases of her skin, in the crooks of her elbows, in her belly button, between her toes, between her breasts, between her legs. She was made of sand. She was a worm cast on the beach, drying slowly, soon to be washed back into the sea again.

But Saint Anne was there to help. Saint Anne – patron saint of unmarried mothers and housewives and miners – had sprung down from the picture and was holding Ellen's hand. Holding her together. Saint Anne was a woman from the Nab, like Beadie on a good day, small and tough and honest. Saint Anne was on Ellen's side.

They could smell Father Scullion – a whiff of incense and rising damp. They could smell the doctor too – old tweed and antiseptic. They could hear Maurice downstairs in the front room – monotone, monologue, telling tales.

Saint Anne shook her head. 'Well, bugger me,' she said.

They could hear Henry wheezing on the landing. They watched Granny Rush come into the room and pull the cradle away from the end of the bed. She pushed it awkwardly out of the door, bang, against the wall, bang, against the door frame.

*

Ellen must have fallen asleep because she was woken by the snow. It tumbled from the ceiling, smothering the carpet and the wet shoes and the woollen coat. It fell over Saint Anne until she was completely covered in it: she couldn't move or speak. The snow-flakes drifted across the bedclothes and buried Ellen's shoulders and her face.

'Go on, make me invisible, hide me away.'

Henry was bending over her.

'It's only for a few days, Nell, until you're better.'

'Don't leave me there, Henry.'

'But it's only for a few days.'

'And look after Jacky. Promise me, Henry.'

The handkerchief was in his hand, twisting round his finger. Round and round it went, white handkerchief, pink finger, white handkerchief.

'Of course, I promise, Nell.'

She put on the going-away dress, the dress she had worn in the Scarborough hotel. Into her pocket she slipped the piece of jet. It was the only solid thing left, a connection between them. She pressed her thumb against the cool, shallow ridges of the flying fish.

He was standing at the upstairs window when they led her through the yard. She couldn't look back because bad things would happen – Jacky would turn into sand and be washed away. But as she reached the gate she couldn't bear it any longer. She twisted her head and waved at the pale blue shadow gazing down at her.

They put her in a car and drove her to the villa. She could see the gates and the gravel drive, but when she stood outside and looked for the view it wasn't there. There was no view. No distance. No time, either, because time *is* distance. Time is the view across the roofs of the town to the sea, to the horizon line, to the point where you can't see anything more. They had taken away the view to punish her.

If she didn't want to be stuck in the white space, she would have to make her own time.

There was the echo in the tiled corridor at the back of the hospital.

She could stand at one end and shout: 'Where's Jacky?' And the words would come straight back at her: 'Where's Jacky?' A faint ghost of a voice that was proof that time was advancing, that she had existed in the past as much as she existed right now.

But they didn't like it, the white women and the white men. They said she was shouting. They sent her to a room that had no echo and they locked the door.

To make time happen there, she had to say each word slowly, in the hope that between the first word 'Where's' and the last word 'Jacky', time had moved forward.

When they let her out of the echoless room, she decided to make time pass another way. She decided to remember the things that had just happened then work her way backwards to the beginning again. It was like digging through layers of snow – easy at first because the snow was wet and fresh. She could make out a pair of gates, but not the gates to the villa. She could see Father Scullion's lined face, and the doctor's white moustache. But now the snow was thick and compacted, too heavy to shift. She had to concentrate. She had to think hard. She saw a wet coat lying on the bedroom floor, a baby's wet shawl, a blue felt hat floating in the water. But the snow was frozen, and her hands skated across the ice without grazing the surface. If she tried to think beyond the hat, all she could see was a wet shawl and a wet coat lying on the bedroom floor, followed by the doctor's white moustache, and Father Scullion's lined face. Finally she saw a pair of gates, but not the gates to the villa.

It was a trap. They had set a trap for her.

It was the sort of time that only looped and turned back on itself. Useless time that went round and round in circles.

There must be other ways. Quiet ways. Clever ways.

There was *Appointments, 1932*.

There was the small pencil attached to the ribbon that had been sewn into the binding.

She wrote:

Henry.

Henry's face.

The scuff marks on the tips of the boy's boots. The sand embedded in the shallow creases of the leather.

The handkerchiefs. The white stitches that hold the white hems in place.

Sand in the air, blown into the ward through the open window.

The brown rosary beads between her fingers.

The blue stripes on Henry's shirt, like … like …

A priest who smells of gravy, standing over her, pushing his face into hers. But she can do what she likes now, say what she likes now. With all her force she thumps her fists against his flabby old-man's chest.

'I hate you, I hate you, I hate you.'

There were things she could remember from before.

List them. List them, so she wouldn't repeat them:

Mrs Tibbs's lace veil that is stitched onto the lilac silk toque that she doesn't wear any more.

'As to the matter concerning the state of the paintwork, I shall leave this entirely in your hands.'

Beadie leaning against a spade in the garden.

The colour of the etched glass globe over the gas lamp in the hallway of the villa.

The silver pocket watch slowly coming to a stop.

A moth. A buttercup petal: 'Beautiful, Jacky.'

The sound of a wailing cat. The view from the window in the back room. The light that flashes on and off, on and off.

'Tell Beadie that Casaubon must be trapped somewhere.'

The burning glow from the sea.

The basement nights when the drums play in the sky. Boom. Boom. Boom. Boom.

The smell of sweet cordite.

The smell of the tower on a pewter day.

The man flying. A firework. A swirling Catherine Wheel. A Fairy Fountain. A Silver Drop.

Mr Churchill on the radiogram. Mr Churchill fighting on Teesby beach. Fat old Churchill covered in Teesby sand.

'Where did Henry go?'

A blue man on the drive. Bang on the window.

'There's Jacky. There's Jacky, nurse.'

'Calm yourself, Mrs Rush. Come away from the window.'

They grasp her shoulders and she lashes out at a flask of water that is standing on a bedside locker. Crashing silver. Water and glass and a bloody hand. A gash that runs across her palm, baubles of shiny blood, a chain of red fairy lights.

'We'll have none of your histrionics, Mrs Rush!'

'None of your histrionics,' whispers the starched uniform.

'Histrionics. Histrionics,' says the bloodstain as it seeps across the apron.

*

335

Fog. Fog. Fog. Snow. Sea mist.

She presses her thumb against the cool, shallow ridges of the flying fish.

Mist. Sunshine.

Sunlight on the tiled floor of the corridor. The button flowers on the groundsel in the drive. The lime trees. A book in her hand, the yellow pages fluttering in the breeze, a swallowtail caught in a net curtain, flap, flap, flap. Grace Archer and Mary Dale on the wireless in the hospital parlour. The moths and the butterflies lying dead on the windowsill.

A suitcase. The wrought-iron gates shut behind her. The road dips and rises, dips and rises, dips and rises.

The smell of the sea. The taste of the sand.

'Da said the Pearsons came out of the sand. He said they were born out of the red clarty sand that sticks to the soles of your boots and the hem of your frock.'

'Settle down, Mrs Rush. Settle down.'

'Enough to drive you mad all this sand.'

It's in her hair, in her ears, in the gaps between her toes, in the corners of her eyes.

'And it's in our blood too.'

There are pots of blue holly at the entrance. A pink leatherette chair in a tiled room. A view of the sea. A view of the television set. Janet of Tannochbrae and Elsie Tanner in the residents' lounge.

'Tell Jacky I want to see him. Tell Jacky.'

ELLEN AND JACK

1981

Our Lady of Sorrows

She likes to be called the Duchess but they always forget – the tray-carriers and the trolley-clatterers and the corridor-mice-creepers. Most of the time they call her: 'Lucky to have your own room'. Or: 'Don't ring the bell, because we won't come'. Or: 'Finish what's on your plate'. Or if they pretend to like her, they sometimes call her Mrs Rush.

She can't be sure how long she has lived here. Time progresses at different speeds depending on the weather. On bright days, when she can see the horizon line through the window in the residents' lounge, time moves quickly. Sometimes it moves so quickly that it skips by before she knows it's gone: an entire day is a mere glint of sunshine on her wedding ring.

When it rains or snows, time moves slowly. It moves so slowly that she can watch the movement of her arm when she lifts a teacup to her lips, it's like watching a film frame by frame. Time moves so slowly that in between each frame, in between each second, she glimpses things that are invisible to everyone else. She can see the cup chattering happily with its saucer on the table beside her. And outside the window, in the rockery, the lichen-covered granite is breathing gently in the rain.

The mouse-creepers give her things to take, pastel-coloured sweets that make her time the same as theirs. Every day they come to her room and hand her a plastic pot filled with sugar-coated pills. They prop themselves against the door frame and watch her slip the pills between her lips. But as soon as they have left, she takes them from her mouth. She has a collection of these pills stuffed under her mattress – the sugar coating rubbed off by her tongue, the bitter medicine still intact.

There is one mouse-creeper who knows about her collection, who always stands in her room and waits for her to swallow. He is a tall thin mean-looking mouse who pushes his tiny paws into his pockets, and stares at her throat.

'You swallowed them yet?'

She nods, tight lipped.

He shakes his head and says, 'Don't tell fibs, Mrs Rush.' And he creeps towards her and thrusts his little whiskered snout into her face. 'I'm watching you,' he says.

On those days she gives in and lets the sweets slide slowly down her throat. When they reach her stomach they burst apart and disintegrate into pink and yellow dust. On those days there is nothing to see but the ordinary things: her dull clothes draped across the chair in her room, her soap and toothbrush in the bathroom, the television set at the end of the residents' lounge.

She tries to think backwards to find out who she was. Each year is a different colour. She can see them curling and twisting away from her like multicoloured ribbons on a hat, blowing in the breeze. White, as numbing as thick snow. Green, the colour of the garden railings belonging to the house on the other side of the lane. Black, like the piece of jet in her pocket.

She remembers the beach, not the wide spread of sand and sea, but the crevices and the rock pools and the white spittle in the waves. She remembers the strand of hair which kept falling into the corner of his left eye, and the gnarled surface of the rock hammer that he used to keep in his pocket. She holds the piece of engraved jet between her fingers, feels the arrowing fish flying through the air, and the word 'Forward' carved beneath the waves.

In the bathroom they wash her face and help her brush her teeth. In the bedroom they dress her as if she is a child again. They pull up her knickers and her woollen tights. They fasten her skirt, button up her polyester blouse and her cardigan. She can remember a time when she did this herself. When she eased a mother-of-pearl button into a silk-trimmed slit at the back of a high-necked blouse, while the shadow of the Monkey Puzzle tree swayed against lilac walls. She can remember the thrash of a bird's wing against a metal cage and the faint whistle from the gas fire as she knelt down on the brown linoleum and buttoned a shirt over a child's narrow chest and his rounded stomach.

'One, two, three, four.'

'What was that, Mrs Rush?'

'Ask Jacky to come, will you.'

The mouse fastens the final button on her cardigan and leans forward.

'Who's Jacqui? Tell us who she is, Mrs Rush.'

The rain is spotting the windows of the residents' lounge. The sky is the colour of slate. In the Teesby gloom, the Duchess sits in her pink leatherette chair and peers at the television set. She can see a gallop of horses' legs and a streak of coloured silks across the screen.

The second race – a steeplechase – has only just begun when the Duchess feels a draught behind her chair. As the swing doors are opened there is a sudden gust that tastes of the sea. Then there are voices, followed by the clatter of heels and the brisk brush of nylon-clad thigh against nylon-clad thigh.

'Someone to see you, Mrs Rush.'

The Duchess doesn't move.

'Someone to see you, Mrs Rush. Wake up, wake up! Look!'

The Duchess turns grudgingly from the television. 'Leave me alone,' she growls.

'But there's someone to see you, Mrs Rush. Don't be rude, now. We'll be having none of your moods.'

Standing by the arm of the pink chair is a woman in a leopard-print coat. She has brown hair and waxy skin that gleams unhealthily under the fluorescent lights of the lounge. In one hand she holds a box of Quality Street, in the other, a large canvas bag. The woman is a Big Shopper: no one that the Duchess knows.

She turns back to the racing, but she can still see the woman reflected on the screen – a pinched face and a faint mottle of leopard print superimposed over the horses' legs. She can make out the drooping shadows under the woman's eyes, and the hard lines that descend from the side of her nose to the corners of her lips. It is a sad face, the face of an unhappy child. The Duchess pictures an empty room and a pale oblong of wallpaper where a picture once hung. She can see a girl in a mirror, dressed in a winter coat and hat. She can see a shining silk umbrella and a Gladstone bag.

She turns back to the woman. With her fingertip she touches the sallow hand that clutches the box of chocolates and tries out names.

'Beadie, Aunt Minnie, Ellen, Nell?'

'Oh, you won't remember me,' says the woman. 'It was far too long ago.'

'Of course I remember you,' replies the Duchess.

The woman smiles. Her cheeks and forehead are heavily lined and there are short, grey wisps of hair growing from her temples.

What colour was Beadie?

Beadie was purple. The swirling yellow-purple of the Victoria plums growing at the end of the garden, the black-purple of the prunes lying in a pool of custard. But the woman blocking the view of the racing from Haydock is red. She is red like Jesus's sacred heart – shiny scarlet, plaster-cold in her leopardskin coat. She is rust-red, freckle-red, hard, glinty, grainy red. The woman with the canvas bag and the box of chocolates is red like the wide, wet banks of sand between Teesby and the Snook.

End of Term

It is unusually hot. The sun is blazing through the windscreen. Jack drives out of Nottingham with the windows wound down, past the hospital and the golf club. At the side of the road the trees sway listlessly. It is early July, but some of the leaves have already begun to fall and the twisted scraps are scattered across the verges.

At the crossroads, he slows and turns right onto the narrow lane that leads to the house. When he straightens the wheel and begins to accelerate again, he sees a bird flying towards him along the road. He assumes it will swoop before it reaches the car, expects it to rise up over the roof at the last minute. But the bird is heading straight towards him. He slams his foot hard on the brake. For a few seconds, all he can see is blackness: a dusty body flung against the glass and a splay of feathers as the bird hits the windscreen then bounces away.

It is sprawled on the road, a starling, jet black with lustrous tips to its feathers: its head shines violet and its chest is almost green. He is certain it is dead. He kneels down and is about to pick it up, when the bird, without opening its eyes, twitches its head. He stands up again, steps away. He wishes the starling *was* dead. He is horrified by the idea of watching it suffer, but worse is the thought of having to kill it himself.

The bird half-opens its dull black eyes and shifts its head from left to right. He waits, breathing gently. After a minute or so, it draws its wings towards its body. And when he begins to walk towards it again, the bird sits upright. It is nervous and alert now, jerking its head from side to side. He cannot believe that the damaged wings will be strong enough to lift the starling, but it shuffles a little along the road and manages to propel itself towards the wall. Then it perches on the stone capping, looking at him, eyes blinking. He waits for a while, leaning against the car, until the bird flies unsteadily to a large Scots pine in the middle of the field, until he cannot see it any more.

It is half past five when he pulls into the drive, too early for a drink. In the kitchen he boils the kettle for a cup of tea and looks through the pile of post on the work surface. There isn't much: a brochure for bed linen, a cyclostyled copy of the village magazine, a telephone bill and a postcard. On the front of the postcard is a quartet of photographs. He fumbles for his glasses in his jacket pocket. The pictures are impossibly bright: the skies are cloudless, the sea is a flat cerulean blue, the beach is lemon yellow. He carries the postcard to the window. In the top right-hand corner is a picture of the High Street. Below it is the Nab. Beside the Nab is the promenade. And in the top left corner is the ruined tower on the Snook. In the centre of the postcard, in bold white Helvetica set on an orange ground, are the words 'Greetings from Teesby-on-Sea'.

Heart beating, he turns the card over and reads the message. The large looping script has been written in blue biro. At the bottom is a telephone number which must have been added later. Six large black numerals make their way along the edge of the card before finally colliding with his address on the right-hand side.

It is only when he reads the message a second time that he begins to understand it.

July 6th, 1981.

Dear Jack,

    Thought I should write. Been to see Mother. She's in Teesby
now. She's not too well – keeps asking for you. Ring me.

    Love

    Cathy

He stands in the centre of the kitchen, gripping the postcard
in his hand. There is a lull like a pause between two breaths,
absolute silence, nothing moves. He feels sick. He puts the card
down on the work surface, opens the back door and breathes
deeply. Anna is in the field at the end of the garden. She is calling for the dog, a high-pitched, melancholic cry, like the call of a
seabird blown off course. He turns back to the kitchen, takes out
a tumbler from the cupboard, draws cold water from the tap and
drinks it. The nausea subsides. He puts the glass in the sink and
leans heavily against the work surface, his hands bearing down
on the white Formica.

He had told himself that she was dead. And yet she was always
with him; she has never gone away. She was with him when he
opened the envelope to the moth and the buttercup, and when
Hannë climbed over the gate and stood on the Snook looking up
at the tower. She was half concealed in the painting of the garden
that he burnt in the studio yard, and she was a faint presence in
the hospital when he held Anna for the first time. He still sees
her. He sees her in the face of one of the secretaries who work in
the art school, and in the gestures of a well-known actress who
appears on television from time to time. And he sees her in Anna,
in his daughter's eyes, in her slightly cockeyed gaze.

Anna has a small squint, nothing serious, but her lazy eye
always reminds him of his mother when she sat in the Winterfield
parlour, clutching the rosary beads. He knows there was no connection between her mental state and her wandering gaze, but he

346

cannot stop himself from seeing one condition as a corollary of the other. He cannot disassociate the memory of his mother's darting eye from the deranged taciturn figure sitting squarely on the bench in the parlour of the county lunatic asylum. Sometimes when he looks at Anna, he fears that he has passed something on, that he is a conduit of sorts.

He looks down at the postcard. He wants to rip it into pieces and hide it in the bin. He wants things to go back to how they were five minutes ago before he saw the card. He remembers standing in the privy and watching the fragments of moth and buttercup fall to the floor. He remembers the note that Beadie gave him in Wilkie's yard. After he had read it, he screwed it into a ball and chucked it into the rubbish bin in the drawing office as he left for home. Jack picks the postcard up again, but instead of tearing it apart, he carries it into the lounge along with the telephone bill and the village magazine.

It is evening, Connie is home. She is sitting on an armchair in the lounge, straight-backed, unsmiling: an imperious little queen. However hard Jack tries, he can never recall what she looked like the day he met her. After all these years, he cannot retrieve that first, bright impression of her as she described the workings of the Robert Seignior clock. She has been replaced by the woman who is perched on the edge of the chair with the postcard in her hand, narrow-framed glasses on her small nose, a sagging mouth, a lion's frown between her eyes.

'Well, it's a bit late for a grand reunion. A bit late for all of you now.'

He is sitting on the sofa with a glass of red wine. The dog is curled at his feet. Anna is in her bedroom, reading or listening to music. It is dark now, but the curtains have not yet been pulled across the windows. In the moonlight, he can see the old apple tree and the roses that clamber over the branches. The air is still.

'And completely out of the blue,' Connie continues. 'What was your sister thinking of. A postcard?'

His wife is stately, reproachful. She resembles Muriel Meakin on the day of the wedding. He pictures the pathetic rabbit's-foot brooch clinging to Muriel's breast, the brooch that now lies in Connie's jewellery box on the chest of drawers in their bedroom.

'I can't believe that your sister contacted you after all this time. How does she know where you live? You haven't seen her for years. And what will your mother be like now? You hardly know her, what will you talk about? It's a bit late now.'

Connie is saying exactly what he has been thinking all evening. And yet he is almost certain that whatever Connie says, he should be thinking the opposite.

'You're not going to go, Jack, are you? As soon as the home knows you're here, they'll expect you to look after her.'

He doesn't reply. He rarely replies to Connie these days and she barely notices. His silences used to irritate her: she would wait impatiently for him to say something, tapping her fingers on the arm of the chair, or smoothing her skirt, or patting her hair. But now she just ploughs onwards, filling the long pauses, answering her own questions.

'You shouldn't go. It'll only make things worse, upset everyone: upset you, upset her. What on earth can she have to say to you, anyway? She's a mental patient, Jack. Ring your sister tomorrow, tell her it's too late. And I don't want Anna to know about it, not any of it, Jack. Do you hear? I don't want her upset.'

Connie gets up from the armchair and tugs the curtains across the windows. Jack swirls the wine in the bowl of the glass and watches the sediment settle.

The Piece of Jet

'Ellen likes looking at the view,' Cathy says, after he calls the number on the back of the card. 'Sometimes I drive her in the car along the promenade. She likes to look out of the window.'

Theirs is a stuttering conversation punctuated by embarrassed pauses. In the gaps, he can hear Connie in the kitchen, taking the dinner plates out of the cupboard then opening the cutlery drawer and picking up the knives and forks one by one.

'Where are you living now?' he asks.

'I'm back in England. I'm living in Felixstowe.'

'Why did you leave the States?'

'Things didn't work out. I wanted to come home.'

There is something odd about the way Cathy sounds. Her voice, the one he remembers, the one he hasn't heard for over thirty years, comes and goes. It is suppressed for a sentence or two by the Arizona twang. Then it returns sounding sharp and cold like the North Sea and the wind on the Nab. Sometimes the syllables of a single word are a hybrid of the old Cathy and the new.

'I'm going up next week, Jack. I'll meet you there,' she says.

Our Lady of Sorrows Nursing Home for the Elderly is situated on the edge of Teesby, constructed on a plot of land that was part of Robinson's farm many years ago. It is a long low building like a classroom block: large panes of glass are bordered by coloured panels of beige and brown. The home isn't far from the snakestone cliffs and the beach. From the road, he can see the sea and the faint grey horizon line which, thanks to the summer rain, has begun to disappear. The sky seems to be dissolving into the waves.

He opens the gate and walks up the concrete path. He is carrying a plastic bag containing a small gift for Ellen – a pink silk scarf. In the breeze, the bag beats against his leg and the handles twist tight around his fingers.

By the entrance to the home is a wooden ramp and there are clumps of pale blue sea holly growing in large plastic pots on either side of the front door. Above the door is a lopsided swoop of gold and silver bunting. The little triangles might have flapped in the breeze had they not been so sodden, instead they hang heavily, dripping rainwater onto the ramp below.

He steps into the lobby and feels a dull ache in his stomach, like a soft paw nudging his guts. He moves forward tentatively, past a glass-walled office and the women's toilets. At the end of the corridor is a pair of double doors which he guesses must open onto the residents' lounge. Set into each of the doors is a square pane of safety glass: he cups his hand against one of them and peers into the lounge.

It is a weekday: there are only women – daughters and sisters. No men, no other male visitors. He pushes the door open and stands on the threshold. The tips of his shoes touch the metal carpet strip that marks the division between the corridor and the lounge. He breathes in the insidious odour of old age. It is like the smell of a wardrobe that hasn't been opened for many years, or the smell of an unclean baby, unpleasant but bearable.

There are chairs arranged around the room, all facing inwards, ignoring the view. They are upholstered in wipe-clean leatherette, in pastel shades, blues and greens and yellows. On the far wall is a large engagement portrait of Prince Charles, wearing a bewildered smile, and Lady Diana, who has lassoed her arms around his neck. Underneath it, draped in another swathe of gold and silver bunting, is a large television set.

She must be here somewhere. She will be one of the grey women in the leatherette chairs, shaking, bent double, mumbling: an arthritic claw clutching at a teacup. But all the residents look the same, old age has rendered them identical. He scans the room for Cathy instead. She will be one of those smooth, airbrushed women that feature in American advertisements for Electrolux or Whirlpool. She will be blonde, wearing citrus colours, oranges and greens: capri pants, a T-shirt. Amongst all the fawn and brown cardigans and woollen skirts, he can see no one who resembles his sister. Cathy isn't in the residents' lounge, he is certain of that.

He retreats, turns away, shuts the door quietly behind him. He creeps past the toilets and the office and steps out of the lobby into the rain.

'Jacky! Wait for me, Jacky!'

He turns around.

She is wearing a pair of brown polyester slacks and a shabby leopard-print jacket. In her hand is a canvas bag with the words 'BIG SHOPPER' stamped in block capitals across the front. She has straight, light brown hair which has been back-combed and lacquered into an outdated beehive. The beehive possesses a strangely synthetic shine, an impression that is reinforced by the band of grey hair growing from her temples. From a distance, she looks like she is sporting a wig which has shrunk slightly and is balanced precariously on the back of her head.

'Jacky.' She moves towards him and grips his arm. 'You didn't recognise me, did you?'

She doesn't smile and her voice is flat. There is no grand reconciliation, she doesn't throw her arms about him. Instead she leans forward and kisses him clumsily on the cheek.

'You should come inside,' she says.

351

'I wanted to see you first.'

He can't decide whether the person standing in front of him is familiar to him, or if she is a stranger. 'I thought we could have a cup of tea somewhere.'

Her lips tighten. He remembers that expression. He remembers Granny Rush standing in the kitchen of the house on Invicta Road, staring at him, hands on hips, small mouth puckering until it almost disappeared.

'I haven't got time, Jacky,' Cathy replies. 'If you want to talk we could have a quick walk on the beach. I've got a thermos. The tea should still be warm.'

He doesn't want a conversation blown about by the wind and interrupted by mouthfuls of sand, but Cathy doesn't wait for an answer. She has already passed through the gate and has crossed the road before she looks back and says, 'You coming, then?'

He follows her reluctantly down the steps to the beach, then labours across the damp sand in his heavy shoes.

'So when did you come home?' he shouts into the wind.

'A year ago.'

When she looks back at him, he recognises the heavy eyelids and the straight nose. It is only her mouth that has changed, narrowed and warped into a replica of Granny Rush's grimace.

'I met Barbara last summer,' Cathy says. 'She was on holiday. She came into the shop – I worked in a gift shop selling Mexican stuff, you know, beads and things. Barbara has a guest house in Felixstowe.'

'What about ... ?' He fumbles for her husband's name.

She shakes her head.

'So you're staying with Barbara now?'

'We live together.' Cathy says this firmly as if she wants him to understand something important. 'It was Barbara's idea that I speak to Ellen. She found her. She found you too. She used to work for the police.'

He looks at the sea, watches the waves hurling themselves at the beach. He feels a stab of resentment at Barbara.

'And how about you?' she asks. 'How's the painting?'

'I stopped painting years ago. I lost faith in it, it wasn't working any more.'

Cathy nods.

'And you're married? You've got children?'

'Yes, a daughter, Anna. She's thirteen.'

'Difficult age,' says Cathy.

'Actually, we get along quite well.'

His sister makes her way to a small pavilion near the promenade and sits down on a wooden bench. He props himself against one of the pillars and digs his foot into the broken shells and grit, unearthing fragments of dull sea coal and bottle tops. From this part of the beach they can see the outline of the Snook on the other side of the estuary.

'I've driven Ellen over there once or twice,' she says. 'But you can't go in the tower any more. The council's going to pull the whole lot down soon.'

He pictures his sister at the wheel of a Mini or a Morris Minor. And his mother is beginning to emerge now: an old woman leaning out of the car window, silent, grim, symmetrical.

Cathy takes a packet of cigarettes out of her bag, puts one to her lips and lights it.

'I never really understood why she was so obsessed with the Snook. She still goes on about it.' She draws on the cigarette and the tip flashes orange for a second or two. 'No one ever told me what happened that day. Uncle Henry wouldn't talk about it and Granny Rush said it was better I didn't know. Dad never said a word.'

The sea mist catches in Jack's throat and he can taste the briny vapour on his tongue. He tries to twist the conversation towards something else.

353

'How is Maurice?' he asks carefully.

'He died about ten years ago – heart attack. He and Joyce were up on the Nab and he just collapsed. I'm glad she was there. She looked after him really well. I wasn't able to go to the funeral.' Cathy taps the cigarette on the arm of the bench and the ash tumbles into the sand. 'Come on Jacky,' she says quietly. 'Tell me what happened that day.'

He looks at the wide stretch of sand and sees the policeman carrying her over it fifty years ago, the wet bundle wrapped in a shawl that had once belonged to Mrs Tibbs. He remembers her lying in her cradle in the house on Invicta Road, the day after his mother left: a placid baby staring blankly at the ceiling.

'She wanted to take you to the Snook. I don't know why. When we couldn't cross the causeway, she tried to wade across the estuary.'

'Yes, I thought it was something like that. Years ago, a girl at school told me that Ellen was trying to drown me and that you saved me. She said you swam in and got me.'

'That wasn't true,' he says quickly.

'What wasn't, the bit about Ellen in the sea, or you saving me?'

'It was the policeman who saved you. But Ellen wasn't drowning you, she was holding you up so the water wouldn't touch you, I could see your face over her shoulder. She'd almost made it. A few more steps, she would have reached the other side and no one would have known.'

He is about to say something more, about sitting in the front room with the doctor and Father Scullion, about what he said to Father Scullion. But there is a sharp squeal from a seagull overhead and they both look up as it sails low across the beach then dives into the water.

'Listen Jacky, I really have to go soon. I've got a long drive.' Cathy is stubbing out her half-smoked cigarette on the arm of the bench.

'Already?' He doesn't want the conversation to end, not like this. There is so much to say suddenly. The words are piling up in his mouth. He wants to tell her about the windowpane check coat and the damp horrible heat and the man shouting at them from the Snook and the boy with the spade. He wants her to understand what it was like, what Ellen was like: how it had been in the front room with Father Scullion questioning him, how angry he was.

But it doesn't seem to matter to Cathy. She puts the packet of cigarettes into her bag and starts to walk back across the beach. As he follows her, the sand slides under his feet. He can still feel the weight of that day with Ellen, he cannot shake it off.

Her car is parked crookedly on the side of the road. 'This is me,' she says, thrusting her hands into her coat pockets and searching for her keys.

He tries to think of something to say, something light, friendly, a way of prolonging the conversation.

'So what happened to all the curls?' he asks feebly.

In the drizzle her beehive has begun to collapse. Thick strands of hair hang flat and straight over her face.

'What happened to what?'

'The curls?' He points to her hair and makes a corkscrew motion with his finger.

'Oh those,' she lifts her hand to her head. 'They cut my hair off in hospital and when it grew again it grew straight.' She tucks a loose lock behind her ear.

'Hospital?'

'Arizona wasn't easy, Jacky. I had my moments.'

'What do you mean?'

'Like Ellen, I had my moments. That's why I didn't go to Dad's funeral. That's why Rickie and I split up.'

The wind batters the plastic bag in his hand, it twists and turns. He can taste the acid in his throat again.

'I should have written, I could have helped.'

'Oh, Jacky, there was nothing you could do. There was nothing you could have done about any of it. Not for me, not for Ellen. It wasn't your fault, you were a child.' Her voice is matter-of-fact. She flashes a bleak smile.

For a second, he can barely breathe, something is unwinding, loosening itself.

She looks down at her watch. 'You should go in before it's too late. They shut the door at five.' She sounds like the old Cathy again. 'Go on, Jacky, get a move on.' She grips his arm tight, leans over and brushes her lips against his cheek. 'You know where to find me now.'

He can still feel the pressure of her fingers on his skin as she walks away from him. He remembers the bright, happy girl on Bleaker's Hill, gazing at the butterfly on the thistle head. He wants to say something more, something meaningful.

She gets into the car and gives him a brief wave through the windscreen.

'Keep sending the postcards,' he calls as she pulls away.

Jack is standing in the doorway to the residents' lounge.

'I'm looking for Mrs Rush, Ellen Rush.'

The assistant points to an elderly woman who is making her way from one side of the lounge to the other. She totters forward tentatively, as if she is crossing a sheet of ice. When she reaches the far end of the room, she lowers herself into one of the chairs, her trembling hands grasping the leatherette arms.

He moves towards her. Her hair is white, bobbed, combed, and parted on one side: there is a sweeping lock that drapes across her forehead. She wears a brooch on the left lapel of her blouse, a parrot with gaudy feathers picked out in green and yellow crystals. Her right hand is resting in her lap, her left is lying uncomfortably in the gap between her hip and the arm of the chair. She is staring

356

straight ahead at the television set. Even when he sits down beside her, she doesn't turn round.

'Ellen.'

When she hears her name she twists slightly. Unlike the rest of her body, which is slumped and flaccid, her neck is long and she holds her head high. She is much smaller than him, but somehow or other she manages to peer down at him, unblinking, like a bird of prey on a telephone wire.

'You a doctor?'

'No, I'm Jack . . . Jacky.'

She studies him, then waves her hand as if she is trying to flick away a fly. She turns back to the television.

In the silence he looks at his mother. The gulf between his memories of Ellen and the woman sitting beside him is so wide that he begins to wonder if the assistant has made a mistake: he can see no trace of young Ellen in this old woman's features. Her eyes, once a luminous blue, are dull and pale, as opaque as the sea mist outside the window. Her cheeks and forehead, which were freckled with pinpricks of pink, are now covered in large stains, the colour of dry sand.

He says her name again, but she is staring intently at the screen now, at a children's programme, something that Anna used to watch. She is mimicking the presenter, mouthing the words, nodding her head in agreement.

Connie was right. It *is* too late. There is nothing left to say.

He touches the old woman's arm lightly. 'Maybe I should go now, leave you to it.'

He is about to get up when he notices the damp plastic bag lying by his feet. He reaches down and pulls out the pink scarf then drapes it over her lap.

'It's a present,' he says. 'I forgot to wrap it.'

She looks down at the silk and strokes it, trying to smooth out the creases. When it is flat, she takes the fabric between her fingers and folds it carefully, matching corner to corner, just as she used to fold Mrs Tibbs's handkerchiefs after she had ironed them in the kitchen. When she has finished, she places the rectangle of folded silk on her lap, and with the tip of her index finger she touches each corner of the scarf, deliberately and precisely.

'One, two, three, four,' she counts. Then she presses her hand flat over the silk and begins again. 'One, two, three, four.'

She repeats the gesture compulsively, five or six times, before he reaches out and grips her hand. She doesn't resist. Her fingers are cold and motionless. He can feel the narrow bones beneath the papery skin.

'You're still blue then,' she says quietly.

She used to tell him this when they lived in the villa. In the evening, when she put him to bed, she would brush the hair out of his eyes or stroke his cheek and say, 'You're so blue, such a lovely shade of blue.' He never knew what she meant.

'Yes, still blue,' he murmurs.

He gazes at her, at the slope of her high forehead, at her long nose, her thin lips. He still cannot reconcile the two Ellens, the one he remembers in the windowpane check coat and the blue felt hat and the new Ellen, the woman dressed in a grey skirt and cardigan, sitting in the residents' lounge. He cannot make sense of it, how one Ellen has become another.

'Da said the Pearsons came out of the sand on the Snook.' She looks up at him hopefully, waiting for a reaction.

'Yes, I know.' He lets go of her hand, and it drops into her lap.

'Bleaker's Hill.'

'What?'

'The beginning of things.' Her face twitches and her hand flaps anxiously in her lap.

He grasps her fingers again. 'Don't worry, don't worry about Bleaker's Hill.'

'The eggs, the eggs, Jacky. Remember the eggs.' She slips her hand out of his. 'Saturday afternoons,' she sighs.

Saturday afternoons on Invicta Road were spent with a mop and a bucket of soapy water, while Granny Rush swore at the dust and the dirt and the parrot screeched in its cage. When they lived in the villa, every Saturday afternoon they used to trek across the Nab to Robinson's farm to buy a dozen eggs. Sometimes they walked to the field with the old shepherd's hut. You could stand at the edge of that field and look over the cliffs at the beach and the sea.

'It's the end of the world,' he used to say to her.

'No, Jacky,' she'd reply, smiling at him. 'No, it's the beginning.'

In the summer, she would wrap two slices of Beadie's fruit cake in a sheet of greaseproof paper, and they would eat the cake by the cliff edge, looking at the view. Afterwards, she would take him for a walk, lead him through the field and point out small things. She would show him a chip of blood-red flint lying in a patch of bare soil by the gate, or the lacy frills of the emerald-coloured moss that grew on the dry-stone wall.

'Everything's worth looking at, Jacky,' she would tell him. 'Even the ordinary things, even the littlest things.'

She used to collect feathers that she found lying in the mud or caught in the gorse. He remembers her clutching them in her hand and saying, 'Soon I'll have enough to make my own bird.' He remembers her laughing.

She told him that the barred pink-and-brown hawks' feathers were too bright: she said that the colours made too much noise.

'How can colours be noisy?' he asked, taking the feathers from her and pressing them to his ear.

'I don't know,' she replied. 'But they're making a bloom-ing racket right now. Can't you hear them, Jacky? Makes my head ache.'

'Yes, Saturday afternoons,' he replies, turning to the old woman. 'I remember Saturdays.'

But she is dozing now. Her hands are knotted in her lap. Her head is nodding gently against her chest.

As she sleeps a thin strand of silver hair slips over her face. He watches it lightly rise and fall with every breath. She reminds him of Anna when she was small, when she used to doze in the back of the car on trips to the Peaks: her head lolling on her shoulder, her lips parted slightly. Ellen is a child again.

A bell rings. She wakes abruptly and opens her filmy eyes. 'Time for my tea. Time for you to go.'

'Yes,' he gets up from the chair. 'Time for me to go.'

He stands in front of her, blocking the view of the television set. She leans heavily against the arm of the chair in an attempt to peer round him at the screen.

'Would you like me to come again?' he asks.

'Don't trouble yourself.' She flaps her hand, impatient for him to be gone.

'I'll be on my way then,' he says.

Without thinking, he bends down and kisses her on her forehead. She smells of calamine lotion combined with a faint hint of Persil. Against his lips, her forehead is cold and dry, it is like kissing Anna when she was a baby. He remembers the slight curve of his daughter's head, the white skin and the delicate network of purple veins at her temples.

'I'll come again.'

She doesn't reply.

He makes his way towards the double doors. As he passes the window, he can see that the day has brightened a little: the rain has stopped and the horizon line is a soft blue band between the sea and the sky.

He opens the lounge doors and begins to walk down the long corridor. He reaches the main entrance then turns back again, he has a faint nagging feeling that he has forgotten something, left it behind in the residents' lounge.

When he pushes the doors again, she is standing by her chair, clutching the arm for support. The pink scarf has fallen out of her lap and is lying on the floor by her feet.

'Ma?'

'The eggs, Jacky. The eggs.' Out of the pocket of her skirt she pulls a small black stone and holds it in the palm of her trembling hand. 'You wanted to know where you came from.'

The Royal Wedding

When he was a boy he was as blue as the view from the tower window. Now he is the sort of blue that is almost silent, just a dull hum in the background. He is blue like Henry's washed-out cotton shirts; like the faded sugar-paper bags on the shop counter in the baker's; like the covers of Mrs Tibbs's old chaise longue; like the long shadows in the early morning when the stone collector built the camp fire by the hut and boiled a pot of water for the tea.

She wanted to tell him about it all: about Da and the Sacred Heart, and Beadie and Mrs Tibbs. She wanted to tell him about the green railings and the whiteness and the Snook. She had told the stories to herself a thousand times, but when she tried to speak the phrases wouldn't shape themselves inside her mouth.

She wanted to tell him about the morning she spent with the stone collector all those years ago. How they had sat by the camp fire and drunk their tea, watching the sun rise above the cliff. If the words had been there, she would have told him that as soon as she had finished her tea, she stood up and said: 'I'll come again, I promise.' And the stone collector had replied: 'Yes, I think I'd like that, Ellen.' But when she had returned in the evening, all that was left of the camp was a black patch of ground where the fire had burned. She cried for a while, but not for long. She sat in the damp field and clutched her belly and felt something shift inside her. It was like the slight, soft movement of the ground underfoot when you walk across the shingle on the Snook.

In her room, as they undress her – untying her shoelaces, unbuttoning her blouse – the Duchess fumbles with her skirt. Her sand-stained hand rummages frantically between the grey polyester pleats.

'What is it, Mrs Rush? What is it you're looking for?'

'Oh, don't trouble yourself,' she mutters.

'Well, if it's something you need, Mrs Rush.'

'No, not right now,' snaps the Duchess.

She wanted to touch the cool, black ridges of the carved sea and the scales of the leaping fish. But all she can find in the pocket of her skirt is a pink plastic button, a loose knot of green thread, and deep in the seams, a few warm grains of Teesby sand.

It is the morning of the Royal Wedding. In the lounge the care assistants have arranged the chairs in a semi-circle round the television and have handed out little paper flags. Some of the residents are wearing tissue paper crowns that were saved from the crackers last Christmas. Everyone is sitting in the lounge: the nurses, the assistants, the cook, the manageress, the secretary and, whether they like it or not, the residents themselves. After the wedding there will be a party in the dining room. The table is already set and the room is decorated with gold and silver bunting and coloured streamers. When the guests in Buckingham Palace settle down to brill in lobster sauce and Suprême de Volaille Princesse de Galles, in Our Lady of Sorrows there will be ham and cheese sandwiches, trifle and fairy cakes with rose-pink icing.

Ellen has selected the green leatherette chair at the edge of the semi-circle: she sits in it with one eye on the television and the other on the window. She has chosen the chair for the view of the sea, so she can watch the tide slide away across the beach without

363

having to turn her head from the screen. Like the others, she obediently flutters her paper flag as the tiny figures, teeth clenched, wave grimly from their carriages. The Queen is lustrous in turquoise, her sister is hard and tart in apricot pink, and the Queen Mother is swallowed up in foamy waves of eau-de-Nil. Poor Diana is a bundle of crumpled silk pressed against the window of the coach: she is a small face enmeshed in a wedding veil, like a sickly-looking North Sea fish trapped inside a net.

On the steps of Saint Paul's there is fold after fold of fabric. They try to unravel her, but she is anchored by the dress, dragged down by the weight of it: the silk train tries to tug her back towards the coach. White is always a mistake, thinks Ellen. White is the colour of the cold, the colour of oblivion, the colour of nothing at all.

'Oh, how lovely,' says one of the assistants.

'What a dream she looks. What a dream she looks,' says the television set.

'Time to go,' mutters Ellen to herself.

When the fanfare begins, the old woman rises stiffly from the chair and starts to make her way towards the swing doors.

'Where are you going, Mrs Rush?' asks the secretary.

'Not now, Mrs Rush,' says someone else.

'Toilet,' says Ellen. 'Don't trouble yourselves.'

'Oh, let her go on her own,' says the manageress, twisting in her chair to look at Ellen. 'But don't go wandering off, Mrs Rush.' She wags her finger in the air. 'We don't want to lose you now, do we?'

Ellen pushes the lounge doors open and trudges along the corridor, past the toilets, to the entrance where the pots of sea holly stand. She shuffles carefully down the path to the gate, then crosses the empty road. With her hands clutching the tufts of grass that grow on the sandy slope, she descends backwards, down the concrete steps to the shore. When she finally reaches the bottom, she stands triumphant. It is the first time in fifty years that she has felt the sand beneath her feet.

There is no one on the beach but Ellen, and nothing moves except the waves. The morning mist has begun to thin now. She can make out the squat silhouette of the tower on the other side of the river. The tower gleams blue. It is the colour of the jay's feather she found on the path by the stone collector's field. It is the colour of the glass insert from Mrs Tibbs's salt cellar in the dining room. It is the colour of Our Lady's cloak in the picture above the bed in the house on Invicta Road. Blue is usually the quietest of all the colours, but she can hear the tower calling gently to her across the estuary.

She starts to walk over the beach, plodding clumsily towards the wooden pavilion, following in her children's footsteps that are still imprinted in the sand. When Ellen was a child she used to run across the beach or stand at the tideline and dodge the waves. Or she would hunt for marbled pebbles and fragments of sea-polished glass and sea-washed bones in the shallow pools of salt water. But now she can hardly lift her feet they weigh so much. And the Snook is just a narrow thread of land on the horizon. And if she raises her arm, she can still grasp the small blue tower in her trembling hand.

She makes her way to the tideline, head lowered, determined: remembering the stone collector gazing down at the pebbles and the shards of jet; remembering Jacky, always a few steps behind her; remembering the red-faced baby crying in the pram. It is easier to walk on the wet sand. Her feet feel lighter: the pain in her legs eases as she grows used to the movement of walking again. She remembers Da throwing pebbles into the sea, making them skim and bounce across the waves. She remembers Henry as a boy laughing at something she said, his head thrown back, so happy. *Oh Henry, where did you go?* She is almost running now, trotting across the bay, her grey hair buffeted by the breeze.

When she reaches the shallow ditch of water that separates Teesby from the Snook, she pauses, catching her breath. She stands at the muddy edge and looks back at the town. This is what it must be like to look at the earth from the moon. Everything familiar seems so far away. She can see the promenade and the corner of the High Street. Above it is the hill that leads to the moor. And in the distance, she can make out the long rectangular form of the brick villa, perched on its narrow shelf just below the Nab.

She remembers things she has long forgotten, small things. The scurry of dried leaves skating across the tiles in the entrance hall. The velvet bell-pull in the drawing room swaying elegantly in the breeze. The burnt logs that lay in Mrs Tibbs's fireplace overnight and always crumbled into ash when she picked them up with the fire tongs in the morning. The soil in the garden where Beadie grew the potatoes – soil that looked so rich you wanted to stuff handfuls of it into your mouth and eat it. The swish of Beadie's apron in the scullery, the echo of Jacky's footsteps in the kitchen.

'This is it,' sings the tower. 'This is all there is, it's enough isn't it?'

She steps from the muddy silt into the salty water, just as the Prince and Princess of Wales move from the darkness of Saint Paul's into the sunlight. As the sea begins to pour into her shoes and seep up her woollen stockings, she can hear the cheers from all the television sets in Teesby. She wades another step and the silt shifts under the weight of her feet. She lurches sideways, her hands splashing the surface of the water, left then right, then left again. In the town the church bells ring out: a rich peal from Saint John the Evangelist followed by a thin, clinking chime from Saint Anthony's on Ryder Street. She manages to steady herself and starts to move forward through the heavy water, her grey skirt and cardigan swaying behind her on the waves. She is close enough to hear the Snook now. It is just ahead of her, beckoning her on. The wide red line is calling to her.

Sand

They find her a few hours later, lying face down on the shore of the Snook. Three policemen and a sniffer dog straining at its lead stumble across her body: though the dog is more interested in the fish-stink of a rotting gull washed up amongst the driftwood.

One of the policemen kneels down and lifts a lock of damp hair with the tip of his biro. 'Looks like it's her,' he says, standing up again and brushing the sand from his trousers.

The wedding is over. There are children playing in the waves. By the mouth of the river someone is flying a yellow plastic kite: it wheels and dips against the sky. No one on the beach notices the ambulance pitching from side to side as it crosses the crumbling causeway. And no one bothers to look towards the Snook as the ambulance crew lifts the small, limp body onto the stretcher. Only a gull on the roof of the tower turns its head as they slide the stretcher into the ambulance and slam the doors. And when the ambulance has gone, all that is left on the shore of the Snook is a damp shallow indentation in the sand.

Jack is in the studio working on a charcoal sketch of the garden when he sees Connie through the window. She is running across the grass, breathless. Her face is white and contorted.

'It's the police,' she says sharply as she pulls open the studio door. 'I don't know what they want. They wouldn't tell me. They'll only speak to you.'

In the house he presses the telephone receiver to his ear. He listens hard but he can barely understand what the voice is saying.

'Your mother walked into the sea, Mr Pearson.'

'What?'

'She walked into the sea.'

Time collapses. He is a middle-aged man gripping the telephone receiver. He is a small boy standing on the beach, watching his mother wade through the water with Cathy in her arms.

He forgets to wash his hands before he leaves the house. It is only when he is waiting to see the body in the mortuary that he notices that the charcoal dust is ingrained in the creases of his palms, and that the tips of his fingers are grey. He thrusts his dirty hands into his pockets and finds the piece of jet she gave him a week ago. He can feel the cool ridges of the engraved fish against his thumb.

The mortuary is white walled and white tiled. It smells of the cold, a sharp, dry odour – clean and chemical – like the inside of the ice box in the fridge. He shivers. He is expecting horrors. He braces himself for a bloated face, bulging eyes, distended fingers and toes. He pictures strands of seaweed entwined around her neck, barnacles clinging to her cheeks, sand caked around her mouth and in her nostrils.

When they pull the blue sheet from her face he is surprised at how young she appears. The sea has washed away the lines on her face and has darkened her hair. He is a boy again, clinging to the bedroom door frame, watching her sleep the evening before they took her away. Her hair was damp then, there were brown coils of it across the pillow, grains of sand caught in the wet locks. The sand sparkled in the evening sun.

'Yes, it's her. It's my mother.' He turns away.

*

368

For a while, he sits in the car watching the terns diving at one another in the sky. He brushes his cheek and remembers the sting of the sand when he stood outside the front door to Mrs Veasey's house all those years ago. He rubs his face in his hands, switches on the engine, reverses out of the car park.

The sun is beginning to set as he drives northwards along the promenade. He parks near the quay where the ferryman used to launch his boat. Without bothering to lock the car, he climbs down the steps to the beach. He cannot face the long journey home, not yet.

He looks across at the estuary and the Snook beyond it. What must have been a narrow channel of water this morning is now a wide, dark gulf that appears to be swelling over the banks of sand. He can see her in her grey skirt and cardigan, lifted off her feet by the force of the waves.

He takes out the piece of jet from his trouser pocket. It is a smooth, flat disc that fits comfortably in the hollow of his palm. In the studio, the day after she had given it to him, he turned it over and over in his hand, trying to understand what it meant.

Anna had noticed him through the window. She had wandered into the studio and perched on the edge of the plan chest.

'What are you looking at?' she asked.

Then together they examined the jet, Anna running her fingers over the engraving.

'Why does it say "Forward"?'

'I don't know,' he replied.

'It's an instruction,' she said.

'Maybe.'

On the beach, the jet seems to pulse with blackness: it is alive, it is breathing. He slips it carefully back in his pocket and makes his way towards the water.

The sea is rising and the waves are spilling onto the shore. They sweep towards his feet then retreat, depositing tiny pebbles, seashells and fragments of wood onto the sand. A few minutes later they return to pick up the flotsam and carry it off again.

The tide is coming in, but he doesn't move. The sea is hesitant at first, it barely touches the tips of his shoes. After a few minutes it grows more confident, begins to splash against the leather soles and stain the leather uppers. The water draws back once more as if it is taking a deep breath then it rushes towards him, and in a single wave both his feet are submerged.

He should move forward, wade through the sea like she did, let it lift him off his feet. But he stands motionless, his face wet with salt water. He watches a cormorant just ahead of him plunge into the sea. The bird will be shooting over the rocks and the gravel and the sand, and the rusting shards of the German bomber, and the bones of the airman, and the rotting remnants of his mother's blue felt hat.

He waits for the bird to appear again. But the sea, now rippling round his shins, is icy cold and his feet are growing numb. He turns away and clambers up the bank of seashells to a patch of dry sand just above the tideline. Wiping his damp face, he sits down, takes off his shoes, peels away his socks. He hasn't sat on the beach for years, not since he sat by the snakestone cliffs with Hannë, the day they wrote their names in the sand.

He misses them all: Uncle Henry sitting on the picnic blanket with his thermos of tea, Marigold clutching a bag of chips in his red bony hand, Lenny with his maps and his monocular. And Ellen: he has always missed Ellen.

He bends over, traces their names on the beach with his index finger: it is all he can do. When he has finished he pushes his fingers into the sand. He had expected it to be cold like the sea, but it is blood-warm and strangely comforting. As he thrusts his hand downwards, the hole that he makes is instantly filled with sand again. Each time he moves his fingers the sand gives way, he feels no resistance. He continues to push until the warm sand

370

is up to his wrist, until it is clasping his fingers and pulling him down. He tugs gently and it gives in, lets him go. In the twilight he can see it clinging to his skin. His fingers, his fingernails, the lines on the palm of his hand are encrusted with glistening grains of red Teesby sand.